A Year at Appleyard Farm

BOOKS BY EMMA DAVIES

EMMA DAVIES

A Year at Appleyard Farm

bookouture

Published by Bookouture in 2020

An imprint of Storyfire Ltd.
Carmelite House
50 Victoria Embankment
London EC4Y 0DZ

www.bookouture.com

ISBN: 978-1-83888-630-1
eBook ISBN: 978-1-83888-629-5

This book is a work of fiction. Names, characters, businesses,
organizations, places and events other than those clearly in the
public domain, are either the product of the author's imagination
or are used fictitiously. Any resemblance to actual persons, living or
dead, events or locales is entirely coincidental.

For Peta, who first believed.

WINTER

Chapter One

Freya slammed the van door closed and leaned up against it, breathing hard, her breath appearing as sharp little puffs in the cold. How difficult could it be? After all, she'd done this countless times before. Except she hadn't, because this year she was alone.

She shivered in the harsh early morning air; whether from nerves or the cold, she couldn't tell, and, in any case, it hardly mattered, the effect was the same. She glanced back at the house, solid and warm and comforting, and tried to damp down the rising sense of panic that threatened to swamp her. She sucked in a breath and, resolutely ignoring the 'For Sale' sign, gave a little nod in farewell. Whatever happened today she was going to give it her best shot; she owed her dad that much after all.

The weather forecast was clear, the very best kind of day. Cold, but with a defiant blue sky that not only cheered the gathered crowds but brought a strong contrast to the holly berries and a gleam to the glossy leaves. She'd dressed for the part too, in her forest green coat and bright red woolly hat and scarf that always made her feel much warmer than she was. The colour brought a rosy hue to her cheeks and made her chestnut hair glow. The punters seemed to like it too. Christmas was just over a month away, and if it helped to look like Mrs Claus, then who was she to argue.

She edged the van out of the gate and onto the lane, reminding herself to breathe normally. It was important to get there early, but she had plenty of time to secure a good spot, and the roads would be relatively quiet at this time of the morning. In an hour's time, she'd make it to Tenbury Wells and could stop fretting.

The familiar landmarks came and went. Freya knew the route like the back of her hand, and, three miles in, she began to feel the first bubbles of excitement welling up inside her. She had first travelled this route over twenty-five years ago when she was just a girl, and every year since, she and her dad had made the journey to the annual mistletoe sales. Her granddad had been there before them too for many a year, and even as a small child, she remembered his tales. Sherbourne mistletoe had been sold at the fair for nearly a hundred years all told, and the thought that this might be her last ever year sat like a stone in her stomach. There would be enough time to think about that though, in the weeks to come; today she had to hold her head high.

It was the boots that Freya noticed first: bright red Doc Martens. She'd never seen him wearing anything else, so maybe he didn't own any other shoes, but today, trudging along the muddy verge, they stood out in stark contrast to everything else. She hadn't seen him for a couple of days, but by the look of him, he was moving on somewhere. She slowed the van on the empty road and pulled up alongside him.

'Amos?' she called.

He turned at the sound of her voice, breaking into a broad grin. 'Well, hello again, Miss Sherbourne, what brings you this way?'

She smiled. It was just the sort of thing he would say, as if it were she who was in the wrong place. 'Well, I live around here, but I don't know about you. And more to the point, you didn't even say goodbye.'

His black eyes twinkled. 'Ah well, you know that's not my style. Besides, I thought I'd finished everything you needed me to do.'

'You did, but it's nearly Christmas, Amos. I could have found a few other things for you. It's not a great time to be without a place to go.'

He dipped his head slightly in acknowledgement of her concern. 'But when I get where I'm going, I'll be someplace, won't I?' He squinted up at her through the sun. 'Anyhow, I think it was time for me to move on.'

Freya blushed slightly. 'Gareth was okay with you being around, really he was. He just... well, he likes things to be... ordinary.'

'And I offended his sensibilities, I understand that.'

'I don't think he understood you, that's all; the choices you've made.' She was trying to be tactful, knowing full well that Amos had heard at least one sarcastic comment that Gareth had made at his expense. Judging by the look on his face however, he understood Gareth's motives very clearly, and really Freya was in no position to argue. She had wanted to help, that was all, but she could also see it from her boyfriend's point of view. Maybe Amos' leaving was for the best.

'So where are you headed to now then?'

Amos surveyed the road ahead, his tight black curls gleaming in the sunshine. 'This way will do.'

'And when you get to the end of this way, where next?'

'Well now, see, that's the best bit. I'll just go the way the wind blows me.'

Freya drummed her fingers on the steering wheel. 'There's a fair wind howling down the A49 today, I reckon. Have you ever been to the mistletoe fair?'

'Not that I can recall.'

'Well, seeing as you helped me to harvest it all, do you want to see what happens next?'

Amos looked at his watch, as though he had some pressing engagement. 'You might need some help then?'

'I might. And I'll buy you lunch and a pint when it's over.'

She leaned over to open the passenger door as Amos shrugged his rucksack off his shoulders. He climbed in, wedging his belongings on the floor of the cab, before taking a deep breath and inhaling the smell of the greenery from within.

'Magical stuff mistletoe,' said Amos. 'But I expect you know that. I've always thought it a rather wonderful coincidence that it appears at Christmas; it seems exactly the right time of year for a miracle or two, don't you think?'

*

Talk about cutting it fine, thought Amos. A few moments later and she might have missed him altogether, and then where would he be? Sometimes, he knew the minute he ended up in a place why he was there, and, sometimes, it took a while longer. This time had been the hardest of them all to call. He'd been in Much Marlowes since the beginning of August, and the jobs that took him there had both been straightforward. Two beautiful cottages rethatched, but no hint of any reason for him to stay. Ordinary families, settled lives, and not the slightest prickling feeling that usually alerted him to his purpose.

It wasn't until he pitched up at the Sherbourne orchard that he began to feel he might be onto something, although at the time he had wondered whether it was the after-effects of too much cider the night before. A drunken bet in a game of cards had cost him his van, and the only reason he had turned up Freya's drive was the hope of quenching a raging thirst. As he walked its length, however, it occurred to him that the apple harvest might be his salvation, and when Freya opened the door, a wave of dizziness had passed over him so strong it had nearly taken him off his feet. He knew then without a shadow of a doubt that he would stay.

Several glasses of water later and two hours' sleep had allowed him to recover, and by then, Freya had already decided to offer him some work. She couldn't afford to pay him much, but he had food, a place to stay, and the weeks had slipped by. By the middle of October, however, he was none the wiser. Freya's boyfriend, Gareth, was a prize pillock but harmless enough, and although their relationship had clearly lost its sparkle (if it had ever had any), they rubbed along peaceably enough. There seemed no real reason for him to be there after all, and so helping her harvest the holly and mistletoe had been his final job. He must simply have been mistaken, and it was time for him to move on once more.

He knew it was her, though, the minute he heard the van slow down, and now as he sat in the warmth beside her, he found he was rubbing the back of his neck repeatedly to calm the prickling sensation he felt there. She had crossed his path again, and he wasn't sure what the mistletoe fair had to do with things, but there was no doubt in his mind that he had to find out.

With the radio playing all the way and the two of them singing songs at the top of their voices, the miles slipped by, so it was only when they turned down a road to join a convoy of other vans that Amos realised they must be close. He glanced at Freya, but she seemed relaxed enough, despite how he knew she must be feeling. She chatted easily to him when it was just the two of them; it was only the evenings when Gareth was around that she clammed up. But this fair meant a lot to her, he knew that much.

The auction yard was busy as they turned in, already milling with people and vehicles as the traders sought to find their spaces and unload their wares. Freya gave an explosive tut beside him.

'Bloody Hendersons,' she said. 'I might have known they'd get here before me.'

Amos followed the angle of her head to a smart lorry, its familiar red livery bright and distinctive in the morning sun. He'd seen them about the lanes quite often over recent weeks, and on the odd occasion when Freya mentioned their name, it was never in flattering tones.

'Look at him, pig-headed arrogant sod; thinks he owns the place.'

It was true that the lorry was now holding everyone else up as it manoeuvred into position, but there was still plenty of room for Freya's smaller van to pass. He glanced at the jut of her chin, deciding not to argue, and pointed out a place further along which she could easily fit into.

Freya was out of the cab in a flash, running over to the pens in a barn which ran along one side of the yard. He watched her walk up and down, her red scarf flying behind her, a coiled little bundle of energy. She paused every now and then before stopping completely, and with a visible little hop, spun on her heels and threaded her way hurriedly back towards him.

'Right, I'm good with that,' she said breathlessly. 'My pitch is right smack bang in the middle, just about perfect.' She grinned at the perplexed look he gave her. 'I'll explain later. Come on, we need to get over to where the rest of the sale takes place.'

She threw a look over to the Henderson's lorry before flinging open the back doors of the van and climbing inside. Amos lost her among the foliage for a second. A riot of green and red and silver greeted him. If you could capture Christmas in a single scene, this would surely come close. He'd really had no sense of it while he was helping her to cut it down, but now, bundled as it was and filling the space, it was a joyful homage to the season.

Freya threw him a pair of gloves as the holly came out first, dark and gleaming. The plant he knew well, but he was certainly no expert on selling the stuff. It was full of berries, though, and he thought that could only be a good thing. She stopped for a moment, her head on one side like a robin, her eyes on his, suddenly anxious.

'Jesus, Amos, what am I doing?'

He really didn't have an answer but smiled in encouragement.

'How can I possibly compete with this lot? I mean look at them. They've easily three times as much as I have. No one's going to want my paltry few bundles. I shouldn't have come.'

Amos picked up a sheaf of the holly, holding it close to his body. He touched a round red berry gently and ran a finger down the spine of a rich dark leaf. 'But this is beautiful, Freya. I would buy it, if I could.' He was horrified to see her eyes begin to glisten. 'Have you been here lots of times before?'

She gave a small nod. 'Yes, but that was… was with my dad.'

'And would you feel like this if your dad were here today? Would you want to give up and go home?'

'No, of course not, but that was different.' She frowned. 'Things were different then.'

'Only if you believe them to be,' he said softly. He reached into the bundle and plucked a small white feather from its depths before taking her hand to help her down from the van. Gently placing the holly on the floor, he tucked the feather into the rim of her hat, pushing it into the woollen folds.

'There are always times when your father is with you, Freya, more often than you know.' He looked up to see her eyes widen in surprise. 'Now, since you're the expert here, can I suggest that you tell me where these need to go; I'm guessing that wherever it is, you'll want them there before the Hendersons?'

Her gaze wandered over his left shoulder just for a second before shooting back to him, her eyes still glistening but now with a new-found glint of determination. She picked up a bundle, seemingly oblivious to the sharpness of the prickles, and, with a grin and a nod of her head, marched off, leaving Amos to trail in her wake.

Once the holly was laid out, they doubled back to the van to collect the mistletoe and began the same process all over again, laying out their bundles in tight little rows in the yard, while prospective buyers milled around, nodding and chatting in fine mood. Amos caught sight of one of them pointing to Freya's bundles, although he made no move to examine it further. He heard the name Sherbourne muttered and smiled to himself. Despite her reservations, her name had obviously preceded her, and her bright blue labels with their distinctive name stamp were doing their job brilliantly.

'I wasn't sure if you'd be here this year, but you made it then.'

Amos whipped around at the sound of the voice, its tone none too friendly.

Freya dipped her head. 'Hello, Stephen.'

The two of them stared at one another for a moment without saying anything further, but Stephen's gaze was travelling up and down the rows of mistletoe, resting on Freya's bundles for a moment too long to be comfortable.

'Berries looking a little green I'd say, Freya,' he said, smiling a smug grin.

His hair was slicked back into a quiff at the front, and a signet ring glistened on one of the fingers he was wiping across his smirking mouth.

Amos took in his green Hunter wellies, waxed jacket and red-checked shirt and frowned. He looked down at the neat rows, but as far as he could see, Freya's berries were glistening little orbs of pearlescent white.

'Much like yourself, Stephen,' Freya replied. 'A little too much sauce again last night, was it? Or is your complexion always that colour?'

Stephen glared at her, his mouth trying to form the clever comeback he so desperately sought, but Freya simply smiled and took Amos' arm.

'All this talk of sauce reminds me; time for a bacon butty, I reckon. Think I'll have an egg in mine as well. Can't beat a fried egg in the morning, can you, all oozing and dripping? Just the thing to set you up for the day. Come on, Amos, my treat.' She smiled sweetly at Stephen who had visibly paled. 'You should have one too, put a bit of colour in your cheeks.'

Freya glanced at her watch as they walked across the yard, heading incongruously for a ramshackle tin shed that looked like the last place you might get a bacon butty from. 'We don't really have time for this just yet, but anything to get away from that slimeball.'

'Would his last name be Henderson by any chance?'

'Yeah,' she replied, a harsh tone in her normally soft voice. 'I've never been able to figure out what his problem is except perhaps an extremely high opinion of himself. It's not as if their farm is any different to anyone else's, but Stephen likes to play Lord of the Manor. Everybody knows that the minute he can, he'll sell up and cash in to fund his lavish lifestyle. He's only interested in money.'

'He has a brother, doesn't he? I've seen him in the village a few times.'

Freya gave a small snort. 'Yeah, Sam will be around here somewhere, hiding in Stephen's shadow. You can bet your life that it was him that did all the hard work to get that lot ready for sale today, though.'

Amos squinted into the sun, a small smile tugging at the corners of his mouth. 'You don't take any prisoners, do you?'

She stopped then, turning around to face him. 'I take as I find, Amos. When my dad died, I soon found out who my real friends were, and believe me, the Hendersons were not on the list.' She glared at him, daring to be contradicted.

Amos decided that changing the subject might be the best move. 'Look if you're pushed for time, I could go and get breakfast?'

Her brown eyes softened again. 'That's a deal then,' she replied, tucking a ten-pound note into Amos' hand.

*

By the time Amos returned to her, Freya had already laid out half the wreaths into her earmarked pens, and was just fetching another load from the van, ingeniously threaded onto a broom pole so that she could carry them. She was pleased with them this year. She'd really found her style now, and it was clear from looking at what the other traders had to offer, that hers were a little different. It had been hard work, though, painstakingly collecting all the greenery to make each wreath identical, and wiring up the fruits, acorns and walnuts that she'd added. She could only hope that she'd get a good price for them.

It was something her dad had encouraged her to do, even when she was small, and he always made it her task to decorate the house for Christmas. Over the years, she had refined her skills and had now been bringing her home-made decorations to the fair for the last five years. Standing back, she checked she had them all laid uniformly, all turned the same way, and, once satisfied, finally turned to Amos to collect her breakfast.

He waved his bap appreciatively. 'Those are beautiful, Freya,' he remarked.

'Thank you.' She blushed, jumping back as a drop of runny egg just missed her coat. She licked her roll, biting off the end of bacon which the egg had dripped from. 'I'll go and get the last of them in a minute.'

She had just taken another oozing bite when someone cannoned into the back of her, followed by an immediate gushing apology.

'Oh my God, I'm so sorry… Oh my God… Freya?'

'Merry!' shrieked Freya in return, throwing her arms around the woman as best she could, hampered both by the roll in her hand and the size of the woman's stomach. 'I didn't think you were coming this year, but look at you!'

The woman pulled a rueful face. 'I know, I'm huge, and bloody due on Christmas Day, can you believe it, of all the luck.'

Freya laughed. 'I think that's the best kind of luck. You have the perfect excuse to let everyone else organise Christmas and sit around with your feet up.'

'Yeah right. Like that's really going to happen. Can you see me sitting still? Not really my style, is it? Anyway, to be fair, Tom has been brilliant. I'm only here today because I've hardly lifted a finger all weekend and am feeling guilty. We do desperately need some stock, though.'

'Well, I don't think you're going to have any trouble finding some today, it's looking like it'll be a great sale. Plenty of buyers around by the look of things, although that might not necessarily be a good thing in your case.' She paused for a moment before adding shyly, 'Are you looking for anything in particular?'

'Well, holly and mistletoe, *obviously*.' She laughed, winking at Amos. 'But Tom would like some decorative pieces for the hotel as well, so I'll drag him over in a minute. Although I have to say, if you get any better, you'll price yourself out of our market. These are looking beautiful.'

'I was wondering if they were a bit too contemporary?' said Freya, biting her lip. 'Not everyone wants something different.'

Merry studied Amos for a moment before turning back to answer. 'It's true, they don't, but I don't think you'll have any trouble selling these. Anyway, enough shop talk for now. This poor man has been standing here patiently while we gossip away.' She thrust out her hand. 'I'm Merrilees Parker, but not surprisingly everyone calls me Merry.'

Amos grasped her hand and nodded. 'I approve, and very appropriate for the time of year.'

'Sorry,' butted in Freya. 'I'm hopeless at introductions. Merry and I have known each other for a gazillion years. She's a florist by trade, although she and her husband also run a hotel in Worcester.

And Merry, this is Amos, and he… well, he's been helping me out a bit on the farm.'

'Still can't get Gareth interested then, Freya? Never mind, maybe he'll come round. It'll hit him one day just how boring accountancy is, and then he'll be brewing cider with the best of them.'

'Hmm, maybe,' replied Freya, sounding doubtful. 'Anyway, there might not be a one day, Merry. I've finally had to put the place on the market. This will probably be my last year.'

Her friend's face fell. 'Oh Freya, no, you can't do that. Is there really no other way? I thought when we last spoke that things were picking up a bit.'

'Not enough it would seem. Believe me, if there was another way, I'd have taken it. Gareth did all the sums, and we're just going to get deeper into debt. I only just managed to get the harvest in this year, but I want to be making cider and juices myself, Merry, not selling my apples to other people so that they can do it. The trouble is I can't afford to pay for help or new machinery, both of which I need.

'There's just me flogging myself to death, and however hard I pretend, it's not enough. Gareth is never going to be a farmer, Merry, and it's wrong to make him try. He's been good to me, you know… since Dad died. I have to respect that.' She blew out her cheeks. 'So… this is it, one last push; out with a bang with any luck, and then I'll be heading for the suburbs and a two-up, two-down.'

Merry pulled Freya into another hug. 'You know we'll help if we can, don't you? I'm not sure what we can do, but we'll think of something.'

'That's very kind of you, but really, it's okay. I'll just have to get used to it. Nothing stays the same forever, Merry.'

There was real sadness in her friend's eyes as Merry pulled away. 'I must go and find Tom. I'll catch up with you later, okay?'

'Okay.'

*

Amos watched Freya for a moment, unsure what to say. He'd had no idea that things were quite so bad. 'Is Merry a good friend?'

Freya's grin was wide. 'The best; we grew up together. Our mums had beds next to each other in the maternity ward, and because they were always together, so were we. We don't see each other as often as we'd like to now that she's married and moved away, but we've always kept in touch. When Mum left, I practically lived at their house.'

'Her name means one who has psychic powers, did you know that?' he replied, swallowing hard. The more he got to know Freya, the more he realised what a bum deal life had dealt her. She had every reason to be bitter but was very far from it. He had a feeling that Freya's holly would always have berries on it.

'What, Merry, psychic?' She laughed. 'She didn't even realise she was pregnant for about five months! It's a nice idea, though.' She looked down at her roll, now cold and congealing in her hand. 'I don't suppose…?'

Amos shook his head vehemently. 'No thanks. But I'll go and find a bin for you if you like. It looks like you have folk waiting to talk to you.' He motioned with his head and, collecting her half-eaten breakfast, wandered off. He had spied Stephen Henderson in the distance and wondered if he might be lucky enough to find a bin in his vicinity.

Things were really picking up now; the place was heaving with people amid good-natured calling and laughing, together with some more serious discussions, and if the conversations Amos had overheard were anything to go by, it looked like bidding was going to be lively. By the time he returned to Freya he could hardly see her amid the bustle that was crowding around. All eyes seemed to be on a tall man in a green coat, who carried some kind of a long stick. As Amos watched, Freya motioned him over.

'That's the auctioneer,' she said, checking her phone again. 'I think we're just about to start.'

Almost as soon as she had voiced the words, a piercing whistle rang out across the yard, and the sound fell away, leaving near silence in its wake. The sale had begun.

*

It was nearly seven by the time Freya walked in, the kitchen still in darkness. She dumped her bags on the table and followed the sound of the television to the living room. This too was in darkness save for the flickering glare cast by the football match that Gareth was watching. She stood for a couple of minutes in the gloom, wondering if he'd even realised she was there, before flicking on the light, making Gareth jump. He whirled around to face her.

'Christ, that's bright.'

'Sorry. Just checking you were still alive as the house is in total darkness.'

Gareth peered back at the screen.

'God, is it that late? I hadn't realised. I only popped in here to catch the score. What a game, though.'

'Popped in with your tea and a beer.'

'Ah, well... yes. I wasn't sure what time you'd be back you see.'

Freya picked up his mobile phone from the coffee table beside him and pressed a button to bring the screen to life. She looked at it for a moment and then handed it silently to him, her text messages all in a row. Then she left the room.

Amos was coming in through the back door as she filled the kettle. She greeted him with a warm smile.

'What do you fancy for tea, Amos? Gareth's already eaten.'

'Um, I'm probably okay, don't worry,' he replied, flicking a glance out through the open door. 'I've put the gear back in the barn, is that okay?'

'Perfect, thank you. I could make us some beans on toast? I'm not sure I'm up for much more than that, my feet are killing me.'

Amos grinned. 'It was a brilliant day, wasn't it? You did well I think?'

'I did fantastically! I can't believe it,' she squealed, giving a little jump of excitement. 'I just hope I can pull it off. It's a lot of work you know.'

'The best things often are, but I'm happy to help. It's very kind of you to let me stay.'

'It's purely mercenary believe me – kindness has nothing to do with it!' She laughed. 'I need your manpower.'

The kitchen doorway darkened for a second as Gareth's bulky frame passed through it.

'Let me do that, love,' he said with a pointed look at Amos. He took the kettle from Freya. 'You must be exhausted. Go and sit down for a bit, and I'll rustle up something for your tea.'

Amos looked from one to the other. 'I'll maybe go and check that the chooks have put themselves to bed, shall I?'

Freya nodded gratefully as Amos made himself scarce.

'Oh, I had the most brilliant day, Gareth,' she launched in before he could start. She really wasn't in the mood for an argument tonight. 'We sold everything, and I got an incredible price for the mistletoe, but not only that, Tom placed an order with me for wreaths and decorations for the hotel. He said he was really impressed with them. Of course Merry might have had a hand in that, but I don't care, they want thirty-two of each for next Saturday; can you believe it?'

He came up behind her, sliding his arms around her waist and nuzzling the side of her neck.

'See, I told you you were amazing. That's fantastic news, Freya,' he said, dropping a soft kiss on the weak spot just behind her ear. 'Is that why he's here?'

She tried not to stiffen. 'I need help, Gareth, that's all. I met him on the road today and offered him a lift. He wasn't going in any particular direction, so I suggested he give me a hand at the fair. He was incredibly helpful today, lugging stuff around for me, and he really got the buyers going. He has nowhere to go tonight; I couldn't just leave him there.'

'And that's your problem because? You can't keep picking up waifs and strays just because you feel sorry for them.'

'He's not a waif and stray; he's a person, Gareth. I know you don't like him, but he's done nothing wrong, and I didn't pick him up because I feel sorry for him. He's not looking for pity if that's what you think; he's willing to work hard for his bed and board. Considering what I've got coming up this next week, I'm going to need all the help I can get.'

Gareth pulled back a little and moved his hands to cup her face. 'I don't want you to get hurt, that's all. You know nothing about this man, and yet you've invited him into our home, at a time when you're feeling very vulnerable.'

'Oh, I get it,' said Freya, pulling her head back. 'You've nothing to be jealous about you know, I've told you a hundred times. Amos is old enough to be my… dad,' she choked, the words sticking suddenly in her throat, and with that, she burst into tears, all the day's tension and anxiety catching up with her.

She clung to Gareth as he rubbed her back, pulling her woollen hat from her head and burying his face in her hair, which he said always smelled of apples.

'I should have made you some tea. I'm sorry, I just didn't think. Look, why don't I run you a bath, and I'll bring you a tray up to bed? You're exhausted, and a good night's sleep will do you the world of good.'

She rubbed her cheek against the softness of his sweatshirt, wanting so much to accept his platitudes and allow herself to be pacified. But there was still a spark of hurt inside her that wouldn't go away. She was tired, she was overwrought and emotional, but more than that she was excited and elated with her success today. She wanted someone to share that excitement with and help her to plan. She wanted interested questions and to share a common sense of purpose. She wanted to feel encouraged. Slowly, she disentangled herself from Gareth's arms.

'Was your phone not working today? Only I sent you quite a few messages. I thought you might have wished me luck.'

Gareth squeezed her arms and turned back to the kettle on the stove as it began its whistling alert. 'Sorry love, it's a bit awkward at work. You know how it is.'

Chapter Two

Amos stood and watched as the car made its way down the track, Gareth's exhaust billowing white clouds into the icy morning air. He'd spotted Freya going into the henhouse a few minutes earlier and hoped that's where he'd find her now. He felt somehow that he should apologise, although he was well aware that he hadn't actually done anything wrong.

She was talking to herself when he got there, or rather to the hens, a continual sing-song stream of chatter as one might talk to a child. He lifted the latch on the door of the coop and cleared his throat.

'Scrambled eggs on toast or an omelette?' said Freya, without turning around. Amos' mouth began to water, and his stomach gave an appreciative lurch. Staying for tea hadn't seemed such a good idea last night. 'Please tell me you didn't sleep in the barn last night?' she added.

When he didn't answer, she whirled around to face him, three eggs in one hand and two in the other. 'Right, come with me,' she said.

Amos followed her meekly back into the kitchen, which, after the air outside, felt rather like a sauna, but right now, the most comforting place on earth. Freya set the eggs down on the table, holding her hand over them just for a second to be sure they didn't roll. 'Sit down a minute.' Amos did as he was told.

A few minutes later, she placed a huge mug of tea and a plate of toast swimming in butter in front of him. She motioned for Amos to start eating. 'Right, while you're tucking into that lot, let's get a couple of things straight, shall we? Firstly, can I just say that I'm sorry that Gareth is being such a prat.'

Amos looked up sharply at her words, but she held her hand up to finish. 'This is my house, and who I invite into it is my business. I know Gareth is my boyfriend, and perhaps I sound a bit disloyal, but he's got no right to moan about you being around, especially when he's so completely uninterested in everything I'm trying to do here. We've got a busy week ahead, and I haven't got time to pander to his selfish and childish arguments.' She stared at Amos to check whether he was still following her. 'Secondly, you have a room in the house and a bathroom which you are very welcome to use, so please Amos, don't sleep in the barn; it's bloody freezing out there.'

Amos took a slug of tea and hacked off the corner of a piece of toast. 'Rant over?' He smiled.

'Rant over.' Freya smiled back. 'I'm glad we understand one another.'

'It strikes me that what we need is a plan of action,' added Amos. 'It's not just the wreaths that need to be made, is it? You'll need more holly and mistletoe for next week's fair, and that doesn't include all your normal jobs. Let me finish this, and we'll make a list.'

'I tell you what, I've got an even better idea. There's plenty of hot water left, so why don't you go and grab a shower and warm yourself up a bit while I make us a proper breakfast; then we'll see where we go from there.'

Amos touched his hand to her sleeve. 'Thank you.'

*

It was noon before they stopped again for a welcome cuppa. They had spent the morning walking the fields and deciding what to cut and when. Freya would need a good deal of greenery for her arrangements, but there were still two mistletoe sales left, and of course she would need a little left over to decorate the farmhouse too. She never tired of the orchards. Whatever the weather, whatever the time of year, there was always some new wonder to catch her eye; baby rabbits running and chasing across the fields, frothy clouds of elderflower blossom in the hedgerow, or row after row of apple blossom, its pale beauty against a blue summer sky a sight she would never forget. Even on the darker days she loved it; those still October mornings when the sky hardly seemed to clear the ground, but where, here in the orchard, the sparkle of dew on cobwebs really was like diamonds, and the air was heavy with the scent of apples.

She had never known anywhere else, and the thought that she might soon have to leave was almost unbearable. She'd taken it all for granted. She hadn't realised until her dad died how much he had protected her from, how much of a struggle it must have been for him to keep things going and how much he had sacrificed over the years. She hadn't realised either quite how much debt they were in, and she felt enormously guilty that she'd never known. Her dad had carried that burden solely on his shoulders, and although she knew he wouldn't have had it any other way, she couldn't help wondering whether it had contributed to his early death; he had, after all, been only sixty-three.

Her mobile had flashed during the morning with a missed call from a number that she had been expecting. She couldn't go on deliberately avoiding these calls and finally decided to voice the nagging thoughts that had been plaguing her.

'Do you think I'm mad, Amos?'

'Possibly,' he replied ambiguously. 'But there's several definitions of mad in my book, not all of them bad I might add, so which variant do you think you might be?'

'Well, all this; doing all these orders, going to sales – for what? The estate agent rang this morning, and I know it's because he's got someone he wants to show around. Sure, I'll make a bit of money from the sales, but it's never going to be enough to save this place, so why am I doing it, why am I putting myself through this?'

Amos took in a long slow breath, considering the question, and then gently let it out again. 'That's not something I can answer, Freya. Only you know why.'

Freya screwed up her face. 'Well, that's no bloody good,' she wheedled. 'Can't you make something up, to make me feel better? Or even not to make me feel better, but to make me see sense instead?'

'Possibly. But I don't know you all that well.'

'You know me well enough. Anyway, you have that wise man thing about you, like you've got everyone sussed. So, tell me why you think I'm doing this.'

'Are you sure you really want me to tell you?'

'Yes, for God's sake,' she groaned. 'Put me out of my misery.'

Amos regarded her for a moment, and then he looked around the room she loved so much, with its warm colours and comfortable furnishings.

'I think it's because there's so much of you in this house, Freya, that you're scared you won't exist outside of it,' he said slowly. 'You've lived here your whole life, and when your mum left, it was just you and your dad against the world, and this place, well, it became your fortress if you like. Now that he's gone, it's the only thing that ties you to him, and now that the house is threatened as well, it's like you're threatened too, like you don't know who you are, or more importantly who you want to be. It's time to find out, Freya, that's all. There's no madness involved. I think if I'd had this life, this house, I'd do everything I could to keep it too. But if it really has to go, then see it as your opportunity to find out what's important to you; and when you do find out, don't let go of it. You never know, things might surprise you.'

'What if I don't know what I want,' she whispered, her gaze still locked on his.

'You will, Freya, you will. Now make the call.'

The agent was prompt, more's the pity. Stephen Henderson came in first, his arrogant manner slightly subdued by the colourful black eye he was wearing, but that didn't stop him from gazing around the kitchen with a very annoying grin on his face. Freya shook his hand, desperate to ask about the eye, but promising herself that at least one of them should show some manners.

The agent was the same one who had come to value the property and draw up the details. She'd gone to school with him, which was a little embarrassing, but then that happened a lot around here. He took Freya to one side almost as soon as he entered the room.

'I know you'll be expecting to show them around, Freya, but can I make a suggestion? Actually, it wasn't mine, it was Sam's, but, on this occasion, I happen to agree. Usually, I'm very happy for the vendor to chat to prospective buyers; it can lend a more relaxed air to proceedings and is often helpful when questions are asked. But since both brothers know the property well, it would seem a bit superfluous, and I wondered whether you might find it difficult, well, awkward, you know. Sam thought this way might be easier for you.' He gave a nervous smile, half expecting to be shot down in flames.

Freya hadn't considered this, but it was a kind thought. She looked at Amos for guidance, who gave a small nod. She was blushing and she knew it, sitting down at the table quickly to hide her colour. For some reason, an old and deeply inappropriate memory had just popped into her head, of her and Sam, from a time when they had been very good friends. But why today of all days when she hadn't thought about him that way in years? It was a good thing that she and Amos were to remain sitting at the table because, right now, Freya really didn't think she'd have anything coherent to say. The moment soon passed, however, as Stephen's voice floated up from the passageway. Ignorant moron, of course it looked like an old-fashioned pantry; that's exactly what it was.

Amos kept up a low babble of conversation the whole time, and she knew it was to prevent her from hearing further snippets of conversation. She was thinking about what he had said, though, and how accurate his assessment of her had been. She shouldn't really be surprised. The more she got to know Amos, the more fascinating she found him, but she hadn't realised she had been wearing her heart on her sleeve quite as obviously as she had. Their discussion had focused her mind, and as much as she hadn't wanted to make the decisions that were facing her, they were long overdue, and all the months she had spent deliberating her various options hadn't brought her any further forward. For some reason, that had changed today, and she knew that she could no longer hide from what was surely the inevitable. It would take a miracle to save Appleyard, but if she had to go, she had to go, and now she must fight for a future beyond this house.

Something cut across her thoughts, and she suddenly became aware of what Amos was saying.

'You never mentioned that before.' Freya laughed. 'That's priceless.'

'Well, I can imagine Stephen Henderson gets himself into all sorts of scrapes from what I've been hearing, and I don't suppose it's the first time he's had a black eye. I might have expected him to get belted by some chap who bore him a grudge, but I never thought it would be his brother.'

'And this happened at the fair? Oh, I wish I'd seen it. Good for Sam. I wonder what they were arguing about, though.'

'I was too far away to hear what was actually being said, but whatever it was, Sam didn't like it. I could see they were arguing, and then Sam turned as if to leave but instead swung round with an almighty punch. He had Stephen on the floor.'

'No wonder he looked a little sheepish when he first came in. Oh, Amos, you've made my day.'

'Ssh, they're coming back; straight faces back on, no laughing,' said Amos sternly.

Freya tried to stifle her giggles. She thought of Stephen poking his nose into all her things, and that did the trick, but then reminded herself that it was a necessary evil. She knew she was biased, but Appleyard was a handsome house; not huge, but a good size nonetheless, of warm red brick and with a pleasing symmetry. It was hard to think about it objectively, but its welcoming rooms were just what people wanted, according to the estate agent.

By the time they'd all arrived back in the kitchen, Freya even managed a welcoming smile. She got up to show them out as they all did the thank-you-for-showing-us-round, we'll-be-in-touch routine. Freya didn't doubt that they would; in a way it hardly mattered what the house was like, Stephen Henderson had been trying to get his hands on their farm for years.

Later that night as Freya lay next to Gareth listening to his rhythmic snoring, she found herself thinking about Sam for some unaccountable reason.

*

Four doors down at the other end of the house, Amos lay on the floor, as was his custom, gazing at the stars through the window. He was also thinking about Sam, but for an entirely different reason. When they'd met earlier, his attention had been consumed by the young man. He'd only ever seen Sam from a distance, but up close, he'd been able to see the family resemblance. He had Stephen's features, but more refined so, instead of looking squashed and pudgy, he was a very attractive man. And while he had none of his brother's stature, his clothes suited him too; he seemed relaxed in them whereas his brother always looked like he was dressing up. He rubbed the back of his neck thoughtfully, another piece of his jigsaw falling into place.

Chapter Three

The call from the estate agent didn't come until Friday afternoon, much as Freya had expected. It was all part of the game, and it certainly wouldn't do for the Hendersons to appear too keen; although Freya imagined that Stephen had found the two-day interval rather trying. Despite his disparaging remarks about her house, she knew it had been on his hit list for years. He'd even had the gall to ask her not long after her dad's funeral when she was putting it on the market. The fact that it had only taken eight months before she'd been forced to, stuck in her craw, but she reminded herself that it was a means to an end.

She actually laughed out loud when she heard what they were prepared to offer. She had expected it to be low, but fifty thousand pounds below the asking price was plain ridiculous. Having reminded the estate agent that they had deliberately priced the property competitively to take into account the time of year, she left him in no doubt that his client either needed to be sensible or quite frankly piss off.

'Do you think they'll come up?' asked Amos as she returned to the table.

Freya picked up another length of ribbon and proceeded to twist it expertly into a bow. 'I think so, although you can never really tell with Stephen. He's that arrogant he seems to think his money is worth more than anyone else's.' She swapped hands, winding wire around the bow to secure it and adding a tail which would fasten it to the wreath. 'Much might also depend of course on how much influence Sam has. You see the thing with Stephen is that he convinces himself he wants something really badly, but then when he gets it, he can't be bothered. He doesn't put the effort into their own farm; it's all down to Sam. Stephen just likes the title of landowner and the ability it gives him to swank about. He's always been the same, ever since he was little.'

'So what's the story with the two brothers then?'

Freya paused for a moment, raising her eyebrows in query. 'What do you mean?'

'Well, I might be mistaken,' ventured Amos, 'but you seem to be rather fonder of one than the other. I wondered if there was any reason for that.'

'Oh there are lots of reasons for that, but none that I'm prepared to go into just now.'

'Fair enough.' Amos shrugged with a smile. 'It was worth a try.'

Freya smiled too. 'Another time perhaps. Now how many of these blessed things have I got left to do?'

Amos counted up. 'Thirty-seven,' he said with a grimace. 'Would another cup of tea help? I'm not sure what else I can do.'

'Tea would be lovely, and you could always peel the veg for tea if you wanted a job. I'm just going to make a chuck-it-all-in vegetable soup, which requires very little effort on my part, but fortunately tastes like I've been slaving over a hot stove all day.'

'So what's the grand plan now?'

'There's nothing terribly grand about it,' started Freya, scratching her nose. 'I do need to sell the house, and pretty quickly too, but after that I have a few options. I had another chat with Merry on the phone this morning, and there are a few ideas I'm exploring with her.' She looked down at the table. 'I love doing all this – making things, the decorations, everything really. I think there's a market for this type of thing, but I need a base to do it from, and once the house has gone, that's what I don't have.'

'Is there no one else interested in this place?'

'Nope. Dead as a dodo. I shouldn't have left it as late as I did putting it on the market, but there you go, one to chalk up to experience.'

'Understandable, in the circumstances.'

Freya tilted her head to one side. 'Perhaps. Not everyone sees it that way.' She laid another wired ribbon on the table. 'Right, I'd better get these finished. It doesn't take long to fix them to the wreaths, but I'd rather get them all finished today. That way I can get them over to Tom and Merry first thing in the morning.'

'Well, this is cosy.'

Freya looked up at the sound of the voice by the door and tutted audibly. 'Don't be such a prat, Gareth. I'm sitting here finishing Tom's decorations off for tomorrow, and Amos is reading. We're not having wild abandoned sex on the rug in front of the fire.' She looked pointedly at the wall on the clock. 'Nice of you to let me know you were going to be late.'

'It's Friday, I always go down the pub after work on a Friday.' He pouted.

'Yes, and you usually let me know. I made soup for tea, which is now stone cold, but there's still some in the pan if you want to heat it up.'

Gareth had the grace to look a little ashamed at this. 'Oh. Er, well, I ate at the pub, sorry.'

'My point exactly, so please don't come in here throwing wild accusations around.' She glared at Gareth.

'Anyway, I've got some news if you're interested,' added Gareth, still a little sulky, but with the beginnings of a triumphant gleam in his eyes. 'I didn't exactly waste my time while I was down the pub.'

'I'll pour some tea,' said Freya, lifting the teapot from the middle of the table. 'Sit down.'

Gareth dumped his work bag on a chair and rummaged around in its depths.

'Well, for starters, I got these at lunchtime. Two of them have just been reduced and are real bargains.' He placed a sheaf of papers on the table and pushed them towards Freya who eyed them warily. When she made no move to pick them up, Gareth rifled through them impatiently. 'This one in particular is a real gem. Very clean and well cared for, but it's been on the market for a while and the owners have already found a place so are desperate to sell.'

Eventually, Freya picked up the property details and scanned through them, returning to the one that Gareth had pointed out and studying it more carefully.

'But these are all on estates.'

'I know, they're brilliant. Full of people the same age as us, with schools and shops nearby, and this one is just around the corner from work. It's on that new estate just up past the business park.'

'The gardens look very small.'

'But you wouldn't want a big garden, would you? Not after this place. And just think, we could move in the New Year; fresh start and all that.'

Freya sighed. 'But that's all supposing I can sell this place. That might take a little time.'

Gareth sat back in his chair with a triumphant grin. 'Ah, but you see that's the best bit. I got talking to Stephen Henderson in the pub tonight. I did a cracking deal with him. Who needs bloody estate agents, eh?'

'Go on,' said Freya in a low tone, her spine stiffening.

'We got chatting, and he mentioned he'd put in an offer on the place—'

'Yeah, I bet he did.'

'Look, are you going to let me tell you or what! I felt a bit of a tit, to be honest, seeing as I didn't even know he'd been to see the place, or put in an offer.'

Freya remained silent.

'Anyway, never mind that now. He's really keen to get this deal under wraps, so we had a bit of a chat. I know you turned his offer down flat, and he doesn't blame you for that, but all he needed was a bit of buttering up. Honestly, Freya, I would have thought you'd realise that. I bought him a few drinks and we chatted a bit more and... what do you think of this... he's agreed to come up another ten grand on his offer, and…' he paused here for effect, leaning in towards Freya with a grin, 'provided we can get the sale though quick, he'll give us twenty-five thousand in cash on the side.'

'No,' said Freya flatly.

Gareth's mouth hung open for a moment. 'What do you mean, no? It's a bloody good deal, only fifteen grand lower than the asking price. We'll have a wodge of cash in the bank to spend as we like and can buy a house outright with no mortgage. Think of how much money we'll have every month not having to fork out on the enormous bills we have here.'

'I said no, Gareth.'

'Oh, for God's sake,' he hissed. 'Will you get over yourself with that bloody man? I've got us a brilliant deal, and you're being stubborn because you don't like him. His money's as good as anyone else's, Freya, and you're not going to get another deal.'

Freya's nostrils flared. 'Firstly, you don't know I'm not going to get another deal, and secondly what I do about this place is very much my decision, seeing as this is my house.'

'Oh well, thanks a bunch, that's bloody gratitude for you. I'm trying to do the best for us, and you throw it straight back in my face. At least I'm trying to do something constructive, not wallowing in self-pity about this stupid house, which, I might add is a noose around our necks.'

Freya risked a glance at Amos, knowing how awkward this must be for him. 'It's a noose around *my* neck, Gareth, not yours. And while we're on the subject, let's just look at everything you're doing for *us*. Let's look at the hours you've put into this place, helping me to keep it going. Let's look at the help you've given me with the harvest, or selling my fruit, or even just getting the mistletoe ready for the sales. A big fat zero, Gareth, that's what. I might not be able to stay in this house, but all I was asking for was a bit of support and understanding of how I feel, instead of trying to ship me out to some soulless brick box. This perfect vision you have for our future, Gareth, is all about you; it's your dream, and you've never considered for one moment how I feel, or what I want.'

'But I'm doing this for *you*, you stupid cow. I'm trying to save you from yourself if you'd only stop and listen. You're so bloody blinkered about this place, you won't think beyond the end of your nose. I haven't put the hours in on this place, as you so charmingly put it, because I can see it would be flogging a dead horse and only encourage you. I want a future for us, Freya, but you're frittering away everything we have, and if you carry on, we'll lose the best opportunity we've ever had too.'

Freya's hands were clenching and unclenching in her lap. 'The best opportunity *you've* ever had you mean. You've never contributed financially to this place, but you'd be very happy for me to sell up and feather your nest with a nice little mortgage-free house. Well played, Gareth, well played.'

Gareth snatched back the estate agent's brochures from the table. 'So is that what it all comes down to in the end, Freya, your money? In my book that's not what a true partnership is all about.' He lurched up from the table, his face beetroot. 'Keep your bloody money. I hope you'll be very happy.'

'I will, because it's not as if you've earned any of it. How soon was it after Dad died that you moved in here, eh? It used to be a partnership, Gareth, but it hasn't been one for a long time; just up to the point where you thought your grand prize was within reach, in fact. I cook, clean, clear up after you, wash your clothes and generally run around after you each and every day as well as everything else I have to do here, while you go out to work. Not that I see any of the fruits of your labour. What exactly do you contribute to this so-called partnership?'

'I've been saving my money for us, putting it aside for our new life actually, if you'd bothered to ask.'

'So how much have you saved then, Mr Accountant? You've had your hands on my books these last few months, but how much have you saved for our future after you've bought that swanky new car, and had your weekends away with the boys? Not to mention that bloody cruise that was a monumental waste of money?' Freya lurched to her feet too, keeping one hand on the table.

Gareth glared at her as she held his gaze. 'Jesus, what are you accusing me of now? I don't have to stand here and listen to this.'

'How much, Gareth?'

He threw the papers onto the floor and gave the chair back an almighty shove before stalking from the room.

'Yeah right... I thought as much,' muttered Freya sadly.

She looked at Amos for a moment who was still pinned to his chair unable to move, and then slowly sat back down, her body deflating like a balloon. She rested her head on the table. 'Oh, dear Lord,' she said to no one in particular.

Chapter Four

Amos certainly hadn't slept much, and he reckoned Freya had slept even less, but somehow, he missed her the next morning. She must have gone out at the crack of dawn. The house was still in darkness as he crept downstairs, checking as he did so that Gareth's car was still in the yard. He didn't suppose that he'd be up too early, but one thing was for certain, Amos didn't want to be anywhere near him when he did.

Taking an apple from the fruit bowl and a hunk of the fresh bread he had made the day before, he slipped on his jacket and boots and softly closed the kitchen door behind him. He didn't know how far it was to the Hendersons' farm, but he knew the general direction it lay in and he'd enjoy the walk at any rate. There was no doubt in his mind that Sam Henderson would be the only one up at this hour of the morning, and there were a couple of things that Amos wanted to chat to him about. He wasn't quite sure why Stephen was so keen to buy Appleyard in such a hurry, but something about the whole thing didn't smell right to him.

He'd only gone a matter of a mile or so when he felt a familiar prickle on the back of his neck. He walked on a little further, the feeling growing stronger with each step until he had to stop by the side of the road and wait for the feeling to pass. If he concentrated hard, he could usually sort out the 'noise' in his head until he understood its sound, but this time, nothing he did could alleviate it. He leaned on the farm gate for a few more moments feeling slightly nauseous when a movement in the field caught his eye, and suddenly he understood. In the distance a rider was putting a horse through its paces and, without a second thought, Amos braced his arms on the top of the gate and swung himself over.

The field was large, and it took him some while to reach them, the horse becoming aware of him first, slowing from a canter to a walk, and finally stopping altogether despite the best efforts of its rider. Amos could sense the confusion in the young man as his horse steadfastly refused to move until, finally, Amos was close enough for him to register his presence. The rider raised a hand, in warning, not in greeting, but Amos paid him no heed. The huge bay stallion walked over to him, eventually standing quietly by his side.

The rider shielded his eyes from the low morning sun as he squinted to get a better view.

'By rights, you should be dead by now, coming up on a horse like that.'

Amos stroked the bay's nose while it blew steamy breaths into his hand.

'You're Sam, aren't you?' he asked. 'Sam Henderson? Sorry, we weren't properly introduced the other day.'

The rider nodded, peering closer until a gleam of recognition appeared in his eyes. He slipped his feet out of the stirrups and slid down from the horse, rubbing its flank for a moment before turning back to Amos.

'You're the chap who's been helping Freya, aren't you? You were with her at the mistletoe sales as well. I'm sorry, I don't know your name.'

'It's Amos. Amos Fry.'

Sam shook his hand. 'Well, Amos, you either know a lot about horses or you're a bloody idiot. Bailey here doesn't normally take too kindly to strangers.'

'I'm sorry I alarmed you, but Bailey and I seem to be getting along just fine,' Amos replied as the horse nuzzled his hand. 'I was on my way to see you actually, Freya mentioned you.'

Sam grimaced. 'Well, I can imagine what she had to say, and none of it complimentary I'm sure.'

'Actually, it's only your brother she dislikes.'

He laughed. 'Really…? Oh, well yes, he does seem to have that effect on people. Anyway, what can I do for you, Amos?'

'Have you spoken to your brother since last night?'

'You must be joking, it's only eight o'clock. My brother won't be up for hours yet.'

'Well, in that case, perhaps we could walk a little, and I'll explain.'

Amos eventually found Freya sitting in the dark on a gate at the far end of the orchard. He'd also found only one car in the yard upon his return, and the scribbled note from Gareth on the side in the kitchen. She'd been crying of course.

He peeled her icy hands away from the cold metal of the gate and led her unyielding into the house where the fire he had laid earlier was roaring. He placed a blanket around her shoulders and a mug of hot chocolate in front of her and then went to sit in one of the armchairs opposite her, where he pretended to read for half an hour before she spoke.

'I don't know why I'm upset really.'

Amos looked up at her. 'It's human nature to mourn something when it's gone.'

She ran a hand wearily through her hair. 'It was stupid, arguing like that. I was tired, and he was drunk, it wasn't the best time to have a discussion.'

'No, perhaps it wasn't. But given a better time, would the words have been any different?'

'No,' she said slowly. 'I don't think they would.' She let out a long sigh. 'I think I've probably been feeling that way for quite a while, I just didn't realise it until I opened my mouth.'

'How long had you been together?'

'Nearly four years. Too long probably. I harboured dreams once that he would ask me to marry him, and we could run this place together, but he never did, and as time went on, it became obvious that he was never really interested. We don't have all that much in common. I mean, he doesn't even much like being outside. A long walk in the country is his idea of hell, but we've always got on quite well, and he was very good to me when Dad died.' She looked down at her mug of chocolate, swilling it gently. 'I wanted someone to share in what we had here, but that person was never going to be Gareth, I can see that now. I've let him down too. He thought I wanted the same things he did, but, in truth, I couldn't live the kind of life he wanted either, a little piece of me would have died each day until we ended up hating each other.'

'Then you've made the right decision. Our choices in life aren't always easy, but if they come from the heart, they're usually the right ones, I've found. Feeling sad for what has passed is normal, but it also frees you to face the future without the weight of hurt and disappointment. These things are often barriers to what lies beyond, and now, without them, you can be open to possibility once more.'

'But what am I going to do, Amos? It's nearly Christmas, and I've probably totally blown it with the Hendersons. I don't want to bow down to Stephen, but I really could do with the money, especially after today.' She took another sip of her chocolate, staring morosely into her mug.

'But I didn't think Gareth contributed financially from what you said. How will his leaving make things any worse for you?'

'It won't, but that's not what I meant. I had a phone call from Merry today. She's had an idea that might give me a way out of all this; without the cash, though, I might not be able to make it happen.'

'That sounds like it could be good news?'

'It is, yes. They've given me a repeat order for the hotel for the next four weeks, right up until Christmas. With that and what I make from the mistletoe sales, it will keep me going through to January, but I will need to find something then, which is where Merry's idea comes in.'

Amos got up to throw another log on the fire. 'Go on,' he said, poking at the embers.

'Well, it seems like they've decided that trying to run two businesses might not be so easy with a small child; at some point they're going to sell the florist shop. They've got someone in there at the moment covering for Merry, but she wants to finish at the end of January anyway. To cut a long story short, Merry has offered it to me to run for a few months while she's busy with the baby with a view to buying it if I find it suits me. Well, obviously, I can't be in two places at once, so I really need to be out of here early in the New Year. Tom has offered me a room at their hotel until I can find somewhere to live.'

'So it sounds as if you have a plan?'

'I might have. But like I said I really need to get this place sold. It's very good of Merry to offer the shop to me, but I can't keep them hanging on, they need to make plans too. The extra orders are good news, but they'll take up a lot of my time as well, and I don't see how I can possibly get everything done.' She rubbed her eyes, which still looked red from her crying.

'Seems to me as if you have no option really. You'll have to speak to the Hendersons and see what happens; just take one thing at a time. As it happens, I bumped into Sam this morning while I was out walking.'

Freya sat up a little straighter. 'You bumped into him?'

'Well, not exactly, he was out riding, but our paths crossed. We got talking, and I happened to mention the deal that Gareth is supposed to have done with his brother. Not surprisingly, given the early hour, he hadn't yet spoken to Stephen and knew nothing about it, but I'd say he was pretty curious. Perhaps you ought to have a chat with him.'

Freya narrowed her eyes. 'Just how exactly do you bump into someone on a horse, Amos? What are you up to?'

'Not a thing,' he replied blithely. 'But it did occur to me that it wouldn't hurt to keep a closer eye on them than usual, just to check that things go according to plan. As it happens, what with Stephen being such a monumental waste of space, Sam is feeling a little busy right now and since the young lad who's been helping him out has come down with glandular fever, when I mentioned that I might have a few hours spare if he needed any help, he rather bit my hand off.'

'Amos,' said Freya in a warning tone. 'That's downright meddling.'

Amos said nothing, but stared into the fire, a small smile playing around his lips.

Chapter Five

Freya really wasn't looking forward to this meeting. It was the first time she and Sam had been alone together in the same room since… well, for a very long time, and in the few days since Gareth had gone she'd realised how much she missed having him around. She hadn't thought they'd talked all that much, but even 'Pass the butter please' was better than no one to talk to at all.

Her dad had always told her how expressive her eyes were; big dark brown pools of her very soul, he teased her, whenever she had been trying to keep something from him. One look and anyone would guess what she was feeling, and now she was rather afraid that she was wearing an I'm-very-vulnerable, please-come-and-rescue-me air which was not the impression she wanted to give Sam at all. She was staring in the mirror again, despite having given herself a stern talking to. She had washed her hair, but that was all. Her face was resolutely devoid of make-up, and her curves were just… well, just plain curvy.

She had wondered if Sam would come on his own, or whether Stephen would muscle in, unable to bear anyone other than him getting the better of Freya Sherbourne. But as it happened when she opened the door, only Sam was standing there, looking very cold and, she was relieved to see, rather nervous.

She made them tea, not because she wanted any, but because it gave her something to do with her hands which suddenly didn't know how to behave. She stumbled for a moment over asking Sam whether he took sugar. Giving it to him without would seem rather knowing and presumptuous, and she wasn't sure she'd be able to look him in the eye. Better to pretend he was a stranger and ask what he preferred, as long as he didn't make some cute reference to it himself. Good grief, since when had making a cup of tea become so difficult? Fortunately, Sam was the model guest, and they managed to end up with a cup of tea each without incident.

His attempt at conversation, though, was rather less successful as he complimented her on the homely quality of her kitchen. Normally, a safe conversational bet designed to put the hostess at ease, but under the circumstances, probably the worst thing he could have said. Of course he then realised and didn't know what to say. Freya flushed bright red and decided that a more forthright discussion was the only way forward.

'Look, Sam, I'm sorry, but to be blunt I want to sell Appleyard, you want to buy it, so let's just discuss the price and then we can hand everything over to the agent and solicitors.'

'Erm, yes, good idea,' said Sam, nodding his head vigorously. 'Right, well, I've had a chat to Stephen, and as expected his memory of the offer he made to Gareth is a little sketchy, but the essence of it was that you would end up with an amount about fifteen thousand pounds lower than the asking price. I'm not sure how you feel about this whole cash business, but it doesn't sit right with me, so I've persuaded Stephen to bin that idea if that's okay?'

Freya nodded rapidly.

'Now the bit you're not going to like is that Stephen has, as usual, been shouting his mouth off to all his cronies and he's found a chap who wants to rent this place. After all, we won't need to live in it, but this mate is going through a messy divorce and needs to move in pretty sharpish. On that basis, Stephen's agreed it would be only reasonable to offer you the full asking price provided that the sale can complete on the 10th of January. That's possible apparently as neither of us has any other properties involved. We don't need a survey, and there shouldn't be any issue over boundaries, etc. You might remember our parents had them checked a few years ago when my dad bought the strip along your bottom field.'

'Still, that seems awfully fast. I'm not quite sure I understand Stephen's massive rush, especially at this time of year.'

Sam sighed. 'I imagine it has something to do with getting a mate out of a fix. You know how Stephen likes people owing him favours because he very often has to call them in. If I'm honest, there will probably be some sort of cash inducement involved as well, but I wouldn't worry about that. If it suits you, Freya, it's still a very good offer.'

Freya bit her lip, knowing the truth in his words. It would give her exactly what she wanted... and exactly what she didn't want. She'd give anything to be able to stay at Appleyard, but as it was clear she couldn't do that, then she must accept that fate was sending her somewhere else. The plans she'd made seemed good ones, and she'd be foolish to miss the only opportunity she currently had.

She nodded her head slowly. 'I know Sam, and thank you. Submit your offer through the agent, and I'll speak to my solicitor later today.' She offered her hand in the traditional manner.

Sam gazed at it sadly before taking it in his own, the warmth of it sending her somewhere she really didn't want to go. He rose to leave.

'Before you go, Sam,' said Freya, also standing up. 'Just answer me a question, will you...? This all seems a bit Stephen this and Stephen that; what's in it for you, besides a load more work?'

It was a grimace really, more than a smile. 'I keep a roof over my head, Freya. And I get to stay doing what I love. Simple as that.'

She nodded and walked him to the door, frowning gently at his answer that wasn't really an answer. 'Will I see you at the sales?'

'Yes. We'll be there next week. I'll see you then.' He walked a few steps down the path before turning back. 'I'll miss you, Freya.'

Freya managed a tight smile before closing the door. She walked back into the kitchen, took down a letter she had tucked into the plate rack, and read it one more time, tears pouring down her face.

'I'm so sorry, Dad,' she whispered.

Chapter Six

Freya fished about in her handbag for some painkillers. Unusually for her, she had the beginnings of a headache, and today the noise was really beginning to get to her. It was the second week in December, and the last sale was always the busiest as the selling season reached its peak, and she could hardly move for people. On the one hand, this was great for business, but she was so tired, she wished she could enjoy it more; the atmosphere was brilliant today. It would also be her last ever sale, and she wanted to savour every little drop, remember every tiny detail to store up for the future. The last thing she needed was to feel unwell.

She found a couple of tablets, and stuffed them in her mouth, swigging them down with the dregs of a cold cup of tea. She watched as a trio of Santa Clauses made its way across the yard and smiled in spite of herself. Even at the ripe old age of 35, she still felt that special kind of excitement that only came at Christmas. She sought out Amos in the crowd, trying to weave his way back to her, carrying his precious breakfast cargo.

She didn't know what she would have done without him these last couple of weeks. If she thought she'd been busy before, that was nothing compared to now, having added packing into the mix as well. Appleyard wasn't a huge house, but it was big enough, and with just her and her dad living there, they had filled every corner of available space. Freya had never had any need to declutter before, and now she was having to sort through over thirty years of memories and the stuff of life. For the moment, everything would have to go into storage, and so the less there was, the better. Given her current state of mind, however, it wasn't a task that she was finding at all easy, and were it not for Amos, she would have given up long before now. He knew when to buoy her up, when to give her space and when to just plain nag. He had been a real lifesaver.

A loud shout in her ear brought her back to the present. The sale would be starting any minute now, the hubbub reaching a crescendo as people shouted their last-minute questions and instructions. Her wreaths were all laid out in the traditional pens, but she'd been hoping to get a look at what the other sellers had to offer too. She beckoned Amos over to give her a hand up onto one of the wide metal railings that bisected a pair of pens. The auctioneers usually stood on these, so that they could see who was bidding, but Freya would only be a minute; she could be up and back down again before the sale started. She walked its length, trying to gauge the other lots and what the likely prices would be. Bidding was expected to be lively today, and she hoped that her offerings would be sufficiently distinctive to command a slightly higher price again. She could see the auctioneer coming to the end of the railings where she was standing and turned to walk back the way she had come.

As soon as she put her foot down, she knew it wouldn't end well. Her scarf had slipped off her shoulder, and she'd trapped the end of it under her boot, throwing her balance off to one side. Instinctively, she tried to throw her body backwards to compensate, but she couldn't move, her upper body pinned by the scarf around her neck. She heard Amos's warning shout but, by then, she had too much forward momentum to right herself. In the instant before the sickening crack, it flashed through her mind that putting out her hands to save her fall was a really bad idea; but by then, she had already landed, her body concertinaed on top of the arm that had crumpled beneath her.

It didn't hurt at first as she became aware of the general commotion around her, but as she tried to sit up, a searing pain ricocheted through her arm, followed swiftly by a violent wave of nausea, and her half-digested breakfast splattered onto the pair of boots in front of her.

She was aware of a soft voice talking to her, but everything else was swimming around most alarmingly and for a moment all she could do was concentrate on breathing in and out.

After a few minutes, the pain had receded to an angry buzz, and she raised her head. She was met by a pair of green eyes, which immediately elicited another groan. Of all the people at the fair today, why in God's name did it have to be Sam Henderson's boots that she'd thrown up all over? He was talking to her, and she tried to focus on what he was saying.

'Where does it hurt, Freya, just your arm?'

She'd always liked his voice. With a supreme effort, she thought about the question. Her knee was stinging, but apart from that all the pain was concentrated in her arm.

She managed a nod. 'I think so,' she whispered. 'Can I sit up?' She was aware of another person by her side and instinctively knew it was Amos.

Gradually, she realised that a space was opening up around her, and she felt a blanket settle over her. It was bright red with white reindeer on it.

'I've called an ambulance, Freya, just lie still,' said Sam.

'What? I can't go to the hospital, what about the sale...? Help me to stand up, I'll be all right in a minute.'

'I bloody well will not, Freya Sherbourne, you're going to do as you're told.'

Tears sprang to Freya's eyes. 'No, you don't understand, Sam, I need to carry on. I need to sell my stuff today... Oh God, I've stopped the sale, haven't I? Are people really cross?'

Sam smiled. 'No one's cross, just concerned. Once we've got you sorted, they'll carry on, don't worry.'

Freya looked up at his face which was alarmingly close to hers. He hadn't shaved for a couple of days and the stubble suited him.

'Perhaps Amos could handle the sale on your behalf, Freya,' added Sam, 'if that's okay? I'm sure he's more than capable.'

Amos grinned. 'It would be a pleasure, Freya, and don't worry, I'll kick up a storm for you. Just relax, and as Sam said, do as you're told. You're in good hands. I'll see you later, okay?'

Sam flashed him a grateful look and tucked the blanket around Freya a little more.

'I can't believe I threw up on your boots,' she said.

'I know, it's not my week, is it? My horse shat on them yesterday too.'

Two and a half hours later, Freya was propped up in bed eating a piece of toast and jam which was, quite possibly, the best meal she'd ever had. A very lovely young doctor had given her a very lovely injection of something equally lovely, and now everything was... well just lovely really; even Sam.

'Do you remember the time at the Harvest Festival dance when I threw a glass of wine at you?' She grinned. 'All over your beautiful pristine shirt. You didn't speak to me for days.'

'Well, that's because I thought you did it on purpose. I hadn't realised you'd tripped over Mrs Courtney-Smyth's enormous feet.'

'And I was doing my best to act all sophisticated, like I drank red wine all the time, when in truth I couldn't stand the stuff and was quite happy to have got rid of it.'

'I remember your dress,' said Sam quietly. 'Deep claret-red velvet.'

Freya remembered her dress too, and she remembered the way Sam had looked at her that night. She looked at him now, on the outside, not that much different; still the same unusual green eyes, darkest brown hair that, although cut short, still liked to curl if it could, and the wide generous mouth that curved into a cheeky grin. On the inside, however, she doubted things could ever be the same, and she pulled her gaze away before she could dwell on it any longer.

'Well, I was thin then, of course, back when we were all bright young things and could wear a bin liner and still look good,' she said, trying to lighten the conversation.

'I never looked good in a bin liner.'

'Well, there were some exceptions to the rule, of course.'

Sam snorted. 'From the woman currently sporting this season's chicest finger to elbow white plaster cast, I'm not sure you're in a position to be quite so judgemental.'

Freya looked around for something to throw, but there was nothing in her cubicle and she certainly wasn't wasting her toast, so she took another bite.

A face peered around the curtain. 'Hey, good to see you're looking better,' said Amos. 'You had us worried there for a minute.'

'Oh, I'm fine, a good clean break. If you're going to break your arm, then you could learn a thing or two from me, apparently. Besides which I'm drugged up to the eyeballs and currently don't care about anything much.'

'Ah,' said Amos, and exchanged a grin with Sam.

'Sorry, I'm being mean, of course I care. How did you get on without me?'

'Well, mistletoe sold, check. Holly sold, check. Wreaths all sold, check, check, check. You got an alarmingly good price for those; I think the punters were feeling sorry for you.'

'So it was worth it then, breaking my arm? That's a relief.' Freya grinned.

Sam looked down at his body. 'I know I wouldn't have got the sympathy vote, but I don't suppose you noticed if we managed to sell anything, did you? That is of course if Stephen even realised the auction had started.'

'No, you're good too, don't worry. I'm not sure what price yours fetched, but it all went. I've left Stephen in the pub, but we can go home once you've finished your toast, Freya. The auction yard shut, so I had to move your van, but we can drop you back there first, Sam. It was good of you to stay with Freya.'

'It was good of you to stay at the sale, Amos, thank you.'

Amos dipped his head and smiled.

'But what on earth am I going to do next week?' asked Freya, suddenly panic-stricken. 'I can't make up my wreaths like this, or cut any mistletoe, and there's still all the packing to do.'

'One thing at a time,' soothed Amos. 'One thing at a time. Let's get you home first.'

'Yes, come on Sherbert, eat up. If we leave it any longer, Stephen will be that drunk, I'll be sorely tempted to leave him behind.'

Sherbert. Now that was a name Freya hadn't heard in a long time.

It's funny how food you don't have to make yourself always tastes better. It was late afternoon by the time they got home, and as the light faded, Amos put the chickens to bed and lit the fire for the evening, closing the curtains and locking out the night. Now Freya was propped up on the sofa with a mug of tea and two thick slices of cheese on toast. Her head was spinning. There were so many thoughts crowded in there, and try as she might, she couldn't get the carousel to stop. She lay back on the cushions for a moment and closed her eyes. She opened them again when she became aware that Amos was looking at her.

'Things catching up with you?'

She gave a wan smile. 'A bit, yes.'

'Then can I make a suggestion…? Finish your supper and then get yourself off to bed or make one up on the sofa here in front of the fire. Take some painkillers and try to get some sleep. Everything else can wait.'

She opened her mouth to argue and then closed it again, the thought of climbing into bed was heavenly. 'You must be tired too?' she said.

'Well, it's not often my days see that much excitement, it's true, but I'll be right as rain in the morning. You, however, might feel like you've been hit by a truck.'

Freya's eyes widened. 'Thanks for that.'

'So what's it going to be, the bed or the sofa?'

'I'll just have a bit of a sleep here I think, but you don't have to make yourself scarce, Amos. Put the TV on or something, I won't mind.'

When she woke several hours later, the TV was quiet, and the room in darkness save for the low flickering of the fire. She shifted slightly, trying to get some relief from the pain in her arm, which was now throbbing nicely, and let her eyes become accustomed to the gloom. She could just make out the shape of Amos lying fast asleep on the rug in front of the fire. He'd pulled a throw from the armchair and balled it up to use as a pillow. She watched his rhythmic breathing for a while and let it lull her gently back to sleep.

Chapter Seven

It was the smell of bacon wafting through the house that woke her the next morning, throwing her into confusion for a minute until she worked out where she was. She was still in her clothes, and what's worse had no idea how to get out of them. She moved her legs to the edge of the sofa and inched them over the side, using her right arm to pull herself forward into a sitting position. So far so good; a few tweaks but nothing like the pain she'd experienced yesterday. She sat for a moment wondering if it was safe to stand up.

Her legs felt like wibbly jelly for some reason, but she made it to the kitchen, largely by clinging to the line of the wall down the corridor. The radio was playing softly in the background, and from the pantry, she could hear Amos murdering her favourite seasonal song, 'Fairy Tale of New York'. A pan was sizzling gently on the cooker. She sat down at the table with an audible sigh and lay her head on her right arm with her eyes shut.

'I know I'm being selfish and whiny, but could you please turn down the chirpiness this morning?' she asked.

Amos walked back past her saying nothing, but the singing stopped. There were sounds of an egg being cracked into a pan and then a soft expletive as the oil spat. A few moments later, a deliciously smelling plate of food was placed in front of her, together with a mug of tea. Her stomach gave a lurch of appreciation.

'Are you trying to fatten me up even more?' She smiled, lifting her head.

'At the risk of perjuring myself, I shall refrain from answering that question.'

'Sam! What are you doing here?' exclaimed Freya, looking around the kitchen. 'I thought you were Amos.'

Sam chuckled and sat down. 'He's out with Bailey. He seems to have struck up rather a friendship with my horse, and anyone who offers to save me from my early morning mucking out duties gets their arm bitten off. So I'm on the breakfast-making rota.'

Freya nodded, taking a huge bite of her sandwich. Egg oozed over her fingers. With only one hand to hold the door stop, her control of it was woefully inadequate.

'This is going to be messy, sorry,' she apologised. Sam merely pushed her plate closer to her.

'Are you not going to have anything?' she asked after a few moments' more contented chewing.

'I've already eaten. I was up a bit earlier than you.'

'Hmm. What is the time?'

'Just after eight.' Sam smiled, amused at her horrified expression. 'Don't worry. We've got a while to go yet before we have to panic.'

'Have you any idea how much I have to do today?'

'Yes,' said Sam, leaning forward. 'Which is why I'm here. Have you any idea how long it takes to get up in the morning when your arm is in plaster?'

Freya stared at him for a moment and then looked away embarrassed. 'I'm sorry,' she muttered.

'I'm just teasing you. It's no bother me being here, honestly, and Amos thought you might need some help. He surmised that I might have more experience of helping young ladies remove their clothing than he has.'

'You didn't tell him, did you?'

Sam studied her for a moment. 'No, I didn't tell him, although I would say that nothing much gets past Amos. I can see it still bothers you, though, so I certainly won't mention anything.'

To her surprise, Freya's eyes filled with tears. 'Sam, don't please, I feel bad enough as it is at the moment without having to think about what I did.'

He looped his fingers under hers gently. 'Don't keep hating yourself, Freya, it was never your fault.'

She looked up at him then, her eyes dark, and shook her head.

'So... Amos is a bit of a find, isn't he?' he said, clearly trying to change to subject. 'I've not seen him around here before; where did he come from?'

'I don't know, actually,' sniffed Freya. 'I wouldn't be surprised if it was from under a mulberry bush. He appeared one day wanting a glass of water and somehow he just stayed.' She stared at her sandwich in speculation. 'I think he'd been working somewhere locally, and I know I should have asked around a bit before I let him in, but it never occurred to me, to be honest. It still hasn't. It's not that he actually evades answering any questions about himself, but somehow, he avoids them. I know next to nothing about him, but I'd trust him with my life.'

'Curious.'

'It's mad is what it is, but someone clearly thought I needed his help and sent him to me, that's all I can think. Of course I could be completely wrong, and by January, I'll be in small pieces under the patio.'

Sam laughed. 'I don't think so.'

'No, neither do I,' said Freya with finality. 'Right then, I can't put it off any longer. I need to go and have a wash and get changed, and while I think I've figured out most things, I cannot for the life of me see how I'm going to get my bra off. So, if you don't mind, and without looking, commenting, or laughing, please could you just unhook me at the back, and I'll take it from there.'

Sam was right, it did take a huge amount of time to get ready, and she'd just about lost the will to live by the time she'd finished. How on earth was she supposed to do all the things she needed to; and Christmas was in just over two weeks' time. The very thought of it made her want to go and lie down in a darkened room.

By the time she got back downstairs, both Sam and Amos were sitting at the table, a large notepad in front of them.

'We need a plan,' Amos said the minute he spotted her.

'I need a double brandy,' she countered.

Both men smiled.

'Not such a bad idea,' said Sam. 'Maybe just a teeny bit early, though. Shall we see if we can make it to lunchtime, at least?'

Freya stuck out her tongue.

'Right,' said Amos in purposeful fashion. 'We need to make a list of what needs doing and by when. Also, what tasks Freya can still do and those that she'll have trouble with. That way we can assign everyone specific jobs so that as far as possible we don't lose any time. Oh, and Stephen sends his best wishes, by the way.'

'Yeah right,' Freya snorted. 'The only thing that man will be concerned about is which arm I've broken, and whether I'll still be able to sign the contracts on this place.'

Sam looked at the table, and Freya could have kicked herself. She must stop doing this. She'd thought about it last night, and although she would cheerfully run Stephen over in her van, she was pleased that Sam would be part of the equation at Appleyard; she knew he would take good care of it for her.

'Well, the first priorities just at the minute are the wreaths and other decorations. They're due to be delivered again on Saturday, which gives us three days. Fortunately, I have all the wreath bases and other additions here, but nothing is wired up, and Amos you know how long that takes. It's lucky my right hand is still okay, but I'm really not sure that I can manage the wiring even so.'

'If things were already wired, could you manage to get them in the wreaths?' asked Sam. 'If you show us how, perhaps Amos and I could do that bit for you?'

'I'll need more holly and mistletoe cutting as well.'

Amos nodded. 'Sam and I have already discussed that, so it's not a problem. We can get what you need for the wreaths to start with and then harvest the last of the mistletoe later.'

'But what about your own mistletoe, Sam?' asked Freya.

He shrugged. 'It'll get done, I'm not that fussed really.'

His tone suggested that she shouldn't argue, and that was the last thing Freya wanted to do. There was one thing she wanted to know, though.

'Why are you doing all this for me, both of you – and please don't think I'm not grateful. You know that's not the case, but I have only broken my arm, and I will manage. It's nearly Christmas, and you both must have a million and one other things to be doing or places to be?'

Amos looked at Sam, who looked back at him. 'Because it's Christmas, Freya, season of goodwill to all men,' he said.

'And all women,' added Sam.

Freya sighed, she could see she wasn't going to get anything out of either of them.

'I also need a ton of shopping, a few Christmas presents and to pack up the contents of the house. That is of course once I've sorted it all out.'

'Okay…' said Sam slowly, 'so what shall we do tomorrow?'

'Oh ha bloody ha,' retorted Freya, and then clapped a hand to her face. 'Oh God, I forgot to order more boxes. I meant to do it at the weekend.'

'Well, I don't think we're going to be twiddling our thumbs, are we?' Amos grinned. 'Those of us that can anyway. Can I suggest that first, I make another pot of tea, and then, Freya, you can get on the internet and order more boxes. Once we've done that, perhaps we can have a lesson in wiring up the stuff for the wreaths and see whether we're any good at it. The rest we'll take as it comes.

*

It didn't help that Freya got a fit of the giggles and then could hardly speak, let alone demonstrate the art of bow making, but they established very quickly that Sam had two left hands. Amos, on the other hand, was a very neat worker, and after a few more practice runs, Freya was happy that he could carry on by himself.

'I think you must be my fairy Godmother.' She laughed, taking up a bow and trying to fix it in Amos' hair. She couldn't of course with only one hand, and so it slipped to one side where eventually it tangled in his curls coquettishly above one ear. Amos said nothing but simply carried on working.

'So, having established that I'm spectacularly shite at this, does that mean I've drawn the short straw and get to sort out the crap in the attic?' asked Sam.

'It does I'm afraid. The boxes won't be delivered until tomorrow, but there's a huge amount of stuff I can probably throw away from up there. Might as well make a start now. You'll need your coat, though, it's freezing up there.'

'Oh deep joy.'

Amos watched them go with a smile on his face. There were occasions when two was definitely preferable to three.

*

Freya was right, it was freezing up in the attic, but the room was amazing – full of crap, but still amazing. It ran the whole length of the house and was lit by five huge windows all set into the eaves, three at the front and two at the back. As an attic, it served its function very well, but Sam could see that the scope for it to become other things was huge. Their own house was pretty impressive, but it had none of the charm and comfort of Appleyard, and after Stephen had finished ripping out most of the ground floor to make a showcase open plan area, there were also very few private spaces. This would make a brilliant workroom; the light was fantastic. He watched Freya walking around disconsolately and thrust his feelings down as far as they would go.

'It's a bit daunting, isn't it,' she said. 'I don't know where to start.'

'Well, I'm yours to command, so pick a corner, and we'll work our way along. Do you want to sit down?'

'I'll be fine for a bit, I think. I might be warmer anyway, moving around.' They hadn't been able to get Freya's coat on, so instead she had a throw from the lounge tied around her. 'If we make a bit of space over on this wall first, we can stack the things that can go. Do we need a separate pile for charity shop donations do you think, as opposed to things that are just plain rubbish?'

Sam groaned. 'I knew you were going to say that; typical woman hoarder.'

'I am not!' retorted Freya. She made her way over to a tall chest of drawers that was standing to the far left. 'See, for example everything in here is just old clothes – jumpers and stuff – but there's nothing wrong with any of it.'

'So why don't you wear them then?'

'Well, most of it doesn't fit any more, and they're ancient and really old-fashioned now.'

Sam said nothing. The silence stretched out while Freya stared at him until a small smile tugged at the corners of his mouth.

'… Oh right, okay, I get it. It's rubbish, let's just chuck it.'

'Ruthless, that's what we've got to be, ruthless. Repeat after me?'

After an hour and a half, they had systematically cleared a whole side, emptying cupboards and boxes, until only the furniture itself remained, or things that Freya really wanted to keep and which could now be wrapped up and packed properly. Sam kept checking on her from time to time, but she seemed to be coping well with the removal of things which must hold a lot of memories for her. He pulled another box towards him into a clear space and tugged open the flaps. At first, he couldn't make out what was inside; it seemed to be just a bundle of cloths until he pulled out a tunic covered in upholstery tassels and trimming, made from the brocade of an old curtain. He knew it was an old curtain because up until he'd been about ten, it had hung in his dining room.

He held it up to get a better look. 'Jesus,' he said, laughing, 'I can't believe you still have these.'

Freya, who was sitting on a trunk leafing through an old book, turned to have a look. 'Is that what I think it is?' She grinned.

'It certainly is. Romeo, Romeo, where for art thou, Romeo,' he squeaked in a high-pitched falsetto. 'Oh, no, sorry that's your line.' He cleared his throat, lowering his tone to a gruff deep voice instead. 'But Soft! What light through yonder window breaks.'

He reached back into the box, pulling out an elaborate headdress. 'Here you go, Juliet, try that on for size.'

She leaned over to take the feathered monstrosity, plonking it on top of her head. 'I can't believe we never made it to Broadway. I mean, we were good, weren't we; really good?'

'Well, your dad said so, and he never told a lie,' replied Sam, with a twinkle in his eye. 'The summer holidays had a lot to answer for.'

'Oh I think this was one of our slightly better schemes. Although I'm not sure taking our three-man plays on a nationwide tour was ever going to truly catch on. I think, as performers, we were much misunderstood.'

'How old were we then?' He grinned.

Freya narrowed her eyes, looking at Sam intently. 'It was 1992, and we were twelve.'

He was surprised. 'You can remember the year?'

'Don't you? That's why there were only three of us. It was the year Merry got glandular fever and spent practically the whole summer in bed. It was the year after we went up to secondary school.'

'Oh God… yes, you're right… and Stephen spent two days in a huff because I got to play Romeo and not him. We had to let him play every other part in the whole play, and the only way he could do it was to wear all the costumes at once.'

'I'd forgotten that bit,' hooted Freya. 'And then, in the one of the rehearsals he couldn't get his tights off and spent the whole of the next scene with them around his ankles. He got so mad at us because we couldn't stop laughing.'

Sam shook his head, smiling as he remembered the hilarity that had engulfed them as children. 'It could have been yesterday, couldn't it?'

'Twenty-three years ago, Sam, that's what it was,' said Freya softly. 'Half a lifetime ago.'

He looked up at her, noticing the change in the tone of her voice. 'Still, good times, Freya.'

She swallowed. 'Yes, they were.' Her eyes filled with tears. 'I'm sorry,' she muttered, brushing at her eyes. 'It's just that—'

Sam was there, by her side, holding her hand. 'I know,' he said gently. 'I feel it too.'

She shivered all of a sudden. 'I don't think I need to keep the costumes,' she said in a quiet voice, slowly withdrawing her hand.

He held her look for just a second before pulling the hat from her head and stuffing it back into the box with the tunic. He gave a quick glance at his watch.

'Another hour or so, and then we'll think about stopping for some lunch. Is that okay?'

Freya nodded. 'I think these boxes are full of old toys and stuff. They can pretty much all go, I think.'

*

Amos placed a teapot on the table as Freya lowered herself gingerly onto a chair. He took one look at her and fetched the painkillers from the dresser. Sam was only seconds behind with a plate of beans on toast.

'Sorry, we should have stopped before now.'

Freya gave a wan smile. 'It's fine really, I'll be okay in a bit once I've taken some of these. It's only just crept up on me, now we've stopped. Besides, it was good to get that last bit finished.'

'It was, we've done well this morning.' He handed her a fork. 'Go on, eat up before it gets cold,' he said, taking a seat too. 'I've cut it up for you.'

'Thanks, Sam.' Freya smiled. 'This looks good enough to eat.'

Sam glanced at Amos and rolled his eyes.

'I can't believe you got so much done this morning, Amos,' added Freya, looking at the pile of greenery and ribbon which they had pushed to one end of the table. 'I think I'll be able to get quite a few wreaths made up with that lot.'

'Well, I was on a bit of a roll,' admitted Amos. 'I enjoyed it actually; it's quite soothing once you get into the rhythm of it. Good thinking time.'

'Oh – and what were you thinking about?' asked Freya, being nosey.

Amos tapped the side of his nose. 'This and that,' he said, 'nothing important. I do have a favour to ask, though? I wondered if I might borrow your iPad for five minutes later. I want to check something on the internet.'

'Of course, just help yourself whenever. There's nothing incriminating on there, unless you count my appallingly bad score on Candy Crush. It's not locked either.'

Amos nodded his thanks and carried on eating.

Freya had to admit that she did feel better after the food, but she wasn't sure she could face another session up in the attic. Things had been just a little too close to home at times.

'Shall we get rid of the rubbish before we carry on, do you think?'

'Amos and I will do that,' said Sam. 'You're going to put your feet up for a bit. And don't argue,' he continued, seeing the look on her face. 'There's no point killing yourself on the first day. Besides which I need to run a few errands while we're out.'

They'd already done two laborious journeys with armfuls of stuff before Freya realised what they were doing. She straightened up from the dishwasher where she was stacking the last of the plates.

'Erm, how are you going to get all that stuff to the tip?' she asked.

Sam looked at her as if she were deranged. 'In the van,' he said slowly.

'Yes, I know that, but it doesn't matter how it gets there, does it? I mean you're just going to throw it all in higgledy piggledy?'

Sam scratched his head. 'Pretty much,' he said, clearly wondering if there was any other way.

'Okay, come with me.' She led the way back upstairs, passing Amos on the landing with another load. 'About turn,' she said, 'and bring that lot with you.'

'No, I haven't got a clue what she's talking about either,' muttered Sam, 'but I would do as she says.'

Back in the attic, Freya crossed to one of the large windows overlooking the front lawn. The van was parked in the yard, neatly to one side.

'Could one of you open the window please?'

Sam and Amos exchanged more looks, but Amos did as she asked, moving the catch on the sash and pushing the window up as far as it would go.

'Now just throw.'

'Pardon?' said Amos.

'It's a hell of a lot quicker than carrying it all down two flights of stairs. Just throw. It's all rubbish anyway, what harm is it going to do?'

'You're mad,' grinned Sam, 'but I kind of like your thinking. Wheelbarrow to the van at the other end, done in a flash.' He picked up an armful of clothing and hurled it out of the window. 'That's strangely satisfying.' He laughed.

'Ruthless you said,' fired back Freya. 'So I give you ruthless.' And with that, she left them to it, smiling to herself all the way downstairs as she listened to the gales of laughter floating after her.

*

Freya was still asleep by the time they got back, right where Sam had left her, tucked up under a blanket on the sofa. He'd put *Love Actually* on the DVD before he left, but it had long since finished, the final credits frozen onto the silent screen. He watched her for a moment, his eyes soft in the dim light, before rejoining Amos in the kitchen.

'Did you find what you were looking for?' he asked. Amos' head was bent over the iPad.

'Yeah, getting there. Just looking at a few things. Does the name Paul Streatfield mean anything to you?'

Sam came to sit beside him so that he could see the screen. 'I don't think so, why?'

'It's just a name I've heard your brother use a few times now, that's all. It pricked my interest.'

'Who is he, anyway?' asked Sam.

'A property developer – look.' Amos angled the screen towards Sam so that he could get a better look.

Sam pulled the iPad closer and studied it for a moment before gazing back at Amos and echoing his worried frown.

'Shit,' he said.

Chapter Eight

It was Sam's idea to visit Worcester, but while Freya could see the logic in it, she wasn't sure she really wanted to be here. There were too many reminders of Christmases past tugging at her brain.

It was three in the afternoon by the time they arrived, having dropped off her wreaths at the hotel first. That had taken rather longer than planned since Merry and Tom insisted they stay for lunch. Merry declared that it was the least she could do since her pregnant state meant she'd been unable to help Freya pack. Hospitality was what they did best, and as Freya looked around the hotel at the other guests enjoying a sumptuous pre-Christmas break, she could see the appeal.

The reception hall was a glittery double height room, dominated by the huge tree which was smothered in white and gilded sparkles. A marble fireplace roaring with flame enticed people onto the squishy deep red sofas, in front of which a table groaned with plates of mince pies, sugar-dusted shortbread and a tower of Ferrero Rocher. Sitting in the dining room, chatting with old friends, it was easy to forget everything else for a while and let Christmas wash over her, an oasis of seasonal charm.

When they finally reached it, the town was still thronging with people. The day was cold and clear, and as they emerged from beside the cathedral, the lights and sounds from the shops drifted over to them. Instead of following the road into town, Sam steered Freya away to the left and through the elegant Cathedral close to the quieter riverside beyond. As they walked through the arch that lead onto the path beside the river, Freya looked at the markers on the huge wall beside them showing the height the river had reached when in flood. It amazed her that some of them were ten feet or so above her head and they were already standing maybe twenty feet above the river itself. It was an important reminder that despite the torrents of life, things endured, maybe not unaltered, but they remained, nonetheless. Right now, when everything she held dear seemed to be slipping away from her, it was hard to see how things could ever get back to even a slight semblance of what they had been before.

Sam took hold of her hand, perhaps sensing how she was feeling, or just wanting to provide support as she walked. His hand was warm and solid, and the feeling of it was as familiar to her as breathing. It would be so easy to allow her feelings to drift back in time, but she knew that Sam was only being friendly, marking time until she left, and finally gave him the closure she had never allowed him before. She should have pulled away, but she was so tired it was somehow easier just to hang on.

She tried to enjoy the chilly air and let her mind drift away from the reality of her current problems, but everywhere she looked tiny sparkles of fairy lights caught her eye and brought her back to the one thing she was dreading. Christmas. She usually loved it all: the shops decked out way before time, the Christmas music playing over and over and the cheesy films on the TV. Most of all, though, she loved the lights; the darkened villages and houses transformed at dusk into winter wonderlands of colour. She loved this over-spilling of joy and exuberance, and although it had only ever been her and her dad at home, she had always strung rows and rows of lights through Appleyard. Until this year.

She walked a little closer to Sam, his thick puffy jacket warm to the touch. The sky was turning violet as the day gave way to dusk, and the lights were beginning to glow off the river. They had walked the whole way in virtual silence and Freya felt no need to talk, but soon they would be heading back into town, and the thought brought her back to the reason for their visit.

'Where would you like to go?' she asked Sam.

He too seemed lost in his own thoughts, and it took him a little while to respond.

'I'll follow you,' he said. 'Wherever you want to go. I can shop any time after all.'

That was undoubtedly true, but when Freya tried to think what she might need to buy, she realised she had no stomach for shopping; she had wanted to come and soak up the atmosphere because it was something she always did, and without it she would feel even more lost. In truth, there was only one shop she wanted to visit, but she was loathe to name it for fear of seeming even more of a sentimental fool.

'Can we just wander and see what happens?'

'No problem,' said Sam, falling silent beside her once more.

They made their way up from the bridge into the town centre, weaving through the crowds into the market square, where the huge Christmas tree stood over the market stalls, ablaze with lights. A Salvation Army band was still playing, and the brass notes rang out rich and clear. She stopped to listen, noting that Sam too had slowed his pace.

'Wouldn't be Christmas without them, would it?' He smiled, fishing in his pocket for some change. 'I could listen to them for hours.'

'Me too. I don't know why, but they always bring a lump to my throat. I think it's the thought that amid all the horrible things that happen in this world, there are still people like them who help, without question, without judgement. That's what I like about Christmas, the reminder that there is still good in the world. Sometimes, it seems so far away.'

'There are still good people in the world, Freya,' he said.

'I know,' she said, moving her fingers in his, and blinking away her tears.

They stood listening for a few moments more, then Sam pulled her gently away, leading her to a stall selling nuts of every variety coated in delicious sounding ingredients, savoury and sweet. Sam bought some spiced honey cashews which they munched from the twisted cone of paper, each time Freya dropping Sam's hand to take one, and each time reuniting it with his.

She almost didn't go into the shop at all. She thought if she kept walking and didn't think about it, then it would be fine, but suddenly the thought of not going in became too much to bear, and she pushed the door open almost with reverence. The first few moments as she stood inside were always the same; that first rush of excitement and endless possibility looming up at her as she stared at every manner of bauble and decoration, assailed by the shapes and colours, the sheer variety. She and her dad would wander around at first, in no particular direction, he going one way and she the other, and then they would meet up for an excited exchange of what the other had seen. Eventually, they would gravitate towards one of the displays as if drawn by an invisible thread, and the selection would begin in earnest. They had bought a new Christmas decoration together every year since her mum had left. It was their special bond, a celebration of another year, and although she wasn't going to decorate the house this year, it was a tradition that she simply couldn't bring to an end. Whatever she bought would remain on her bedside table until it too was packed away.

Almost as soon as they were through the door, Sam dropped her hand and headed off to take a closer look at something that had caught his eye. The shop wasn't busy now, and she was happy to wander alone, pleased to find that the usual sense of wonderment she felt on coming inside was still with her.

She had paused by a display of neon decorations, which were gaudy but strangely attractive when she became aware that Sam was hovering by her side.

'This place is amazing,' he said. 'How did you find it?'

'I can't remember, just stumbled across it one year. It's only here at Christmas of course, the rest of the year it sells giftware.'

'Are you going to buy something?'

'I'd like to… it's sort of a tradition.'

Sam gave an understanding nod. 'How on earth do you choose, though?'

'I don't know really. The one I want seems to find me.'

'Okay, well happy hunting.' He grinned at her and wandered off again.

Freya had only moved a little way around the corner when he was back again, almost fizzing with excitement.

'You need to come over here,' he urged, and grabbed her hand, not caring about the other shoppers in their path.

They were near the back of the shop now, standing in front of a small section of more expensive decorations, all made from the most beautiful glass, a myriad of colours and sizes. Her eyes scanned this way and that, and then she saw it, seconds before Sam's hand reached out to take it gingerly down from its hiding place. It was about the size of an apple, a handmade glass ornament of pale cranberry glass, a single perfect white feather curled within it in perfect suspension. Her breath caught in her throat as she reached out a trembling hand to take it.

'What do you think?' asked Sam anxiously.

Freya held her breath, hardly daring to move. 'I can't believe you found it,' she said, her voice choked with emotion. 'This is it; this is absolutely it.' She turned to him, her eyes shining. 'How did you know?'

'I didn't, I saw it… and it just seemed… right. Like the sort of thing you should have.'

Freya was still gazing at the ornament in her hand. 'Can we buy it?' she asked, handing it back to him. 'Is it very expensive?'

Sam cleared his throat which felt a little constricted. 'It's twenty pounds. I'm sorry, I should have checked the price first, but Freya…' He faltered for a moment, trying to find the right words, 'I want you to have this… I'd like to buy it for you… please.'

She paused for a moment, but then to his surprise, she gave a slight nod. 'I'd like that,' she said, looking up at him. 'Because then I'll have something to remember you too.' And she did something she'd sworn she'd never do again. She kissed him.

'I don't want to sound rude, Amos, but I was wondering what your plans for Christmas were?'

Amos looked up from his book and gave her a warm smile. 'Not rude at all,' he said. 'It's a busy time of year, only natural that you would want to know.' He placed his bookmark back in the book and laid it on his lap. 'I've been thinking about it too as it happens, and I thought maybe I would go at the end of the week if that's all right with you? The work will pretty much be done by then, and there's heavy snow coming in after.'

'Is there?' Freya replied, surprised. 'I hadn't heard that... but... what I meant was more, well, whether you had definite plans, that sort of thing. Do you have somewhere you're meant to be?'

Amos considered the question for a moment. 'No, nowhere I'm meant to be, but often the place I am, well, it's the same thing.'

Freya grinned, giving an amused tut at his enigmatic answer. She was beginning to expect nothing less from him. 'Good, because what I really meant was, if you don't have to be anywhere in particular, would you like to stay here for Christmas? It won't be very grand because everything will be in boxes, but I'd like it if you were here.'

'Then I accept,' replied Amos. 'Thank you. I didn't like the thought of you being here by yourself. It didn't seem right.'

Freya stared into the fire for a moment. 'No, me neither,' she said finally, giving a huge yawn. 'I might head up to bed now actually. I'm so tired, and it's going to take me an age to get ready anyway.'

'Do you need anything?'

'No, it's fine, thanks, I'll just take my book.' She eyed the glass bauble sitting on the mantelpiece.

'I could bring it up for you if you like?' ventured Amos, watching her.

She smiled again. 'Sorry, I just thought I might have it beside my bed.'

'Then that's where you shall have it.'

When her head eventually met the pillow, she lay for a few moments looking at the bauble, lost in thought. This morning she had wished that she could be on her own for Christmas. She had thought she wanted nothing more than to see out the last few days at Appleyard by herself so that she could say her own goodbyes, but something had changed during the course of the day. She'd realised it in the car driving home earlier that afternoon, and she was trying desperately hard not to admit it to herself. Perhaps having Amos stay would help to keep the thoughts chasing around her head at bay. Perhaps. She closed her eyes and willed sleep to come and claim her.

Chapter Nine

'And here's another festive treat for this fine Monday morning to get you in the mood. After all, the big day is now only four away.'

Sam switched off the radio irritably, he didn't need any more bloody reminders of how little time he had left. The last week or so had passed in a blur. He drained his coffee mug and stared morosely at the toaster. He was due back at Appleyard tomorrow to help with more packing, and although he had no great expectations of the day, at least it meant he wouldn't have to suffer Stephen's smug comments at home. He could hear him now, arguing on the phone with someone. It was only nine o'clock in the morning, for God's sake.

He concentrated on buttering his toast, trying to ignore his brother's strident tones as they grew louder. Stephen was still a little wary around him since getting punched, but it didn't stop him from reminding Sam at every given opportunity that he would soon own Appleyard too.

'Have a heart, mate, even the wankers – sorry, bankers – don't work at the weekend. I'm doing the best I can. My man's on it, believe me, and I'm expecting to hear from him later today.' Stephen paused for a moment, nodding intermittently. 'Yes, of course, I will, cheers, Paul.'

He ended the call, pulling an exasperated face at Sam. 'That man has no bloody idea, but you have to keep 'em sweet, don't you?'

'Do you?' countered Sam. 'I really wouldn't know,' he added, feigning disinterest, although the mention of the name Paul had caught his ear. He knew better than to quiz his brother, though; that was the quickest way to get him to clam up.

'Course I wouldn't have a problem if your doe-eyed little girlfriend wasn't being quite so picky.'

Sam said nothing, but his eyes glittered dangerously.

'Oh, of course, she's not your girlfriend, is she, sorry.' Stephen smirked. 'Anyway, give her a message from me, would you? Tell her to pull her socks up on the sale; we're running out of time. Her bloody solicitor won't progress until he has written confirmation of the mortgage offer, and we haven't got time to be pissing around.'

'That's standard practice I believe, Stephen. Haven't you done your homework?'

Stephen swiped a piece of toast. 'Just bloody tell her,' he growled, and stalked off.

Sam allowed a small smile to curl around the corners of his lips; he liked to see his brother riled, especially when it forced him to show his cards. He hadn't known until now that Stephen needed a mortgage to buy Appleyard; which was interesting. For the first time in a long time, he saw a way that he might just be able to outmanoeuvre his brother. He would call his solicitor as soon as Stephen was out of the way.

Chapter Ten

Amos and Freya had already made good progress by the time Sam got there, having sorted another whole section of the attic. When he found them, Freya was holding up some threadbare tinsel that had discoloured to a diseased-looking green. She held it between thumb and forefinger in case whatever it had was catching.

'When you said you weren't going to bother putting up the decorations, I thought you were being boring, now I can see why. That's pretty disturbing.'

'Morning, Sam.' Freya laughed. 'It is, isn't it? I think the box must have got damp, it's all like this which is a shame because I was looking forward to putting these out.' She fished inside the box and pulled out two very moth-eaten-looking reindeer, which at one time in their lives had been furry but now had a severe case of alopecia. 'I'd forgotten we even had them.'

'Blanked it from your memory probably,' said Sam with a shudder. 'Stuff of nightmares.'

'Look, are you going to stand there criticising my family heirlooms, or make yourself useful and cart this lot over there with the rest of the rubbish?'

'Yes, ma'am,' grinned Sam, picking up a box. 'Being serious for a minute, though, are you going to put anything up this year? It seems such a shame not to do anything, especially as tomorrow is Mistletoe Day.'

'But it's just one more thing to have to do, when I could leave it all in its boxes, ready and packed.'

'It wouldn't take long... and we'd help, wouldn't we, Amos?'

'Oh for heaven's sake, you're as bad as him,' she said, pointing a finger. 'Okay, you win. Take the stuff downstairs and leave it in the dining room, and then I can decide. It's those boxes over there,' she added, wafting her good hand at a pile by the door.

Sam did as he was told, a plan forming in his mind.

The dining room was stacked high with boxes already packed, and it took a few minutes to move the others around to make way for those coming down. He was trying hard not to think about what they meant, and how little time he had left. He pulled his mobile out of his pocket as it buzzed with a message. It was from his brother, three words in block capitals.

CALL ME NOW

Sam clicked the sleep button, watching with satisfaction as the screen went dark again. *Oops*, he said to himself. *I missed that one.*

He was just moving the last few boxes when Amos appeared with another couple.

'These are all decorations too,' he said, putting them down where Sam indicated. 'Just in case they're needed at all,' he added, winking. 'You must tell me about the customs of Mistletoe Day some time. It sounds fascinating.'

Sam laughed. 'As if you didn't know. You don't fool me, Amos Fry.'

'And you don't fool me either, Sam Henderson.' Amos grinned. 'One other thing, though. Can I suggest that we go and get the shopping fairly soon, there's snow coming, and I don't think we should leave it too late.'

The day outside was clear and blue, just as it had been for days. 'I know it's nearly Christmas, but that doesn't mean it's going to start snowing. Have you looked outside?'

'Yes, and I know that snow hasn't actually been forecast.'

'But?'

Amos winked again. 'I tell you it's coming.'

'Okaaay,' said Sam, humouring him. 'Let's go and grab the rest of these boxes, and then we'll see about putting a list together. Not because I believe a word you're saying about the snow, but because the supermarket will be like your worst nightmare, and I'd rather not leave it any longer.'

Sam had a total of four more text messages and two missed calls by the time they eventually emerged from the supermarket hours later. Freya had wanted to come, but Sam insisted she stayed at home. There would be too many people around all pushing and shoving, and he thought she'd find it very uncomfortable. Instead, she had provided them with a list that made the Declaration of Independence look like a scribbled note on the back of a napkin. The list contained things that neither Sam nor Amos had ever heard of, but they had been determined to find everything she asked for.

Now, with the bags stashed safely in the boot, Sam pulled out his phone to look at the messages again and tried to concentrate. The texts were all from his brother, more shouty messages, getting more ridiculously threatening by the minute. Sam had no intention of answering them. This was not his battle to fight he had decided; not this time. He had assumed that the missed call was also from Stephen, but although there was no message left, he recognised the number, and checking Amos was okay to wait, he returned the call.

'That was good news I take it?' said Amos, looking at the Cheshire cat grin on Sam's face.

'The very best,' he replied. 'Do you mind if we make a quick detour on the way home? There's one last shop I need to visit. Got my Christmas present to pick up.'

Amos glanced at the sky. 'No problem, we've still got time.'

The High Street was packed with people, but by some miracle, Sam managed to find a parking spot in a side street and nipped out to finish his shopping.

'I won't be long, I promise.'

It was gone three o'clock by the time they navigated their way out of the car-choked streets and began to head for home. They were only a couple of miles into their journey when Sam took his sunglasses off. The late sun, hanging low in the sky made visibility particularly difficult at this time of year, and he never went anywhere without them. Now, though, he realised he was having trouble seeing, not because of the glare, but because of the sudden reduction in light. He dipped his head to look below the sun visor, shaking his head as he did so. The sky was split in two; one half still the brightest winter blue, and the other banked with dark clouds sporting an ominous pink tinge.

'I don't bloody believe it,' he remarked, driving on.

As he drove, the line of cloud sank lower and lower to the ground, and by the time they turned into the driveway at Appleyard, the first flakes of snow were falling.

'So what is it with you then, Amos? Got a direct line to the big man upstairs or what?'

Amos gave him an innocent look.

'Don't give me that, you know what I'm talking about, the whole "snow is coming" thing.'

'My bones have been around longer than yours, that's all.' He grinned. 'They sense these things.'

'Bullshit!' said Sam succinctly, and jumped out of the car to haul the first of the shopping inside.

Freya was chopping vegetables by the sink, or at least she was trying to. She had pinned a carrot to a board with her cast and was slowly making progress with her good hand. She looked up as they came in.

'I got bored sifting through the papers upstairs, so I thought I'd make a start on tea. It's taken me rather longer than I thought, though.'

'Interesting technique,' said Sam.

'But strangely effective, so don't mock.'

He dumped the first of the bags on the table and went to inspect the pans on top of the stove.

'That's not what I can smell, though,' he said, lifting one of the saucepan lids, and inhaling deeply.

'No, I made some mulled wine for later too. I thought we'd have a casserole, and as it took me so long to get the wine open, I thought I might as well use it all up.'

'I like your thinking,' said Sam, 'although I wish I'd been here. I'd have paid good money to see you trying to get into a bottle of wine.'

Freya gave him an amused look. 'Yes, well, if you were clamped between my knees for that long, you'd surrender too.'

Sam turned away so that she wouldn't see the smile on his face. My, that was a vivid image.

'Right, well, I'll help Amos bring the rest of the shopping in, and then I'll give you a hand. We bought enough to feed an army.'

'Good, just what you need at Christmas: faith, hope and gluttony.'

*

'I'm not sure I should be drinking this,' said Freya, with a total lack of concern. 'Are you allowed to drink alcohol with painkillers?'

'Bit late I think,' offered Amos. 'How many glasses is that now?'

'I haven't been counting, but more than one.' She squinted up at him. 'Oh hell, never mind. I don't have to go anywhere.'

'No, but Sam does, I'm not sure it was such a good idea.'

'It's only two miles away, and at this time of night no one will be on the road. He'll be fine.'

Amos frowned at her.

'I wouldn't normally say it was okay to drink and drive,' she said, 'before you give me a lecture, but if the roads are a bit snowy, he'll have to go at a snail's pace anyway.'

She hoped she didn't sound too much like she wanted to get rid of him. She'd rather enjoyed standing side by side with him cooking their tea, the way they'd giggled at silly reminders of their childhood. She'd also enjoyed the way he leaned into her to get her to move along the work surface a bit, and the way his green eyes lit up when he laughed. She'd enjoyed the way his hand brushed against hers as he reached for her wine glass and the affectionate way he teased her during dinner.

Then she had enjoyed sneaking little glances at him as he relaxed in the chair, drowsy with wine and food, and the thought of what it might be like if he were there every night; and that was why she very much wanted him to go, because actually she didn't want him to go at all.

She sneaked a peek at Amos now, wondering just how much of herself she might be giving away, when Sam came back into the room.

'Um… you might want to come and have a look at this,' he said, the wool of his coat glistening with snowflakes in the room's soft light.

Freya pulled herself up out of the chair, giving him a quizzical glance and then following him through into the kitchen, where he went to stand by the back door. She could see the wet imprint of his footprints across the tiled floor.

'We've had the curtains closed all evening, and it's, well, um, snowed a bit.' He pulled the door open.

The light was on just outside the back door, throwing a small bright circle out into the night. Against the patch of lit sky, a torrent of snow was falling, thick and steady. Of the grass, path and driveway there was no sign. Even the car was just a muffled outline.

Freya peered out into the whiteness and then back at Sam. 'How the hell did that happen?' she exclaimed, turning to look at Amos.

'Why are you looking at me?' He grinned.

Freya and Sam exchanged glances. 'No reason, no reason at all.' Sam sighed. 'I could walk, I suppose?'

'You could, if you were stark raving mad,' she replied, firmly closing the door, and turning the key in the lock. 'If I show you where the linen is for the spare bed, could you help me make it up?' *Keep it businesslike*, she thought to herself, *it's the only way*.

Sam trailed after her.

'It'll be cold in here I expect, the room hasn't been used for a while, but if we put on the radiator and turn down the covers once the bed is made that should give it time to air before you turn in.'

'Listen, don't worry, I'll have another glass of wine, and then I won't feel the cold anyway.'

'I've got plenty of blankets if you need extra,' said Freya, hating herself for sounding like a Blackpool boarding house landlady. 'They're all in this drawer here, and the sheets and duvet cover. Bit pink I'm afraid.'

Sam crossed the room and looked out through the window for a moment before closing the curtains. 'No problem. I tend to sleep with my eyes closed and the light off, so I won't notice what colour they are.'

Freya snorted before she could stop herself. Oh my God, was she drunk? It wasn't even that funny. She struggled to pull the drawer open.

'Here, let me do that,' said Sam, his hand brushing against hers, again.

'Thank you... I should just go and get you the spare duvet, it's in the airing cupboard, and if you want any more pillows, they're in the wardrobe there.'

She walked back down the landing, blowing out her cheeks in an effort to relax her face which currently felt like she'd had ten Botox injections, stiff and wooden yet strangely liquid all at the same time. She reminded herself that Sam had been in her house now for the best part of a month on and off with no problem whatsoever. That was it, she must be drunk, or hormonal, or both.

Trying to contain the duvet under one arm, she kicked open the bedroom door once more. 'Do you need anything—' she started, and then she stopped because standing in the middle of the room was Sam, holding a wedding dress. Her wedding dress.

She hadn't a clue what to say, so she just stood there looking at Sam, looking at her dress, looking at her.

After what seemed like an age, Sam started to apologise. 'I went to get a pillow... I'm sorry, I didn't know it was in there.'

Freya rubbed her forehead distractedly. 'No... I'd forgotten it was. It's my fault.' She could feel her eyes filling with tears, and she couldn't breathe. 'I'm so sorry,' she whispered, turning to run.

And then Sam was there, holding her, pulling her to him, stroking her hair. 'You don't have to run, Freya,' he murmured. 'Not any more. Please don't run.'

She wished with all her heart that she could believe him.

Chapter Eleven

Mistletoe Day

Sam woke the next morning to the sound of hammering on the back door. He raised a bleary eye to the clock, suddenly sitting up as he realised the time. Pulling on his jeans, he grabbed his fleece from the chair and went to investigate. He could tell from the white glow behind the curtains that the snow was still around, so there couldn't be that many people up and about, even if it was ten o'clock.

He winced as his feet met the cold quarry tiles in the kitchen. Someone was obviously up, as the blinds had been raised, and through the windows, he could see the snow still blowing into huge drifts. He hadn't expected there to be quite so much; even as he pulled the door open, a small pile slumped inward and onto the floor. And he certainly hadn't expected to see the person who was standing there either.

His brother looked dreadful. He was obviously cold, his face looked pinched and mottled in places, his nose bright red; but his eyes were wild, bloodshot and staring. He practically fell into the kitchen.

'Why the hell aren't you answering your bloody phone?' he snarled. 'I've been ringing you all morning.'

Sam's gaze fell to the table where his phone lay exactly where he had left it last night.

'I've only just got up,' he said flatly, not in the mood for one of his brother's arguments. 'How did you get here anyway?'

'I followed the sodding snow-plough, it's taken me nearly an hour.' Stephen looked around the kitchen which still smelled faintly of last night's mulled wine. 'Can I at least have a cup of coffee?'

Sam filled the kettle, feeling a little uneasy about doing so in Freya's absence, but reasoning that it might be the quickest way to get rid of Stephen. He slid it back onto the Aga's hotplate, and turned to face his brother.

'So where's the fire?' he said evenly.

'Don't bloody joke about. Is she here?'

Sam could feel his anger rising and did his best to stay calm. 'If you mean Freya, I haven't seen her yet this morning.'

'Oh, like I believe that. From where I'm standing, it looks as though your slippers are well and truly under the bed.'

'Yeah, well, that's what you would see when you're standing in the gutter, Stephen. For your information, I stayed last night because I'd had a drink or two, and the snow came down too heavy. It wasn't safe to go anywhere. Besides which, the company here was rather more pleasant than that at home.'

Stephen glared at him. 'Stop being such a snide little fucker, Sam, I'm not in the mood for pissing about.'

Sam glared back at him, tempted to simply throw him out, but as he stared at his brother, he was astonished to see something else in his eyes which he couldn't ever recall having seen there before. Aside from the habitual arrogant defiance, there was a glimmer of fear, and it made a shiver run down Sam's spine. He threw some coffee into a mug and stood drumming his fingers against the Aga while he waited for the kettle to boil.

'So, do you want to sit down and tell me what this is all about, or will you carry on playing the big I am, because if it's the latter, I'm going to throw you out now and save us all the bother.'

Sam could see that Stephen was treading a knife-edge here. His natural instinct would be to shout and bully to get his own way, but instead he was trying to choose his words carefully, and moderate his behaviour. It didn't come naturally to him; in his view, it was tantamount to admitting he was wrong. Whatever it was must be very important, or worse, something that he needed Sam's help with.

'I wondered whether Freya had heard from her solicitor, that's all. The timing's getting critical on the sale, and they seem to be dragging their feet.'

'Well, she hasn't mentioned it, but then it's not something we've discussed. Under the circumstances, I don't think she feels it's a subject she can bring up.'

'Perhaps you could have a word with her, ask her to give him a ring and check that everything is in place. They'll shut down for Christmas tomorrow, and we could really do with getting it moving today.'

Sam moved the kettle off the hotplate. 'Do you really think that solicitors are going to be interested in anything today? Besides drinking sherry and eating Quality Street with their staff, that is. Stephen, everything's pretty much shut down already.' He watered the coffee and handed it to his brother.

'But you don't know that. There's a lot riding on this, Sam. I thought you might be more interested.'

'Not particularly.' Sam shrugged. 'Not any more.' He held his brother's look for a moment, trying to read him. 'What exactly is riding on this, Stephen? It's only a house sale, they happen every day; and some of them don't happen, but it's not worth getting hysterical over.'

'Are you being deliberately obtuse? For Christ's sake, Sam, I'm your brother, try to remember whose side you're on. I just need to know if the money is the only thing holding the sale up. I need her solicitor to confirm that and I need it today.'

Sam smiled then, the penny finally dropping. 'So you're having trouble getting the mortgage through then, Stephen. But why is that? You shouldn't have any problems at all I'd have thought, especially not when you're using our place as collateral.'

Stephen's gaze was fixed at the level of the table, but Sam could see his jaw working in anger. Slowly, he looked up, his face red and blotchy. 'You smug little shit,' he hissed.

Sam ignored him. 'How much, Stephen? Eh? Just how much do you owe?'

Stephen shifted slightly in his chair. 'It's just a few gambling debts, that's all. Nothing I can't handle.'

'Jesus, Stephen, when will you stop? When will you ever learn that enough is enough? How much is it? Twenty grand? Fifty grand?… A hundred grand…?'

'I won't owe anything if I can get this house, don't you get it?'

Sam sat down at the table, leaning closer to his brother. 'Then you'd better tell me, hadn't you,' he said, shoving his face closer still.

Something crumpled behind the façade then, and Stephen clung to the table before lowering himself onto a chair. He ran shaky hands through his hair and closed his eyes.

'I met a bloke in the pub a while back. We had a few beers and then a few more and before I knew it, he'd suggested we had a game of cards. He was an arrogant bastard, but he knew what he was doing, and at the end of the night, I owed him five hundred quid.'

'Oh, and let me guess, you thought you could beat him? Just one more game, eh?'

'They were serious guys, Sam, you wouldn't understand. They didn't just play for a few pounds, they played for big bucks, and not just cards either. It wasn't unusual to win or lose twenty grand during a night.'

'So you gambled your inheritance to get the better of some bloke down the pub. Nice one, Stephen. What did you do? Re-mortgage the house?'

'So what if I did? None of this will matter if I can get this place, everything will be okay.'

'Explain.'

Stephen rolled his eyes. 'I'm not as stupid as you think, little brother. While you were out there slaving away picking bloody apples for peanuts, I was making connections, and a couple of months ago, I hit the jackpot; a property developer who was looking for a new investment project.

Two houses, two orchards, a lot of land; it's a desirable venture for an astute businessman with money to spare.'

'Except that you don't have two houses and two orchards, do you? Only the one, and a whole heap of debt.'

'Which is why I need your bloody help. I need to get the sale through on this place, otherwise I'm going to lose my buyer. This is small fry for him, he won't hang around. Don't you get it, Sam? When you have that kind of money, it's just a game, and he's getting impatient.'

'But you just said you can't get a mortgage?'

'I need the funds, Sam, that's all. You could lend me the money, couldn't you? It would only be for a short while, until the sale of the whole lot goes through, and then you'll get it back twofold, I promise.'

Sam jerked his chair away from the table as he stood up sharply. 'No,' he said coldly, his mouth a thin line. 'It's about time you learned to stop playing with people's lives, Stephen. You can't have everything just because you want it; life doesn't work that way.'

'Oh, but it does, doesn't it?' bit back Stephen, his bravado returning. 'I can have everything I want, can't I? Anything of yours, that is. I can take what I like, remember?'

'Don't you dare bring Freya into this!'

'Why not? I'm not the only one making plans around here. Don't think your knight-in-shining-armour routine is fooling anyone, not for one minute.'

'And neither is your big-man, I-can-do-anything routine. You've lost this one, Stephen. Accept it.'

Stephen lurched up from the table, his face contorted with rage. 'So what the hell am I supposed to do?'

'What other people do,' replied Sam mildly. 'Act like a grown-up, get a proper job, pay your way. Take responsibility for once in your life.'

'But the people I owe money to won't take no for an answer. How am I going to pay them off now?'

'Sell the house. Settle your debts, start over.'

'Look, I don't even need your cash. You could act as guarantor on the mortgage or something. Just have a chat to the bank, Sam, please. They're the ones that have caused all this mess. It would only be for a short while and—'

'The answer's still no, Stephen. The banks have had their fingers burned too. They won't lend you the money no matter how hard you beg them to, and neither will I.'

The back door opened then, catching them both by surprise as Amos came through, stamping his feet on the mat to release the snow from his boots.

'Merry mistletoe!' He grinned at them both, holding aloft a glistening sprig. 'Morning, Stephen. I hope you're on your way back home soon. The snow's coming down again, and by the look of the sky, there's a heap more on its way. In a short while, nothing will be moving.'

Stephen glared at them both, then flung his chair back under the table with such force that the whole thing rocked, slopping undrunk coffee everywhere. With a final glare at Amos, he stormed out of the door, leaving it wide open.

Sam went to close it gently. 'Well, that was good timing.'

'Wasn't it?' agreed Amos. 'I've been standing outside the door for the last five minutes just to make sure.' He grinned. 'My feet are freezing!'

Sam wiggled his own bare toes. 'Yeah, mine too. I wasn't expecting to have a long conversation when I answered the door. Where have you been anyway?'

'Where do you think?' he said, waving the green sprig in the air. 'It's Mistletoe Day; that stuff doesn't get picked all by itself.'

'You've been out harvesting in this weather? Amos, that's downright dangerous!'

'Well, I wasn't sure you softies would like being turned out of your nice warm beds to come and help. Besides which, I've got nine lives me, and as you can see, I'm perfectly fine. Tradition dictates that the mistletoe is freshly picked for her special day; it's not my place to argue with that. It's all in the barn anyway, plus a little extra surprise.' He winked. 'So when we've had some breakfast, you can give me a hand to bring it in.'

'Ah,' said Sam slowly. 'I think the agenda for today might have changed a little. I'm assuming you heard some of the conversation with Stephen?'

Amos nodded. 'I did, but that doesn't necessarily change anything. I'm not surprised of course.'

'But it changes everything. Freya will have lost the sale on the house. I know she didn't want to sell it to Stephen, but she did want to sell it.'

'Admittedly, but I wouldn't worry too much if I were you,' he replied, giving Sam a direct stare. 'I had rather thought that she was selling it to both of you as it happens, but it would appear not. That's the only bit I've not quite understood as yet, perhaps you could fill me in.'

'Over a bacon sandwich?'

'That will do nicely.'

*

Freya sat on the edge of the bed for a moment, trying to come to terms with quite how late it was, but also the events of the day before, which she was even more unsure how to come to terms with. She hadn't said a word to Sam about the wedding dress, and he hadn't asked her either, just held her close, telling her everything was going to be okay. For quite some time, it felt like it might be, but now in that annoying morning after the night before kind of way, she wasn't so sure. How could it be?

By rights, she should probably be feeling awful. It was a long time since she'd drunk alcohol like that, and mixed with strong painkillers, it was a heady cocktail she had consumed. She was surprised to find, however, that she felt remarkably fine, and even – spurred on by the delicious smell of bacon – ready for an enormous breakfast.

She pulled on her furry slippers and went to see which way the land was lying.

'Aye aye, the boss is up, Sam, more rashers required in the pan,' said Amos, as she walked into the room. 'Good morning, Freya, Merry Mistletoe!'

'Merry Mistletoe, Amos,' she returned. 'I'd forgotten what day it was.' She paused for a moment, head on one side. 'It seems a bit daft I know… with everything that's happening, but I wondered if we might bring the mistletoe in today anyway, like we would usually do… just for old times' sake.'

'Already taken care of. Sam and I were just going to have some breakfast, and then we're ready to go. It's all in the barn waiting.' He eyed Sam. 'It might still be a bit wet, mind, it's been snowing pretty heavy again this morning.'

She crossed to the window to have a better look, pulling her dressing gown around her a little more tightly. 'Hey, look at that lot. Typical isn't it, the one year there isn't a white Christmas forecast, and it catches us all out.'

Sam cleared his throat. 'Actually, it might not be a bad idea to bring the mistletoe in this year. We might need her help.'

Freya turned to look at him, and tried out a small smile. 'What do you mean?'

'Well, I've just had a rather difficult conversation with Stephen. Perhaps you'd better come and sit down.' He waited until she was seated before pouring her some tea, relinquishing his bacon cooking duties to Amos.

'I probably don't need to bore you with the details as such, I know you're well aware of the things that Stephen gets up to, but I have to admit that his latest escapade is breath-taking even by his standards. I think you should probably give your solicitor a ring, Freya, just to check, but unless Stephen's bank has had a radical change of heart, they aren't going to lend him the money he needs to buy Appleyard.'

She stared at him blankly.

'You're going to lose the sale on the house, Freya,' he added, just in case there was any doubt.

'Yes, I got that,' she replied, feeling her face pale. 'What intrigues me, though, is your use of the possessive pronoun.'

'I'm sorry?'

'*He* needs to buy Appleyard,' she reiterated, 'that's what you said. Things *Stephen* gets up to, *Stephen's* bank. Where is the 'we' in that statement, only I thought I was selling the house to both of you?'

Amos moved the frying pan off the heat. 'We were just about to have that conversation, Freya,' he said. 'You're lucky you missed Stephen, he was extremely unpleasant. A very foolish, irresponsible young man, and rather manipulative too, I think.'

Freya ignored his intervention. 'So what did he come around for then, Sam? I doubt it was to break the news to me gently. And coming over here in all this snow? Stephen never puts himself out for anyone, so he must have been pretty keen to see someone, and I can only surmise that must have been you.'

'Stephen came around to ask for my help basically, to bail him out of his latest scrape by lending him money so that the sale could continue on this place. I refused.' He swallowed.

'Big of you,' she said. 'I still don't understand.'

'Well, it's not unusual in situations like this for a mortgage to be raised against one property to help to buy another. That's what Stephen was trying to do. Trouble is that unbeknownst to me, he's already mortgaged Braeburn to help pay off some of his debts, debts which incidentally still exist. The bank won't lend him the money, it's as simple as that. I'm not involved in any of this because I don't own Braeburn, Stephen does.'

Freya stared at him. 'What do you mean you don't own it, since when?'

'Since Dad died and left everything to Stephen.' He held up his hand. 'Hang on, let me finish. What did your dad used to say about mine?'

'He called him a wily old bird, the sharpest business brain around.'

'Exactly, and he was, and he also knew both his sons very well. He called us together a few years before he died to discuss his affairs, and he gave us a choice. He could leave Braeburn to both of us, or only one of us, in which case the other would inherit financially but would never own the orchard. If he left it to both of us, we had to run the business together, and if he left it to only one of us, the other would be granted permission to live there for as long as Braeburn remained in the other's possession. He was giving me an out, Freya.'

Amos placed three plates of sandwiches down on the table. 'As you say, a very astute man.'

'No, I still don't get it. Why would you give all that up, Sam, why let Stephen win?' asked Freya.

'I haven't let him win. Dad knew that Stephen would never want to give up Braeburn, but he also knew that if we had to run the farm together, it would be a disaster. I would have hated it, so he did the best thing he could think of, which was to give me the opportunity to carry on living there but to leave me with an investment that I could use for my own future when the time was right. I think he hoped that Stephen would change his ways and make the best of the opportunity he'd been given too, but he's done exactly what Dad worried he would do. He's frittered everything away, and now he's lucky if he'll have anything left. I didn't realise it at the time, and I know Dad hoped everything would turn out fine, but he wanted to protect me from going down with the ship. I think I've just realised how astute he actually was.'

'And how much he loved you,' said Amos.

The words hung in the air for a few moments, settling between them all.

'So everything at Braeburn's is Stephen's, the fancy lorry, the posh house, everything?'

'Yes.'

Freya picked at the edge of her cast. 'And Stephen came to you this morning because he wanted to borrow money from you, so he could buy this place?'

'Essentially, yes.'

'And what did you say?'

'I told him no... I'm setting myself free, Freya. Finally.'

She considered this for a moment. 'But do you have the money?' she asked quietly.

'It's not what you think, Freya,' he said quickly. 'Please just let me explain.'

'What's to explain, Sam?' she flashed, turning on him. 'I can see exactly how it is. You didn't feel the need to explain any of this before, and I wonder why. Oh, yes, because this is what it's been about the whole time, isn't it? This stupid bloody rivalry between you and Stephen. And now after all these years you've finally got the revenge you've waited so long for. I've been like a lamb to the slaughter, haven't I? You've been keeping me sweet so that you could swoop in at the last minute and buy my house out from under me. Do you even want it, Sam, or is it just to get back at Stephen?' She got up from the table. 'Well, I'll tell you one thing, I'm not going to be piggy in the middle any more. I know what I did was wrong, but I was just beginning to let myself fall in love with you all over again. I didn't realise you still hated me quite as much as you do. You can think again about buying this place, Sam. Over my dead body you will.'

She turned and looked at Amos, the tears spilling from her eyes. 'Excuse me, I need to go and get dressed… and you,' she added, pointing a shaky finger at Sam, 'can get out of my house. Now.'

*

Sam braced himself for the sound of slamming doors, but none came. Just a deep and all-encompassing silence. He lay his head on the table and groaned. 'As if I couldn't see that coming. It's been inching ever closer, coming at me straight between the eyes, and there didn't seem to be a damned thing I could do to stop it. She's not going to listen to me now, is she? What the hell am I going to do? I can't lose her, Amos, not again.'

Amos laid a hand on his shoulder, and paused for a moment, thinking. He took a deep breath.

'You're going to do what you were going to do before, and that is to help me bring in the mistletoe.'

Sam lifted his head a fraction. 'And that's the sum token of your sage advice, is it?'

'It's very sound advice actually. One, because it will keep you busy for a few minutes, two because it will give Freya the time to fully take in what she's just learned before you go and speak to her, and three, very importantly, because it's Mistletoe Day, and the mistletoe needs to be on the inside, not in the barn.'

'Amos, this is important.'

'Yes, it is, I'm glad you agree. Come on then.'

'I meant… this whole thing with Freya.'

'I'm fully aware what you meant,' he replied, not taking his eyes off Sam for a minute.

Eventually, Sam heaved a frustrated sigh, but rose from the table just the same. He stared at Amos, his eyes dark and questioning.

'It will be worth it, Sam, believe me. I'm sure you're well aware of the old-fashioned name for mistletoe. It's not called Allheal for nothing.'

*

Freya sat on the edge of the bed, cold and numb. She wished with all her heart that she had got it wrong. She had even dared to believe that things could be different after last night, but truly, even after all these years, he still hated her. The thought reverberated around her head. It was all lies, everything he'd done for her these last weeks was all a ruse, all a pretence to soften her up, lure her into a false sense of security before he played his final hand. She knew what she'd done had hurt him terribly, but she'd truly never meant to. She had thought she was in love. At least now she knew where she stood. She had no idea what to do, but she knew that Sam would come and try to talk to her, and she definitely didn't want to talk to him. In fact, there was only one person she did want to talk to. She had to get out of the house.

It was still such incredibly hard work getting dressed, but she pulled on what she could, not caring what she looked like and went softly back downstairs. The kitchen seemed quiet, but she doubled back just the same and went through into the main hallway, pulling open the cloak cupboard quietly and wriggling into the coat that she found there. It was huge on her but meant that at least she could get it around her arm and still button it up. She pulled her red knitted hat on as well and pushed her feet into her boots, opening the front door as quietly as she could. She had no desire to see anyone and instead slipped unnoticed into the white world outside.

The snow was drifting gently down now, small feathery flakes that settled with the lightest touch onto the mounds already there. Snow on snow. She breathed in the cold air deeply, letting it settle around her, and enjoying the sensation. It seemed right to feel cold somehow. She walked down the path and out onto the lane, picking her way carefully through the ruts. She had no idea how long it would take her to walk, but that scarcely mattered; she had all day.

She had always enjoyed walking, loving the way it sent her brain into freewheel. She could surrender to the sheer enjoyment of being outside, putting life into suspended animation until she chose to rejoin the world once again. Thinking only about putting one foot in front of the other had always calmed her and made her feel in control once more, but today even this feeling deserted her. Her head was just as full of white noise as the day outside, and she couldn't make any sense of it.

Their lane turned right onto the main road after about half a mile, and it was trickier here where the snow-plough had gone through. The snow had compacted to ice under its wheels and deep piles of snow had been pushed to the sides of the road. It was safer to walk on the verges – less slippery – but with each step, her foot sank by about twelve inches, and in only ten minutes her legs felt like lead. She stopped for a moment, tears of frustration fuelling the anger that suddenly reared up inside her. She didn't want to turn back, but at this rate she knew she'd never make it to the village either, and she was just about to howl with rage when she heard the rumble of a tractor close by.

She hadn't realised quite how bad the roads were. Even the tractor had found it difficult to navigate at times, but despite the farmer's caution, Freya was still adamant that she wanted to be dropped off in the village. Like most local folk, he'd known Freya most of her life and dressed as she was in her dad's oversized coat, there could only be one place she was headed for today.

The church looked especially pretty with its blanket of snow, the dark yew and holly hedges vibrant under their white topping. A bright wreath adorned the lych-gate and, tucked inside the porch, a Christmas tree twinkled with light. At any other time, Freya would have appreciated its picture-postcard quality. Today the gate creaked fiercely as it opened, but it did so with ease, the path having already been cleared, no doubt in preparation for tomorrow's Midnight Mass. She stepped away from it almost straight away, wading through the thick snow amongst the gravestones.

It saddened her to see the floral tributes half-buried, their colours lost beneath the snow, the weight of it bowing the stems of the roses and chrysanthemums. She crouched beside a grave and lifted the wreath she had placed there over a week ago, its shape only a soft mound in the deep snow. She gently brushed the snow from the greenery, freeing the holly and mistletoe from its cloak and shaking loose what she could. She brought it to her lips for a moment before laying it softly against the icy marble, sweeping the snow from the top of the stone so that none would fall on it.

'Hello Dad,' she whispered.

She hadn't even realised she was crying until a sudden squally gust of wind stung the wetness on her cheeks. She felt hollow inside all over again, just as she had when her dad had died. The last few months had been some of the most painful in her life, but gradually a sense of purpose had filled her, and she had woken each day knowing that, although different, her life was still hers to make of it what she could. She had felt some of her old spirit returning, and each day confirmed what she was beginning to feel: that she would be okay. Now, it felt as though someone had viciously scrubbed out these pages of her life, leaving them obliterated and ragged, the paper torn and scratched so that nothing could be rewritten onto them.

The wind was really beginning to whip up now, blowing white flurries of snow across the graveyard, and she shivered as an icy trickle forced its way down the back of her neck. Her arm was beginning to throb from the cold, and she stood wearily, the stiffness in her legs making her realise just how long she had been crouched there. A robin swooped to perch on the gravestone, its feathers ruffling in the cold wind. It cocked its head to one side, then flew off, landing on a neighbouring stone and immediately swooping away once more. She lost it for a moment before a flash of movement caught her eye. Without thinking she followed it into the church porch where a trug of holly lay next to the Christmas tree. The robin was perched on the handle, a ruby berry held delicately in its beak. It watched her for a moment, its tiny eyes bright, and then flew off once more, leaving a small white feather floating on the wind. In that instant a thought cut through her like a knife.

She saw Sam's face as he had looked in the kitchen that morning, not triumphant as she had thought, but desolate at what he believed he had lost. There was nothing in his expression that had been laughing at her, or smug, or even close to hatred. He loved her, after all this time. He had forgiven her in spite of everything she'd done, and she'd give anything to see him again.

She looked up then, seeing the whiteness outside as if for the first time, and realised that this was no longer the place she should be. She wanted to be among the living. She wanted to be the little robin, who even in the bleakest of times could find what he needed to survive. She pulled her coat around her a little tighter, realising just how cold she was and suddenly scared about how long it would take her to get home.

A jangling noise in the stillness made her jump, echoing around the enclosed porch. She pulled her mobile out of her pocket, trying to hold it with the hand of her injured arm while she frantically tried to remove her glove with her teeth. The ringing went on.

'Hello,' she managed eventually, 'hello.' But the line just crackled as the voice cut in and out. 'Sam,' she tried again, but all she could hear were short bursts of noise and then the line went dead. She stared at her phone. How quickly things had changed. In only a few hours, there was no one else whose voice she'd rather hear.

With shaking hands, she dialled Sam's number, watching anxiously as the snow began to fall thick and fast, but the call went straight to voicemail. As she stared at the display, it suddenly lit up and she jabbed at the accept button, her heart hammering wildly.

'Sam,' she started, her face falling as she realised that he wasn't the caller after all. She was struggling to hear, and moved closer to the edge of the porch trying to angle her body out of the wind and snow that tore at her hair.

The voice cut in loud and clear all of a sudden. 'Merry!' she exclaimed, a smile automatically forming on her lips. 'Oh it's so lovely to hear your voice.' A sudden rush of emotion brought the tears rushing back to her eyes. 'Everything is such a mess, I don't know what to do.' Another thought caught up with her then. 'Oh God… how are you? Is it the baby?'

'I bloomin' well hope so, what else could possibly hurt this much?'

'Oh Merry!' said Freya, smiling not at her friend's pain but at her typical matter-of-fact reaction to the things that happened in her life. 'Where are you, at the hospital?'

'No, just about to leave. Tom is doing the whole running-around-in-a-panic thing, and I thought I'd give you a ring to see how everything is. I thought it might take my mind off things, but it seems as if I've rung at just the right time.'

Freya listened to the overly casual tone in Merry's voice, one that Freya had heard her adopt on many occasions over the years. It hadn't fooled her then, and it wasn't fooling her now. 'I see… you're sure it's not because Sam has rung you and you're checking up on me?'

There was silence for a moment before Merry heaved a sigh. 'Do you know I thought it might work this time, you know, seeing as we're not face to face, but I can never seem to get one past you, can I?'

'Nope. You never could lie at the best of times. You are actually in labour I suppose? You haven't made that up as well?'

'No, I bloody well have not. I'm in agony here. Listen, Sam's just worried about you, Freya. He couldn't get hold of you, said something about an argument and being out in the snow.'

'We had a fight... well not really, but I've done it again, Merry, jumping to conclusions, running off without giving him the chance to explain.'

There was an answering silence. That grew longer. 'Merry?' whispered Freya. 'Are you still there?'

Merry drew in a sharp intake of breath that was readily audible this time. 'Freya... I think my waters just broke... Oh God, my waters just broke, Freya, I'm going to be a mummy!' Her voice rose with excitement mixed with pain. 'I've got to go, Freya, sorry... I'll ring you, okay?'

'Yes, go, go!' replied Freya urgently.

'Listen, just one thing, Freya Sherbourne, and you damn well listen this time,' she panted. 'My whole life is going to change today, nothing will ever be the same again, but it's a good thing. It's the right time for me and if you let it, it can be the right time for you too. Promise me you won't fight what you're scared of, Freya. Breathe through the pain and at the end of it, well you just might have yourself a miracle.'

'Okay.' She nodded. 'I will, I promise.'

She could almost hear her friend nodding, words temporarily deserting her until she got her breath back. 'Good, don't let me down, will you? Okay, I'm going now. Wish me luck...'

'Merry Mistletoe!' shouted Freya against the wind, but her friend had already gone. She slipped her phone back into her pocket and, wiping her eyes, set out from the shelter of the porch into the whirling storm. If she was lucky, she would find someone who could take her home.

The church was in the very centre of the village, but even so by the time she had navigated the village green and emerged onto the high street, she was exhausted. The little row of shops huddled together, their twinkly lights shining bravely out into the dimming light, but this was the only sign of the season. The place was deserted; even the butcher's which would usually have a good-natured crowd spilling out onto the street as people queued to collect their turkeys, was eerily quiet. She thought of her own warm house, with its homely kitchen, and roaring fire, fragrant from the apple wood they burned, and her stomach turned over with a tiny shiver of fear. She was finding walking increasingly difficult, her arm still in its sling throwing her off balance, and her wellies, although waterproof, with next to no grip on the snow.

In desperation, she walked towards the baker's at the far end of the street. Millie's husband was a farmer, and it was just possible he might be able to come and collect her. As she walked, she heard a light tinkling noise and then, 'Freya?'

She turned to see the door of the off-licence closing. Stephen stood on the pavement, a carrier bag in his hand. He looked as surprised to see her as she him.

'What are you doing here, Freya? Jesus, you look cold.'

To her further surprise and humiliation, she burst into noisy tears, all her pent-up emotion finally catching up with her.

'You bastard!' she shouted, flailing her arm at him. 'This is all your fault. Why couldn't you just leave me alone?'

Stephen put down his bag on the pavement with a clank, and tried as best he could to get both arms around her as she struggled against him. He said nothing, just tried to calm her, his natural height and build giving him the advantage, and after a while, although the whimpering accusations continued, she eventually stopped wriggling and sagged against him.

'Come on,' he said gently. 'Let's get you home.' He picked up his bag again, and still holding onto her as best he could, moved her slowly down the street to where his car was parked.

'I'm not going anywhere with you,' she sniffed, eyeing his car warily. 'Not if you've been drinking.'

He drew a slow breath in. 'Jesus Freya,' he said, studying her for a moment, her face a picture of abject misery. 'You really do hate me, don't you? No, don't answer that. I haven't been drinking, not yet anyway. You'll be perfectly safe. Come on, get in.'

He folded her inside, and then set about clearing the windscreen, which even in the short time he had been shopping had completely covered in snow. After a few minutes, he climbed in beside her, and started the Range Rover, turning the heaters up to full.

He was about to put the car into gear, when he suddenly stopped and looked at her.

'Not that it will make any difference to you, but for what it's worth I wanted to say that you're quite right. I *am* a bastard, and it *is* all my fault.'

Freya turned to look at him, sniffing gently, her eyes still full of tears. 'Stop playing games, Stephen, enough is enough.'

'You know, I don't blame you for not believing me, but actually this time, I mean it, Freya, I'm telling the truth. I should never have done what I did. You were young, and I took advantage of that. I knew exactly what I was doing.'

'So why did you then?'

Stephen toyed with the air freshener on the dashboard. 'Because I've always been jealous of Sam, right from when we were children; of the way he made friends when we were young, of the way he made people laugh. Stupid and irrational I know, but there you are. I can't think of one single reason why I should have felt like that, but I did, and anything he had, I set out to take from him... including you.'

Freya's lip trembled. 'And I let you take me,' she said sadly. 'I'm just as much to blame.'

Stephen reached for her hand, even now feeling her flinch as he took it. 'No, it wasn't your fault, Freya. I pursued you like a hunter stalks a lion. I showered you with compliments and presents, planted dreams of what our life could be like if we were together, of the riches we would have, the places we would travel to.'

'Empty promises...'

'Yes, but you weren't to know that. You were eighteen, not old enough to know what you wanted.'

A tear trickled down Freya's cheek. 'But I did know what I wanted... and I let him go.'

The silence stretched out between them for a few minutes, both lost in a time over 15 years ago. 'He wanted to go after you that day, after the wedding, did you know that? But I stopped him. Even then, after all that had happened, he would still have gone after you, but I punched him and knocked him to the ground.'

Freya looked up in shock. 'I never knew that,' she said, her eyes wide. 'But you were angry, Stephen, I'd stood you up in front of all those people. I knew weeks before that I didn't want to marry you, but I let it go too far. I was scared; your dad had done so much, all those beautiful flowers, the marquee, I couldn't bring myself to tell anyone. I just thought I would go through with it and in the end it would all be okay. But on the day… I just couldn't… I should never have done that either.'

He squeezed her hand. 'We both made mistakes, but I don't blame you for what you did. Marrying me would have been a disaster. I've never said this to you before, but I am truly sorry for what happened.'

Freya looked down at her hands.

'Why are you telling me this now, Stephen?'

'I don't know… because it's Christmas… because I've fucked up my life and it's time to do something about it… because my brother has loved you since primary school and you should be together…' He shrugged. 'I could go on.'

'What will you do?'

Stephen gave a rueful smile. 'Go home and get bladdered one last time and then try to sort my life out. Try to salvage what I can of my home and my business, maybe marry someone like you, try being a grown-up for a change.' He pushed the gear stick forward. 'But first I'm going to get you home.'

Appleyard was only a three-mile drive from the village, but the snow was coming down so fast now that Freya wondered if they would make it at all. The wind had blown huge drifts against the hedges and in places there was barely room to pass. Even with the car's four-wheel drive, they struggled up the lanes, visibility almost zero, but Stephen drove slowly on, his teeth clenched in his jaw. Freya sat forward in her seat and urged them onwards.

Eventually, the gates to the house came into view and Stephen carefully brought the car to a standstill.

'Are you sure you'll be all right from here?' he asked anxiously.

Freya touched her hand gently to his. 'I will, I'm sure of it.' She leaned over to kiss his cheek. 'And thank you.'

Stephen smiled at her touch, as if in recognition that for once in his life he had done the right thing.

She had only made it halfway up the drive when the back door opened and a familiar figure half ran, half stumbled towards her. She could feel her heart pounding in her chest as she took the last few steps, until finally she felt Sam's arms go around her and there, swaying gently in his warmth with the snow whirling around them, cold and exhausted, Freya finally came home.

'I thought I'd lost you again,' murmured Sam as they clung to each other in the quiet solitude of the kitchen. They held each other close, the years catching up with them until a peaceful silence settled on the room, and this was how Amos found them, in a silent embrace, standing oblivious under the mistletoe that they had hung from the rafters only hours earlier. He closed the back door firmly and turned the key in the lock before coming to rest a hand on Sam's shoulder and kiss Freya's cheek.

'Merry Mistletoe,' he whispered.

It was fully dark by the time Freya awoke, stretching luxuriously under the weight of the blankets. After gallons of tea, hot buttered toast and jam and a rather giggly one-armed bath, she'd had no objection at all to being told what to do, and had fallen into a deep sleep.

It was quiet downstairs as she made her way along the landing, pausing for a moment as she spotted Sam sitting at the bottom of the stairs, an open book on his lap. He turned as he heard her footsteps.

'I didn't want to miss you,' he said, holding out his hand and waiting for her to reach his level. 'Come with me.'

She followed his lead along the hallway until he stopped at the door to the lounge. 'Close your eyes,' he instructed, a smile on his face.

She did as she was asked, stepping gingerly into the room, a child-like leap of excitement filling her. The door closed behind her, and she strained her ears, but there wasn't a sound that she could hear.

'Okay you can open them now.'

She peered between her fingers, the room still completely dark, and suddenly she was aware of a familiar fragrance. In the split second that she realised what it was, the room came to life with what looked like a million points of dancing light.

'Oh,' was all she could say, her mouth round as she inhaled a sharp breath of surprise.

In the room before her were a myriad Christmases past; holly and mistletoe heaped along the mantelpiece, woven with tartan ribbons and gilded pine cones, bright red woollen stockings at either end – stockings she herself had knitted. Strings of fairy lights hung across the alcoves on each side of the room, and the edges of the bookshelves were covered in twinkly gold stars. Her patchwork Christmas quilt was thrown over the cream sofa, and the jolly felt reindeer and elves she loved so much stood on the coffee table to one side.

Her gaze swept the room each time seeing something new, but each time coming to rest on the huge tree that stood in one corner, a beautiful spruce of the brightest green and now bearing only the simplest of decoration. As Freya moved closer, something caught in her throat as she realised what was hanging there; each and every one of the beautiful baubles she and her dad had collected over the years, each with its own story to tell and each still as perfect as the day they had bought it. She looked at them all in turn, every one bringing a smile of memory until she saw right near the top, the most recent addition: a shimmering rose globe, caught in the light to reveal its perfect feather frozen in time within. It was utterly, utterly beautiful and left her devoid of words.

She felt an arm go around her, warm and comforting and familiar.

'I thought you might like it,' murmured Sam in her ear. 'It seemed such a shame to leave them in their boxes; all those memories locked away. They need to dance again, don't you think?'

A soft smile lit up Freya's face. 'I think it's the most beautiful thing I've ever seen. When did you do all this?'

'This afternoon while Amos was out looking for you. I wanted to stay here in case you came back, but I had to have something to keep me occupied, I was going out of my mind with worry.'

'I'm so sorry I ran away. I should have let you explain,' said Freya.

Sam placed a finger gently across her lips. 'I seem to remember a time when I should have listened to you, but I let a lot of years go by, letting my stupid pride have its way. We should look to the future now, not the past.'

Freya kissed his fingers, entwining them with her own. 'It was Stephen who brought me home you know. He actually apologised for what happened between us, said it was all his fault. I've carried the guilt of that around with me for so long, Sam.'

'I know.'

'I think he's going to be okay, though, Stephen I mean. He might even be growing up finally.'

Sam smiled, his eyes twinkling in the light. 'Well, it is Christmas, Freya, stranger things have happened.'

She looked at the mistletoe on the mantelpiece, deep in thought. 'Where is Amos by the way?' she asked.

'Gone to bed, he said he'd see you in the morning.' He touched Freya's face once more. 'You know he'll be gone soon, don't you?'

Freya stared wistfully at the bauble on top of the tree, thinking of the man who had come into her life so suddenly and would no doubt leave it the same way. He would remain in her memory for a very long time. 'Yes, I know. He'll go whichever way the wind blows him.'

She watched the light for a moment sparkling on the rose-coloured glass, her eye now drawn to something she hadn't seen before: a bright red velvet box, tied with golden thread.

Sam followed the direction of her eyes. 'It was supposed to be your Christmas present, but you could have it now if you'd like.'

Freya grinned, trying hard not to jiggle with excitement. Sam lifted the box from the tree, motioning for Freya to come and sit down beside him.

He waited until she had wriggled herself comfortable, sliding onto his knees beside her and drawing a steadying breath. 'Before I give this to you, will you let me tell you what I meant to say this morning? In fact, I should have said this a long time ago… I don't blame you for what happened with Stephen, I never did, Freya. I pushed you away as much as he pulled you to him. I'd lived so many years losing things to him, that I viewed it as inevitable in the end. He'd taken so much from me over the years that when I saw him begin to take an interest in you, I thought I never stood a chance. I should have fought for you. What's worse was that I never gave you the opportunity to tell me differently, and I've had to bear the consequence of my stupidity ever since.'

'We're both to blame, Sam. I was flattered by Stephen's attention, and I let myself be seduced by his stupid promises. I knew deep down that he never loved me, but I so desperately wanted to believe everything he told me. I wanted to stay here, among the orchards, to follow in my father's footsteps, raise my own family here. I thought that's what he wanted too, but I knew really it was never the case. Time has shown me that.'

'But is that what you still want, Freya, a life here?'

Her lip trembled. 'More than anything. I thought I could start a new life, buy Merry's shop and move away, be something different, but I can't. This is where I belong. I have to try to find a way to make it work.'

He pressed the box into her hands. 'Open it, Freya,' he said.

She pulled at the thread holding the tiny parcel closed and let it fall away until she was left, with shaking hands, holding the lid. She closed her eyes and opened it.

Inside was a key.

She looked up puzzled for a moment, until it suddenly struck her what it was.

'I'm giving you back Appleyard, Freya, so that you never have to worry about leaving again. The Sherbourne orchard has been here far too long to let it go, I want us to breathe new life into it… together.'

'But—'

'I'm asking you to marry me, Freya. To let me live here with you, and work alongside you, as equal partners, 'til death do us part and all that. We can make Appleyard whatever we want her to be, what she deserves to be.'

The clock on the mantel chimed midnight as Freya reached down to pull Sam to her, her lips only inches from his. She smiled softly. 'It's Christmas Eve,' she breathed, 'I wonder what we should do now?'

'Well,' grinned Sam, his lips tantalisingly close to hers. 'I could always help you unpack.'

In the room, just above them, Amos gave a soft sigh and turned over in his sleep. He pulled the covers a little tighter around him, snuggled into his pillow, and smiled.

SPRING

Chapter Twelve

Merry screwed her eyes tight shut, and then opened them again. 'Nope,' she said, laughing, 'it's still a mess. Remind me again why we did this, Tom.'

Her husband slid an arm around her waist and surveyed the yard they were standing in. 'Well, now let me see…' He smiled at the baby strapped to Merry's chest, reaching out to touch her downy cheek. 'This little one made us think that we needed a different challenge, that running a country house hotel with a pretty huge income and a nice little pension pot was not the sort of thing we needed in our lives any more. So, we swapped all that for a house that hasn't been lived in for a year, and a derelict shop that will need a miracle to get it open again.'

Merry nodded absently. 'Yes, I thought that was it,' she said. 'We are actually stark raving mad, aren't we? I mean who in their right mind would take this on?'

Tom gave his wife a sideways glance. 'Don't you like it any more then?' he asked.

'No,' replied Merry. '… I absolutely love it! I've never been so excited before in my life. I can't wait to get in here and get started.'

Tom grinned widely.

'What time did Freya and Sam say they'd come over?'

Tom looked at his watch. 'In about half an hour or so. We should feel very honoured, you know. I'm surprised they could tear themselves away from each other for long enough to come and visit.'

Merry slapped his arm. 'Stop it!' she said. 'I think it's lovely. And so what if they are love's young dream, they've waited long enough.'

'True. That they have.' Tom looked about him, shuffling his feet. 'Well, we've got half an hour to kill before they arrive. Whatever will we think of to do?'

'I've absolutely no idea,' Merry replied with an impish grin. 'Want to go and look in the house again?'

'I'll race you,' said Tom. 'Last one in's a cissy!'

'That's not fair, I'm carrying Robyn!'

'Who said anything about fair?' he retorted, and shot off across the garden.

Merry watched him go, a slow smile spreading across her face. She shielded her eyes from the sun and looked up at the old building. 'Well, Five Penny House, I think we're going to be very happy here. It's nice to be home.'

*

'Does my bum look big in this?' Freya laughed, skipping away from Sam's playful hands. She reached the bedroom door and turned for a moment, her peachy bottom wobbling as her naked body came to a halt. She picked up a cushion from the chair beside the door and threw it back towards the figure slumped beneath the covers.

'Come on, lazybones, time to get up!'

Sam gave a muffled groan as the cushion found its mark. 'Slave driver,' came his voice from the depths of the duvet but warmed with a smile.

Freya grabbed her dressing gown from the back of the door and headed downstairs. She winced as her feet made contact with the quarry tiles on the kitchen floor. The temperature outside might be warming up a little, but those tiles were never anything other than freezing. It would help if she could remember where she had left her slippers, but, as the memory of the night before came back to her, bringing a rosy blush to her cheeks, she knew that her slippers would not be the only item of clothing she'd be looking for this morning...

She spied her wellies propped up by the back door and crossed the room to put them on instead. They were bright pink with white spots, and clashed violently with her purple dressing gown, but Freya merely shrugged and wriggled her feet into them. Having filled the kettle and set it to boil, she unlocked the back door and slipped out into the morning air.

The sun was still a little hazy and as yet had no real warmth to it, but it was only early in the year, and the day looked like it had some promise. There had been a slight change in the air recently, a lightness and softness to it that was hard to define, but which to Freya was unmistakably the herald of spring, and as she crossed the yard she swung her arms, breathing deeply. She was late this morning, but it was the weekend after all, and she knew the hens would forgive her.

Her breath caught in her throat as she reached the barn at the top of the yard. The door was a tiny bit ajar, and although she knew that the cause was probably only the faulty catch, a little nugget of hope still flared inside her. She pulled open the door cautiously, peering into the dim space, and pausing until her eyes became accustomed to the gloom. It was empty, and she allowed herself a small sigh. The barn wasn't empty of course; it was full of all sorts of equipment, some of it junk, some vital to the running of the farm, but none of it was Amos Fry, the man who had drifted into her life one afternoon a few months ago, and then wafted away with the wind one day, just as she knew he would.

It was hard to define exactly what Amos was; a man with no fixed abode who came and went as he pleased, moving to wherever the next job took him, but a man who had come into Freya's life just when she had needed him the most; enigmatic, wise beyond his years, and now someone she considered a dear friend. He had left at Christmas time, when the snow still lay thick on the ground; to where, Freya never knew. In fact, it was quite possible that even Amos didn't know where he was bound for, but she still harboured a hope that one day she would open her barn door and find him there, asleep on her blankets, just like she had before.

Freya collected the pellets for the hens and walked back out into the yard. She looked over towards the house, where just for a moment a shadow crossed the kitchen window, and she smiled. Amos had brought her Sam, a man she had loved for years, but who she had thought was lost to her, and, in turn, Sam had given her back Appleyard. She stretched out her hand in the low morning sunlight to admire the ring on her finger. Sam hadn't just given her back Appleyard, he had given her a future, as his wife.

By the time she returned to the kitchen, the smell of bacon cooking was already beginning to waft out into the yard, and she hurried inside. It was a bit too early for most of the hens, but she still had two warm ovals in her hands, which would go down a treat with the bacon.

Sam had already made the tea, and she shivered as she accepted a mug from him, the sudden warmth of the kitchen a contrast to the day outside.

'Have you no shame, woman?' he asked, one eyebrow raised in question. He motioned towards her dressing gown, which was now gaping rather at the front.

Freya giggled. 'Well, the chickens never seem to mind!'

Sam reached forward with his free hand and pulled slowly at her dressing gown tie. 'No, neither do I…'

'The bacon's burning.'

'Is it?' murmured Sam. 'I like it crispy.'

An hour and a half later, Freya and Sam finally pulled out of the drive, turning into the lane that led down past Appleyard Farm into the village.

'I knew we were going to be late,' remarked Freya mildly.

Sam merely smiled. 'Merry's your oldest friend, she'll understand.'

'That's rather what I'm afraid of,' replied Freya, knowing just the sort of teasing comments her friend was likely to make. She pulled at her skirt a little self-consciously. 'I'd rather not be, that's all. This is a big day for them, and we need to show our support.'

Sam took one hand off the steering wheel and laid it on her arm. 'I'm sorry. Blame it all on me. It was my fault… to begin with…'

Freya blushed again, although revelling in the joy of their relationship, which just a short while ago was something she'd never thought she'd find again.

'And don't forget,' added Sam, 'Little Robyn is only three months old, so Merry and Tom will still be packing the enormous amount of stuff that she requires into their car, they're bound to be late.'

'Hmm, that's true. I can't wait to see the baby again, I bet she's grown heaps.'

Sam pulled neatly into a passing space in the narrow lane to let a tractor past. 'Totally ruling the roost no doubt. I know what they're doing makes sense, but even for Merry, this is a bit of a tall order. I hope they haven't bitten off more than they can chew.'

Freya had been thinking the same thing. She and Sam had a lot of work ahead of them, but they didn't have a small child to worry about too.

'I do understand why Merry feels that this is the right time for them to do something different, though. They've run the hotel ever since they've been together, and whilst that was fine when they were just the two of them, having Robyn changes everything. It's not the kind of life they can sustain any longer, and well… you and me of all people should know that sometimes you have to take a chance on things.'

Sam nodded at the truth of her words. 'Point taken. I shall say no more.'

They drove in peaceful silence for a few minutes until the car swung round the final bend, bringing them into Lower Witley.

'I can't remember the last time I was here,' remarked Freya. 'And I still can't picture where this new place is they've bought. Merry says it's up past the green, nearer the top of the hill, but I don't remember there ever being a shop there.'

'Well, we're about to find out,' replied Sam, slowing to a crawl as the village green came into view.

On a day like today, it was easy to see what had attracted Merry and Tom to the village. At its centre stood a circle of warm red brick, or black and white timbered houses, in front of which was a traditional village green, complete with pond. A weeping willow swayed lazily at one end of it while three ducks bobbed about aimlessly, without a care in the world. The road widened, sweeping onwards in a wide circle, revealing another cluster of cottages behind low brick walls, with paved paths and blossoming cherry trees. The pale blue sky provided the perfect backdrop as they drove on.

The village was bigger than it first looked and, as they crossed over the small bridge and followed the road up the hill, Freya looked back to see the church which stood on the other side of the village. It was certainly all very appealing.

The road gave one final bend before Five Penny House came into view.

'Look, there it is,' pointed Freya. 'I can see Tom's car.'

Sam turned into the wide courtyard to the side of the house, admiring the handsome lines of Merry and Tom's new home.

Freya was out of the car in a flash. 'Halloo,' she shouted. 'We're here!' waving her arms at the two figures she could see in the garden. She ran across the lawn. 'I remember this place now, isn't it beautiful?' she said, and reached up to give Tom a kiss.

Tom beamed at her and Merry, in turn. 'We think so, don't we?' he replied.

Freya stood back to look at Merry. She looked tired, although happiness shone from her face. A baby carrier was strapped to her front, from which two legs dangled, encased in bright red woolly tights. Freya automatically bent to grasp the baby's toes, grinning as Robyn tried to pull her legs away. 'Look at her, and look at you,' she exclaimed, giving her friend a hug and a kiss. 'You both look gorgeous!'

Merry pushed a lock of dark hair off her face. 'Well, I don't feel gorgeous at all, but this little one certainly is. She's beginning to grow at last too.' Freya knew how worried Merry had been during the first month or so after Robyn was born, as the baby steadfastly refused to put on weight. 'She's pretty much caught up now.'

'See. I told you everything would be all right,' replied Freya, tickling Robyn's toes again. 'Not that I know anything about babies of course, so you're probably wise not to listen to me.' She paused for a minute, watching Merry closely. 'And who said you weren't looking gorgeous? Give me their name, and I'll have them taken care of.'

Merry gave Tom beside her a furtive glance, and leaned in towards Freya. 'It's hard to feel gorgeous when your boobs feel like they're on fire. Jesus, they're sore, Freya. No one told me that breastfeeding would hurt this much.'

Sam arrived at this point which forestalled any further discussion, something which Freya was secretly relieved about. She winced inwardly at the thought of her friend's nipples being mashed to a pulp.

Tom shook his jacket, listening for the jangling that would reveal in which pocket he had stashed the keys to the house. He fished them out with a flourish.

'Come on then, who wants to look around?' he asked needlessly. 'Although don't get too excited; like Merry said, it needs a lot doing to it. The décor is a bit well… you'll see.'

He led the way up the path to the stout front door and wrestled with the lock for a moment before beckoning them all in.

'So what's the story with this place then, Tom?' asked Sam. 'Freya said something about a family dispute?'

Tom nodded. 'It was owned by two sisters and a brother, inherited when their great uncle died a year or so ago. The brother contested the will actually, believing that the property should have been his alone, but, even though he didn't win his case, he flatly refused to sell the house either, and so it's been empty ever since.'

'So how come you were able to buy it?'

'The brother died, just before Christmas,' replied Tom. 'A bit spooky actually; he fell through the ice on a lake in a freak accident while on holiday. He went for a walk apparently, and never came back…'

Freya gave an involuntary shudder. 'Oooh, that's a bit creepy.'

'No, it isn't,' retorted Merry. 'Tom, will you stop with the ghoulish stories. It was an accident, nothing else; very tragic I grant you, but no more than that, and before you say it, no, the house isn't cursed either.'

Freya's eyes widened. 'It isn't, is it?' she asked, looking around the hallway.

'So they say…' replied Tom, a smile curving his mouth upwards.

'Don't listen to him,' said Merry firmly. 'It's just some silly story he heard in the village.' She took Freya's arm. 'Come on, let's start upstairs, the view from up there is amazing.'

As Freya gazed out of the window, she felt a deep peace wash over her. It felt right, this house. She hadn't seen that much of it yet to be fair, as Merry had led the way upstairs, and although the décor was… unusual, the house had an undeniably comfortable feel to it. It felt welcoming, despite having been empty for a while, and Freya, who set great store by such things, felt warmed by this feeling. Buying this house was a big change in her friends' lives, and she would hate for it to be a mistake. And Merry was right; the views were simply stunning.

Five Penny House sat just short of the top of the hill, and from the windows upstairs the whole village lay spread out before them. It was like looking down onto a model village, so wide was the view. The other side of the house looked out over open countryside, the swoop and sway of the fields stretching away into the distance.

Freya could hear the others moving about the bedrooms and reluctantly pulled herself away from the window to join them.

'Blimey, what colour would you call this!' she exclaimed, walking into the next room, which was painted a shockingly bright shade of purple.

'How about "over my dead body"?' quipped Tom. 'It's not staying.'

'Ahh, shame.' Freya laughed, as she followed him out into the hallway. 'Are they all like this?'

'See for yourself,' said Merry, catching up with her. 'It's weird… It looks as if the house should be falling apart, but in truth it's been well looked after. It's had new electrics, new plumbing and even new windows in most places, but the one thing that hasn't been touched is the decoration. Some of it is newer than the rest, but as you can see, every room is a different colour, and they're not what you'd call easy on the eye.'

Freya wandered about, taking in the exuberant hues of lime green, cherry red, teal blue and zesty orange. It really was quite extraordinary.

'Wait till you see the kitchen,' said Merry, catching hold of her arm, and winking.

It was like stepping back in time, straight into a 1950s' diner.

'Oh my God, Merry. Is this original?'

'Yep.' She grinned. 'I knew you'd like it.'

'It's amazing. It must be worth a fortune!'

Merry pulled a face. 'Only to those who appreciate it, sadly. You know the saying, one person's trash is another's treasure.'

Freya ran her hand over the pristine cabinets. 'Please tell me you're not going to rip all this lot out?'

'I've already told Tom I'll divorce him if he does! Fortunately, he loves it too. It needs a bit of tidying up, but even so…'

'I think I'd have bought the house just for the kitchen alone.'

'It is rather special, isn't it?' Merry agreed. 'The paintwork I can do without, thank you, but the house itself, I'm totally in love with.'

Freya smiled at the excitement on her friend's face, which was obviously catching because Robyn's arms and legs began to jiggle up and down as if she was dancing.

'I think you're going to be very happy here,' she said to them both.

'Hold that thought.' Merry grinned in return. 'You haven't seen the shop yet.'

Optimistic, thought Freya; that was one word she'd have used. Or imaginative, that was another good one. You'd have to be both to see anything shop-like about the building to the side of Five Penny House. It was at least made of brick, but as Tom pulled open the door into the dark space beyond, it was evident that the only things still in one piece were the walls. A large part of the ceiling had collapsed in one corner, and opposite that, where the rain had poured through a broken window, the plasterboard had sagged and buckled away from one whole side of the building. Apart from that, the room was full of dirty and dusty junk.

'Okay…' said Sam slowly. 'I've seen the mess in Freya's barn, but if you don't mind me saying, this is rather more than that.'

Tom scratched his head, as a trail of cobweb settled on it. 'Yes, it's not the property's crowning glory, I'll give you that. But at least the structure's sound. Even the ceiling is not as bad as it looks.'

'Well, I said I couldn't remember there ever having been a shop here, and no wonder,' said Freya. 'It can't have been open for decades?'

Merry nodded, being careful to keep Robyn out of the dust. 'Probably before we were born,' she replied.

'But what do you think?' urged Tom. 'Are we mad or what?'

Freya gave Sam a long look, her lips pursed together. He obviously wasn't entirely sure what to say, but Freya wasn't quite so reticent.

'I think you're completely bloody mad,' she said succinctly. 'Although, actually, I wouldn't expect anything less. The house is brilliant, but you've certainly got your work cut out for you here… When did you say you wanted this place open?'

'June. At the latest,' commented Tom. 'Three months, that's all.'

Freya snorted. 'Well, good luck with that.' She stopped for a moment, peering back into the gloom of the dingy room. 'Seriously though, I am thrilled for you. It's a brilliant opportunity, and I know you're not afraid of hard work. Please just promise me that you'll ask for help when you need it, especially with little Robyn here.'

She looked at Merry and Tom's smiling faces. 'We should have some champagne really, I'm sorry I didn't think.'

'Oh, plenty of time for that when we actually move in.' Merry smiled. 'We'll just have to pretend for today,' she added, raising her hand as if holding a glass.

'For all of us facing our new beginnings,' she said. 'To the future!'

'To the future!' they chorused.

Chapter Thirteen

It was still raining. Freya stood at the kitchen window looking out into the yard, and waited for the kettle to boil. There wasn't much else to do on a day like today. Or the day before for that matter; it had been raining for ages. She was longing to get out into the orchard, to walk the rows and rows of her precious apple trees, but all that would accomplish was a thorough soaking. It was a little too early in the year for the flowers to appear; they were still in tight bud, but it was the promise of them that she loved. The thrill that she always got on the day when she spied the first delicate pearly pink blooms beginning to find the sky, was something she would never tire of. It wouldn't be today, though.

'Looking at the rain won't make it stop,' came the voice from behind her.

Sam was sitting at the kitchen table, an open laptop in front of him. 'Come and have a look at these and see what you think,' he said, motioning to the chair beside him.

Freya sighed and went to join him. She was bored, and she knew that she should be taking more of an interest in the equipment they needed if they were going to rejuvenate Appleyard. But it wasn't the lumps of metal and machinery that excited her; it was the alchemy of the thing. It was seeing the blossoms filled with bees and knowing that soon tiny apples would appear as if by magic. It was feeling the kiss of the summer sun on her skin, knowing that its golden rays were turning the starch within the apples to sugar and, eventually, eking out the glorious autumn days until the fruit was so ripe that the tree offered it up as a gift. This was what fuelled the fire in Freya's veins.

She peered at the screen in front of her, trying to concentrate on what Sam was saying.

'See, this is what I mentioned the other day,' he said, pointing. Stephen was adamant we buy these, but I've always favoured the Voran. To my mind, they're much superior. They might cost a little more, but the efficiency of juice extraction will pay for itself in the end. Plus, the machinery will last twice as long.'

Freya blanched when she caught sight of the price quoted on the website. 'We can't afford that, surely?' she said.

Sam had the grace to look a little embarrassed. 'We can, actually,' he replied, taking hold of her hand. 'Freya, I meant what I said at Christmas. I want us to breathe new life into Appleyard, but I want us to do it together. I won't do anything you're not comfortable with.'

Sam's hand felt warm in hers. She smiled. 'This means a lot to you, doesn't it?' she said gently.

A soft sigh drifted across to her. 'I think I've been waiting my whole life for this,' he replied. 'To get you was the best Christmas present I could ever have wished for. To get a chance to run Appleyard with you as well, is the icing on the cake really, but now that I can, it would seem rude not to have a big slice, wouldn't it?'

She chuckled. 'You have such a way with words.'

Sam watched her closely for a moment. 'And before you ask, no, I'm not just doing this to get one over on Stephen, or be flash with my cash. I want us to succeed, and to me, this makes sound business sense.'

Freya would never have dreamed of making such an overt observation, but Sam knew her so well. It was true, this thought had crossed her mind on more than one occasion. She wouldn't blame him if he did feel this way; after all he'd spent so many years in Stephen's shadow, and now that he was finally able to make a life for himself, particularly one that included Freya, it was only natural that he would want to feel a little smug.

She got up to make the tea, collecting the mugs that were already on the table as she went.

'So how is Stephen anyway?'

It was an innocent enough question, but Freya listened keenly for Sam's answer. She still felt a bit sad for Stephen. Even though he deserved much that had come to him, he had looked so forlorn on the day he had rescued her from the blizzard last Christmas.

'I think resigned is probably the word I'd use,' Sam replied. 'He seems to have got over that whole thing with his property developer friend. When the sale fell through, I think Stephen realised that he hadn't actually lost anything at all; he still had a perfectly good business, and he'd better get on and run it. Now that I'm no longer under his feet arguing the toss over everything, I think he feels a little more settled.'

'Hmm, but he's lost his best worker of course... everyone knows that you did all the work there, Sam.'

'Yes, well, it won't hurt him to get his hands dirty for a change either.'

Freya brought the mugs back to the table. 'You know, what we really need to do, is find him a woman. Not one of those bimbo nymphet types he usually goes for, but a soulmate, someone who will love Braeburn and him in equal measure.'

'You don't have to feel that sorry for him, you know.'

'I know... but I did nearly marry the bloke. It was a long time ago, but I do feel partly responsible all the same. There's nothing wrong with wanting him to be happy too, is there?'

Sam's green eyes were soft on hers. 'Feeling the way I do right now? No, there's nothing wrong with it. I wish everyone could feel this way.'

Chapter Fourteen

Freya wasn't entirely sure Merry would ever actually leave. The plan had been simply to drop Robyn off, but half an hour later, Merry was still going strong, anxiety written all over her face. Little Robyn, however, lay fast asleep in her car seat, utterly oblivious to the drama she was causing.

'It's her feeds I'm really worried about,' said Merry again. 'She's never had a bottle before.'

'Merry,' replied Freya, her hands on her hips. 'She'll be fine. It looks like breast milk, tastes like breast milk, what's not to like?'

'But it's very different from a bottle, it's the sensation. Babies' mouths are so sensitive, and she'll know.'

'I'm sure she will, but she'll also drink it if she's hungry, surely? Look—'

An impatient toot cut across her. Merry looked to the door, and then back again, indecision clouding her face. Freya could understand her friend's concern, but this wasn't helping. She put on her 'no-nonsense' face and decided to take charge.

'Right, come on, you need to go. Give me that,' she added, plucking the bag from Merry's hands. 'I promise I will heat her milk to *exactly* the right temperature, and I promise I will apply Sudocreme *liberally* to her bum when I change her. I also promise not to let her roll in the mud or eat chicken poo, and by the time I drop her off, she will have learned her three times table and all the letters of the alphabet… now go!'

She all but propelled Merry through the door. 'And don't forget to enjoy yourself,' she called at her retreating back. 'This is the start of your new adventure!'

Tom's brake lights flashed a couple of times as he made his way down the drive, and Freya wouldn't have been surprised to see Merry leap from the car with something else of vital importance that she'd remembered, but in the end they made it safely out of the yard and onto the road. Freya watched them until the car was out of sight.

She closed the back door and leaned up against it, feeling suddenly exhausted. Perhaps if she closed her eyes it would look better, but no, when she opened them again, her kitchen table was still littered with one hundred and one items, most of which Freya could never see herself needing. There were spare clothes, and then another change (just in case), nappies, lotions, potions, cloths, bibs, toys, milk, a spare bottle and milk (just in case), a couple of towels, a baby monitor, front carrier and, Freya was sure it was there somewhere, a partridge in a pear tree.

Until that moment, Freya had always considered herself to be quite a maternal person. She had even allowed herself a few sneaky dreams of what it might be like if she and Sam had a baby, but right now, the little person fast asleep in her kitchen might as well be an alien species. Freya had no idea it was this complicated to look after a baby, or that she would need so much stuff. Merry could run a thirty-bedroom hotel with one eye closed and a hand tied behind her back, but three months of motherhood had clearly tested even her talents. It was a scary scary thing indeed.

Freya eyed Robyn warily, but the baby was still peaceful. She could do with another cup of tea, but surely the noise from the boiling kettle would wake her? Perhaps she could move the baby into another room while it boiled, but then again, wouldn't the movement wake her anyway? She felt trapped.

It was at times like these that Freya found herself thinking of Amos again. He had been so wise, so comforting, always knowing exactly the right thing to say at exactly the right moment. Or so it had felt. He was like Mary Poppins, or Nanny McPhee she thought to herself, smiling as she remembered a line from the film: "*When you need me but do not want me, then I will stay. If you want me, but no longer need me, then I must go*." It wasn't quite the same thing, but it pretty much summed Amos up. It also made her realise the extraordinary gifts that he had given her. She had felt so lost and alone after her father died the year before, but Amos had given her the courage to start living again, to face her future with conviction and believe in herself once more. Her chin lifted as she thought of him.

A deep breath calmed her even further as she crossed the kitchen to fill the kettle. She set it to boil with a wry smile and started to tidy up the mess on her table.

Everything was fine, for the first hour. Robyn woke about half an hour after Merry left, looked around her and then started to bounce her legs up and down in her seat so that the toys strung across the front, danced and jangled. She accompanied their noise with cheerful gurgles and much drooling, and as Freya pottered around the kitchen, she kept up a steady stream of chatter.

Freya had only left the room for a couple of minutes when she was summoned back to the kitchen by an ear-splitting wail. Gone was the happy chortling, and in its place was a furious, red-faced baby. The toy that Freya sought to calm her with was resolutely dumped over the side of the chair, and the noise intensified. Further offerings were given the same treatment, until there was nothing for it but to release Robyn from her seat.

The minute she picked her up, the reason for the baby's distress became apparent. Freya almost gagged as the overwhelming aroma reached her. And to make it worse, something ominous had leaked through Robyn's Babygro as well. Balancing the baby on her hip, whilst trying to keep her away from her own clothes, Freya grabbed the changing mat and hurried to the bathroom.

Explosive diarrhoea at nine o'clock in the morning was not something that Freya had much experience of dealing with. She lay Robyn down on the changing mat and gingerly began to undo her clothes. *Just keep breathing through your mouth,* she told herself, *and you'll be fine.* Oh Dear God…

She was just beginning to congratulate herself on surviving the ordeal when Freya realised her mistake; she had left Robyn's changing bag with all her nappies and spare clothes downstairs. She couldn't leave the baby on the floor, even if it was unlikely that she could go anywhere, and so grabbing a towel off the rail, she wrapped it around her and went back downstairs. By the time she returned, Robyn had weed all over the towel, and laying her back down again, Freya added the towel to the sodden assortment of items on the floor beside her. She was only tiny for God's sake, where did all this stuff come from? A few minutes later, with Robyn safely back in her car seat, Freya gathered up the stinky clothes and threw them in the washing machine. There was no way she could give them back to Merry in the state they were in. She had never had cause to think about the existence of nappy sacks before, or indeed their usefulness, but as she gingerly lifted the soiled nappy and pile of wet wipes into one, she said a prayer in gratitude to Merry for providing them. And then finally, as the clock edged past two, Freya could see the end of her challenge in sight. There had been more wee, more poo, and a sticky moment when, despite screaming with hunger, Robyn had flatly refused to drink from the bottle. In the end, reasoning that perhaps babies were like animals and could smell fear, Freya fixed her with a steely glare and said, *listen sunshine, my boobs will be of absolutely no use to you, so it's this or nothing. If I were you, I'd shut up and give it a go.* Much to her surprise, it had done the trick. After that, she and Robyn had agreed a truce; the baby fell asleep in her arms, and Freya, lulled by the tiny snuffling noises, nodded off as well, her lips brushing the top of the baby's downy head.

Tom and Merry were leaning up against a pile of boxes in the kitchen, eating Mars bars as if their lives depended on it.

'Don't tell me that's all you've had to eat all day,' remarked Freya, as she deposited the first of Robyn's bags on the table. 'Haven't you had any lunch?'

Tom licked his lips. 'No, we had lunch. These are emergency fuel rations.' He waved his empty wrapper. 'Anyway, onwards… shall I give you a hand?'

Merry followed them straight out to the car, just as Freya knew she would.

'She's been absolutely fine, Merry, honestly. Although you might have warned me about the amount of bodily fluids she was capable of producing.'

'What and spoil all the fun?' She wrinkled her nose. 'It wasn't too bad, was it?'

Freya handed Tom another bag out of the car. 'Well, no, not all the time; I had rather a baptism of fire this morning that was all. I've done a bit of washing for you as a result, although I'm afraid it's not quite dry yet.' She turned and looked back at Merry. 'More importantly though, how have things gone today? Are you all in?'

'We are,' replied Merry. 'The removal men were gone by twelve, and we've worked like stink this afternoon to get things sorted. I've even managed to get the beds made up already.' She looked around her to the fields beyond the house. 'You know, I already love it here. And yes, the house is hideous in places, but it's only on the surface. I think we're going to be really happy here.'

Freya squeezed her friend's arm. 'I know you will. Even the sun came out for you today,' she said, eyeing the sky, which was already darkening a little. 'Come on, let's get back inside before it decides to rain again.'

Chapter Fifteen

Merry could hear the rain battering against the window, but that didn't stop her from rushing to look out. With no curtains up yet, she had woken early, even earlier than Robyn, and was filled with a sudden rush of excited energy.

She'd been completely exhausted of course, when she'd finally gone to bed, but had slept like the proverbial log. Even the lime green walls hadn't intruded into her dreams. Now, as she stood looking out onto the spread of the village below, she felt a deep calm and contented peace. Tom still lay snoring gently in bed, and knowing that it couldn't be long before Robyn did wake up, she slipped from the room and went downstairs.

As moving days went, it had all gone like clockwork. There had been no dramas, no mishaps, and even no sticking points over furniture. Most of the rooms still held piles of boxes, but here in the kitchen, the last few to be unpacked held all her china and glassware. As she flicked the kettle on, she opened the lid on the uppermost box and started to pull out its contents.

Within twenty minutes, the kettle had been forgotten, and instead the kitchen floor was littered with newspaper, as she emptied the first box and then the second. The table was covered with a selection of wine and spirit glasses, and having room for no more, Merry started to ferry them to the dining room. It didn't escape her notice that it would have been easier to unpack them in situ, but she enjoyed walking back and forth, and the way it made her feel a part of the house.

The dining room, which faced the road was still in darkness, heavy curtains drawn to shut out the night. They were thick and cumbersome, dark, with a faded flowery pattern, and although she'd leave them in place for the time being, Merry eyed them dispassionately; they would have to go. She struggled to throw them back, wrestling with their weight and amazed that after her tugging, the rail still remained fixed to the wall.

Her eye was immediately drawn to the view outside, or more specifically to the figure which stood by their gate, staring up at the house. The day was foul, and yet it seemed to make no difference to the woman, her raincoat, already soaked and buffeted by the wind. She stood motionless, her gaze trained on an upstairs window, and if she saw the curtains opening, she certainly gave no indication that she had. Merry turned away, smiling to herself. She wasn't sure yet what form the local jungle drums took, but she had a fair idea that whoever was standing by her gate would be one of the main drummers. Their arrival had obviously not gone unnoticed.

Whilst it was better with the curtains open, the light this morning was minimal and did little to expel the gloom. The dark, almost navy-blue walls weren't helping either, but Merry opened the doors on her dresser and started to replace the contents: glasses which had only been removed for packing a few days earlier. She enjoyed this, the routine and rhythm of making the house theirs, and breathing new life into it with their things. They had a long day ahead of them, but it was exciting, and as she bent to load the last few glasses into the cupboard, she realised that she hadn't felt this good for a long time.

She straightened up once more, surveying the room, her artistic eye looking forward in time to her vision of how she wanted it to be, but first things first; now it really was time for that cup of tea. She crossed the room, instinctively looking back towards the window; but whoever it was who had been outside, was gone.

By some miracle Robyn hadn't woken until half past seven. Merry had even crept upstairs to check on her once or twice, but the baby had been fast asleep. Now though, she seemed to be making up for lost time with an extra-long feed, and Merry winced as she latched on once more. Tom had made copious quantities of toast this morning, and she munched on slice after slice to keep her mind off the pain, while they chatted over their plans for the day.

Tom was itching to get started on the shop; clearing it out ready for the refurbishment that needed to take place. Although there was still much to be done in the house, he reasoned that the quicker they made a start outside, the quicker they could ascertain what work needed doing and start to make plans. It was going to be their livelihood after all, and the sooner it was open, the sooner they would start to see some return on it.

'Besides which, once we get everything else unpacked, we're going to have a huge amount of rubbish to get rid of. This way maybe we can do it all in one fell swoop, perhaps even get a skip.'

Merry considered her husband for a moment, knowing that there would be no deterring him from something he had already decided to do. So, rolling up her sleeves and helping him was the only real option. She glanced down at the now, sleeping baby, and levered herself out of the chair. No time like the present.

In truth, the shop was more than one room. The front part that was visible from the road was the largest of the rooms, split almost in two by another wall with a wide archway through to the rear portion. From here, another door led into not one but two separate storerooms, and it was these rooms which had really fired their imagination. The second of these was L-shaped and formed the top of the courtyard. It sat beyond the house, providing a backdrop to the rear garden, and in time was an area they hoped to develop into a showcase for local speciality products.

The other thing which had appealed to both of them was currently still in place, although covered in assorted rubbish, and, Merry suspected, had long been out of operation. The little black pot-bellied stove would have once been here purely for practical reasons, but it was such a homely addition to the space and fulfilled every vision that Tom and Merry had for the place. Now, eyeing the flue warily, it seemed that an extraordinary leap of faith would be called for to ever get it working again.

They decided to start on the storerooms and, checking that the baby monitor was switched on, Merry pulled on a pair of gloves. Robyn usually had her longest sleep in the morning, and if Merry was to be of any help to Tom today, now would be the time. She flicked on the old light switch and surveyed the space in front of her. Spiders she could cope with (up to a point), but dear God, let there not be any rats.

The space was dim at best; on a day like today, little natural light fell through the tiny window at the rear, and despite her surprise that the single overhead bulb actually lit, the glow from it was disappointing. The only thing that Merry could establish was that to get to her goal – a row of wooden cupboards at the rear of the room – she would have to wade through a huge number of damp and rotting boxes. She picked up the first, but it fell apart as she lifted it, the smell of decay, sour and strangely verdant.

She wandered back out into the main room.

'Tom,' she called, searching the room for her husband.

A head appeared from behind the archway, already white with dust.

'Found any buried treasure yet?' He grinned, wiping away a cobweb.

'Not exactly… I was just wondering whether that agent had ever got back to you. Did you find out what the shop used to sell?'

'General produce was his best guess. I googled it too and found some old references from the 1950s when it seemed to be a family grocer's. There was a picture with an old delivery bike propped outside. Other than that, only what a chap from the village told me: that it was a gallery of some sort. Why, what have you found?'

Merry held up a wodge of sodden papers. 'Not much… a box of mush mostly, but from what I can make out, they could have been drawings, sketches, at one point. The rain has got to them though, and they've pretty much dissolved.'

'Well, that would fit then, with it being a gallery?' replied Tom.

'Hmm, I suppose so. It's just that there is a whole box of these, all stacked together. It seems a bit odd.'

'Now't so queer as folk, so they say. Let me know if you find anything interesting.' Tom had already returned to his task.

She looked down again at the papers in her hand, lost in thought for a moment before finally dumping them in the wheelbarrow by the door. The rest of the box appeared to be the same, the condition of the paper noticeably worse at the top where the rain had dripped onto it through the leaky roof. She bent to pick up the last of the pile, papers from the very bottom of the box which had toppled sideways as she lifted it from the floor. A face stared up at her.

At first, she thought it was just a random pattern on the paper, making it appear familiar, like seeing shapes in clouds, but as she peered at it a little more closely, she could definitely make out a sweep of hair and at least one eye peering out at her. She stopped for a moment, looking back at the mess on the floor. She was looking for others; pages that might not be quite so damaged, but as she turned them over they were all illegible. On a whim, she lay the paper on top of a box a little way from her. Perhaps when it was dry some further detail might appear.

She worked solidly for the next half hour, heaving out the sodden contents of three more boxes. More papers, but this time what looked like bills and receipts of some kind. She was just about to start on her fourth box when a loud squawk alerted her to the fact that Robyn was awake once more. She grabbed the baby monitor to go and check on her daughter.

In truth, with the busy events of the day behind her, Merry wouldn't have given the sketch another thought had it not been for the strange encounter, later that day.

Chapter Sixteen

'I'm sorry, can I help you?'

Merry was on her way back into the house having delivered a cup of tea to Tom. What useable daylight they had left was fast fading, and he promised only to be another half hour or so. Robyn wriggled in her arms, as she hurried, trying to get out of the rain. The baby hadn't fed at all well this afternoon, and with the prospect of their own dinner preparations looming, Merry was anxious to try to settle her.

She almost didn't notice the woman standing by the gate once more. In fact, she might have missed her altogether had the dog by her side not given a small bark. Merry pulled her coat a little more closely around Robyn and tugged her hood further forward to shelter her own face.

The woman raised a hand in greeting, which was a start at least. She looked just as she had that morning: as still as stone, her face all but expressionless, as she waited for Merry to join her.

'You're in then?' she said in greeting, pushing a hand down onto the dog's back. It sat down instantly. 'I came by this morning, but it didn't look like anyone was up. I thought it best not to disturb you.'

'Oh yes, I saw you…' Merry frowned gently at the rain dripping off her hood. 'Would you like to come in? It's grim out here.'

'That would be very nice, thank you,' came the reply, polite and quietly spoken.

Merry led the way back into the house, not quite sure if she was up for entertaining. She was about to enquire about the dog when it trotted past her, pausing momentarily on the doorstep to scuff its feet at the doormat, for all the world as if it was wiping them clean.

A voice shot past her. '*Ma*-nners, Rupert!' It wasn't exactly a shout, but there was a touch of the Sergeant Major about it none the less. Rupert stood smartly to one side to let Merry pass.

'Now then where would you like me? I don't want to get in your way.'

Merry, who was busy shrugging off her wet raincoat, gave a nod towards the kitchen table.

'We could sit in here, if that's all right? I've just made tea actually – would you like a cup?'

'If it's not too much trouble.'

'No, no. Have a seat. I won't be a moment.'

She adjusted Robyn who was fussing gently in the carrier. Her gaze wandered to the dog, which still stood by the door.

'Erm, he can come in if it's okay. Will he be all right with the baby?'

Her visitor, now in the middle of taking off her own coat, gave a wry chuckle. 'I can see you've never met Rupert before. I think it's time some introductions were performed, don't you? Probably better if you sit down.'

'Oh,' said Merry, a little amused. 'Okay.'

With a gentle nod of permission, Rupert approached Merry's chair and sat beside her, where he held out a polite paw. She laughed and took it as the dog gazed into her eyes before resting his head against her leg.

'Well, I've never seen anything like that before!' she exclaimed. 'How ever did you get him to do that?'

'Well, manners cost nothing I've always said, even from our canine friends. I'm Cora, by the way,' said her visitor with a smile, holding out her own hand, the fingers bent with arthritis.

'Merry. It's lovely to meet you. Do you live nearby?'

'Oh yes, just over the hill, in more ways than one.' The piercing blue eyes twinkled. 'But, I have Rupert, and he keeps me sane. Well, that's what I tell people anyway.'

'Sanity's greatly overrated in my opinion. He's a beautiful dog, though. What are they called again?'

'He's a Weimaraner.'

Merry couldn't help but warm to the slender figure. Her self-deprecating manner was endearing, and she suddenly realised that her colouring was almost identical to the beautiful grey dog with the blue eyes.

As though reading her mind, Cora said, 'The only difference of course is that Rupert has rather fewer wrinkles and, to my knowledge, doesn't suffer from arthritis.'

'Well, it's lovely to meet you too, Rupert, although perhaps I could have my hand back now so I can make some tea.' Amazingly, the dog did as it was told.

Once Merry had placed the tea down on the table, the conversation resumed where it had left off.

'So, that's me and Rupert, how about you, and this little one?' asked Cora. 'Is she your first?'

Merry laughed. 'Is it that obvious? Over-protective-mother-syndrome I expect. But yes, she is. Born on Christmas Eve, the little darling. Her name's Robyn.'

'Oh very fitting. I like that.'

'Well, she was such a tiny little thing when she was born, it seemed appropriate. She seems to be making up for lost time now, though, and usually guzzles her food except for this afternoon for some reason. That's why she's a bit cross.'

Cora watched them both for a moment. 'And your husband?'

'Tom is the filthy one who'll be coming through the door any minute now. He wanted to make a start on getting the old shop cleared out as soon as possible, but it's pretty gruesome work.'

'I can't remember a time when the shop was last open, but I expect you have lots of plans. You must tell me all about them one day when you're not quite so busy.'

'I'd like that, thanks. Right now, it feels as if we're mad as hatters, taking on all this.'

Cora smiled. 'Well, I expect you are, but I guess you have very good reasons for it. A friend once told me that sanity is a very overrated thing anyway.'

Merry gazed at her in astonishment, feeling the warmth in the words. She smiled back.

'My husband mentioned something that one of the villagers told him, about a curse on the house…'

'And you want to know whether I think it's true?' asked Cora. 'Well now… I've lived in the village a very long time, but I'd much rather know what you think.'

'It's not really something I want to think about if I'm honest, seeing as we've just moved in… but, no, this feels like a happy house to me. I don't think it would feel that way if it were cursed.' The dog shifted against her leg.

'Quite. And I agree. I've been here on many an occasion, and always felt very peaceable. It's had an unhappy history over recent years certainly, but I think the villagers allow superstition to cloud their judgement. Either that, or a good dose of cider in the Apple Cart on a Friday night. Isn't that where all the best stories come from?'

Cora paused, and for a moment Merry thought she was going to elaborate on her story. Instead, with a glance at the clock on the wall, she stood, holding out her hand. 'Now, I've already taken up too much of your time, Merry, but it's been lovely meeting you and your beautiful daughter. You must come and visit Rupert and me, anytime. As I said we're just over the hill, the little cottage with the bright blue door. I shall be walking Rupert for a bit now, but I'll pop back later with a cabbage for you if that's all right?'

Merry took the proffered hand, feeling a little guilty that she would have no gift to give in return, but she clasped it warmly. What a lovely neighbour to have found.

True to her word, at a little after six, there was a knock on the back door, and Merry opened it to find Cora and Rupert on the doorstep.

She pulled the door wide to let them in, but Cora remained where she was.

'I won't keep you, while you're so busy,' she said. 'But I did promise I'd bring this for you. Keep it in the fridge, it works better that way.'

Merry looked down at the green vegetable, not quite sure what to say. 'Did you grow this yourself, Cora? It looks beautiful. I'm sorry I haven't anything to give you in return – we're not quite up to speed yet, but I'll be sure to bring you some cakes next time I'm baking.'

Cora stared at Merry for a moment and then let out a peal of laughter.

'It isn't for you!' she exclaimed. 'Well, it is, but not in the way you think. No, it's for them,' she said, pointing at Merry's chest. 'If I'm not mistaken, you've a nasty bout of mastitis on the way. Best cure of all is a cabbage. Two leaves down the front of your bra. Leave them there until you can't bear the smell any longer, and then put fresh ones in. You'll be right as rain in a day or so.'

Chapter Seventeen

Freya laughed like a drain. 'Merry, that's priceless, but did it work?'

'It bloody did, I couldn't believe it! Oh, but Freya, it hurt. I thought she was a bit nuts when she first left. I mean everything felt fine, but then after tea when I tried to feed Robyn, things felt a bit weird. By bedtime, my left boob had blown up like a Belisha beacon, and the heat coming off it was something else. I went to sleep wearing the cabbage, woke up stinking like old socks, but by yesterday evening it had all but gone. And I'm fine today.'

'Is Robyn okay?'

'Oh she's grand… Listen, I don't suppose you fancy coming over do you? I think I'm going ever so slightly mad. With all this rain, we can't get out, and I'm not really any use to Tom. Besides which, he's gone back over to Worcester today to speak to a builder chum of his.'

'I'm on my way. Give me twenty minutes.'

An hour later and they were both sitting on the floor surrounded by half-emptied boxes and piles and piles of books.

'You never mentioned slave labour when you rang,' grumbled Freya. 'How on earth did you get to have so many books?'

'It didn't look this many in the hotel somehow. Still, I love this room, particularly because the bookcases take up two whole walls so there's not quite as much paint on show as there might otherwise have been.'

Freya looked around her. 'Actually, I don't dislike the colour in here,' she said, eyeing the damson walls. 'It's just that they clash rather with the green carpet, don't they?' She got to her feet. 'Right, come on then. This isn't going to get them all put away. Are you one of those hideously OCD type of people who has to arrange their books by colour or something weird, or can we just put them all on the shelves?'

'Fiction and non-fiction?'

Freya picked up the first book. 'I can cope with that,' she said.

They worked solidly for the next hour or so, steadily decreasing the number of full boxes.

'They look nice, don't they?' commented Freya. 'Really homely.'

Merry stood up, stretching her back out a little. 'I never really feel at home until all the books are out, and this is going to be such a light and airy room, it'll be a great reading room cum office.'

She squinted at the desk in one corner of the room. 'That's going to be my next target,' she added. 'Getting the computer set up and, with luck, working. I'm so used to being in touch with everything, I feel a bit lost at the minute. Out of the loop.'

'You're not missing the hotel surely? Think about all that stress you've left behind, Merry.'

'I know.' She sighed. 'And I don't miss it, not really… I know we have a huge amount of work to do here, so we'll still be very busy, but…'

Freya watched her friend, who was anxiously biting her lip now. It was an old habit of hers, and Freya knew the sign well.

She put down the book she was holding. 'Merry?' she said gently, 'what's wrong?'

To her surprise, Merry burst into tears.

Freya was at her side in an instant, pulling her into a hug; no words, just the comfort of another's warmth. She stroked Merry's hair, just as Merry had hers countless times in the past.

'What's this really all about? Come on, Merry, tell me.' She fished a tissue out from up her sleeve. 'Here, come and sit down.'

Merry raised her head, her cheeks streaked with tears. She moved to pull away, looking over to the baby who was bouncing in her chair, quite contentedly. 'Robyn…' she murmured.

'Is fine,' said Freya firmly. 'So no changing the subject. Come on, spill. I won't leave you alone until you do, so you might as well get it over with.'

Merry wiped away a stream of snot, sniffing loudly, before hiccupping a little.

'I don't think I can do this, Freya,' she started. 'It's all my fault, and I…' She sniffed again.

'What is, Merry, what's your fault?'

'Robyn… I can't even feed her properly… I'm so hopeless, and all the other mums have no trouble at all, and I know I shouldn't say it, but I hate it.' She broke down into choking sobs once more. 'It's my fault she's so tiny.'

'That's utter bollocks!' exclaimed Freya. 'I'm sorry, but it is. You're an amazing mum. Look at her, Merry, she's gorgeous… happy… *and* she will adore you whether you continue to breastfeed her or not. She's pretty much reached the right weight now; you said so yourself. So what if it took her a wee bit longer than some of the other babies, they're all different, even I know that much.' She gave Merry's arm a rub. 'Give yourself some slack. You've just moved, which is one of the most stressful things on the planet, your hormones are probably still all over the place, and now you've had mastitis as well.'

'But I shouldn't give up, it's not fair on Robyn.'

'Says who? Robyn probably won't even notice. And, excuse me, but you're not giving up. That makes it sound like you've failed in some way, which you haven't. You have already breastfed her for three months, don't forget! If you do decide to bottle-feed her, all you're doing is finding a solution to a problem. That's what you're good at, Merry, you do it all day, every day. Don't make this any different, just because you feel pressured into behaving a certain way.'

The sobs had subsided a little now, and only small sniffing sounds remained. 'Have you spoken to Tom about this?'

'A bit.'

'And?'

'He said it was daft to carry on when it's making me this unhappy.' She wiped her nose again. 'And I think he'd quite like to be able to feed her actually…'

'There now see? Why are you giving yourself such a hard time over this?'

Freya watched Merry fidgeting uncomfortably. 'Ahh, I get it… If it's not one thing, it's your mother, right?' Her lips curled upwards into a smile, as she repeated what had become a stock phrase between the two of them in their younger years.

Merry looked up, and then away to Robyn. 'She gave me such a lecture… How I was utterly irresponsible for moving here and taking on such a big project when I should be thinking only of Robyn. How she could understand such selfishness in Tom, but not from me. How I'm a mother now, and it's about time I started behaving like one. How the younger generation don't know what hardship is, and how we're all so ready to take the easy way out these days. You know how it goes.'

'Yes, I do. And so do you, so why do you listen to her? All she ever had to do was keep house, and get your dad's dinner on the table at half past six. You've had to keep house, run a thirty-bedroom hotel and a florist shop, and still have Tom's dinner on the table.' She held up her hand. 'And yes, I know he does his fair share, I'm not saying that. All I am saying is that you have a wonderful, supportive marriage, a beautiful daughter, and now the opportunity to take on a new and exciting challenge. Whatever your mum wants to believe, things are different for our generation, and the truth of the matter is she would probably have given her eye teeth to have the chance to fulfil her dreams the way you have. So don't let her bitterness and jealousy sow doubts in your mind about what you're doing here. Put your energy where it's needed, Merry, not into fretting over something like this.'

Merry was quiet for a moment, plucking at the tissue in her hands.

'Have I won you over yet?' Freya smiled, giving her friend a playful nudge. She could see the beginnings of a smile on Merry's face too, as she nudged Freya back.

'Sorry,' she muttered.

'What for? There's no need to apologise, but let's be honest. How much of this was down to feeling guilty about not wanting to breastfeed Robyn any more, and how much was you feeling a teeny bit anxious about what you're taking on here, which your mother has now magnified tenfold?' She gave Merry a stern look. 'Because, you're not fooling me one little bit. Since when have you been afraid of tackling anything…? Right, have a good blow. I'm going to put the kettle on and find some biscuits, and then I'll help you make up some bottles for Robyn – that is if you've got any milk?'

Merry smiled wryly. 'Actually, I bought some with my shopping this week, and then hid it in the back of the cupboard. It's still there.'

Freya burst out laughing. 'You daft bat!' she said, shaking her head in amusement.

Chapter Eighteen

Merry pushed open the door to the storeroom and took a deep breath. A tingle of excitement rippled through her.

After her release of yesterday, she had slept like a log, as had Robyn who, just as Freya had said seemed to notice no difference to her feeds and suckled contentedly on a bottle. Tom had even given her the last feed of the evening, and the sight of the pair of them snuggled into the armchair almost brought tears to her eyes. She couldn't believe she had become quite so worked up about something, which now, in the cold light of another (albeit rainy) day, seemed so trivial.

Freya had ended her visit by offering to have Robyn for the whole day today, so that Merry could have a bit of a rest, and do whatever she liked. After the hard days' graft of late winter, pruning their trees, things were quieter at Appleyard at the moment, and Sam was more than happy to carry on without Freya for a day or two. Merry had wanted to refuse her offer at first, but as she thought about the possibilities of what a day to herself might bring, she practically bit her friend's arm off.

Now though, of all the relaxing, peaceful things she could have chosen, the minute she'd opened her eyes this morning, she'd had a yearning to carry on clearing out the storeroom, and was now full of energy.

There were more boxes of sodden papers, old cans of hideously coloured paint, and an assortment of paint brushes, the bristles stiff with age and their handles pitted where the varnish had blistered. It was unlikely they would ever be of any use again, and Merry discarded them without a thought. Then she peeled open a box and picked up a few, much smaller brushes, and, as she lifted them, she could see that these were quite different. They were finer, with a longer handle and, although obviously well used, the brushes had been meticulously cleaned. The bristles had been carefully wrapped and were still soft and pliable.

It would seem a shame to throw these away when they were in such good condition, and a long-buried yearning made itself known to Merry. She put them to one side on the floor beside the barrow and carried on with her task.

There really was no semblance of order to the room, and for the next half hour or so, she threw away box after box of sodden papers. She had worked her way towards an old trestle table and, although the table itself had been damaged, she realised that it had protected what was underneath it from the rain. These boxes were different from the others too: they had been sealed with care. Merry peeled back the tape holding them closed, and peered inside. There were more brushes, again wrapped with care, nestling in some newspaper, and under that something more solid, square.

It was the colour that leaped out at her first as she held the small canvas in front of her. Although a little marked and faded, the square was covered with bold blocks of colour in lime green, orange and bright blue. She immediately thought of the walls in the house, and wondered whether the painter was one and the same. She turned the canvas over, but the back was entirely plain. The painting was completely abstract but had a certain symmetry about it and reminded Merry of the pieces she had seen recently in a local interiors shop.

Her excitement mounting, she pulled another square from the box. This time the whole thing was painted an eye popping red with a single white flower in the middle of the canvas, a bright green centre to it. On the reverse she could just make out two initials, CM, and a date: 1973. She scrabbled about in the box, fishing out three more canvases, and then sat back on her haunches for a moment staring at them in surprise. They were not what she had expected to find when she came in here this morning.

The box empty, she hurriedly grabbed another, ripping off the tape and pulling open the lid. She could see straight away that there were no more canvases here, and her stomach sank in disappointment. There was, however, tube after tube of paint, and palettes too, along with various bottles of what looked like some sort of solvent.

Merry tucked her thick hair behind her ears impatiently and began to gather up her finds, cradling them in the folds of her old sweatshirt. She went back through to the main house, entering the kitchen and laying the canvases down carefully on the table. She shouted for Tom, flicking on the kettle at the same time.

By the time Tom wandered into the kitchen, Merry had laid all five pictures out in a row, and was standing back admiring them, cocking her head from side to side. Apart from the first one she had looked at, which was right at the top of the box, they were in very good condition, considering that they were now over forty years old.

'Good God,' exclaimed Tom. 'Where on earth did you find those?'

'In a box, in the storeroom… What do you think?'

'That I understand why the walls in this house are such shocking colours.' He picked up a canvas, peering at it for a better look. 'They remind me of something actually, although I can't quite put my finger on what.'

'I thought that too, but I've just remembered. That orange one there reminds me of the wallpaper we had in our kitchen when I was little. It was outdated then, and I used to think it was hideous, but now I'd probably think it was very cool.'

'You're right,' he said. 'Classic seventies design.' He too was looking at the back of the canvases. 'Have you seen the dates on the back of these? They're bloody well authentic. I actually really like them.'

'Me too. As pieces of artwork, I can't tell whether they're good, bad or indifferent, but there's something about them.' She grinned back at her husband. 'Are you thinking what I'm thinking?'

'Too right I am,' he flashed back. 'Sod the bloody paperwork. That can wait until another rainy day.'

Laying the canvas back on the table, Tom followed his wife back through the door. Behind him, forgotten, the kettle turned itself off with a click.

It took until lunchtime, with both of them working solidly to empty the remaining boxes. By the time they had finished, they had found another seven canvases, making twelve in total, along with more paints and equipment and bizarrely, several tubes of paper, which were printed with similar designs. The rolls were not unlike wallpaper but only about half as wide, and although one was severely water damaged, the others had survived pretty much intact.

Merry stood back to survey their morning's handiwork. The room was now virtually cleared with only some larger pieces of furniture remaining. Most of what they had sorted through was utter rubbish, but the few gems they had found had made the work worthwhile. Merry was well aware that most people would have consigned the canvases to the rubbish heap, but she had never considered herself and Tom to be most people.

She wandered back into the main shop, which still required such a huge amount of work. In spite of the debris and the hanging plaster and sagging ceilings, she could see how the room would look in the future with its huge window transformed and flooding the place with light. They had wanted to sell ordinary everyday things alongside the slightly more unusual, and Merry had always had in her mind a strong theme of some sort to pull it all together; she just hadn't known what. Today she had found her answer, even if, just for now, she was going to keep it to herself.

Tom was looking at the pieces of furniture, in particular a couple of old tables which were stacked against one wall. The patterned Formica on their top was chipped in a couple of places and the paint was peeling from them badly, but even from where Merry was standing, she could hear the cogs turning. She smiled to herself, knowing exactly what was running through his mind; it was one of the reasons why she loved him so much.

She slipped an arm around his waist and laid her head on his shoulder. 'I need food,' she murmured. 'Come on, I think we should stop for a bit.'

He kissed the top of her head. 'I'll be right there, just give me a minute. I want to check something.'

And Merry knew exactly what that was too.

Her stomach gave a ferocious growl as she crossed the courtyard once more, trying to decide which she fancied more, cheese on toast or some lovely warming soup. She didn't see the figure pass her gate, but she heard the cheery 'Good afternoon' from behind her.

She swung around. 'Cora! Hello,' she said, walking to the gate. 'And hello to you too, Rupert. How are you both today?'

'Wet,' came a cheery smile. 'Again. Still, it could be worse. It's not freezing cold, and that's something.'

'Are you just going, or have you been?' asked Merry, wondering how many times a day Cora walked the fields.

'Just been. Homeward bound now I'm glad to say.'

Merry paused for a moment, a little shy, and wondering how much she should say. In the end, she decided that less was more. Cora didn't need to hear about her massive wobble yesterday. 'I wanted to say thanks for the cabbage by the way, it certainly did the trick, although I'm not really sure how you knew I'd be needing it…'

Cora said nothing, but simply stood and nodded.

'…Well anyway, I made some cakes yesterday. Nothing special, just a few muffins, but as you're on your way home, I wondered if you might like to take a few, to have with your tea.'

Cora beamed. 'Particularly if they're chocolate ones.'

Merry gave her a look. 'They are actually… Do you want to wait here, and I'll pop in and get them?' She hurried back to the kitchen.

Relieved of her cakes, Merry was just saying goodbye when a thought slipped into her mind. 'Cora, before you go, could I ask, do you know if the chap who had the house before us was an artist of some kind?'

'That's very perceptive of you.'

Merry laughed. 'Not really...' She was going to tell Cora about the canvases that they'd found, but something stopped her. 'We found some boxes of old paints and brushes in the storeroom, artists' materials. I just wondered, that's all.'

'Well, you wondered right. Yes, he was an artist, although I'm afraid I don't know terribly much about his work. Christopher was his name; Christopher Marchmont. I expect you could find out about him, if you wanted to.'

Christopher Marchmont, CM, thought Merry to herself; so, in all likelihood, the paintings were made by him. She waved a cheerful goodbye to Cora and hurried back inside.

The fire made her feel drowsy, but as Merry sat on the sofa that evening, there was just one more thing she wanted to do before she went to bed.

It was late evening, and Robyn had been returned to them, safe and happy, and was now fast asleep. Beside her, Tom was leafing through a copy of *Grocer* magazine, but she could feel he was struggling to concentrate. She pulled her laptop over, and waited while it started up.

Christopher Marchmont, she typed, waiting for the search engine to spring to life. Immediately, the page was covered in text, most of it relating to a firm of architects, but there, almost at the bottom, was an entry from some art journal, with Christopher's name, and one word that caught her eye: designer.

She clicked open the link and the page was filled with images, some of them startlingly similar to the canvases they had found today. One, in particular, caught her eye and, as she peered at the screen, she suddenly realised that she was looking at the design on the orange canvas that she had liked so much. Here, it was interspersed with another pattern, and repeated over and over. It was a wallpaper design. She sat up a little straighter.

As she scrolled down the page, a flicker of excitement began to run down her spine. She gave Tom a nudge.

'Look at this, I think I've just found our mystery painter.' Her lips twitched as she carried on reading.

'It must be him, see? It says here that he lived in Herefordshire and in his early career was a portrait painter, but his love of bold design and colour led him to experiment with patterns and textiles, until eventually in his forties, he gained renown as a textile and print artist, until the… Oh…' Merry's hand flew unbidden to her mouth.

'What is it?' asked Tom, leaning over to see.

Merry's eyes filled with tears. 'Oh no, that's horrible.' She pointed her finger to a place on the screen. '… Until the death of his wife and child within a year of each other forced him to abandon his career.'

Tom sat looking, first at his wife, and then back to the screen, not knowing what to say. It would seem that Christopher's career had been over just as soon as it had begun.

Merry shoved the laptop into Tom's hands. There was something she needed to see. She rushed into the dining room, where for now the canvases and other items they had salvaged were laid on the table. At first, she couldn't find it, until she remembered she had placed it under a heavy book to help flatten it out. She lifted up the sketch that she had found on the first day, and held it to the light. She had left it to dry out in the storeroom hoping that as it dried more detail might appear. She was right, and as she gazed at it now, the sweep of hair, the bright eyes, and the hint of a mouth, she knew with upmost certainty that she was staring at a sketch of Christopher's dead daughter, Catherine Marchmont.

Chapter Nineteen

April

Well, at least it wasn't raining, thought Freya, as she forked another load of mulch onto the ground. After the horrible wet March they'd endured, there had been a week of beautiful spring days, and the blue skies had lifted her spirits like no other. Today was mild, but overcast, and she hoped for a return of the sunshine as she worked. It was as if the orchard held its breath. In another couple of weeks, with an exuberant release, it would lift its riot of blooms to the skies, gently filling the air with their perfume, a whispered enticement for the bees, like a lover's caress. She eyed the delicate buds above her and prayed for the sun.

From the other end of the line, Sam waved to her, as he too moved among the trees. It wasn't a race because it was important to do the job properly, but as Freya looked up from time to time, she knew that she would make sure they arrived roughly in the middle, and not at some sixty/forty split down the line. She had never dreamed she'd be working alongside Sam, and it was important to her that she held her own. After the death of her father last year, she had barely had time to accomplish all the tasks in the orchard by herself, and at times it had seemed overwhelming, but she had got through it. She was stronger because of it, and this year she was determined that Appleyard would be the very best it could be.

It was hard physical work, but the rhythm of it soothed her, gave her mind time to wander, and dream a little. It was the time when she came up with her best ideas, and as Merry and Tom's shop was coming on a pace, it wouldn't be long before they started to think about what products they might stock. Freya was anxious that this year, she would not dwell on where she had been, but only where she was going. Inevitably, her mind turned to her neighbouring farm, Braeburn, and its now sole occupant: Sam's brother, Stephen.

She had only seen him a couple of times since Christmas and, despite her previous opinion of him, the help that he had given her in her hour of need was not something she would forget. Gone had been the cocky irritating manner on that occasion with, in its place, a rather more thoughtful, grown-up version of Stephen. She hoped it was a change he could maintain; she didn't like to think ill of anyone, and it was time Stephen found some real happiness of his own, and not one fuelled by booze or a succession of women. Something told her that the transition wasn't necessarily going to be an easy one, though; a leopard doesn't change its spots that quickly.

Sam was still working away, and Freya watched the steady rise and fall as his body bent and straightened in his task. She wondered how he was feeling, putting in the hours here, rather than at the house he had called home for all of his life. Everybody knew it was he who had kept the Henderson's orchard going, and he must feel odd being so distant from it now, leaving his brother to do all the work. On the surface he seemed okay with it all, but she would make sure she asked him about it soon.

As it happened, Sam must have been thinking the same thing. As soon as they were close enough to hear one another, he called across to her. 'So how do you reckon Braeburn's trees are faring at the moment then?'

Freya squinted in the general direction of their neighbouring farm. 'I don't know; I'd like to think they're doing well, but—' She broke off as she noticed Sam's rather forced nonchalance. 'Would it hurt to go round? Not to check up or anything, I can't imagine Stephen being chuffed with that, but just as a "how are you" sort of a visit. You might be able to glean how things are going.'

'I know I shouldn't even be thinking about it, but you know... old habits and all that.'

'Sam,' said Freya sternly, 'it was your home, and it's natural to care about what happens to it; in fact, it would be unnatural if you didn't. You invested a lot of your life and hard work into making it a success, it would be impossible just to turn your back on it and pretend it didn't happen.'

'I know, but I don't want you to think—'

This time she silenced him with a kiss. 'I don't think anything of the sort, you numpty. I know how committed you are to me, and to Appleyard. In fact, it only makes me love you more knowing that after all that happened with Stephen you still care.'

Sam smiled, knowing that, as usual Freya had summed up the situation pretty accurately. He pulled her closer. 'So if you love me even more now, I'm, er, wondering how much that is exactly...'

Freya skipped backwards, raising her pitchfork slightly. 'Oh no you don't!' She laughed. 'We've still got far too much to do yet. Besides if we finish up here earlier than planned, you could use the time to pop over to Braeburn, couldn't you?'

There was a loud groan. 'Sometimes, Freya Sherborne, you can be far too practical for your own good.'

She stuck out her tongue. 'I'll meet you back here in the middle in about an hour then, yes?'

The pork was sizzling nicely as the kitchen door opened later that day. Freya poured in a healthy glug of cider and watched contentedly as it bubbled away, before turning around, the welcoming smile on her face dying in an instant.

'Well, that went well,' muttered Sam, kicking the door closed. 'I hate to say it, Freya, but your dreams of us all living happily ever after might be a little premature. The bastard all but threw me out.'

She opened her mouth to speak, but before she could get a word out, Sam cut across her.

'And before you say anything, no, I did not go in there playing the arrogant I-told-you-so card. I was as nice as I could be, but his opening line was still, "Come here to gloat, have you?" There wasn't an awful lot I could do.'

'Oh dear.' Freya turned the gas out from under the pan. 'That good, eh? Listen, maybe Stephen's just had an off day.'

'I can hardly remember when he had an 'on' day, it's been so long. Don't make excuses for him, Freya.' He sat down wearily at the table, hunched, and still in his jacket.

Freya went over and knelt beside him, leaning forward to kiss his cheek. 'Don't give up on him, Sam. His pride's hurt, that's all. He'll come round as soon as he realises that we're not out to make fun of him. Our two orchards have co-existed side by side, more or less happily for decades. There's no reason why that should change now.'

Sam stared at her. 'You know, I really wanted things to be better between us, but actually I'm not sure that Stephen has it in him. I think he's an arrogant sod, and deserves all that comes to him, end of.'

'I know you don't really mean that, Sam Henderson, so you can drop the big tough guy routine. His attitude is disappointing, admittedly, but I still think it's a touch of bravado.'

'Yeah, well I'm not so sure,' he replied glumly. 'You know, the longer I'm away from Braeburn, the more I realise how much I put up with over the years. I was happy to give Stephen a hand, only if he needed it, mind, but I don't think he'll ever change. If he wants to make a competition out of it, then he can have one. Right now, as far as I'm concerned, it's every man for himself.'

Freya watched sadly as Sam took off his jacket and went to hang it up. Stephen was such a fool at times, and he made her mad enough she could slap him. It pained her to see Sam so defeated, but a sliver of unease also crept into her thoughts. She knew better than to press things now, but she would not let Appleyard become a battlefield.

Chapter Twenty

Merry had found it hard to sleep the night before. The discovery that it was Christopher Marchmont's daughter in the sketches she had found unnerved her for some reason. She had stood staring at the sheet of paper in her hand for so long, that eventually Tom had come to find her, still carrying the laptop she had shoved at him.

Together they sat at the dining room table trying to discover more about the man who had lost his family so young; but although there were plenty of descriptions of his early work – and photos too – it was as if time had stood still for him after the tragedy. There was not a single description of his life after their deaths, and yet it was clear that he had been hugely successful and his work much sought after. It was almost as though he had died himself.

This morning, standing in the cold, dim storeroom once more, it seemed so sad that his work had been left to rot here, and Merry thought back to the boxes of papers she had already discarded. There were hundreds of pieces of paper in some of those boxes, and whilst many of them were obviously paperwork, with hindsight she knew that a good many of them had been sketches like the one she had salvaged. She could hardly bear the thought that all of it was gone, and wondered when he had drawn them. An image came into her head of a bearded man, sitting deranged by grief, desperately trying to capture the image of a daughter whose face was fading from his memory day by day. A shiver ran the length of her spine and she had to go outside for a few minutes to clear her head.

Just as she had thought he would, Tom had dragged the last bits of furniture out of the storeroom and left them in the main shop. He had even given one of the table-tops a cursory clean, and she smiled as she saw which way her husband's thoughts had been headed. She could hear him banging now from the other storeroom and went through to investigate.

Surprisingly, the door to this room had been locked and, having tried all the keys they had been given, Tom's only recourse had been to remove the door to gain access. It was a smaller room than the first store, lying immediately to its left. As a room on its own, it would not be of much use other than as a store, but with the wall between the two rooms knocked down, the space would become a more attractive proposition. As Merry joined her husband, she could see he was trying to weigh things up.

'Will it work, do you think?'

Tom was standing in the middle of the room, sandwiched between an old desk and what looked like a very distressed sideboard. His hands were on his hips, and he waggled his head from side to side, looking through the open doorway into the room beyond and trying to gauge the overall size.

'Well, it's wider than I thought, but maybe not quite so long. What do you reckon?'

Merry adopted her husband's stance. 'It's deceptive isn't it, but the width is good. I think you'd get a fair number of units in here. Maybe even some low island ones in the middle if there's space to move either side of them.' She looked back to her husband. 'I think we should go for it. I know it means more work initially, but better to get it all done at the start than change our minds after we're open and have to put up with the upheaval then.'

'That's true.' He stared at her for a minute as if trying to deduce what she was thinking. 'Are we completely mad?'

'Oh, utterly,' Merry agreed. 'But when has that ever stopped us? I think it's absolutely the right thing to do. General groceries is one thing, even newspapers, but I honestly believe that we need to diversify if we're going to succeed. We need something to give us a bit of an edge… so gourmet goodies through there and gorgeous gifts through here. How does that sound?'

Tom merely smiled back at Merry, years of experience having taught him that she had an unerring eye for spotting the potential in things, and it was futile to try to change her mind. Fortunately, most of the time he agreed with her one hundred per cent.

He nudged his hip into the desk. 'And what about this lot?'

Merry peered further into the gloom. 'It's hard to see what there is really, but the idea of reclaiming some of it appeals to me.' She glanced at her watch. 'We've probably got about an hour before Robyn wakes up. Shall we try to shift some of it into the main room so we can get a proper look at it?'

There seemed to be an inordinate number of broken chairs, but in among the debris, they discovered a corner cabinet, another table, a glass fronted bookcase, several kitchen type units as well as the desk and sideboard. There was also what looked like a whole set of oak balustrades. Merry could only imagine that it had all come from the main house, and although each piece of furniture was different in terms of style, colour and condition, there was something about the motley collection that fired her imagination.

'We shouldn't throw these away, Tom,' said Merry, running a hand along the length of the desk. 'I know we can't leave them here, but could we store them in the house for a bit, in one of the spare rooms? I'm thinking thoughts here, but they're not quite fully formed yet.'

Tom's response was simply to smile. 'I can see you're thinking thoughts, Merry. You've got that look on your face again. The one that usually means a lot of hard work.'

Merry stuck out her tongue. 'Isn't that why you love me? Life would be so boring otherwise.'

Tom raked a hand through his hair, a wry smile on his face. 'It's one of the reasons I love you,' he said. 'Come on then, let's shift what we can before our little bird needs feeding again.'

As it was, they only got the desk as far as the end of the hallway before they heard the first indignant squawks.

'I'll go and get her,' replied Tom. 'It's probably time for a cup of tea anyway.'

'I might even have one or two muffins left. I'll go and see what I can find.'

Robyn was halfway through her bottle of milk when there was a small tap at the kitchen door, and a grey head peered around it.

'Anybody home?'

'Cora! Come in... How are you?'

The small figure stood on the doorstep, holding a carrier bag. 'Very well, thank you. And grateful to see some sun for a change.' She smiled. 'Now would you look at that, Rupert, isn't that a sight for sore eyes,' she said, glancing down at the dog and then back up at Tom, who had Robyn nestled in his arms. 'What a picture. It does these old bones good to see such a thing.'

'Come and sit down, Cora, and join us in a cup of tea.'

'Only if you're not too busy.'

She unclipped Rupert's lead, and took a seat at the table, the dog immediately taking up a position beside Tom's chair, where he sat quietly, his blue eyes resting on the baby.

'I told Rupert that Robyn is only little and that he must look after her when he's with her. He usually takes me at my word.'

'So I see.' Tom laughed. 'You have him extraordinarily well-trained.'

'Thank you,' said Cora simply, both at Tom and to the cup of tea that Merry placed beside her. 'Now, I've just been for my weekly visit to the library, and I brought this back for you, I thought it might be of interest.' She handed the bag across the table to Merry. 'It's as old as the hills, and I suspect the library have had it since it was first published, so it's rather dog-eared too, no offence, Rupert, but you might find it worth a read.'

Merry removed the book from the bag, a large hardback, with a very dated and faded front cover.

'Oh,' she said, looking up at Cora, 'How brilliant,' she added, swivelling the book round so that Tom could see the title: *Seventies, Design and Style.*

'I thought you might like to have a read about Christopher. There's quite a large section about him in there. I suspect that's why the library have hung onto it for so long.'

Merry opened a page at random, the bright red design from one of the canvases they had salvaged leaping out at her. 'This is amazing,' she said, her head still bent to the book. 'We were just looking at some information about him yesterday, weren't we, Tom?'

Cora remained silent and sipped her tea.

'It all seems so sad, what happened.'

'It was a difficult time certainly. And one of the saddest things is that he stopped working completely after it happened. He was a very fine artist, and quite young when they died. I would have liked to see how his new work developed, but it was obviously never meant to be.'

A loud burp suddenly broke the rather sombre mood.

'Oops, pardon you, young lady.' Tom grinned, wiping a dribble of milk off his daughter's chin. 'I guess that's you filled up again.'

'She really is quite adorable, isn't she?' said Cora, a wistful smile on her face. 'Just like a little bird. Such bright intelligent eyes.'

A proud look passed between Tom and his wife, which Cora missed entirely.

'Would she like to come out for a walk, do you think? Admittedly, it was a long time ago, but I seem to recall that my own daughter liked nothing better than being in her pram in the fresh air.'

'I didn't know that you had any children, Cora?'

'Yes, just the one. Her name's Sian, but she and her husband live in Australia now. She comes home when she can, bless her.'

'It must be lonely for you,' said Merry, watching the expression carefully on Cora's face.

'At times,' admitted Cora. 'But I have Rupert. There's never been a Mr Evans, I'm afraid. I was seduced by a flash ne'er-do-well in my youth

I'm sorry to say, and he left us when Sian was a little over a year old, so there've only ever been the two of us.' She took another sip of tea. 'A child born out of wedlock didn't go down very well in the small Welsh village where I was born, but here, people seemed to accept us, and so we stayed, all these years… Happy years, though, I hasten to add.'

Merry could feel her nose beginning to smart, a sure sign that tears were on their way. Her pregnancy hormones were still playing havoc it would seem, although she'd always been a bit of a cry baby. She sniffed, blinking rapidly, pretending to read something on the still open page in front of her.

After a moment, she gave Cora a wide smile. 'I'm sure Robyn would love to go for a walk with you, if you're sure it's okay?'

'We'd be delighted to have some company on our walk, wouldn't we, Rupert? And you mustn't feel like it's an imposition, before you say so. I can see how busy things are for you at the moment, and if this helps in any way, then I shall be glad.'

Merry, who had been just about to say exactly that, closed her mouth again.

Fifteen minutes later, after changing and dressing Robyn warmly, Merry waved them off down the path, Cora smiling broadly, and Rupert walking neatly at the pram's side, keeping pace with it perfectly. She felt her husband's arms slide around her waist.

'Are you okay with this?' he asked softly, knowing how hard it was for any new mum to let her baby out of sight for more than a minute.

Merry watched the little trio for a few moments more before turning in Tom's arms. 'Oh yes,' she said. 'Absolutely.'

Chapter Twenty-One

It was the start of a beautiful friendship, and one that set a new rhythm to Merry's days.

Every morning, towards eleven, Cora would appear to collect Robyn for a walk, the sight of the three of them setting off down the path never failing to bring a smile to Merry's lips. Robyn herself seemed more settled, her legs bouncing in delight whenever she caught sight of Rupert. She was feeding better, and Merry could hear her daughter's contentedness in her steady stream of burbling noises.

For Merry, it brought a welcome couple of hours of unstructured time, and although she felt a little guilty, Cora's admonishment soon made her put it aside and enjoy the opportunity it gave her to do whatever she pleased. Most days, this meant being able to help Tom more usefully, but on others she caught up on a little housework or did some baking.

This morning, Merry stood in the more formal of their two living rooms and looked at the pieces of old furniture gathered there. The plans had come back on the new shop design, and with the actual building work beginning to get under way, she was keen to explore some of her ideas.

Merry couldn't explain her feelings about the shop, but whereas everything in their hotel had been of the highest quality and the last word on elegance, it was not a look that she wanted to replicate here. She'd always had a savvy eye for recognising a bargain or the potential in things that others might overlook, but she had tended to save these items for their own living accommodation. The shop was different, though. She and Tom had trawled through brochure after brochure of shop fitments and bespoke units, and although she could see their practicality, none of them drew her eye.

If she had to pick one word to describe what was in her head, *kitsch*, was probably the best she could come up with, but even to her, this sounded horrifying. However, she was beginning to have a very clear idea of how she wanted the shop to look, and now was as good a time as any to see whether any of this furniture would prove to be useful, or indeed would fit the space. She took out her tape measure and began to jot down some measurements.

The desk was ideal; its surface a little pitted and stained, but once painted, this wouldn't matter one bit, and, in Merry's opinion, would only add to the look she was trying to create. It had one large drawer that ran the whole width of the top and once in place, with the drawer pulled open, it would add to the overall display space. The desk itself wasn't too deep, and she checked again with the tape measure. The drawer was locked, but she gave it a tug, feeling it move slightly, and then tugged again, just to be sure. They wouldn't need the lock after all.

One side of the drawer had moved out much further than the other, and Merry dropped to her knees for a better look. She popped out to the kitchen, where Tom's toolbox now seemed to live more or less permanently and returned with a long-handled flat screwdriver. The lock was a little loose on one side, and Merry was sure that with a bit of help, she could persuade it to part company with the wood.

She tucked her hair back behind her ears and gritted her teeth, as she brought her weight down on the end of the screwdriver. She wiggled it from side to side, and pushed it further and further as the metal began to buckle. She didn't want to damage the front of the desk but reasoned that a small amount of repair would be necessary anyway. Eventually, the lock pushed away from its housing completely, and Merry jiggled the drawer open.

Packed almost to overflowing, it was full of huge sheets of paper, and bundles of notebooks secured with elastic bands. The tallest of these piles was wedged against the top of the drawer, so that Merry had to use the edge of the screwdriver once more, pushing down in order to totally free it. On one side was an old Oxo cube tin, and Merry lifted it out, a smile on her face. Her mum still had one just like it, where she kept her needles and threads. This tin was full of old keys, and Merry tipped them out onto the desktop in wonder.

She lifted out one of the piles of notebooks, the band holding them falling away, long since perished. Thirty seconds later, her heart thumping in her chest, she ran through the house, shouting for Tom.

She found him in the shop where his head bobbed up from behind the little pot-bellied stove in the shop, black smudges all across his forehead.

'You have to come and see this!' she exclaimed, breathless, reaching out for his hand. She stopped when she caught sight of it. 'But don't touch anything!'

Tom followed her back into the house, trailing in her excited wake.

One of the notebooks still lay on the desktop where she had left it.

'Look Tom, look at these,' she directed, holding it open so that Tom wouldn't have to touch it with his sooty hands. 'They're sketches, designs, some of them just tiny details, almost doodles, but others cover the entire page.'

Tom looked up at her flushed face, with dawning realisation of what he was seeing.

Merry nodded. 'They're all Christopher's work, pages of the stuff. And there must be... fifteen or so books in here. I haven't looked at them all, but that's not the only thing.'

She gingerly lifted up the corner of one of the sheets that lay flat in the drawer, revealing its underside.

'What are these, mock-ups or something? Proofs?' Tom looked at the coloured sheets, a long rectangle filled with vibrant colour, not painted like the canvases, but printed onto shiny paper. He glanced ruefully at his hands, and Merry knew he was itching to get a better look.

'I almost daren't lift them out.'

'Just take out the top one, carefully,' Tom suggested.

Merry did as she was asked, holding her breath until the paper was safely down on the desktop again. She stared at it in amazement.

'Jesus,' she said. 'We can't keep these. What do we do?'

Tom stared down at the artwork in front of him. 'The sad thing is, Merry, that no one will probably want them. I agree we need to find out, though. I'm not sure if they have any historical significance, but what're left of his family ought to know at least.'

'I can't believe all this stuff was left here to rot.'

'Well, that's families for you, especially estranged ones. I expect to them this is merely worthless tat.'

'Do you think the family knew all this was here then?'

'There was an inventory of sorts from the estate agents, but I can't remember how much detail it went into; not much I'm guessing… Let's put all this back for now and see what we can find out.'

Merry took a deep breath. 'I want to use this, Tom – Christopher's work. I want to use it in the shop, and this furniture. I can't explain it, but it feels right somehow. It's the thing that's going to make this place come alive again, I'm sure of it.'

Tom took hold of his wife's shirt, pulling her close until their noses were just touching. 'Come and show me,' he murmured. 'And bring those keys.'

They were standing in front of the row of wooden cupboards in the first of the storerooms, cupboards which appeared to be fixed to the wall behind them, and the ones that Merry had been working towards on the first day they started to clear out these rooms. There were three in total, each with two doors, and although neither of them had said as much, both thought that the cupboards would make excellent display units. It was such a shame to have them languishing unused in the storeroom, but as the doors were locked they hadn't been able to investigate any further.

'It's a bit of a long shot, I know,' said Tom, 'but how about we try some of the keys? I thought about taking the doors off, but it would be much better if we could just open them.'

'Do you suppose there's anything still inside?'

Tom gave his wife a wide grin. 'Wanna find out?'

He upended the tin of keys onto the floor.

'Back into the tin if they don't fit, right?'

Merry snatched up a handful of keys. 'I wonder if the same one fits all the locks,' she said, trying the first of the little brass keys. 'That would make life a whole lot easier.'

'I'd say it's probable, hardly high-level security, is it? Anyway, I'm guessing that at one time there were cupboards like this throughout the main shop. It would make sense given the age of the place… It might also explain why there are quite so many keys,' he added. 'There must be fifty or so here.'

The tin rang with the sound of keys dropping back into it, and Merry lost count of the number before Tom gave a sudden shout.

'Bingo! A wee bit stiff but nothing that a can of WD40 won't fix,' he said, looking across at her. 'So that was door number one, let's try number two, shall we?'

Merry's answering grin got wider as she saw the key turn in the second lock.

'Go on, the last one's yours,' added Tom generously, handing her the key. 'Let's make it a hat-trick, shall we?'

With a final shove, the key grudgingly turned the last of the way. Merry gave Tom an excited glance. 'You know they're probably empty, we shouldn't get too carried away.'

'I know… but on three?'

'One… two… three!' yelled Merry, swiftly turning the handle of the door nearest to her.

'Oh my God,' came Tom's astonished voice from beside her.

Chapter Twenty-Two

'Why are you so determined to think the worst?' demanded Freya, getting crosser by the minute. 'It doesn't help anybody, least of all you.'

Stephen regarded her from over the top of the newspaper he was trying to read. 'I'm not. I rather thought I was stating the obvious.'

'But that's exactly what I mean!' countered Freya, her eyes blazing. 'Why would a visit from your brother automatically lead you to think he was gloating? Couldn't it just be a catch-up visit; that's what happens in normal families I believe. There doesn't always have to be an agenda, Stephen.' She snatched the newspaper from his hand, and plonked it down on the table. 'This is just your guilty conscience talking here, you do realise that, don't you?'

Stephen's look was cool. 'I didn't invite you over here, Freya. If all you came here to do was insult me, you might want to consider leaving.' He narrowed his eyes. 'What's it to you anyway?'

She gave him an exasperated look. 'Because in case you haven't noticed, I'm marrying your brother soon; you're going to be family. We're neighbours, and I don't want there to be any bad blood between us. It's about time all this was put to an end.'

Stephen opened his mouth to speak, but Freya ignored him and ploughed on. 'I'd have thought that much was bloody obvious… and I haven't forgotten what you said before Christmas. I really thought you might have begun to view things in a different way… or was that just the booze talking after all?'

'You really don't like me very much, do you?'

Freya dropped her head to the table and groaned. 'Yes, I do. I do like you, Stephen, that's why I'm here.'

Jesus, it's like talking to a small child, she thought.

'Okay, let me start again. Forget the fact that you and I were nearly married once upon a time, or that you've treated your brother appallingly for most of his adult life. That was all in the past, which is exactly where it needs to stay. I'm not bothered about that. What I care about is the here and now, and where we go in the future.' She looked up to see if he was listening at all. 'At Christmas, you showed me the real you, not the puffed up act you put on for everyone, but the Stephen you can be, the rational adult who does things for the right reasons and who understands that what he has around him is all he needs to be happy. You told me you were going to put all this nonsense between you and Sam behind you and try being a grown-up for a change. You were going to make a go of your business too, instead of swanning around like the big I am, and leaving everyone else to do the actual work. And yet here we are only four months later, and pardon me, but what's changed, Stephen?'

'That was quite some speech.'

Freya could feel her cheeks getting hotter and hotter. Stephen's gaze was on her, mocking her, and it was more than she could bear. She shot up from her chair, making for the door. She was such a fool for thinking things could ever be any different. She shouldn't have come.

Suddenly, she felt a hand on her arm. 'Freya, don't.' And then, 'I'm sorry. I shouldn't have said that.'

She whirled around to face him. But his usual look of arrogance had been replaced by something else. A softening around the eyes, and uncertainty... even fear?

'Please, come and sit down.'

She let herself be led back to the table, where she sat watching Stephen, his eyes closed.

He opened them after a minute and got up, moving across to a cupboard where he took down a tin and brought it back to the table.

'Not the answer, but would you like a chocolate biscuit?' He smiled hesitantly, and Freya returned it.

'Thank you,' she said.

Stephen let out a long sigh. 'Sam probably doesn't even know you're here, does he?'

'I thought I'd see how things went before I mentioned it to him.'

'Ah, I see. Not going terribly well, is it?' He took a biscuit and broke it in half. 'You're a good person, Freya.'

'So are you, you know… if you let yourself be.'

Stephen looked up in surprise. 'After all I've done, and you can still say that.'

'I'm like the proverbial guardian angel, always willing to believe that there's a spark of good in everyone, even if on the outside they behave like an arrogant prat.' A small smile played around her lips.

'You're teasing me now, which isn't fair.' He regarded his biscuit for a moment. 'It's all true, though… It's just that it's so hard, Freya, you know? All of it. I think I've been a prat for too long.' He smiled ruefully.

Freya said nothing, but merely nodded her encouragement.

'I think I've spent far too much time in the pub, drinking and gambling. I've been doing business of another kind, and I've taken my eye off the ball with my own. I've lost touch with everything, our suppliers, our customers. Christ, I even find it hard just walking the fields.' He patted his rather round belly. 'Some days, I don't even know where to start.'

'At the beginning is as good a place as any, I find.' Freya smiled. 'I know it's hard doing this on your own, I've been there, remember. The work is physical, it's relentless some days, but this is all you've known, Stephen, since you were a little boy following your dad around the orchard on your toy tractor. It will all come back to you, you just need to give it time. Get out there, breathe it in. Let the rain soak you and the sun warm you… feel the seasons, the rhythms again. You'll get there.' She took a bite of her biscuit and wondered how best to frame her next sentence.

'It might not be what you want to hear right now either, but Sam would still help you, we both would. You only have to ask.'

'That would go down really well, wouldn't it?' Stephen replied glumly.

'Better than you'd think probably. But you won't know, if you don't try.' She glanced at her watch, and shoved the rest of the biscuit in her mouth, chewing thoughtfully. 'Look, I need to go now, but think about what I've said, Stephen. Don't let any more months go by without making use of the opportunity you've been given. You told me you wanted to sort your life out, let's do it now, shall we?'

She was almost at the door before she heard Stephen's reply.

'Thank you, Freya, and I mean that. I know you're right, but listen… don't say anything to Sam, will you? About today I mean. It should come from me.'

'I won't. You men and your bloody pride. I know you need to find a way to do this and still save face – just don't leave it too long, okay?'

Chapter Twenty-Three

Merry opened another door, and another. They were all the same.

'Look at this lot!' she exclaimed, 'I've never seen anything like it, it's like a museum.'

She stared at the rows and rows of tins and packets. Breakfast cereals, boxes of tea. Washing powder and soap. Tins of soup and hot chocolate. Sweets galore.

Tom inspected his hands before taking down a packet of cocoa powder carefully. 'Blimey, I remember this from when I was a child, at least it's similar. This is even older, I think.'

'How old is it?'

He turned the packet over. 'I don't know. Older than the stuff we had certainly. Maybe 1960s or '70s perhaps?'

'Cora would know, I bet.'

'We could put glass across the front.'

Merry stared up at him, lost in her own thoughts.

'Out there,' Tom pointed. 'Wouldn't it be fabulous to have these on display in the shop? We'd have to cover the fronts of the shelves with something to preserve the stock, but people would love it.'

'Oh, they would,' breathed Merry, jiggling up and down. 'This is just perfect. I told you we needed to reuse all these old things, and now we have the absolute icing on the cake. It's like it was meant to be.'

Tom gave her a sideways glance.

'And there's no need to look at me like that. Don't you feel it too?'

Tom, who didn't, simply smiled. Merry knew it made sound business sense to him, and that was all he needed to know.

'Come on, let's try these other keys,' he said. 'At least to see if we can find some spares, and I'll let you get back to your furniture. We'll shut everything away again. They've been here for years, another few weeks won't make any difference.'

Merry had almost forgotten about the furniture after the excitement of finding all Christopher's things.

'I should ring the estate agent, I suppose, and put him in the picture. Not that I want to, mind. I don't think I could bear to lose all these things now. I haven't even looked at what else was in that desk drawer.'

'Better to be safe than sorry,' said Tom. 'We'll only get into hot water if we've got no claim to any of it.'

'I know,' agreed Merry morosely, picking up the rest of the keys. 'I'll ring them in a minute.'

'Well, admittedly they had just lost their brother, and grief can do funny things to you, but I wouldn't say the family were at all close. Their instructions were quite clear: get rid of everything.'

'But did they know what was here? Had they had a look at any of it, do you know?'

The estate agent was reassuring. 'I would imagine so. If you recall, their great uncle died quite some time ago and the family made enquiries then about selling the property. It was only because of the disagreement between the siblings that the house never came to market and that only changed at Christmas as you know. They would have had plenty of time to check the house during the time it was empty, it did belong to them after all.'

'Yes, of course, they must have, mustn't they?' agreed Merry gratefully. 'So you don't think there would be any comeback?'

'I wouldn't think so. The property and any remaining contents now belong to you.'

A muffled bump sounded above Merry's head, and she lost the thread of the conversation for a moment.

'So basically, we shouldn't worry, and there's no need to contact the previous owners, is that it?'

'Pretty much. From what you've said, it doesn't sound as if it would have much value anyway. Sentimental perhaps, but as I've said, I don't think the family went in for that very much.' Merry could hear the smile in the estate agent's voice.

'We're not planning on selling any of it, just to use it in the shop, either for practical purposes or for decoration.'

There was another bump from overhead.

'Then I really wouldn't worry.'

Merry thanked him and hung up, quite distracted now as it sounded as though something was bouncing on the ceiling overhead. She put down her phone and hurried up the stairs.

As she reached the top, she could hear that the noise was coming from one of the smaller bedrooms, a room as yet unoccupied but housing a number of items of furniture from the hotel that they had still not made up their minds whether to keep or not. There was another thump as she reached to open the door.

It was the smell that hit her first, acrid and sharp, catching in the back of her throat; but she soon took in the sooty black mess which covered a large portion of the room. The source of the noise was immediately apparent as a terrified crow blundered repeatedly into the window, seeking an escape.

Merry closed the door and hurried across the room, making soothing noises without even realising she was doing so, as she talked to the frightened bird. She tried to get the window open, but the catch was stiff, and the crow's wings beat against her as she reached past it, dirty puffs of soot rising up into her face. The bird's eyes were wild, its mouth opening and closing repeatedly although no sound came out.

It darted past her again, flying in a low swoop around the room before hurtling towards the window once more. Merry was sure it would hurt itself if it carried on. She leaned on the window catch again, feeling it suddenly give way as her fingers slid off, banging her knuckle painfully against the metal. She took a step backwards, trying to calm her own heart which was beating hard in response to the bird's frantic efforts. She started to talk once more, making shushing noises as she would to her daughter, trying to soothe her.

She reached forward with both hands, trying to stop the bird from its ceaseless flapping and suddenly, almost as if it could sense Merry's intention to help, it stilled, hunched against the corner of the window, its chest heaving.

'That's it, little one, don't be scared. Let's get you out.' Merry managed to get both hands around the bird, and gently brought it into her, wrapping the bottom of her fleece around it in an effort to make it feel safer. She managed to free one hand and pushed as hard as she could at the window, flinging it wide. A sudden rush of air flew in, bringing with it a patter of raindrops as she offered the bird up to the wind. It stood perched on her hands for a moment more, and Merry sensed the moment it would fly as it took off, soaring high above her before coming to rest in a tree at the edge of the garden. A minute later and it was gone.

Merry smiled, leaning forward to reach the window and close it once more, only then catching sight of her hands. They were filthy, as was her jumper, and she slowly turned around to see the state of the room. How could one bird make so much mess? And how on earth was she going to clean it up? The chimney had obviously not been swept for a while; a huge ball of soot had fallen with the bird and burst onto the hearth, a black circle of dust fanning out and covering everything in its wake. Where the crow had sought to free itself, black marks covered the walls and carpet, and the furniture stored in the room was dark with the sticky mess.

She knew better than to touch it. She had only seen this happen once before when she was a teenager and still living at home. A crow had come down the chimney in their dining room, and her mother had been adamant that the worst thing they could do was to rub it to get it off. It had to be lifted while it was still dust-like. With a grim expression on her face she went downstairs to get the vacuum cleaner, cross now at the interruption in her day.

A newspaper had been pushed through the front door on to the floor in the hall, and as she bent to retrieve it, she became aware that there was still someone standing outside. A very tall woman was scribbling something onto a piece of paper, and she looked up at the sound of the door opening.

'Oh, hello. Sorry I didn't think anyone was home. I did try the bell.'

Merry looked at her quizzically.

'I'm Pat,' the woman said. 'From the village. I wondered if you might like the evening paper delivered. I was just leaving my details in case.' She handed Merry the sheet of paper.

As Merry reached out to take it, she caught sight of her hands once more. 'Ah, sorry. I'm a bit mucky. We've just had a crow come down the chimney. Could you just leave it with me, and I'll have a look when I'm less, well… covered in soot.'

Pat gave a nervous smile, looking up at the roofline. 'Was it still alive?' she asked, with a slight shudder.

'Oh yes,' said Merry cheerfully. 'I managed to get it out of the window, it was fine. Ungrateful so and so, though, didn't even say thank you.'

Merry's humour was met with a stony stare. 'Well, that's something I suppose, it's even worse bad luck if they're dead.'

Chapter Twenty-Four

Freya pulled her hood further over her face, but the wind was blowing in gusts this morning, and her raincoat did little to deflect the rain. It also seriously impeded her vision.

Impatiently, she reached into her pocket and pulled out a hairband, throwing back her hood, and offering her face to the weather. She scraped her hair back as best she could, tucking the loose ends firmly behind her ears. Freya was used to being outside in all weathers; in fact, it was one of the things she loved about her life. It didn't matter how cold and wet she got during the day, there was nothing that a nice hot shower, a mug of hot chocolate and a bacon sandwich couldn't cure. People often remarked that there was no such thing as bad weather, only inappropriate clothing, but Freya disagreed. Some days it didn't matter what you were wearing, but the one thing she had learned over the years was that skin, at least, was waterproof.

Hair secured, she returned her attention to the task in hand, anxiously reaching for another branch of the apple tree beside her. The pregnant buds were beginning to swell into beautiful tight promises that would soon offer glimpses of their delicate blushed petals. There was no sign of that this morning, but Freya was standing on the side of the orchard that faced the sun, so these were the buds that would blossom first. She thanked her lucky stars that March had seen a particularly sharp cold snap which had lasted for a couple of weeks. It had held these buds back and, as she surveyed the black pall of the sky above her, she thought once more of the extraordinary alchemy that was Mother Nature. Had spring come early, these buds might be in flower by now, and the driving rain which was now into its third day would have ripped the petals apart. She eyed the sky again, and prayed for an end to the deluge.

After a few minutes, Sam joined her, a grim expression on his face. 'We've another couple of weeks I reckon, what do you think?'

Freya nodded, wiping a droplet from the end of her nose. 'I think we'll be okay, just as long as this doesn't go on much longer. We might lose some of the Devonshires, but the cider apples are okay.' She screwed up her nose. 'I'm not so sure about the perry pears, though.' She looked up at Sam, trying to gauge the expression on his face.

He had turned away from her, and was staring out across the fields. She knew there was no way to see Braeburns's fields from here, but it didn't stop Sam from looking.

'I rode out by Stephen's this morning, his trees are already like galleons in full sail.'

'But we've had good days of warm sunshine up until this week, and there were plenty of bees around, maybe he'll be okay? He might still get a good crop.'

Sam sighed. 'I'm not sure I care any more, Freya. It's been two weeks since I went to see him, and I thought that perhaps he would have had time to calm down and think about what I said; that maybe he would have got in touch… I'm just fooling myself, thinking things will ever be any different.'

'Sam, you can't blame yourself. Stephen is a grown man, he has to take responsibility for his own actions, and that includes how he runs Braeburn. You've offered to help, that's all you can do.' She took his hand, wondering whether to mention her own conversation with Stephen, but knowing that this wasn't really the right time. 'Come on, let's get back inside. We've a lot of homework to do.'

Merry took hold of her friend's coat later that afternoon, and hung it over the big butler sink in the utility room. Even the short dash from the car into the house had been enough to soak her through.

'That's the second time today.' Freya laughed as Merry rejoined her. 'I got drenched this morning as well,' she added, holding up her bedraggled hair as proof. 'And it's so windy, the car practically blew itself here.'

'Dreadful, isn't it?' agreed Merry, pulling a face. 'Rain is most definitely stopping play right now, which is fantastic just as we've got the builders actually organised to turn up. I hope when they do arrive that they can put on a turn of speed; everything else is dependent on when they finish, and I'm getting rather impatient.'

Freya smiled. 'It's all very exciting. Come on, show me what else you found.'

Merry led Freya through to the dining room where the table was covered in a layer of papers and notebooks. 'These are the latest things,' she said. 'They were stuffed into the drawer of an old desk we found but look at the colours on them. They'll make gorgeous posters.'

Freya picked one from the pile closest to her. 'What are they?'

'We think they're printer's samples. I've looked up some of the designs, and they were all used for wallpaper.' She shuddered. 'I'm not sure I would ever be up for that amount of colour in a room, but I think these are lovely. I'm guessing they were printed from Christopher's original designs, perhaps to check the colours, or the detail maybe. Once all was okay, they'd go on to run the rolls of wallpaper.'

'And you're going to use all these in the shop?'

'Hmm.' Merry nodded. 'In fact, we've just had some drawings back from the architect, do you want to have a look? Tom's in there now.'

A fire was roaring in the grate in the study as Tom sat working at the computer. He smiled a greeting, immediately vacating his seat so that Merry could sit down.

'Here, I'll let Merry show you round,' he said. 'I'll just pop and check on Robyn.'

Merry rolled her eyes. 'Don't you dare wake her up,' she said, clicking on a file on the screen in front of her. 'She's been a right grumpy mare this morning,' she added to Freya. 'Cora's been taking her out for a walk most mornings, and I think she's rather got used to it. With all this rain she hasn't been out for the last few days. Do babies get cabin fever? I dunno. Anyway, she refused point blank to go to sleep this morning and consequently didn't know where to put herself this afternoon… Right, here we are.'

Freya looked at the screen as directed. A bright image had appeared, that even to her untrained eye, clearly showed the shop space, now transformed from an empty dilapidated shell to an impression of what it might look like once open for business.

'We want to use as much of the salvaged furniture as we can, but as space is at a premium, Nigel did a survey for us, showing the best fit to maximise the selling area. Bless him, I didn't ask him to, but I'd emailed photos of some of Christopher's work to give him an idea of the look we wanted and he's incorporated those too.'

'He knows you too well,' stated Freya, knowing that Merry's relationship with the architect they had used so often at the hotel went back years. 'It's really good, though, it gives you a much better idea of how it will look.'

'It will also save us no end of time. We were going to have the walls a soft green, you know a bit heritage Farrow & Ball, but when you look at this, it wouldn't work at all. We can also see exactly how the units will look, and what we might display where. I don't want to spend hours renovating the furniture, only to hate it when it's all in position.'

Freya nodded at her, seeing the truth in her words. She was just about to ask about the extraordinary collection of groceries they had found when she became aware that Tom had returned to the room, standing in the doorway. His face was ashen in the dim light.

'Merry,' he began, but he needed to go no further. One look at his face, and she was out of the chair and crossing the room. Freya raced upstairs after them.

'I thought she was sort of snoring at first, and I nearly left her to come back downstairs. Merry, I nearly left her, I could have walked away…'

Merry lifted Robyn from the cot, her daughter's head flopping backwards, her breaths coming in short fast puffs.

'What's wrong with her?' Tom's voice was an anxious whisper. His hands were shaking, Freya noticed.

She crossed to take his arm, while Merry laid Robyn down on the changing station, the back of her hand resting gently against her daughter's forehead. 'She's burning up.'

Merry lifted up her little pinafore, smoothing the skin on her belly and quickly pulled down the top of her woolly tights. 'Oh, no, no, no,' she muttered. 'Please no.'

The skin was mottled and blotchy, and even Freya could see that Robyn's responses were low. Merry looked straight up into her eyes, her own wide with panic and fear.

'I'll call an ambulance,' said Freya.

The waiting room was like any other, full of hunched nervous people. Freya's eyes scanned the doors at either end of the room, hoping for a glimpse of Merry or Tom through one, and Sam through the other.

She had followed the ambulance as it pulled out of the village, the siren setting her heart pounding as she wove through the lanes after it, praying that the roads were clear, willing it onwards. They had caught it early said the paramedic. They had done the right thing. But it was still Robyn's tiny body inside the ambulance, a place she had no right to be, and Freya drove, forcing all thoughts from her mind, save getting to the hospital. The rain lashed at the windscreen, the car buffeted by the wind as they turned onto the main road. The wipers screeched across the screen as they fought the weather, but Freya remembered nothing of the journey.

Only now, alone in a room full of other people did it all come flooding in. What would have happened if Tom had thought his daughter was merely sleeping? What if he hadn't been there at all, as she and Merry chatted away without a care in the world. What if Merry hadn't recognised the signs; how did she even know? A singular moment of responsibility that Merry had reacted to by instinct, some innate maternal guide giving her the sixth sense she needed, right at the crucial time. Freya had never felt so helpless. She wanted to hug her friend, and hold her, to tell her everything would be all right, but that reassurance was not hers to give. Only time would offer it, if they were lucky.

She had no idea how long she had sat there until she became aware of Sam by her side.

'I came as soon as I got your message,' he murmured. 'Where is she, is she okay?' He grasped Freya's pale hand, warming it between his own.

'I don't know, Sam. I haven't seen anyone.' Her eyes began to fill with tears. 'She looked so poorly…'

Sam pulled her into him, and they sat unspeaking as the minutes stretched out. The door opened several times as people came and went, but nothing changed.

Freya was thinking about Amos. She knew it was daft, but she couldn't help it. He would have known what to say, or what to do, and she missed his gentle words of encouragement and wisdom. He had come into her head a few times over recent months, usually when she'd been out in the fields, or walking the lanes by their house. She had no idea where he had gone, but she knew he would have found his way to somewhere he was needed; that's the way his life worked. She felt Sam's warm body against hers, and gave an inward smile as the realisation hit her that it was not Amos she needed at all. Everything she required was deep inside her; the courage to say those things that needed to be said, and to fight for those things she knew to be true. That was the real wisdom that Amos had brought to her, and to Sam.

'I can't wait any more, Sam. I need to see Merry and Tom. Whatever's happening we should be there. She's my oldest friend.'

'We don't want to be in the way.'

'If someone tells me I'm in the way, then I'll leave, but until then I need to find out what I can. I don't know if there's anything we can do, but I'd never forgive myself if there was and we were just sitting here… I'm going to see if anyone has any information.'

The receptionist was tired and busy. A telephone behind her rang incessantly, and her colleague, deep in conversation, ignored it. Her smile at Freya was tight, but at the mention of the baby, a flicker of something passed behind her eyes. She's a mother too, thought Freya; she knows how it feels. She pointed back behind her, motioning through the double doors.

'There's another waiting area down the corridor, which leads off the ward. I should wait there if I were you. Someone might be able to help.'

She couldn't do any more, Freya knew that. They weren't family and had no right to any information. She glanced back at Sam, and together they hurried through the doors. The atmosphere here was different, purposeful. There were no bored expressions or resigned faces. Here, everyone was alert and watchful, waiting for the next conversation, the next event which might either take them on the road to recovery or lead them further into an even darker day.

Freya caught sight of Tom almost immediately. He was sitting halfway down the corridor, his back tight against the chair, his pose rigid. He was staring straight ahead, his hands still, cradled in his lap.

His head whipped around the minute he became aware of someone, and a small flicker of disappointment was visible as he realised she wasn't a doctor. Freya's heart went out to him, as his look changed to one of gratitude at seeing them, and she wished with all her heart that she could give him more.

He rose as they approached and reached for Freya just as she reached for him, their hug saying more than the words they struggled to find.

'I had to come out for a minute,' said Tom, 'but Merry... someone should be with her.'

'Where is she, Tom?' asked Freya. 'I'll go to her.'

'Through there,' he managed, pointing at another doorway. 'In the middle.'

'I'll find her,' she replied, looking at Sam.

'Go on, go. I'll wait here,' he answered.

It felt so intrusive, walking past other people in beds, but as she neared the middle of the row of cubicles, she heard Merry's voice, soft and gentle, and knew she had found them.

A nurse smiled a welcome as she paused by the door, replacing a pen in her top pocket, and Freya felt a slight easing of the tension in the room. The nurse made room for her to pass and in a moment, Freya had her arms tightly around Merry.

It took a few minutes before either of them could speak. Freya felt Merry take a deep breath, and pulled away slightly so that she could see her friend's face. Her cheeks were wet, but although her eyes were still brimming with tears, Freya was relieved to see more than the despair she had expected. A tiny glimmer of hope, perhaps?

'They think she's going to be okay, Freya,' said Merry, in a rush of breath. 'I was so frightened.'

Freya looked down at the small figure lying on the bed; the baby's cheeks were flushed, but her breathing was more peaceful as she slept. One arm lay on top of the loose covers, a tube snaking away from it to a drip at one side of the bed. Freya couldn't imagine how Merry must be feeling and the terror that she must have felt.

'Is it... is it what we thought?' she asked, not wanting to say the word out loud.

Merry nodded. 'They've confirmed it's meningitis, and they're pumping her full of antibiotics just to be on the safe side, but they won't know for certain which type it is until the results of the tests come back. We've caught it early, and there's no proper rash which is a good thing. They're pretty certain it's viral, which isn't as serious as bacterial...' Merry trailed off. There was no need for her to say any more. 'It all happened so fast. No one said very much in the ambulance, but the minute we got in here, the room was suddenly full of people, sticking needles in her, doing tests. It makes you feel so helpless, just watching... and I wanted to pick her up and cuddle her, but I couldn't...'

Freya watched as a single tear spilled out onto Merry's cheek.

'We might have lost her... we still might.'

'But you didn't, and you won't.' She pulled Merry close again, stroking the back of her hair, just like she had done so many times in the past. Just like Merry had comforted her all those years ago when she thought she had lost Sam for good.

'Do you remember what you said to me when you were in labour, Merry?'

Merry lifted her head.

'You were very eloquent if I remember. Even though you were in pain, you made me promise to listen to you. I thought *I'd* lost everything that day, first Appleyard, and Sam too, but you told me to fight, to let go of what was making me scared, and breathe through the pain. You said that at the end of it, I might find myself with a miracle. Well, I got mine that day, Merry, and so did you. A beautiful little girl, born with a snowstorm raging outside, and named after one of the smallest birds there is, but a bird brave enough to see the winter through. She's got her mum's fighting spirit, so don't you dare give up on her.'

Merry inhaled a shaky breath, and pulled away, wiping her eyes.

'Who suddenly made you so wise?' she whispered.

Freya thought for a moment, the answer on the tip of her tongue, but she said nothing, just smiled.

Chapter Twenty-Five

Cora and Rupert were there to welcome them home two days later. Cora hovered at the edge of the driveway as Tom turned the car in, barely able to contain her excitement, or so it seemed at first. The real reason became apparent as the car came to rest around the back of the house.

Merry stared through the windscreen in blinking disbelief. What more could possibly go wrong? She pushed open the car door, grabbing onto it as the wind fought to tear it from her hands. From the back seat, Robyn slept on peacefully.

Some ten metres in front of her, the space where Merry's car was parked had completely disappeared, and in its place was tree. Nothing else, just tree, although somewhere, underneath it all she supposed her car was still there. She looked around her, following the line of destruction into the field beside the house, where the enormous roots of the tree had ripped a jagged crater in the soft soil.

'Don't look at that now,' urged Cora, coming round to stand beside Merry and Tom, trying to crane her neck for a better look at Robyn inside the car. 'It's worse than it looks, and all under control.'

Tom gave her an incredulous stare. 'How can that possibly be under control?' he asked, mouth hanging open.

Cora ignored him. 'Come on, let's bring the little one inside, I've the kettle on for you,' she replied, trying to shepherd them along.

'But I've only been gone for two hours…'

'Yes, well, it doesn't take long for a tree to fall down once it's a mind to. Come on, in we go.'

Merry looked around her and up at the sky as if she expected another tree to appear from nowhere. She leaned back inside the car to unclip Robyn from her seat and allowed herself to be led inside. Cora shut the door firmly after them.

'It came down not long after you left for the hospital, Tom, but I've called Brian, and he'll be along shortly. I'm afraid he and his chainsaw are rather in demand today, but he'll come and see to it for you. I suspect his sons will be along too to lend a hand, so that's fine.'

'Cora,' insisted Tom. 'We've just come home from the hospital to find a ruddy great tree sprawled across our driveway, and if I'm not very much mistaken, Merry's car will be flattened underneath it. In what way is everything fine?'

'Are you all right?' she asked by way of reply. 'Is Merry? Is the baby, and the house…? Well then, in my book, everything is fine. The car is just a heap of metal that can be replaced. Sit down while I pour the tea, and you can tell me how Robyn is, although I must say she looks chirpy enough now.'

Robyn was indeed chirupping away merrily at Rupert, who as usual had come to sit by her side. Her toes bounced up and down with delight. Merry sighed and accepted the cup of tea with a weary smile.

'Real tea,' she said. 'Thank the lord.'

The last couple of days had been relentless. The sheer panic and terror of not knowing what was happening to Robyn had given way to a listless relief when she was pronounced out of danger. But she was still in a place where Merry had felt unable to reach her, to care for her. It was far from home, and she had felt the pull of Five Penny House keenly. Now she wanted to feel the house around her, to sense its security and comfort and, while she knew she was probably too tired and emotional to think straight, it felt as though this was a place where Robyn could get strong and well again. As the soothing warmth of the tea slipped down, even the devastation of the tree outside seemed an irrelevance. It was fine, Cora had said, and Merry believed her. She let herself sit and be comforted.

'Thank you, Cora,' she said, as she finished the last of her tea. 'That was the nicest cup of tea I can ever remember having.'

'Well, that's because it came with a hefty dose of contentment. It's good to have you all home again. We've missed you,' she said, laying a hand on Rupert's head. 'Especially this fellow. He takes his guard duties very seriously. I think if they'd let him in the hospital, he would have been there like a shot.' She watched Robyn for a moment, a smile playing across her face. 'What have the doctors said? Do you know where she picked up the virus?'

Merry was quick to reassure her. 'It could have been anywhere, but somewhere full of people – the supermarket most likely, and certainly not from being out with you and Rupert.' She ran a hand through her wind-blown hair. 'It's ironic really because she's not long had her immunisations. She was just unlucky, that's all.'

'Or lucky,' Cora replied.

Merry tipped her head. 'How so?'

'That it wasn't the more serious form of meningitis.'

Cora's words settled in the room for a moment, as Merry recognised their wayward truth. How strange to be grateful for something so awful, and to feel that even after the horrible time of the last few days, there was still something to feel glad about. Everything was relative, that was all.

Tom reached down for the baby's things. 'I'll go and put these back where they belong,' he said, laying a soft hand on Merry's head.

As soon as Tom had left the room, Merry turned to Cora.

'How did Christopher's wife and daughter die? Please, I want to know.'

Cora's expression was not quite as shocked as it perhaps should have been. 'It was a long time ago, Merry. I'm not sure it helps... but I do understand why you asked.'

'Then will you tell me?'

The minutes of silence stretched between them, as Merry's eyes flickered back and forth towards the door, waiting for her husband to reappear.

'You're quite right in what you feel,' answered Cora eventually, watching Merry carefully. 'But if you've felt that much, then you know that Robyn is in no danger. Christopher Marchmont was one of the nicest men I've ever met. In life there wasn't anything he wouldn't do, either for Catherine, or for his wife, Marina… and similarly in death, nothing he wouldn't do to protect their memory. If you've felt his presence, then I'd say it's only because he's pleased you're here.'

'Nothing like this has ever happened to me before. I sat in the hospital on that first evening, watching Robyn sleep. I felt so peaceful. I felt like I was watching her through somebody else's eyes, but they were kind eyes, Cora. They cried when I cried, and in the morning when I knew that Robyn would be okay, when I looked in the mirror I saw my own relief, but I saw another's there too, mirroring my own. All I wanted to do was to get home.'

Cora nodded. 'And home you most certainly are.' She smiled. 'Although it's unfortunate that the weather chose this particular moment to spring a surprise all of its own.'

'Do you know, I don't think I even mind about that too much now. The rain worries me, though. I noticed how high the river was when we drove through the village, and I have friends who run an orchard; this rain will be wreaking havoc with the apple blossom.'

'Then we must hope that this temporary break brings a welcome respite to all.' She patted Rupert's head once more. 'Now, we must go and leave you three to settle back in. You both need your rest, and on a day like today, it's the perfect excuse not to venture out very far.'

There was the sound of a door closing in the hallway. 'You didn't answer my question, Cora,' said Merry.

Her smile was immediate. 'Oh, I think you'll find I did,' she replied. 'Maybe not the one you asked, but most certainly the one you wanted answered.' She leaned over and kissed Merry's cheek. 'And one day, a little while from now, I shall tell you more, but today is not the time… Now, you know where I am if you need anything, and if Brian doesn't appear to sort out your tree, you give me a ring. He's a good man, but a bit forgetful at times.'

Merry stood to escort Cora to the door. 'You go safely home now too,' she said. 'Get out of this weather yourself.'

'I have an excellent puzzle to finish, which I'm rather looking forward to,' she said. 'So I shall be absolutely fine.' She had one hand on the handle before she turned back towards Merry. 'Just one more thing before I go. It suits you perfectly, but yours is such an unusual name. Is it short for something?'

Of all the things that Cora could have asked her, this was certainly not what Merry had expected. She laughed and pulled a face. 'It's Merrilees of all things,' she said.

'Of course,' Cora replied. 'I rather thought it might be.'

'There's not much else it can be I suppose, except perhaps Meredith.' She rolled her eyes. 'I still don't know what on earth possessed my mother to give me such an unusual name. It's handy at Christmas, but—'

'Well, my dear,' interrupted Cora. 'I know what the name Merrilees means, and like I said… it suits you.'

Merry looked puzzled.

'Apart from the more obvious joyful, it can also mean someone with a strong will or spirit, even someone with psychic powers. Quite appropriate, don't you think?'

Chapter Twenty-Six

Freya bit her lip for the umpteenth time that day. She knew that Sam's mood was symptomatic of how he was feeling about Stephen's continuing silence, but even so he was skating perilously close to the wind. She picked up the discarded brochure that lay on the kitchen table and sat down for a moment, flicking through the same pages that Sam's fingers had lingered over only minutes before. She really didn't need the thoughtfully turned down corners of the pages to know where Sam had been looking, nor to confirm her suspicions: the guilty look on his face had been enough. The trouble was that Freya wasn't sure whether it was guilt at daring to think of taking Appleyard in a direction that she didn't want it to go in, or simply guilt at having been found out. She laid the brochure back down on the table and collected the two mugs that sat there. Ordinarily, she would have been quite happy to leave them there until the next cup of tea was due, but today, washing them up gave her the opportunity to stall for time.

It was only a few short months ago that she had sat in this very kitchen and listened to Gareth's dreams of their future together. A future that didn't include Appleyard at all, but instead suburban bliss in a two-up, two-down and a tiny garden, thank you very much. She reminded herself that her relationship with her old boyfriend was nothing like the one she now had with Sam. She and Sam were a partnership, and had been since they were small, playing games in the school holidays with their friends long before their relationship was anything other than friendship. Even her old friend, Willow, had once told her she thought them destined to be a couple. If Merry thought about it in a level-headed way she knew that the complexities of Sam's relationship with his brother were such that they could never be resolved in just a matter of weeks. The trouble was that today's conversation had rung the same warning bells in her head that the conversation with Gareth had all those months ago, and Freya didn't like that one little bit.

It had started out as a perfectly reasoned argument. Decisions needed to be made soon over what equipment to buy if they were ever going to produce anything from the apples that they hoped would soon be growing in abundance. But Freya's natural inclination towards prudence meant that she found this difficult. Neither did it agree with her independent spirit, one founded out of necessity over the last few years. Everything that they needed to buy seemed to cost such a huge amount of money and, as the conversation progressed, it became increasingly obvious to Freya that money was the one thing that Sam was at pains to dismiss. She knew that in part it was only because he was trying to be generous, to help her bury the fears she'd once had for her future; but the more he talked, the more she heard something in his voice that she didn't think was Sam at all.

She returned to the table once more, Sam's head still bent over the laptop.

'Did you have these at Braeburn?' she asked, looking over his shoulder.

'Something like it, yes. Although Stephen could never see the point in shelling out for these.'

Freya looked at the face she loved, the gentle green eyes and the soft curl of the hair above his ears. She knew how hard it must be for him even to be here. To have moved out of the house he had lived in since childhood, and now be taking his place by her side on land that wasn't his, in a house that wasn't his, and to put his heart and soul into a business that wasn't his. They weren't yet married, and even when they were, she couldn't help but wonder how it would all feel to Sam. But the generous mouth she had covered so many times with her own was pulled into a pout that said more than words ever could. She needed to tread gently.

She leaned forward, trying to attract his attention.

'I'm not sure that I can see the point either, to be honest,' she said. 'They're far too big for what we need. Couldn't we manage with something a bit more modest?'

'But it gives us no room to manoeuvre, Freya. As we expand, we'll only have to replace them, so where's the logic in that?'

Freya had a feeling they were going to go round in circles, and much though she didn't want to raise her head above the parapet, another part recognised the need to take the conversation to another level. She decided to bite the bullet.

'Are you sure you're not just going with these because they're bigger and better than what Stephen has?'

Sam's head swivelled around immediately, and Freya heard his sharply inhaled breath.

'Is that what you think?' He glared. 'That this is all some game to get back at Stephen? Has it never occurred to you that I might want what's best for us?'

Freya refused to take the bait. She considered her next words carefully. 'I think you believe that these things are what's best for us,' she said, 'at the moment. But I also think you're fooling yourself, telling yourself what you want to hear, and I think that has everything to do with Stephen. If you were thinking straight, and Stephen wasn't around, I think your decisions would be different, and those are the ones that would be best for us.' She picked up the brochure, looking straight at Sam. 'Because they would be decisions made by the two of us, together, with no third-party involvement.'

For a moment, she thought she had got away with it, but then Sam's eyes clouded and his mouth set in a hard line.

'I thought you might have had a little more faith in me at least. Talk about throwing it all back in my face—'

'I'm not being critical, or ungrateful,' bit back Freya, interrupting him. 'But what I am doing is trying to put an end to this endless fighting between the two of you. It's got to stop, and I'll be damned if I let Appleyard become your own personal battlefield.' She was aware that her voice had risen considerably, and she forced it back down again. 'Look Sam, I do understand how it is for you, but you have nothing to prove as far as Stephen is concerned. I love you. Appleyard is as much yours now as it is mine, and what's important is that we do things for us, because they're right for us, not to prove a point to anyone else. Stephen can do what he bloody well likes. He said he'd talk to you and I happen to think he will, but if I'm wrong, then let him get on with things; it's his business not ours.'

Sam's shoulders sank a little lower as he took in Freya's words. He reached for her hand with a small sigh, a rueful smile softening his expression.

'Shall we go back to the beginning again?' he said, shaking his head in amusement. 'I'll close this poncey website down, and we can get back to our original list of things we need to think about.'

Freya gave him an answering smile, and rummaged on the table for her notebook and pencil. She was flicking through the pages when Sam's harsh voice cut through her thoughts.

'What do you mean Stephen said he'd talk to me, Freya? Just when was this exactly?'

Bugger.

'Don't you start,' grumbled Merry. 'I've had enough with the villagers telling me we're doomed without you buying into the whole silly curse thing as well. This house is not under some dark spell and neither are we.' She stood beside her husband looking down on the road beneath their bedroom window as her crumpled car was slowly towed away.

'So that phone call from the builders telling me they can't come back for three whole weeks isn't more bad luck?' replied Tom, rubbing at the dirty windowpane.

'It is bad luck, yes, but nothing more. These things happen.'

'Well, they seem to be happening to us rather a lot at the moment,' he said, his finger squeaking against the glass.

Merry stilled his hand. 'Will you stop that, look, you're making it all smeary.' She was determined not to credit Tom's concern. Admittedly, her thoughts had been straying in that same direction a few days ago, but that was before Robyn had become ill, and since then, bizarrely, amid all the anguish and confusion that had been heaped upon them, Merry now felt a profound peace. She also felt inclined to stick up for Christopher and his house.

'You know you could look at what's happened from another point of view; that the crow chose to come down the chimney in the only room in the house full of furniture we're not using, that it was still alive, and I got to hold its body in my hands before setting it free. That Robyn's illness wasn't the more serious form, and that we caught it quickly… even the tree came down when no one else was here, and of all the places that it could have fallen, it missed the house and the shop completely. Given all the things it could have landed on, it picked the one thing that in relative terms wasn't worth a great deal.'

A small smile played across Tom's lips. 'And what about the work in the shop?' he asked, pulling his wife to him in a playful hug.

'Well, I haven't quite worked that one out yet…' Merry smirked. 'But, I'm sure I shall.' She turned her attention back to the window and the rivers of rain that ran down it. Outside, a dark wall of cloud proclaimed little change in the weather.

'Anyway, I don't think we're the ones in need of luck,' she remarked, tilting her head towards the cluster of houses that sat at the bottom of the hill. 'I wouldn't want to be down there right now. Look how far the river has come up in the last few hours.'

Tom followed her line of sight and stared out of the window as if seeing the rain for the first time.

'It wasn't like that this morning,' he said. 'I wonder if it usually floods.'

'I've no idea,' frowned Merry. 'But Cora would probably know. I could give her a ring?'

Tom glanced at his watch. 'Perhaps you should,' he agreed. 'I might just go out and take a look before it gets dark. Will you be okay here?'

'*We'll* be fine,' said Merry pointedly. 'But you'll get soaked going out there. Do you really think it's necessary?'

'I've never really noticed it before now, but look at the bend in the river and the slope of the hill. If it goes over, it will take out all the houses below it down by the pond. They're directly in its path.'

Merry stared at Tom, her heart beginning to beat a little quicker. 'I'll go and ring Cora,' she said.

It was a full hour before Tom returned, dumping his boots by the back door and standing in the kitchen, his waxed jacket dripping a steady stream of water onto the floor.

'It's come up even higher just in the time I've been out,' he said, as Merry and Cora looked up anxiously from the table. 'If the rain continues, it will flood for definite, I'm sure.'

'But that's what I don't understand,' said Cora. 'The flood plain has always taken the weight of the water before it ever gets this high. That's what it's there for.'

Tom looked puzzled for a moment. 'None of the fields is flooded Cora, I've been the whole length of the village and back again. Where is this flood plain?'

'Out on the left as you go through, opposite the new estate. That's why the houses are only on one side of the road. The developers fought long and hard to get permission to build on the other side as well, but all the villagers petitioned, and the town council quite rightly refused permission. The flood plain can never be built on, it would be a disaster.'

'But there's no water there, Cora. None at all. In fact, if anything, I'd say the water level is lower on that side of the village.'

Cora got up from the table, her face anxious in the dimming light. 'That doesn't make any sense… unless… unless the bridge is somehow blocked. That might explain it. Did you take a look at it, Tom?'

'Only from the car. The water's high, but I couldn't see any obstruction.'

'Then might I suggest you get down there again and have another look. At the very least we ought to warn the folks who live down by the pond. Perhaps Merry could ring Bill at the pub in the meantime; he and his wife know everyone in that row of cottages. They'll know what to do. And if you know of anyone with big strong muscles who could give you a hand, I suggest you ring them too. There might be a bit of furniture that needs moving.'

Merry nodded as she watched Tom shrug his coat back on. By the time he reached the door, she had already picked up her phone.

*

'Don't be so ridiculous,' argued Freya, 'you're completely overreacting.'

'Oh am I,' snarled Sam, his eyes blazing. 'Put yourself in my shoes, Freya. You go and see my brother behind my back, in an attempt to convince him to do the very thing I'd already asked him to, and yet you claim to have every faith in me. It doesn't look like it from where I'm standing. You've questioned everything I've said today, so go on, admit it, you're still not sure I'm man enough for the job, are you?'

Freya stared at Sam, her mouth hanging open. 'Oh for goodness' sake, how many times, Sam? How many times do I have to tell you—?'

A shrill noise interrupted her, and it threw her for a moment as she tried to work out where the sound was coming from. She tried to ignore it and remember what she was saying, but the noise was accompanied by a harsh vibrating that made everything on the table shudder. Freya fished her phone out from under some papers and tutted in exasperation. She was about to silence the call and switch off her mobile when she caught sight of the name on the display. She held up a hand to Sam.

'Merry, what is it, is Robyn okay?' she asked in a panic, all thoughts of their argument forgotten. 'Oh thank goodness for that.'

Sam was standing right in front of her, and she saw his shoulders relax at her words. She listened to Merry's anxious voice, her thoughts racing away from her at what she heard. After a moment, she gave a swift nod and ended the call. She looked down at the phone in her hands and then back up at Sam.

'We need to get over to Lower Witley as soon as possible,' she said. 'So go and get your boots and your mac on, we're going to get wet.' She turned to go and fetch her own from the hall closet. 'And no arguments, go and ring Stephen, we need his help too.'

Chapter Twenty-Seven

'Can you see anything?' shouted Sam, his voice snatched away by the wind as he leaned out over the bridge.

Below him, Tom edged gingerly down the bank beside the road. One hand grabbed a bush as he tried to lower himself further, and the other inched its way down the wall, loath to let go of the parapet. The noise was ferocious.

The thick bushes thrashed in the wind, and it was impossible to tell what he was looking at. Tom knew he would have to get lower still if he was to see what was going on. He swung his body round for a moment, throwing his weight forward into the bush as he sought to get a firmer grip with his feet. He let the bush take his weight as he braced himself against it, and slid one hand down to grasp a thicker branch. His feet moved further down the bank and there was now nothing to save him if he fell, but a tumble of grasses and low lying shrubs which would part easily if any weight were put on them.

His feet met water as he strained forward, finally seeing what had caused the river to rise so dramatically. A small tree had become completely wedged under the bridge, its trunk stuck fast against the walls with a tumult of debris straining behind it. Several smaller logs and branches were bouncing about the water seeking an escape. He shook the rain off his face and tried to lever himself backwards, his feet slipping in the sodden mud.

A hand reached down to pull him the last few steps as he neared road level once more, and Sam's concerned face came into view. 'Did you see anything?' he shouted again, shuddering as a fresh draught of rain trickled down the back of his neck.

Tom motioned towards Sam's pickup where they could talk a little easier. He climbed inside, passing a hand over his face to remove a curl of hair that dripped water over one eye.

'The bridge is partially blocked,' he said. 'Right in the middle. A tree has come down stream and wedged itself against the bridge walls. The weight of water and other rubbish behind it is only pushing it tighter. Some water is getting through, but it's acting like a dam. If we don't move the tree, the river will flood further back for sure.'

Sam nodded, a grim expression on his face. 'Any ideas how we get the tree out?' he asked.

Tom shook his head. 'Not one. Not yet anyway. How is everyone else doing?'

'Bill has rounded up as many folk as he can to help, and so far Freya and Stephen have a team in each house, shifting what they can of the furniture upstairs. There are six houses down by the pond altogether, it's not going to be a quick job.'

'Okay, I need to ring Merry and let her know what's going on. Then I suggest we get our heads together to see what we can do about that tree.'

*

Merry pushed the plate towards Cora. 'It's ridiculous, isn't it? I feel so helpless up here, while they're all slogging their guts out down there. I can't think of a single thing to do except eat cake and drink tea.'

'Well, I for one am very grateful,' replied Cora, helping herself to a chunk of the fruit cake. It's fiendish out there. These old bones have seen a few rough storms in their time, but this is up there with the best of them, that's for sure.'

Merry picked at a crumb on her plate. 'I'm scared, Cora,' she said with a small smile. 'What if something happens to any of them?'

'I think perhaps we need something to do while we wait,' she answered, neatly sidestepping the question. 'It's not good to dwell on our fears. Why don't you show me all the wonderful plans you have for your shop? Robyn is fast asleep and now would be as good a time as any.'

'Or you could tell me about Christopher… you did say you would,' replied Merry, refilling her friend's teacup.

Cora sighed. 'Well, I can see that you're not going to give up pestering me about that, although I'm not so sure that now is the right time to be talking about it.'

'Oh, I don't think Christopher will mind,' Merry replied, a twinkle catching in her eye. 'And if you think about it, maybe it's exactly the right time.'

'Well, he would certainly approve of what you're doing here, that I do know.'

'I'm glad you think so.' Merry smiled wistfully. 'It's so strange when you think of all the unhappiness this house must have seen recently, and yet it's never felt like a sad house to me, particularly now.'

'Do you believe in ghosts, Merry?'

The question surprised her a little, although she supposed it was entirely logical, given what they were discussing. It was hard to put into words how she felt exactly. She didn't think she was a believer as such, but neither did she discount things out of hand. She did believe in instinct, or fate, and at times things had felt very right to Merry, and at others, very wrong.

'I wouldn't exactly call them ghosts,' she said, 'but I do think that sometimes strong emotions or energies can be left behind. Maybe that's all ghosts are, anyway, I don't know. I've been in places sometimes that I couldn't wait to get away from, the hairs have literally stood up on the back of my neck although I've never known why, and yet at other times I've felt profoundly peaceful.'

'And is this how you feel about Five Penny House?'

Merry tipped her head as if listening out for something. 'Kind of. Although actually now I feel energised by it. Maybe the time of year has something to do with it, but I can't wait to get the shop open and see how wonderful everything looks. Despite all the setbacks, I sense a real optimism about things. I don't think Christopher is haunting us, or anything like that, but like you say, I think perhaps he approves of what we're trying to do.'

Cora took another sip of her tea and nodded at Merry's words. 'You know, I always felt as if Christopher had become stuck, in life I mean. He was such a vibrant man when I first knew him, the whole family were, and you only have to look at his art to know that, but in later years he became so deeply buried in his grief that that part of him became lost, and he could never seem to find his way back to it. I think he meant to, he just didn't know how.'

'He must have been devastated by his wife and daughter dying. I can't imagine how you could ever recover from something like that.' Merry gave an involuntary shudder. 'I hope I never have to find out.'

'It was all so sudden, I suppose. That was the hardest thing,' added Cora. 'One minute Catherine was here, and the next she wasn't. Just a simple cold, and to start with she didn't even seem that poorly, but within days it had turned to pneumonia. She died in her sleep, two days later.'

Merry's eyes filled with tears, thoughts of the last few days rushing back to her. She raised a hand to her mouth in shock at the thought of what could so easily have been her devastation. Her heart went out to the man she'd never known but was beginning to understand a little better.

'Perhaps we should leave this for another day,' said Cora gently. 'It must be a hard thing for you to hear so soon after Robyn's illness.'

But Merry shook her head. 'No, I want to know. Robyn is fine now, but it makes me realise how lucky we are... and how much I want to bring Christopher and his family back to life, if only through his art. I can't understand why his family don't seem to want to remember him; that he should be forgotten is the very worst thing.'

Cora fixed Merry with a grateful smile. 'I think he would feel honoured to have someone do all this for him.'

Merry hoped so. She stole a glance at her watch, wondering how things were going in the village. It seemed ridiculous that in her head she should be asking for Christopher's help to keep them safe, but that's exactly what she was doing.

*

Freya looked at the sea of worried faces around her and wondered what else she could say to allay their fears. Apart from one younger couple, the occupants of all six houses that stood beside the village pond were elderly, and as she sat now in the lounge of the Apple Cart, she knew that the next half hour or so would be crucial in determining their future for the next few months.

The publican's wife brought over another tray of drinks for them all, motioning Freya to one side with her head.

'Bill has just gone over to help shift the last of their furniture,' she whispered, 'but he reckons they'll be cutting it fine. Your young man and his brother are getting a winch thingy set up, but goodness knows how they'll get the tree out; it's stuck fast right underneath the bridge he said, and the water's fair near to the top now.'

Freya tried to recall the strong warmth of Sam's arms around her as she had wished them luck, just ten minutes ago, but already it seemed like an age had passed. She had tried to apologise for their argument, but Sam silenced her with a fierce kiss and a violent shake of his head. None of that mattered now he said, but it did to her. She had watched as he hurried back to Tom and Stephen, the rain-laden wind battering her face and felt the hollow feeling in the pit of her stomach get bigger and bigger.

'It's not just the furniture, though, is it?' she replied, turning her attention back to the kind face in front of her. 'It's what damage the water will do to their homes. That lady in the green coat has lived there for over forty years she told me. Can you imagine how many memories are in that house? It doesn't bear thinking about.'

'No, that it doesn't,' came the reply. 'Let's just hope it doesn't come to that, and Daisy and all the others get to sleep soundly in their beds tonight.' She touched Freya's sleeve. 'Come and sit back down by the fire and have something to drink. We've a bit of a wait ahead of us yet.'

Freya had wanted to stay outside with the others, but both Tom and Sam were forceful in their insistence that she stay away. She knew there was nothing she could do to help, and although standing by helplessly looking on would be almost unbearable, at least she would feel that she was supporting them somehow. The fact that they wanted her out of the way was chivalrous, but she also recognised that it meant she would not be around to see what they were really getting up to, and how dangerous it was. And that scared her more than anything.

She made her way back to the table and sat down with a bright smile. The small Yorkshire terrier that belonged to the couple in the third house down jumped onto her lap and Freya gratefully curled her fingers into its warm fur.

Chapter Twenty-Eight

Stephen was adamant that he should be the one to go. It made more sense he argued. There was no way Tom was going, not with a wife and child, and Sam… Stephen didn't need to say her name for Sam to know who he was referring to. Stephen had no dependents, and it was also his idea.

'You know guys, none of us actually has to go,' said Tom. 'We've done the best we can for the folk whose houses will be in the firing line. What we should do is call the fire brigade and let them deal with it. I never intended that either one of you should volunteer to get the tree out.'

'No, but you and I both know that these people don't have that kind of time. I reckon we've got twenty minutes tops. The only tricky part is getting the tree strop over the branches, after that the winch will have no trouble.' Sam fixed his brother with a steely stare. 'And I'm going, Stephen. One, because like it or not I'm much fitter than you, and two, because the equipment is yours and you know how it works, you know the speed the winch goes and how to play the line out.'

The three men looked backwards and forward between each other, weighing up their options.

'So are we going to do this thing or not?' asked Sam abruptly. 'Only time is ticking on.' He saw the small acknowledgements of the other two. 'Jesus, Freya is going to kill me,' he said.

Stephen fished the Landy's keys out of his pocket. 'She may not have to,' he muttered, walking off towards the truck.

Tom put his hand on Sam's arm. 'No playing the hero, right. If it isn't going to work, we back off, agreed?' He waited until he saw the answer in Sam's eyes.

Moments later, Stephen had backed the Land Rover a little way down the road, angling the vehicle so that the winch cable would run in a straight line to the tree he was using as a winch block. He worked quickly and methodically, his instructions to Tom and Sam brief, but articulate. Once the cable had been set up around the winch block, it would run out to the fallen tree at a forty-five-degree angle to the first cable. It was the only safe way to ensure that the cable wound without becoming kinked and damaged. Stephen had only seen a steel cable under tension break once in his life and it was not something he wished to repeat.

Down by the riverbank, Sam shivered. He'd been wet through for what seemed like hours, barely noticing the cold, but now the thought of what was ahead loomed large, and he felt the wind keenly. He tried to shut out the roar in his ears as the noise made it hard to focus, but there was nowhere for it to go, and he gritted his teeth, taking deep calming breaths.

A shout further up the bank alerted him to the fact that Tom, his first anchor point, was ready. Shortly after, he felt Stephen guide the harness around his shoulders, and he took hold of the strap that would connect with the cable, testing the weight in his hands. There was only one branch of the tree that he would have any chance of passing the strap over, and his throw would need to be accurate if this was to work at all. He would be leaning as far out over the water as he could, but if he slipped… He focused his vision away from the churning surface of the water, and concentrated on the branch. The boiling mass of debris bouncing around the tree need only be of concern to him if he fell in, and if that happened, his only hope for survival would be if Stephen and Tom managed to haul him out quickly.

He looked back at Stephen to check that he was ready to begin, and slowly made his way further down the bank. His feet sank too quickly into the soft mud at the water's edge, and he panicked for a moment fearing he would slide even further. Then he realised that it was not traction he needed, but a place where his feet could anchor, where the squelchy surface would suck at his feet and render then immobile. He shifted position slightly, squaring himself to the task, and allowed his weight to sink his feet further into the mud. Behind him he could feel Stephen digging in.

'Let's do this now, Sam… I've got your back.'

Stephen's words floated past him for a moment before being lost to the wind, and he took a deep breath. Whatever had happened between them, Stephen was his brother, and would always have his back, he knew that.

He balanced the weighted end of the strap in his hand, narrowing his vision until he saw only the branch in front of him. He leaned forward, feeling the pull as both Stephen and Tom took his weight, and he stretched out, his body following the trajectory of his throw. A singular moment, a deep breath, and he threw, not daring to breathe until he saw the perfect arc of the strap as it dropped. It landed in a tangle of branches, but Sam had watched it clear the main branch and that's all that counted. He could see the metal shackle hanging clear, and his head sagged in relief. Now all he needed to do was pull the two ends together.

He heard Stephen's triumphant shout behind him, and knew that he would be trying to pass him the long pole, but his body was angled so far forward that reaching any distance behind him was impossible. He couldn't see either, and any movement of his head to either side simply blew a torrent of rain into his eyes. He made sure that the shackle on his end of the strap was fastened to his harness and threw his weight backwards; the last thing he needed now was to drop the bloody thing. His feet came free from the mud with a loud squelch and he sprawled on his back, chest heaving amongst the undergrowth.

His hands came into contact with cold metal as Stephen slithered down beside him, placing the pole where he could reach it.

'You're doing great, Sam, are you okay?'

'If I can get up again, yes,' he replied through gritted teeth, trying to find a place where he could dig his heels in and stand once more. He felt his brother's body against his back as Stephen tried to provide some leverage, and he pushed off blindly, hearing Stephen's grunt as he pushed down on his shoulder. Immediately, his feet tried to slide away from him as they found his original footholds, now made bigger by his exit and he sank quickly. Water filled his boots as he realised how much farther down he had slid, or was it that the water level had risen even in that short space of time? He stared out over the river, trying to focus on the tree branch and the strap he had thrown. He could still see the shackle, but it was now only inches above the water's surface. If he didn't loop it quickly, it would be underwater and there would be no way he could see it. He shouted back at Stephen, praying that he was ready to take his weight once more. He had no choice but to go for it now.

He fed the long metal pole through his hands, feeding the hooked end out into the wind, trying to counterbalance the movement and sway, which became worse the further out he reached. The muscles in his shoulders and arms began to burn with the effort of keeping the pole aloft, and his arms shook in response. He was now only inches from the dangling strap. He stopped for a moment, letting the pole drop slightly, trying to ease the ferocious ache that was building uncontrollably, and centred his weight over his legs, taking some of the strain through his body. He took a couple of deep breaths and raised the pole again, grunting with the effort. The shackle swayed tantalisingly close, but just as Sam thought he had it, the wind danced it away once more. The pain began to radiate down his back, and he knew he couldn't maintain this for much longer.

His vision began to blur, either from the rain or exhaustion he couldn't tell, but as the wind gusted once more, he thrust the pole forward with everything he had left. The hook passed clean through the hole of the shackle, the downward movement of the pole now totally beyond Sam's control. All he could do was hang on as it swung violently, pulling him forward. The last thing he saw before he hit the water was the hook still engaged with the strap.

The cold was absolute, dark and violent as he sank beneath the river, and he knew that the instinctive breath he had taken would not be enough; he hadn't the strength to hold it. An icy burning began to fill his body before the sudden sharp jolt of his harness bit against the rope that secured him to Stephen. For a moment, he was motionless, but as he felt the pull on his harness, he kicked out with the remaining strength he had. A sharp pain tore across one cheek, but his hands remained gripped to his precious cargo as he felt himself being pulled free of the water. He sucked in a huge breath, coughing, face down in the mud, as his brother hauled him over the tangle of roots at the water's edge, and he came to rest toppled against him. Stephens's grip was solid across his shoulders as if he would never let him go.

They lay there panting for a few seconds, hearing Tom's shouts above them, as he finally let go of the rope that had been holding them both and crashed down the bank to join them.

'I'm okay,' spluttered Sam. 'I'm okay...' And he held up a hand for them to let him speak. 'Now for God's sake get the bloody winch clipped onto this,' he spluttered, rolling onto his side with a groan so that they could see the pole still pinned under one side of his body, the webbing of the tree strop still miraculously attached to it, and coiled around one of Sam's legs.

Stephen scrambled up the bank, throwing himself onto the winch cable and pulling it down to clip through the shackle underneath Sam. Only then was Sam finally able to move, suddenly finding a sea of hands above him which reached down to help. He staggered up the bank, still clutching onto Tom; wet, cold, exhausted and muddy, and rather surprised to find his heart still beating.

'I need you all clear of the winch block,' shouted Stephen. 'To the left of it!'

The noise back up on the bridge was almost as loud as that down by the river, as the shouts from the gathered villagers mingled with the noise from the winch and the wind which still hurled rain across the road. Sam had had no idea there was anybody else here, and he was still trying to work out what exactly was going on when a warm body hit his and Freya's arms pulled him close. He allowed himself to be led clear of the winch cable, where he sat at the side of the road cradled in her lap. Her hair was fragrant against his cheek.

He felt rather than heard the cheer which went up as the tree freed itself from under the bridge and the water surged beneath it, the sudden freedom carrying the swell safely down to the part of the river where the flood plain would gently absorb it. The water level upstream would drop almost instantaneously. The houses were safe. Someone threw a blanket around them both, and Sam wearily closed his eyes.

Chapter Twenty-Nine

Merry leaped up the minute she heard the car pull up outside. Cora had gone to give Rupert his tea and the last half hour waiting on her own had been almost unbearable. Dusk was falling now and the light from inside made it hard to see, but be it friend or foe, she threw the door open anyway.

'God in heaven, what on earth has happened to you?'

Freya led the way, her hair still plastered to the side of her face, and one half of her wearing a coating of mud where Sam had leaned up against her. Sam himself trailed behind, finding it hard to walk with no shoes and a pair of trousers that he was struggling to keep up. The woolly fleece that the publican had lent him alongside the trousers was equally roomy, and he looked like a schoolboy in his brother's hand-me-down clothes.

'We're the advance party,' said Freya, with a grimace. 'Only because Sam is more in need of hot water than anyone else. A roaring fire and several brandies may have warmed him up a bit, but he could do with a bath, Merry, if that's all right. He's filthy and rather whiffy.'

Sam rolled his eyes, although even he could smell the river mud that clung to every part of him.

'What happened?' Merry asked, crossing automatically to flick the switch on the kettle. 'You look like you fell in.' And then her hand flew to her mouth as she realised that that's exactly what had happened and the seriousness of it all.

Freya filled her in while Sam leaned wearily against the door post.

'Tom and Stephen will be along in a bit. They're just helping to move one or two bits of furniture back downstairs for folk, although I have to say it's coming down a lot quicker than it went up.'

Merry put down the mug of tea that she had just made and went and stood in front of Sam. She looked straight into his face for a moment before plonking a huge kiss on his forehead and pulling him into a hug. 'We got up to damn stupid things when we were kids, Sam Henderson, but in all that time you have never, ever, done anything so bloody stupid as this. I could murder you.'

He smiled weakly. 'Join the queue,' he muttered, throwing a rueful glance at Freya, who glared at him.

'May I go and run a bath, Merry, before the others get back? They'll both be cold and wet as well.'

'And hungry too no doubt,' tutted Merry, releasing her hold on Sam. 'Shall I make some bacon sandwiches, do you think? Or toast and jam, dripping in butter, how about that?' She saw Sam's eyes light up at the thought of it. 'Go on, go up, and I'll bring it along in a few minutes.'

*

Freya added a good dollop of Merry's scented bubble bath to the steaming water, and watched as it swirled around.

'This will make you smell like a girl, which is no more than you deserve,' she said, leaning over to test the water with her hand.

Sam had already removed all his clothes and stood on the bath mat stark naked. Little bits of dried mud had fallen from his underwear and lay like ash beside him. He trembled slightly, whether from cold or emotion, Freya couldn't tell.

'I mean, it's not as if you're a total hero for saving the day, is it? Or that eleven people, three cats and one dog all have a home to go to now because of you.' She tested the temperature of the water again. 'Go on, you can hop in now,' she added, hands on hips.

She watched as Sam gave a lopsided smile, still not sure how much metaphorical hot water he was in.

'It wasn't just me,' he offered, through lowered lashes.

'No, I know it wasn't... you're all as bad as each other.'

He gingerly put one leg over the side of the bath, and then the other, lowering himself rather jerkily until he was sitting, practically submerged. Only then did she see the strain begin to leave his body, his muscles stop fighting and begin to relax. Her bottom lip began to tremble.

She waited until he had settled himself, facing her, before gently stretching out to touch the gash on his cheek. He winced slightly as her fingers made contact.

'Where does it hurt?' she asked, her face pulled tight with emotion.

'Pretty much every bloody where,' he replied, his features contorting as he shifted slightly, trying to get comfortable.

Freya closed her eyes and swallowed. 'Please, please promise me you will never do anything like that again,' she whispered, laying a trail of bubbles across his chest with the sponge.

Sam's eyes were dark in her shadow. 'I'm sorry,' he whispered, guilt wrought large across his face, the enormity of what had happened that afternoon beginning to take its toll. 'It seemed like the only thing we could do at the time, but I probably wasn't thinking straight... I seem to be good at acting like an idiot just lately.' He let his eyes rest on hers for a moment. 'I'd never do anything to hurt you, Freya, I hope you know that.'

'I know,' she whispered back. 'I know it was all well intentioned,' she added, and they both knew their conversation had gone way beyond the events of the afternoon. She moved the sponge a little lower, in soothing circles. 'I love you,' she said.

Sam lifted a hand half-heartedly. 'Sorry, Freya, but I can barely raise a smile,' he said, misreading her intentions.

She gave a low laugh. 'You muppet.' She smiled fondly. 'Just lie there and close your eyes.'

'I love you, Freya,' he said, and then did as he was told.

She scooped up a pile of bubbles and with the gentlest of touches began to soap every inch of his skin, finally washing the day clean from his body.

Chapter Thirty

Stephen licked his lips, and took a huge gulp of tea, replacing the mug on the table with a satisfied sigh. He looked down at the empty plate in front of him, where not a trace of the enormous breakfast he had just eaten remained.

'Merry, that was superb, thank you. And just what the doctor ordered.' He watched her at the stove where three frying pans were currently on the go. She was in her element.

She turned to face him, brandishing a pair of tongs. 'Jolly good. Now be a love and take that lot through to the dining room for me, can you?' She nodded towards the tray on the table, piled high with an assortment of mugs, two plates of biscuits and an enormous teapot. 'Can't keep the troops waiting.'

Stephen did as he was told and Merry eyed her watch once more, wondering how long her husband was likely to be. She couldn't wait to see the smile on his face when he returned to the house. He was in for such a surprise. She turned her attention back to the frying pan nearest to her, where six rashers of bacon were crisping nicely. Freya and Sam had better hurry up or she'd be banging on their bedroom door.

She was just turning out three perfectly fried eggs when Sam shuffled in, Freya hot on his heels, a solicitous arm on his back.

'Ah,' she winced. 'Yesterday catching up with you, is it?'

Sam groaned. 'Don't. I can hardly move this morning. Freya had to put my bloody socks on for me.'

Freya nodded brightly, confirming his words. 'Sad, but true. I've told him not to get used to being waited on hand and foot, mind. It's only for the next day or so, while he still has hero status.' She smiled fondly at his stooped figure as he gingerly lowered himself into a chair.

'Well then, maybe this lot will make you feel a little more human,' said Merry, placing an enormous plateful of food in front of him, similar to the one that Stephen had just demolished.

Freya sat down beside Sam. 'Thanks Merry,' she said, accepting her breakfast with a grin. 'This is fantastic; I hadn't realised quite how hungry I was until I began to smell this lot from upstairs. It was very good of you to let us all stay over.'

Merry simply waved her tongs in acknowledgement. 'Nonsense,' she said. 'It's the least we could do.' She looked down at her own breakfast. 'And this is just like the old days; cooking for the masses. I've rather enjoyed it, to be honest, and quite relieved to know I can still do it.'

Freya raised an eyebrow. 'Another opportunity to be explored perhaps... Five Penny House B&B?' Merry said nothing, but Freya knew her too well to expect an answer. 'Where's Tom anyway?' she asked instead.

Merry speared a mushroom. 'He's just popped into the village to see how things are this morning,' she said, blushing a little. '... And if I'm honest to go and shake a few hands. Cora came to see us first thing and apparently news of yesterday's events has spread far and wide. There isn't a soul round here who doesn't know what you've all done for the village.' She eyed Sam warmly. 'So I'm afraid you're going to have to get used to being the centre of attention for a while.'

Sam grimaced, but continued to eat steadily. He swallowed and looked around him. 'So where's Stephen? He hasn't gone home, his truck is still outside.'

'No, he's still here. He's just gone to take some tea to our guests. I expect he's still nattering.'

Sam looked about him. 'Guests?' he said.

She was about to reply when Freya cut across her. 'My God, where did that come from?'

'Quite something, isn't it?' replied Merry, without looking up. She knew exactly what Freya was referring to.

'It's beautiful. But it wasn't here yesterday surely? I would have noticed it.'

'No, you're right. Cora brought it round this morning.' She laid her knife and fork down on her plate. 'She thought that now might be the perfect time to return it, even though of course, strictly speaking it belongs to her.'

Freya swung her chair round a little so that she could get a better look at the painting which was propped up against the far wall. 'Is it who I think it is?'

A huge smile crossed Merry's face. 'Yes,' she said simply. 'The Marchmont family. Christopher, his wife, Marina, and their daughter, Catherine.'

'But, it looks like it was painted yesterday.'

'I know, that's the most remarkable thing, isn't it? I think they're pleased to be home.'

Sam put down his own fork and looked at the oil painting which had so caught Freya's eye: a portrait of two women, and a man, a little behind, his arms around them both. Happiness shone out of their faces, the paint gleaming as if lit from within.

'Is that your painter?' he asked, remembering some of the conversations that Freya had relayed to him.

'One and the same,' nodded Merry. 'It hasn't hung in this house for a very long time. Cora said Christopher couldn't bear to look at it after they died, and he removed it to an upstairs room where it stayed in the back of a wardrobe. It's so sad.'

'So how did Cora get hold of it? I don't understand,' asked Freya.

Merry gazed at the painting, a soft expression on her face. 'Because he could never truly bear to be parted from it, even in death. I think he understood that after he was gone no one would care for it, least of all his rather grasping relatives, and so he left it to Cora in his will. It's hung in her dining room ever since, waiting for the time, she said, until she could return it to its rightful place.'

Freya gasped, her eyes unexpectedly filling with tears. 'Oh, that's beautiful, Merry.' She sighed, her hand lying over her heart. 'You will put it up, won't you?'

'Oh yes,' said her friend softly. 'I know just the place.'

Sam looked between the two women, both of whom he had known since childhood, both the truest of friends, and now one a woman he loved with all his heart. He looked back at the painting, recognising the feeling that shone from Christopher's eyes, and he smiled.

'Well, you'll be pleased to know that the house is no longer cursed.'

All three looked up suddenly at the intrusion into their thoughts as Tom strode into the kitchen. His face was wide with delight. 'It's official apparently, according to the landlord of the Apple Cart. Seeing as how we all saved the village, the curse has been lifted. What do you think of that?'

Merry looked up at her husband, noticing the expression on his face. Her laughter rang out loud around the kitchen. 'I should think so too.' She giggled. 'Although that's not all,' she added. 'We have a few guests who'd like a word with you...'

'Yeah, what's with all the vans outside? Where did they come from?'

'Well, the blue van belongs to the landlord's brother-in-law, who's a builder as it happens. The green van belongs to his mate, a plumber, and the white van to his mate's brother who's an electrician. Apparently, they'd heard of the issues with getting this place ready, and in honour of you helping to save the village from flooding, they wondered if you might be needing a hand with anything?' She grinned. 'So, I've plied them with tea and biscuits.' She winked at Sam. 'They're in the dining room; ready when you are.'

Tom snatched the last chunk of sausage from his wife's plate. 'Well then, I best not keep them waiting any longer, had I?' And with that he strode back out.

Merry smiled to herself; there was a man on a mission if ever she saw one. She looked back at Sam, a contented sigh escaping her. 'And have I managed to fill you up?' she asked, 'or do you need even more breakfast?'

Sam patted his stomach. 'Well, I didn't think I would manage that, but I surprised myself actually.' He glanced towards Freya. 'So thank you, Merry, but we really should be getting out of your hair. Now that the rain has stopped, I think we need to go and see what sort of a crop we're going to be left with this year.' He passed a weary hand over his face, tired, but resolute in the face of what he needed to do next. 'And when we've done that, I need to focus on what's really important at Appleyard and stop being such a prat. No more fanciful stuff, just concentrate on what we're good at, which is producing beautiful fruit, our way, and no one else's.' He leaned across the table and took hold of Freya's hand. He opened his mouth to carry on, but Freya forestalled him.

'Actually, I've been thinking about that,' she said, holding Sam's look and returning the pressure on his hand. 'I'm not sure it's fair to carry on as we are, Sam—' She caught sight of the expression on his face and quickly laid her other hand over his. 'What I mean is that it was unfair to think that you could move into Appleyard and simply carry on as if your life before never existed. It's too big a leap, and it's far too close to home having Stephen on our doorstep doing exactly what we do. There have to be changes if we're all going to get along. I wanted everything at Appleyard to be as it always had been, but I was wrong, Sam.' She took a deep breath. 'It's time for things to change, to make Appleyard ours, not mine with you just having to slot into the way I want things. You're right when you said we should do what we're good at. We've always been about making beautiful fruit, about taste above all else, so what do you say we stop producing cider and do something different instead?'

Sam sat up straighter in his chair. 'Like what exactly?' he asked, a little cautiously.

'Well, Merry and Tom have a shop opening soon that is going to stock gourmet produce… handmade, local, gourmet produce… Why don't we start making juices instead? Beautiful single variety pressed juices, clever blends, so there's something for every palate? Cordials, old-fashioned apple curds?'

Freya let out her breath bit by bit as she watched the slow smile start to gather on Sam's face, the corners of his mouth begin to twitch, and the light flare in his unusual green eyes.

'I think that's an absolutely bloody fantastic idea!' He turned to look at Merry for confirmation. 'Freya Sherbourne, you are without a doubt, one of the most amazing women I have ever known.' He gave Merry an answering nod before turning back to Freya, his eyes soft. 'Thank you,' he said simply.

A small noise behind him made him turn and his face immediately fell.

'I couldn't agree with you more,' said Stephen, coming into the room. 'She is an amazing woman.' He came up behind Freya and placed both hands on her shoulders, dipping briefly to kiss her cheek. 'And one who talks an awful lot of sense too,' he added as he sat down. 'In fact, she's really very eloquent when she gets going, isn't that right, Freya? She certainly told me a few home truths.'

He let his words hang in the air for a few moments, knowing that his silence was making Sam feel even more uncomfortable, but knowing too how important it was that he got this right. He turned his attention full on his brother.

'I want to apologise, Sam,' he said. 'I know I've been a complete pig-headed bastard, for years in fact, not just recently, although my latest outburst was exceptional, even for me. You came to offer your help, although why you think I deserve it is beyond me, but still you did, and all I could do was throw it back in your face.' He paused to push the hair out of his eyes. 'You see I was scared of what I was going to do. For years I've belittled you, made things difficult for you, whilst all the time letting you take care of all the business... I couldn't help overhearing what Freya suggested just now and I think it's a brilliant idea, not because it's one less competitor for Braeburn, but because I want you to have something, for yourself, like Freya said, something that has nothing to do with me.' He offered his hand for Sam to shake. 'The only thing is,' he added ruefully, 'that I wondered whether I might ask for your help first, just to get me on my way. I haven't got a bloody clue what I'm doing, and you're the expert after all.'

Sam stared at his brother, his mouth hanging open. He took the proffered hand and swallowed hard.

'Well,' said Merry brightly, clearing her throat and picking up the plates from the table. 'I can't believe the weather this morning. There's no trace of yesterday's storm. It's going to be the most beautiful day.'

Chapter Thirty-One

Six Weeks Later

Freya wasn't sure which were brighter; the colours in the room, or Merry's and Tom's smiles as they posed for the photographer. He, like everyone else seemed stunned by the transformation of the shop he was standing in, not simply because the array of goods on offer looked so inviting, but because, in all his thirty-two years of life he had never been inside a village shop that looked the way this one did.

In fact, Merry was the only one who wasn't surprised by the way things had turned out. As every cabinet had been moved into place, every display case installed, every picture hung on the wall, hers had not been the only guiding hand, of that she was absolutely convinced. Even Tom had stopped making suggestions, seeing the resolute look on his wife's face and the day-by-day transformation she was wreaking. She knew exactly what she was doing, and bit by bit the shop grew around her.

First to be installed were the cupboards they had found all those weeks ago, dusted off, and with glass fronts protecting their contents, but otherwise completely untouched from the last time they had appeared in this shop – a time before Merry and Tom were even born. They were a perfect time capsule, and having been given pride of place on the wall facing whoever entered, they were as much a talking point as the vibrant art on the walls, or the reclaimed and renovated furniture which offered up whatever the locals could possibly need.

A selection of wooden tables running the length of the room held baskets packed with local produce. Jersey Royals jostled for space with fresh young carrots, and golden loaves of bread that brought the memory of the cornfields with them. Desk drawers were pulled open and filled with an array of tins and packets, and huge bookcases leaned against the walls filled with packets of flour and sugar and the biggest eggs that Freya had ever seen. A sign on a far wall pointed the way to Gorgeous Gifts and Gourmet Goodies, a space to invite and captivate, where many a weak-willed moment would occur as goods found their way into baskets.

And pride of place, carefully arranged on every inch of spare wall space were all of Christopher's art works; bold and brilliant, an exuberance of colour and joy.

Merry stood behind the till now, her husband just behind her as they chatted to the last customers of the day. The last of a very long line in fact, of which many would soon become friends. She knew that today they had been a curiosity, perhaps tomorrow too, but soon in the very near future, their customers would be back, by routine, out of necessity, or simply because The Five Penny Shop was a part of their community, and it belonged to them now.

With a final warm goodbye and a thank you, Merry turned slightly to acknowledge Cora, waiting patiently with Robyn. She gave a nod to the portrait behind her. Hung on a pale lemon wall, a portrait of a man, and his wife and daughter, their beaming smiles radiating out across the space and returned by all who gazed on them.

'So what do you think now, Cora? Have we done well?'

'Oh, I reckon so. I think Christopher would be very proud, and rather honoured too.'

Merry surveyed her friend for a moment.

'Then I'm glad. But not just because I hope that Christopher and his family will never be forgotten, but because at times I did wonder if I wasn't just the teensiest bit mad. It's only when I see all this that it makes sense, to me anyway. It feels like it was meant to be.'

'Then that's exactly what it is. You know this could have been such a difficult time for you and your family. A new house, a new business, a new baby. It could so easily have overwhelmed you, and I think it's something most people wouldn't be brave enough even to try. I think that perhaps Christopher wanted you to make a go of things too, and his story became… an encouragement if you like.'

Merry cocked her head to one side.

'How so?'

Cora fiddled with the rattle on Robyn's pushchair. 'Well, Christopher became so overwhelmed by his grief that he closed the doors to everything else in his life; he lost his fight and his spirit; he forgot how to chase the dreams he had as a younger man. He, more than anyone perhaps, understood how hard life can be sometimes; maybe he wanted to remind you that with all that happens in our lives, we must remember to live.'

She smiled up at the portrait. 'And now you've brought him and his family back to life too, well their memory at least. I know they're dead, Merry, but there's a part of me that wonders if that makes no difference. I keep expecting them all to come walking back through the door, smiles on their faces, laughing like they always were.'

Merry looked up into the happy faces on the wall and then back down to her husband and friends who were deep in conversation. 'I know exactly what you mean, Cora. Life really is what we make it, isn't it, and right now, I can't think of a better one.'

From their space on the wall, overlooking their new home, Marina and Catherine seemed to approve. If she didn't know better, Merry could swear their smiles were just that little bit brighter than usual.

SUMMER

Chapter Thirty-Two

Jude Middleton was a very lucky man. He was also terrified of being poor. This fear, given to him by his father, and which had stalked him since his teenage years, now resonated through every part of his being as his powerful car whispered through the grimy streets and away from the city. How did people live like this? In dirty streets, and dirty houses, the cigarettes and booze they fed on the only things that got them through the day. These props were a necessity, he could see that, but they destroyed so much, used up too much of their meagre amount of money, and left nothing good behind, least of all hope.

It made him shudder to think about it, but the city was a necessary evil; from the over-air-conditioned and sterile offices, to the cheaply made clothes of the arrogant young go-getters he met with; from the smell of the traffic fumes to the overpowering perfumes worn as part of a uniform. But whilst they were necessary, they were also forgettable, and Jude had been trained in the art of self-preservation for years. As the miles disappeared beneath his tyres, Jude shed their layers from his skin as a snake might. Within half an hour, it was all a distant memory.

The nights were beautifully light now and the scent from the stocks along the edge of the house rose up to greet him as he made his way up the path to his front door. A child's bicycle lay abandoned on the front lawn, ready to be picked up again tomorrow once school had ended for the day. The trailing white rose which burgeoned over the porch, had stems heavy in bloom, and their heads brushed his as he placed his key in the lock.

Willow was waiting for him in the hallway, her eyes shiny at seeing him, just as they always were. She had on another of her wafty dresses (as Jude referred to them); it suited her, with her long, wavy blonde hair and slight figure, her bare feet covered by its trailing hem on the thick carpet. He dropped his bag by the door and gathered his wife into his arms, breathing in the smell of orange blossom which she always brought with her. She slipped her hand into his and led him towards the kitchen.

As always, the table and work surfaces were a jumble of school bags and books, toys, hair slides, and the general detritus of a busy day of childhood. It was the same every day, and Jude felt reassured by their presence. The girls were munching their way through fish finger sandwiches by the look of things; great doorsteps of homemade wholemeal bread, dripping with butter. His stomach rumbled at the thought of what Willow might have made for his own supper, the unsatisfactory steak he had eaten at lunchtime having done nothing to appease his appetite.

He stood in the doorway for a minute, anticipating one of his favourite times of day, and sure enough a few seconds later Beth spied him, giving her customary squeal. In an instant, both girls had released themselves from the table and rushed to his side.

'Daddy!' they choroused.

He swooped each of them up in turn, swinging them sideways and planting a trail of kisses across their wriggling stomachs.

'Do you know I think you've got even more beautiful during the day? Now how can that have happened?' he asked, laughing.

Amy, the eldest by eleven and a half minutes and far more forthright than her sister, gave a giggle. 'Don't be silly, Daddy,' she declared. 'That's impossible.' She smiled up at him through her long fair lashes. They were both so like their mother.

Willow came and took his jacket from him, folding it over her arm as she collected a glass from the cupboard and placed it on the table.

'Come and sit down, and I'll pour you some wine. Did it all go as planned?'

Jude thought of the meeting earlier that day, a meeting that had gone well on the way to sealing probably the biggest deal of his life. He wasn't ready to share the details yet, though, not when so much was at stake. His freedom from Andrew would be the biggest prize, but also the hardest won, and he would need to tread carefully if he was ever to pull it off.

'Well, there are still one or two finer points to be agreed on, but I'd say, yes, it went very well.' He smiled at Willow, wondering what else she would expect him to say. He didn't want to lie, but perhaps under the circumstances... 'Andrew was very pleased at any rate,' he added, watching her face carefully. He knew she didn't have much time for her father-in-law, believing him materialistic and callous.

'Then that sounds like it could be the perfect end to the week, I'm so pleased.' She reached into the fridge and took out a bottle of chilled wine, pouring him a glass before leaning down and kissing the top of his head. 'Supper will be half an hour yet, if you want to grab a shower. You must feel horrible after a day in the city.'

Jude nodded, and glugged back a large swallow of wine. He grimaced. 'God, this is revolting,' he said, the vinegary taste hitting the back of his mouth. 'What is it?'

Willow turned back to the fridge and waved an airy hand. 'White wine, that's all I know.' She grinned. 'It was on offer.' She took out the bottle and handed it to him. 'Isn't it any good?'

Jude shook his head affectionately. 'One day,' he admonished her, 'I will get you to appreciate the finer points of wine's great beauty. Until then, please don't buy rubbish. We have a cellar full of the good stuff, so just choose one of them. We don't need to scrimp and save.' He took the bottle from her and stuck it back in the fridge.

He pulled Willow towards him and kissed her, at first only intending for it to be a brief touch of the lips, but she smelled so good and his desire began to rise. It was only when there was a loud chorus of 'euww' from the girls that he pulled away, laughing.

'Isn't it time these rascals went to bed anyway?'

'We might not always be able to afford nice things,' Willow said.

Jude thought of the conversations that had ranged back and forth this afternoon. In a few weeks, his signature would be on the bottom of the papers that were being drawn up, and then… maybe she had a point, after all. The deal would secure him a good deal of money initially, but after that their life would most definitely have to change. He reminded himself that this was what he wanted, but old habits die hard, and he wasn't sure if he was ready for the sacrifice. But Willow must never see the doubt on his face, so he quickly shrugged it away. He flicked a playful finger against the end of her nose, and kissed it. 'What are we going to do with your mummy?' he said to the girls. 'Tell her to behave herself.'

Willow merely smiled, thinking of the little nest egg that her prudent housekeeping had saved her, and she turned back to the girls.

'Come on now scamps, daddy's right, it's time you were getting sorted. Finish your sandwiches, and then it's time for your bath. If you're quick, we'll have time for an extra couple of chapters of *Winnie the Witch*.'

Both girls looked imploringly at her, just as she knew they would. 'But no staying up tonight, mind. I know it's Friday, but it's our big day tomorrow, don't forget.'

'Strawberries!' shouted Beth. 'Yummy!' And she grabbed Amy's hand, practically dragging her from the table.

The light was finally leaving the day now, but the sky was still clear and wide. The first and brightest stars were beginning to appear, and Willow hoped that tomorrow would stay fine. The forecast was good; like today, blue skies, but not too hot, and no rain, that was the main thing. She pulled the bedroom curtains closed and went to turn on the shower, the pale glow of the lamp beside her bed illuminating the curve of her skin as she walked.

She was aware that Jude had been watching her from the bed. He lay fully clothed; his city suit shed, and now relaxed in jeans and a T-shirt. She knew he'd join her in a few minutes, for what would be the perfect end to the day, and a languid smile passed over her face as she thought about soap sliding over skin. Willow inhaled the fragrant steam that billowed around her with the fresh scent of lemons and shivered in anticipation of his touch. She was already lost in the sensation when she felt Jude behind her, his naked body padding soundlessly into the wet room, and a small sigh escaped her as she felt his hand slip across her stomach and over one breast. She turned, moving her own hands.

It must have been towards three in the morning when she awoke. A slight shift in her consciousness that alerted her to the fact that Jude was no longer beside her. But even as she registered his absence from the bed, she knew that this was not the only reason for her wakefulness. Fleeting images came back at her, still veiled in a fug of sleep, yet unpleasant enough to wake her. She tried to grasp at them, but the wisps of memory disappeared. A moment later, she heard the toilet flush and as Jude returned to wrap his warm limbs around her back, she smiled to herself. There was much to do tomorrow, and finally, time to start putting into place the plans that she had begun to make a few weeks ago. Plans, in fact, that had come to her during another night of restless sleep plagued by strange dreams but plans which were so exciting that she now couldn't wait for the morning. As her thoughts drifted towards the recipes in grandma Gilly's notebook, she slept, the troubling images she had seen in her sleep all but forgotten.

Chapter Thirty-Three

It was her art teacher who once told Willow that no sky could ever be this blue. She hadn't believed him then, and today was confirmation of that. The colour was unbroken, stretching out into the cloudless sky until it reached the horizon, only then paling slightly. The air was soft – not harsh with the fierce heat of late summer, but a gentle pervasive warmth that made her skin smile.

The fields were ready, and in a few moments, Willow too would be all set. She just needed to post one more tweet and then she could do no more. But people would come, of that she was sure; they always did. She collected the bottles of water and snacks she had prepared and, snatching up her sun hat on the way out, she walked down the hallway. She paused for a moment by the back door, looking towards the room on her right as if weighing something up, and then with a glance at her watch, she pushed open the door.

Her grandma's old notebook was still on the table where she had left it yesterday, and she reached for it now, running her fingers across the cracked surface, its yellowed pages spilling out from the confines of the navy-blue cover. The little silver moon on the top right-hand corner of the cover flashed in the sunlight, and Willow smiled. She needed no further testament that her actions were the right ones. She closed the door behind her softly, and walked out of the house and down the path, her fingers brushing the tips of the lavender that grew there as she went. She skirted around the apple trees and made her way to the gate which stood in the corner of the garden. She smiled and took a deep breath, whispering a thank you to the sun. The strawberries were waiting.

Even this early in the morning, there were a few pickers around. They didn't officially open for another half an hour, but no one was ever turned away. The folks who came this early usually picked with a vengeance. They were not the spur-of-the-moment afternoon crowd looking for a punnet of delicious fruit to have with their tea, nor were they families revelling in a day in the sun. They had purpose these early birds; the whole day ahead of them, and by sundown, jar after jar would be filled with sweet sticky jam.

Jude had already opened the wide gates into the car park and set out the signs directing people where to go. He now stood beside their little wooden shop with his back to her, looking up the slight slope of the field, watching Amy and Beth ahead of him. They were in good hands, thought Willow. Peter, their student here for the summer doted on the girls and wouldn't let them out of his sight. Their enthusiasm for picking would wane in the weeks to come, but today, on their first day of opening, they were just as excited as she was.

She sidled up behind Jude, planting a kiss on the nape of his neck, the pale skin as yet uncoloured by the sun. All that would change soon, even though hats were a must, as was sunscreen, long days in the fresh air would soon bring a golden glow to them all.

'All set, Captain?' He grinned.

Willow smiled at his greeting. It was how he always addressed her here. Middleton Estates might own all this land, but Willow had never had anything to do with the day-to-day running of their company; that was Jude's domain. These fields, though, were hers to command.

'All set,' she replied, with a smile of her own.

'So where would you like me, Sir?' he asked, doffing an imaginary cap. 'I can pick, or I can man the barricades?'

Willow glanced at her watch. 'Actually, could you pick for me? I'd like to stay here for a bit, you know, to catch up with folk for a while.'

'Get the gossip more like,' argued Jude benignly. 'I know what you're like.' He motioned with his head towards the few women who were steadily picking fruit.

'Humour me,' she said. 'I don't get that many opportunities. Besides which, Freya is going to pop over in a bit. We've a few things to talk about.'

Jude narrowed his eyes. 'Oh ay. I heard they were having a bit of a change of direction at Appleyard. That wouldn't be what you're planning to discuss, would it?'

'It might be.' Willow grinned, laying a finger along the side of her nose. 'That and to see how things with Sam are working out.'

Jude rolled his eyes. 'Right, well, I'm definitely off then if it's going to be all soppy girl talk.' He picked up a stack of empty punnets from the table beside the shop doorway and threaded them up his arm. 'Enjoy your natter.' He plonked a kiss on her lips and set off up the field.

Willow watched him go, the soft linen of his summer 'uniform' sitting comfortably on his lithe body as he moved easily across the ground. God he was gorgeous.

At times, manning the barricades was a pretty apt description of Willow's morning as her customers jostled for room in the shop. But it was all good-natured, as people came to pay for their fruit or to collect punnets in readiness for picking. Many stayed to talk, light-hearted chatter with their neighbours, or with Willow herself, and a few, feeling weak-willed, succumbed to one of Willow's tempting cakes as well. And throughout it all, the summery smell of strawberries pervaded the air, pungent and sweet, with their heady invitation to be eaten, fingers and lips stained red with their juice. If Willow could bottle the smell and sell it, she'd do that too.

After a couple of hours, the initial swell of opening day visitors calmed and returned to the more usual steady movement, and suddenly there was Freya, grinning at Willow like a Cheshire cat.

'Oh, I haven't seen you in such a long time,' she cried. 'Much too long!'

'It has been,' agreed Freya. 'We mustn't ever let it get so long again. I don't even know how it happened.'

Willow stood back to get a better look at her friend, with her gleaming chestnut curls and wide green eyes. She wore an air of contentedness that brought a glow to her cheeks and a softness to her face. 'Life is good then,' she surmised.

'Oh, life is very good,' gushed Freya in reply. 'Very good indeed. Hard work, mind...'

'But since when has that ever stopped you?'

'I know... but it's different now somehow, you know?'

Willow giggled. 'Oh, I do know, Freya Sherbourne. It's coming off you in waves. Love. That's what it is, pure and simple.'

Freya blushed. 'Is it that obvious?' She grinned. She stood back to let a customer pass by. 'And what about you? You look great too, and busy by the look of things.'

'Oh, always,' she replied. 'And about to get busier if I have my way.'

'Which knowing you, you will.' Freya laughed. 'So, come on then, tell me what you're up to. I know you've got something up your sleeve, you sounded really mysterious on the phone.'

'Well, that rather depends on whether what I've heard is true...' Willow trailed off, feeling a little guilty that she hadn't seen her friend for a couple of months and now here she was about to spring a proposition on her.

She was just about to continue when Jude appeared, carrying half a dozen more punnets full to the brim with strawberries. He took off his hat, and came over to kiss Freya.

'You look well,' he commented, catching Willow's eye. He stood back for a moment, looking between the two women. 'Oh, I'm sorry,' he directed at Freya, 'I don't think you two have met, have you? Can I introduce my wife, the slave driver?'

'Oh, ha bloody ha,' muttered Willow.

Freya giggled. 'Get on with you, Jude, you love it, you know you do… you might want to watch the staff, though, Willow, this chap seems to have eaten half your stock.'

It was true, Jude's shirt had a very obvious dribble of strawberry juice down the front.

Jude pulled a face. 'I'm a walking advertisement for the deliciousness of the crop, that's all.' He looked back at Freya. 'I don't even get paid…'

'My heart bleeds for you,' said Freya, miming playing the strings of a violin.

'Actually Jude, now that you're here, would you mind watching the shop for a minute? I just want to have a chat with Freya, you know, lovey dovey girly stuff, and I thought we could pop back to the house for half an hour or so… I'll bring some drinks out afterwards.'

Jude's smile was warm. 'Of course it's okay. Go on, I'll take over here.' He kissed Freya's cheek again. 'If I don't get to see you later, say hi to Sam for me. Tell him to give me a ring, it's about time we had a pint together.'

Freya nodded as Willow took her arm. She waited for a few moments until they were well clear of the shop before speaking again.

'What on earth was all that *wanting to talk about lovey dovey stuff* back there? That's not the impression you gave me on the phone.' She narrowed her eyes. 'What are you up to?'

They'd reached the garden gate now, and Freya paused while Willow fiddled with the catch. 'Only that I know it's a subject pretty much guaranteed to have the menfolk backing away in droves. I want to show you something, but strictly on the QT for now.'

'Okay…' said Freya slowly, following Willow up the path.

Once inside, Willow led the way back into the kitchen.

'Look, let's grab a drink and I'll explain.' She reached into the fridge and took out a glass jug decorated with daisies.

'Is elderflower okay?' she asked.

Freya nodded enthusiastically, looking rather pleased.

Once they each had a glass, Willow beckoned Freya back down the hallway, leading her into the room she had been musing in earlier. It was warm inside – a bit tired and musty, as though it had been shut up for too long. Apart from a sink, a long pine trestle table which held her grandmother's notebook, two chairs and a series of shelves running the length of one wall, it was completely empty.

Freya's eyebrows were raised. 'That's quite a transformation,' she said. 'When I last saw this room, it was full to the brim with coats, boots and toys. When did you do all this?'

'A couple of weeks ago. Three actually.'

Freya looked up, concern crossing her face. 'You gonna tell me why?' she asked softly, taking a seat at the table. Willow followed suit.

'I don't think I've ever actually shown you this,' she said, and pushed the notebook across the table towards Freya, where it sat looking suspiciously like a can of worms.

Freya stared at it.

'I'll explain. I know you all thought I was weird when we were kids, especially Stephen—'

'Stephen thought everyone was weird…'

Willow smiled at the memory of Sam's brother. 'Yes, maybe. But we all joked about it, me included. I know my mum was different from everyone else's, but do you remember what she said just after you and Sam, well, you know, the Stephen thing.'

'You can say it you know, Willow. After I dumped Sam, ran off with his brother and then jilted him at the altar,' said Freya. 'I vaguely remember it. Your mum said everything would come right in the end and that I'd get Sam back again one day. But everybody told me that, Willow; they were just trying to make me feel better. No one was more surprised than me when it actually happened…' She looked down at the notebook and then back up at Willow. 'Actually, thinking about it, *you* weren't that surprised when I told you what happened at Christmas…'

Willow picked up the book and eased off the tie that was holding it closed. She took out an envelope tucked between the pages and held it out to Freya.

'Here it is in black and white,' she said. 'Mum sent me this letter at university, just after your wedding should have taken place. The first page is general chit chat and goings-on in the village etcetera, but you might want to read the second page.'

Freya took the letter, looking bemused. It was a long time ago, after all. She took out the thin white sheets and began to read.

… I saw Freya in the village shop only yesterday, and she looked awful, poor love. It was a brave thing to do, though; Jenny and Sarah were in there, clearly talking about her. They stopped of course when they saw her, but it was so obvious. I wanted to talk to her then to tell her that things would be okay, but by the time I'd paid for my things, she'd gone. She must have legged it pretty quick, and who can blame her. Anyway, please tell her next time you see her, my dream was very explicit. It will take a long time, years even, but she was definitely with Sam, and it was definitely Christmas time, I could smell the pine from the tree like it was in the room with me. There was someone else there too, someone with black curly hair, but I couldn't see any more…

Freya looked up in shock.

'From what you told me that was pretty much how it happened, wasn't it?' asked Willow.

Freya nodded mutely. 'So Jessie knew,' she continued. 'She actually knew…'

Willow leaned over to touch Freya's hand. 'There were other things of course, things I never told you about back then; you all thought I was weird enough. I don't blame you for not believing me, but to me she was just my mum.'

'And just like her own mum I'm guessing?' Freya said, eyeing the notebook still in Willow's hands. 'So that's granny Gilly's, is it? Her book of spells.'

Willow looked at the ceiling. 'I know it sounds far-fetched, but you should see what's in here, Freya. Some amazing recipes apart from anything else, which is one of the reasons why I wanted to talk to you. But aside from that there are some… well, let's just call them remedies, shall we?'

Freya stayed silent for a moment, weighing up what she'd just been told. 'So why am I here?' she asked eventually.

Willow inhaled deeply, letting her breath out in a slow, controlled movement.

'Because I've had a few weird dreams of my own lately, nothing that momentous, but they've got me thinking about what we do here, or rather the potential for what we might do here. Once I started to think about it, I couldn't stop… only I might need your help.'

'Me?' asked Freya, surprised. 'What can I do?'

'Well, I heard on the grapevine that you and Sam are changing a few things at the orchard and that maybe you're not going to be making cider any more?'

Freya sighed. 'The jungle drums work well, don't they? My fault. When Sam and I got back together, I didn't realise quite how difficult it would be for him to up and leave the family business and his home. He's totally committed to Appleyard now, but still, having his brother as our main competitor down the road wasn't easy, and you know what Stephen's like.'

'Is he ever going to grow up, do you think?'

'Well, actually, it's early days, but I think there might be some progress in that direction. There's been something of a truce called lately, but I don't count my chickens where Stephen is concerned. I thought moving away from cider production and into juices instead might help Sam feel more settled, more like it was our business and not just mine any longer.'

Willow took a sip of her drink. 'And has it?' she asked, over the rim of her glass.

Freya's reply was immediate. 'Oh yes,' she said. 'Just try stopping us now; we've got that many plans. A range of our own juices for definite, perhaps other products too, and we're also going to set up a community juice pressing service so that locals or other small growers like ourselves can come and press their own fruit.'

Willow's grin was getting wider and wider by the minute.

'I take it that was what you wanted to hear.' Freya laughed.

'It might be... Do you remember the ice cream I made for Louisa and Phillip's ruby wedding anniversary? Well, that was one of granny's recipes, straight out of that notebook, and there are plenty more, all using the kind of soft fruits that I grow here. I thought I might try and have a go at making them again, properly I mean, to sell. What do you think? I could start with the gooseberry perhaps.'

Freya took another sip of her drink, holding the glass aloft and peering at the dew-coloured liquid. She squinted up at Willow. 'I think you might need to borrow some of our elderflowers,' she said, amused. 'And what a totally brilliant idea!'

'Well, I'm not sure that 'borrow' is quite the right word, but if I could harvest your elderflowers, perhaps you might like to have some of the syrup I make back in return. You could use it for your own juices.'

'Serendipity!' Freya grinned. 'Although I really don't need anything in return, Willow. I didn't put the elderflowers there, Mother Nature did... but, now that you come to mention it... apple and elderflower... mmmm.'

'So do you think we might be able to come to some sort of an arrangement?' asked Willow.

Freya sat back in her chair. 'I'm certain we could. I'd want to run it by Sam of course, but it's just the sort of thing he'd love, I know it. God this is exciting.'

'That's what I thought,' nodded Willow. 'And it could be just the thing we need.'

Freya paused for a moment, her face falling a little.

'So I get why you've suddenly cleared this room out,' she said, obviously wondering how much to say. 'It would make a great workroom, but...' She cocked her head on one side, watching Willow closely. '...

earlier on you said this was all on the quiet, as if you didn't want Jude to know about it. Is... is everything all right between you two?'

'Oh God yes, it's nothing like that. Well, it sort of is, but not in the way you mean.' She threw her hair back over her shoulder. 'Let's just say that I'm worried Jude is in danger of making some very bad decisions soon; business decisions, but ones that will affect our whole family. I'd like there to be an alternative, that's all, but I don't want to involve him until I'm sure it's something worth pursuing.'

Freya raised her eyebrows. 'Oh I get it, and then it will be his brilliant idea, right? That's the oldest trick in the book, Willow.' She smirked. 'You get exactly what you want, but Jude thinks it was his idea all along.'

Willow smiled in reply. 'Something like that,' she said.

'Well, I won't say a word, trust me. And I'll make sure that Sam keeps his mouth shut too. I should probably let you get back to your strawberries now, but why don't we meet up again one day in the week when Jude is at work, and then we can have a proper chat? There's someone else I think you should have a word with while we're about it. Someone who might also be able to help.'

'Anyone I know?'

'Oh yes, from way back, but let me have a chat to her first. If she's up for it, I might bring her along too.'

Willow rose from the table. 'Well, now I'm intrigued.'

'Good.' Freya winked. 'I'll give you a ring, shall I?'

Chapter Thirty-Four

Something wasn't right here. Willow shouldn't be able to feel the rain like this. Normally, when she stood by this gate, the canopy of trees overhead protected her from the worst of the elements. It wasn't until you reached the end of the wooded lane that the trees thinned out as the path sloped down towards to the clearing. Only then did you get a full view of the sky.

She shielded her face from the raindrops that the wind was whipping into her eyes and looked up, raking the skyline for any clue. Maybe she wasn't where she thought she was, but the sky was inky black, so there would be no help from the moon tonight. As she watched, an explosion of light struck out across the expanse of dark and she raised her shoulders, flinching in anticipation of the crashing noise that would surely follow as the lightning cracked open the night.

For a split second in the flare, the ground was illuminated before her, jagged scars cut through the fields, gouges through the pastoral landscape. Grasses, flowers, trees, all gone, just cracks of soil split wide, their muddy guts piled up in heaps. Willow could feel her feet oozing in the deep mud, rooting her to the spot, forcing her to look at the desecration in front of her.

She turned her head, another flash of lighting searing across her vision and this time row after row of houses stood, stretching out to the horizon, and above her head a huge wooden sign standing sentinel. She tried to pull her feet free from the soil, but as she struggled, sank ever deeper. The hairs pricked on the back of her neck, and panic rose in her throat…

Her breath came in heaving gasps as she woke, her nightdress heavy against her chest, sodden with her sweat, and it took her a few moments, eyes staring wildly out into the dark before Willow realised that she was safe, back in her room. She stretched out a hand to feel the smooth expanse of the sheets beneath her, the gentle cocoon of the pillow cradling her head. Beside her, Jude's rhythmic breathing stalled for a moment and she held her breath, but then it released once more in a sigh and with a faint snuffle, he resumed his peaceful sleep.

The clock beside the bed showed half past midnight; the dream had come quickly to Willow tonight, stronger than ever, and there was no longer any doubting its truth. She reached under her pillow and brought out the bundle of cloth which lay there, a small blue stone nestled within its folds. Even constrained within the soft muslin, its message had been a powerful one, and she was careful to keep the lapis lazuli from touching her skin; to do so right now would cause it to burn her like fire.

Very gently, she leaned across and slid open the drawer beside the bed, popping the bundle inside and, with a cautious glance at her husband, she lay back down and tried to calm both her mind and her breathing. Over the years there had been odd occasions when Willow had known without a shadow of doubt that things were going to happen, or she had seen things which had later come true. Intuition her mum had called it, being in tune with your feelings, and as a child Willow had been so used to her mum's eccentricities that she never thought anything of it. The things Willow had seen could be explained away, the feelings passed off as well-informed hunches. There had never been anything like the dreams she was having now. These were vivid, powerful even, and the truth was that they scared Willow a little; not only because of their intensity but because of the message they brought. She felt for Jude's fingers, feeling them close over hers as he slept. She looked at him fondly, but sadly.

Oh Jude, she sighed, *what have you done…?*

*

Freya was met with a cloud of fragrant steam as Willow opened the door to the stillroom for her.

'Blinking heck, you don't hang around, do you?' she commented, breathing in the delicious fruity smell. She and Willow had sat in this room only a few days before but it was now no longer bare. Instead a new wooden work surface ran the length of one wall set with a huge cooker.

'That smells amazing,' Freya remarked, crossing over to get a better look. She hung her head over one of the pans that bubbled there. 'What exactly is in that?'

Willow came to stand beside her. 'Gooseberries, lemons, sugar and elderflower cordial. Summer in a saucepan. What do you reckon?'

'You got that right,' she agreed. 'Is that how your ice cream starts? Only much as I love that, I'd be quite happy spooning this lot up straight from the pan.'

'You wouldn't really. It smells divine, but it's very, very sweet, and very, very sticky.'

Freya looked around her once more. 'I don't think I realised quite how quickly you were going to get this all up and running. What did you do, wave a magic wand?'

'Naked incantations by the light of the moon... hardly...' Willow laughed. 'No, I waved a chocolate cake, a tub of ice cream, three punnets of strawberries and some runner beans under one of our friend's noses, and being the wondrous carpenter that he is, he put this together in an afternoon.'

'Ah, sorry,' said Freya, acknowledging the slight admonishment. 'Been reading too much Harry Potter.'

'Besides,' continued Willow, with a wink. 'That is most definitely not why you perform naked incantations by moonlight...' Her smile was warm as she took Freya's arm. 'And look, come and see these.'

She led the way over to the work surface where a pile of elderflowers was waiting. Beside them a muslin cloth was suspended over a large bowl, the syrupy mixture it contained slowly dripping through.

'This is my cordial. You have to steep the flower heads for twenty-four hours in the syrup before straining it, so I made this lot last night. I pretty much have to keep a batch going the whole time.'

Now that she was closer, Freya could smell the sweetness of the creamy flowers. There was nothing she liked more on a summer's day than to wander through her orchard, the sunlight glancing off the hedgerows filled with these frothy heads. She picked up a bunch and inspected it closely before bringing it to her nose. The last time she'd done this, she'd inhaled a small bug straight up her nose.

'So what do you think?' asked Willow. 'Am I mad, or do you think there's a possibility that this might work?'

Freya's head had done nothing but spin with ideas since she had left her friend at the weekend. With her and Sam's own plans for Appleyard now beginning to look like reality, this was quite possibly the most amazing opportunity for them both, and for their friend Merry too if Freya wasn't mistaken. Merry and Tom had only opened their shop a few weeks ago, and were now on the lookout for small local businesses whose produce they could showcase. The opportunity for them all to work together was serendipity indeed, and would give them the helping hand they needed to fulfil their individual dreams, of that she had no doubt.

'I think there's every possibility it will be bloody brilliant, Willow. It's a shame that Merry couldn't come today, but when I talked to her at the beginning of the week, she seemed really keen. Have you made the list of things you're hoping to produce?'

'Yes, it's on the table. Come and sit down and I'll show you.' She handed Freya a piece of paper. 'I still can't believe I didn't know that Merry had sold the hotel in Worcester and bought a shop up here; that has to be the biggest coincidence.'

'I know. It's brilliant what they've done with it, you won't believe it until you see it.'

Freya took a few moments to read what was in front of her, and even though Willow had simply listed the products, she knew her

friend well enough to know that they would all be beautifully packaged; the ice cream would be softly whipped inside smart tubs, the
blackcurrant cordial would glow ruby red from glass bottles, and
her gooseberry and elderflower jam would look like the pale golden
glow of a winter sun. As for the smell when their lids were removed;
Freya was out in the fields already. They would look perfect against
her range of juices.

'I think Merry will be thrilled to stock these. I'm going to see her
on Thursday, why don't you come with me? You could discuss how
this could work for you both, and to be honest, Willow, I'd love to
get involved. I think what we're both trying to do could be the perfect
complement to each other.'

Willow smiled a little shyly. 'Are you sure it doesn't seem a bit rude?
I mean, I haven't seen Merry for ages, or much of you for that matter,
and now I feel a bit like I'm throwing this all in your faces.'

'That's the way of life, Willow, we're all busy. Those strawberries
out there don't grow by themselves, do they, and I certainly don't think
you're being rude, and neither will Merry. In fact, far from that, I'd like
to view it as a wonderful turn of fate – the perfect opportunity for all
of us. Perhaps after all we make our own fate...'

Freya held Willow's look for a moment, recognising that she knew
the truth of what she had said. Hopefully one day soon, she would find
out the real reason why Willow was so keen to start this new venture.
There would be a reason, there always was.

*

Willow sat still for quite a while after Freya had left, pondering the
direction their conversation had taken, and wondering whether she
should confide everything. There was something different about Freya,
a kindred spirit perhaps, something that despite their years of friendship
she had never seen before. Freya had had a tough time last year, losing
her father and what had seemed then the only hope of keeping her
beloved Appleyard alive. She had come close to selling up, but now

she seemed more alive than she had ever seen her, more in tune with things. Perhaps she would understand after all.

With a sudden start, the smell of the room hit her again, and she got up swiftly. She had ice cream to make, and then she must go and see Henry. She had a favour to ask.

Henry Whittaker should have been a banker or a stockbroker, or even a solicitor, anything but an artist; it just didn't suit his name. You'd only need to glance at him, though, to know that he'd never picked up a copy of the *Financial Times* in his life. If he owned any clothes other than aged, paint-splattered jeans and T-shirts, Willow had never seen them.

He was, in fact, the model tenant. He'd been with them for over two years now, coming to them with impeccable references and a firm, if paint-speckled handshake. He paid his rent on time, every month, and took great care of the property; in fact, his vegetable patch rivalled Willow's own, albeit on a smaller scale. He never had wild parties, and although Willow had made tentative enquiries, there didn't seem to be any girlfriends on the scene; or boyfriends for that matter. She often wondered in a motherly way whether he was lonely, but two energetic spaniels accompanied him wherever he went, and that seemed to be enough. As time passed, the lines in their relationship had become blurred from tenant and landlord, mainly at Henry's insistence and now Willow found it hard to look on Henry as anything other than a good friend.

Today, like most days, he was sitting at his computer, headphone wires trailing across his shirt. She'd been pulling faces through the window at him for over five minutes before he spotted her, his face creasing into a broad grin the minute he did. He waved at the door indicating that she should come in.

'That's the one thing I can never quite understand about you,' she remarked, after she'd spent a few minutes making a fuss of the dogs. 'Every time I come in here, you have headphones glued to your ears, and yet who's going to hear your music? We're too far down the road and Jude's office is right on the other side of the courtyard, even when he is there.'

Henry held out one of the headphones. 'Do you want to hear what I was listening to?' he asked, his clear grey eyes dancing with mischief.

Willow took the wire tentatively in one hand, imagining her ears being pounded by some raucous thrash metal. Instead, all she could hear was a hissing noise. 'Oh, it's stopped,' she said, but then registered his amused expression. She held the wire up again, listening to the rushing noise once more. 'What is it?' she asked. 'Some kind of weird white noise or something.'

Henry took back the headphones. 'It's pink actually. Slightly lower frequency than white noise. It helps you to concentrate, in a calm, relaxed kind of way.'

Willow pulled a face at him, and he shrugged. 'Now you know why I play it through headphones.' He grinned. He eyed the contents of the bag in her other hand.

'I sincerely hope there are strawberries in there. And I sincerely hope they're for me.'

'There's also a bribe dressed up as ice cream, so don't get too excited.'

Henry peered at her over the top of his glasses and then took them off altogether. 'Might this have something to do with our conversation from a few days ago then?'

'Possibly…' admitted Willow.

'In that case, I can see this is going to be one of those conversations that requires a cup of coffee as well,' he said. 'I'll go and fire up the beast.'

Willow looked at the bag in her hand and back to Henry's workstation. He wasn't painting today, but designing something instead; his computer screen showing half of some sort of flash racing car, but she'd still interrupted him. He was working, so she shouldn't even be here, but apart from the favour, she didn't have anyone else she could talk to about this, not yet at any rate. She bit her lip, torn.

In the end, it was Henry who decided for her, taking her arm, relieving her of the bag she was carrying, and marching her across the room to the collection of sofas and armchairs which were centred round a huge fireplace. He pushed her down into the middle of one of the settees, where she was immediately joined by a dog at her side and one at her feet. She sank back against the cushions, grateful for the opportunity to sit for a moment. So far, she had been travelling through her day at a hundred miles an hour, and she suspected it would continue to be like that for several weeks to come.

After ten minutes or so of silence apart from the slurping and hissing of the coffee machine, Henry returned with two huge foamy cappuccinos which he settled on the coffee table in front of her. She smiled up at him gratefully, already feeling a little more at ease, although that may have been in part due to Dylan's heavy breathing, the beautiful blue springer spaniel, whose head was heavy in her lap.

'So what's the bribe for then?' asked Henry after a moment, licking a strip of frothy milk off his top lip. 'And before you answer, I'll remind you that I'm open to bribes of any kind where your food is considered payment.'

'Well, that's just it, the bribe is the bribe. I just want your opinion on the ice cream really... but—'

Henry chuckled. 'Is that all? Christ, I wish all my clients were this easy to please.' He got up and went back to the kitchen, returning with the tub of ice cream and a huge tablespoon.

'Henry, I didn't mean now! You can let me know in a day or two, when you've had time to eat it.'

He looked at her steadily. 'What is this day or two of which you speak?' He grinned and pulled off the lid, plunging his spoon into the creamy mass. It emerged with a huge dollop on the end, and he put the whole thing straight into his mouth.

Willow winced, expecting imminent brain freeze, but Henry just sat back, eyes closed, letting the sweet concoction melt in his mouth. He gave a series of swallows and then sat up once more, looking at her. He plunged the spoon in again and repeated the process. Willow said nothing.

After the third mouthful, Henry sat up straighter and lowered the spoon. 'Okay, I like it,' he said impassively.

Willow's face fell. That wasn't exactly the reaction she'd been hoping for.

'Willow,' he said, 'that was absolutely spectacular. I was just teasing!' He grinned, and she could see now that he was. He took another spoonful, smaller this time.

'I don't know how you do it,' he added. 'One minute I'm here and the next I'm out there, in the field, picking gooseberries, the sun on my arms, the insects buzzing. It's like when the fruit is so ripe and you pop one in your mouth, all the juice and seeds suddenly exploding, and then after that first tangy hit, you get the sweetness, mellow and creamy, hedgerows full of frothy elderflowers, the smell... I'm probably not doing it justice.'

Willow blushed. 'Really?' she asked. 'Is that what you feel? You're not just making it up?'

'No, I'm not just making it up,' he said. 'Scout's honour... although, I am wondering why my opinion matters so much.'

Willow reached for her coffee and took a sip, feeling Henry's eyes on her.

'I need the opinion of someone neutral. Everybody else I know is too close to home.'

'Well, I've been called many things in my time, but never "neutral" before.' He waved his spoon. 'And before you leap to apologise, I'm only teasing again. If you don't mind me saying you look really nervous, which is unusual for you... however, I do understand what you mean, and I'm flattered that you've asked me.' His grey eyes were smiling at her. 'Does that make you feel any better?'

Willow swallowed and nodded. 'It does actually, thanks. And you're right, I am nervous about this.' She paused for a moment, wondering how much to say, but Henry wasn't stupid, he'd have worked it out. 'You see I'm thinking that I might start making ice cream, and one or two other things, properly, you know to sell, but I've never done anything like this before, it's all a bit nerve-wracking.'

'Ah, so now we're getting to the bottom of it, but Willow, you run a fruit farm. How can you be nervous about this?'

'That's different. I don't make the fruit, it grows all by itself—'

'I think there's a bit more to it than that,' interrupted Henry, 'but perhaps I should put you out of your misery. I think what you want might be in that folder there.' He directed her towards the table with a look. 'I took the liberty of completely disregarding the cock and bull story you tried to sell me the other day, and started to mock up a few designs for you. Have a look and see whether they're what you're after. I've tried to come up with a few differing ideas, but they might be a bit too… masculine maybe.'

Willow's mouth hung open. 'How did you know that's what I wanted?' she managed.

'Because when someone comes in here asking me to 'doodle' a couple of pictures of some gooseberries and strawberries for you to put on a sign in your little wooden shop, and that person knows that among other things I'm a concept artist, I'm generally able to read between the lines.'

'Oh,' said Willow, a little embarrassed now. 'Was I really that obvious?'

Henry laughed. 'Have a look. I might have got it completely wrong.'

Willow pulled the folder towards her and opened it cautiously. Whatever was inside could potentially mean this thing was about to come alive, and although a part of her was ready for it, a large part of her was not.

She picked up the first piece of paper, struck first by the beautiful colour of the artwork, a soft green, like a summer meadow. Then there were pale golden hues, a gorgeous pink – the colour of the setting sun, a deep cranberry and a dark purple, the exact shade of ripe blackberries. There were bold scripts, elegant scripts and modern edgy patterns. Willow couldn't believe it. She looked up in astonishment.

'How did you do all this, it must have taken you an age?'

Henry simply smiled. 'I was on a roll,' he said. 'Do you think any of them are what you're looking for?'

Willow gazed on in wonder. 'I think they're stunning. How will I ever choose? Every one of these could make a perfect logo, and I love the way you've put them onto some packaging already. It makes them so much easier to see what they would look like.'

'It's what I do.' Henry shrugged.

A rush of excitement hit Willow like a wave. 'Can I take these away with me, to have another look? I've got a couple of friends I'd like to show them to as well, if that would be all right.'

Henry waved a hand. 'Sure, they're yours for as long as you want. They'll probably need some tweaking too, so just let me know what works and what doesn't, and we can go from there.'

'Oh my God,' squealed Willow. 'Thank you so much!' She lurched up from the sofa much to Dylan's disgust, coffee forgotten. 'I'll bring you some more ice cream,' she gushed as she rushed to the door. 'Thank you so much, Henry.'

*

Henry watched her go, an amused smile on his face. His hunch had been right then. He gave a sigh; time to get back to work. But then he checked his watch, picked up his spoon once more, and worked his way steadily through the entire carton of ice cream. He liked Willow, in fact he liked both of them. He'd shared a pint or two with Jude and always found him very likeable. He had pots of money of course, and a love of the finer things in life; but it rarely got the better of him. Most of the time, he appeared to be an ordinary bloke, much like himself. Only now and then had Henry seen a little seam of something darker running through him, but Jude was a very successful man, and Henry supposed it came with the territory. He wanted Willow to succeed, for her sake and, actually it was sweet that she was so reticent about her capabilities. She shouldn't be. Henry was a pretty good cook himself, but Willow was amazing. Her food was so full of flavour, so full of life. He suspected that she could make even a cardboard box taste exceptional.

*

It wasn't until Willow got to the bottom of the lane again that she remembered her dream. It flashed in front of her as her hand touched the gate to open it. An explosion in her mind, much like the lightning that she remembered, and she turned quickly to look behind her. The wind was filling the canopy of the trees above her, lifting the leaves in a song above her head. Beyond them there was nothing but more trees and the dusty ground of the lane which reached back towards Henry's house and the clearing where Jude also had his office. She knew that she was in the right place, though; that beyond the trees was a gentle sweep of pasture land almost as far as the eye could see, land which at the moment was a carpet of grasses and wild flowers, of hedgerows and swaying corn. It wouldn't take much to reduce it to the muddy hell hole she had seen, just a few diggers and an unhealthy greed. She shuddered, gripped by the force of the images and clutched Henry's folder to her. She had to hope that time would be on her side.

Chapter Thirty-Five

'How long is it since you moved here, Merry?' asked Willow. 'Only it looks like you've been here forever.'

Merry laughed. 'Well, that's only because everything is so old... myself included. I can't believe how tiring it is, running a shop. I thought we were busy before with the hotel, but I guess I'd forgotten how much I used to delegate,' she added ruefully. 'But it is absolutely the best fun ever. I wish we'd done it years ago.'

Willow eyed the garishly coloured fittings and decoration. 'It shouldn't work really, should it?' she commented. 'All I remember from the seventies is that it was dubbed the decade that taste forgot, but this is stunning, inspired even.'

Merry and Freya exchanged looks before Merry grinned and pointed to a rather grand portrait on the wall. 'It was inspired, actually,' she said. 'Meet Christopher, our artist in residence, his wife, Marina, and their daughter, Catherine. They're all dead by the way.'

The painting was very striking, but Willow wasn't quite sure what to make of it. It looked almost as though it had been freshly painted. 'I'm not sure I follow,' she said. 'How can he be your artist in residence if he's dead?'

'I'll tell you all about it some time,' said Merry. 'But all the work you can see on the walls is Christopher's. He was quite a well-known artist in his time; he designed wallpaper and textiles, that kind of thing. He once owned the house, and we found all these things just packed away when we moved here. It seemed right to reuse them, and they gave us the theme we were looking for.'

'It's amazing,' answered Willow. 'I love it. But you said you've still got things to do, more plans for the place?'

'We have,' said Merry. 'There are things we'd like to try, but what I'd love to show you is this little space out the back here.'

She led the way through the main part of the shop, past tables overflowing with produce, and through an archway into the rear. The smell in here was even more amazing. An array of old cupboards and bookcases lined the walls, every inch of which was covered with bottles and jars, or packets and boxes. What set these apart from the items for sale in the rest of the shop was the packaging itself and the labels. None of the items looked mass-produced, and all had an air of quality about them. The labels were classy and individual, they looked hand-lettered. It was exactly the look that Willow herself was hoping to achieve.

Willow looked about her, picking her way around the room, peering at the contents on display, and wondering whether she would be able to compete; moreover, whether anything she could produce would actually fit in here, the room was crammed to the gills as it was.

'View these as only temporary,' said Merry. 'We wanted to introduce some speciality products alongside the everyday staples we offer, but we didn't have enough time before we opened to seek out the suppliers we really wanted to use: local people with fabulous local produce. We're taking our time discovering who, and what is out there, people like you, Willow. So bit by bit, we plan to replace this lot with new lines as we find the right suppliers. What was more important in the beginning was to establish whether or not these type of products would sell, and admittedly we haven't been open that long, but people do seem to like them. I'm convinced that we'll continue to do well with them.'

'But I'm not sure how long it will be before I'm up and running,' said Willow. 'I don't want to hold you up, and I'm not sure yet what kind of quantities I'll be able to make.' She picked up a jar of bramble jelly, very similar in fact to the jars that lined her own pantry shelves at home. It was so exciting to see the possibilities of what the shop might offer her, but it also brought home just how much hard work this would involve, and what a big leap it would be for her. She still wasn't sure whether it was something she should go ahead with, but all her instincts were telling her it was. Perhaps it was the fear of what she suspected was coming next that prevented her from making the next move.

'Well, why don't we take it a step at a time,' said Merry. 'Your fruit is amazing right now, and I would certainly love to sell some for you. Can you imagine how the strawberries would smell in here? Why don't we start with some of the fruit varieties, and perhaps some bottles of your cordial, and that would give you a little more time to think about your other products, particularly the ice creams. It would also give you some time to have a play at home before you agree to provide us with anything.'

Willow didn't mean it to, but her face fell a little. She should be treading more carefully here. It wasn't that she didn't trust Merry, but this was a small community, and the village shop was the fount of all gossip. What would happen if people found out what Jude was planning before she'd had a chance to put her own plans into place? It didn't bear thinking about, but time was of the essence now.

She was just about to reply when she noticed that Freya had put down the jar of olives she was studying, and was watching her intently. It threw her for a minute, and she scrambled to say something quickly. Too late.

'Willow, is everything all right? You can tell me to mind my own business if you like, but we've been friends for too long for me not to notice when things aren't quite right. A couple of times now when we've talked about this new venture, you've seemed almost panicky, as if things weren't happening quickly enough. I mean, one minute you had a utility room, cleared out, but just a blank space, and almost the next day it was kitted out as if you were going into full production. Something doesn't quite add up here…' She stopped for a moment, thinking about what she had just said.

'It's not the business, is it?' she asked quickly. 'Everything with Jude is all right?'

The question caught Willow off guard. She thought she had hidden her feelings well, but Freya had put her finger on it with unerring accuracy. To her surprise, she felt tears beginning to well up. What on earth could she say? She had no proof that her suspicions were true; they were based on dreams for heaven's sake, and to admit them out loud was tantamount to admitting she was going mad. She would also be accusing Jude before she had any facts at all. It would seem like a betrayal when all she was really trying to do was help. Just as quickly another thought came to her – a memory of a conversation with Freya in her kitchen, when she'd told her about Christmas and the stranger who had caused her to think a little differently. And here was Merry talking about a dead painter who had somehow provided her with the inspiration for her brilliant shop. Perhaps they would understand after all.

'You're going to think I'm quite mad,' she started.

Freya laughed. 'Oh, I've always known you're mad,' she said. 'But since when did that ever stop us being friends?' She smiled warmly, and when Willow looked across to Merry, she saw the same expression echoed there too.

'It's really hard to know where to start,' she began. 'Everything with the business is fine, and with Jude too; more than fine, and perhaps that's part of the problem. Despite his mother's best efforts, his father brought him up in his own image, and although Jude thankfully is nothing like Andrew in many ways, they share the same relentless materialistic streak. It's something I've always recognised in Jude, something that's always worried me a little, to tell the truth, even though for the most part he manages to keep it well in check. Even my mum warned me about it when we first got together.'

Freya came around the side of the table and perched on the corner of it. 'Actually, I always liked your mum. A bit kooky admittedly, but she always seemed so vibrant, so alive. Don't forget my own mum bailed out on us when I was only little. I loved my dad, you know that, but when I was younger, your family always seemed so happy, and I always used to think how much fun it must be to be you.'

Willow touched her hand to her mouth. 'I never knew that,' she said, eyes starting to smart again.

'Well, I'm telling you now; one, because it's true, and two, because I know you had a hard time when you were younger, kids calling your mum names just because she was a bit different to everyone else's. But looking back, all I see is a bunch of kids who never knew any better. My life has shown me, more so over the last year, that not everything that happens to us can be explained. And neither is everything black-and-white; if we allow it, life can be the most wondrous collection of colours, in every shade of the rainbow.'

Merry was nodding her head. 'I agree. The things that have happened to me over the last few months probably don't make any sense. If you ask my husband, he'd tell you a very different story. Whenever I try to tell him exactly how I feel about recent events, he gives me that weird look, you know, the one that says *you've just had a baby and your brain is still a pile of mush.* Whatever you need to tell us, I don't suppose I'll be the least bit surprised – just say it as it is.'

Willow smiled gratefully. 'A few months ago, I started to have dreams, nothing specific at first, just a vague feeling of unease. And it was at about the same time that Jude first mentioned he had a meeting up in Birmingham with his father. This alone was enough to set warning bells ringing.' She nodded at Merry. 'You probably don't know, but Andrew is still a silent partner in the business. He and Jude started Middleton Estates mostly with his capital, and even now the strawberry fields, meadowland, our house, and everything else belongs to the business. It will all transfer to Jude at some point or another of course when Andrew dies, but it's always made me feel uneasy; I feel beholden to him, even though I know he can't take any decisions without Jude's agreement. Jude has always run the company day to day, but he had a big meeting with his father at the very moment I started having my dreams. Other people might not see the significance, but to me it's like a shining beacon.'

'So what do you think is going on?' asked Freya. 'Couldn't you just ask Jude?'

'I could.' Willow paused for a moment, wondering how best to phrase her next statement. She was painfully aware that any minute she'd be laughed out of the shop. 'A couple of nights ago, I had a vision that all the land around us was completely desecrated, torn up to make room for houses. I'm convinced this is what Jude is planning, or, more likely, is an idea that his father has hatched, and Jude is going along with for some reason. I know it makes me sound like a crazy person, but I almost don't need to know any more than that. There's no way I can talk to Jude about it, when everything I feel is based on dreams; he'd think I'm mad. So, the only thing I can think of is to offer Jude a real and valid choice, an alternative future and, importantly, a reason to go against his father's wishes.'

'Hence the new business venture?' suggested Merry.

Willow nodded sadly. 'And the need to get it up and running in far less time than is really feasible.'

Freya crossed the room to stand by her friend's side. 'Then it sounds to me like we need a hefty dose of girl power to help things along. What do you reckon, Merry? It's scary trying to do things like this on your own, and what could be more wonderful than Merry and me helping you out? Merry has the perfect place to sell your produce, plus business contacts coming out of her ears, I have some of the raw materials you need to get up and running, and I know where I can get more, and you have granny Gilly's notebook. From where I'm standing, that's a pretty powerful combination.'

Willow looked around the room one more time. All her instincts were telling her that this was the right thing to do, and they had never let her down before. Besides what other choice did she have? Her future with the man she loved, and that of her children, were at stake here. It was time to fight.

Chapter Thirty-Six

Willow called Peter over to see her the very next morning. It was not long since his breakfast, but despite the early hour he'd already been hard at work for a while. It would be mercilessly hot out in the fields today with no shelter, and the strawberries were much better if picked when they still held the morning's freshness.

She had a mug of tea waiting for him as he sauntered through the door, his enormous flip-flop-clad feet squeaking across her floor.

'Ah, cheers,' he said, as Willow handed him his drink. 'Is everything okay?'

Peter was one of the best students she'd ever had. Over the years they had ranged from the gormless to the adequate as long as she kept an eye on them, but Peter was different. Apart from Rachael who had been with them for the past three years, he was the only one with any initiative. He was quiet and studious, with floppy brown hair and a big bushy beard, but his unobtrusive manner belied a keen intellect and a sharp wit. They got on like a house on fire. Trouble was there was only one of him, and right now Willow needed six or seven.

She gave him a bright smile. 'Wonderful,' she replied. 'How's it looking out there today?'

'Busy, and hot,' he grinned. 'But mostly hot.'

Willow looked at her watch. 'Well, let's see how it goes. If the sky stays this clear, by two the heat will be unbearable. No one will come to pick, so you must call it a day. I don't want you keeling over on me.'

Peter was six foot three and had muscles like Popeye, and his expression let her know in no uncertain terms that she was fussing, but she waggled her finger at him anyway.

'Actually, I wanted to ask a favour if that's okay? I've been having a bit of a think recently about branching out a little; making some cordials, ice creams, that sort of thing, but I'm a bit short on manpower. I don't suppose by any happy chance you have a handful of mates who'd like some work over the next day or so? They'd need to be like you, mind, not afraid of hard work.'

Peter wiped a hand across his lips as he drained the last of his tea. 'Is that what the amazing smell is all about?' he asked. 'I was wondering. Can I see?'

He crossed to the sink and rinsed his mug under the tap, upending it on the draining board before turning back to her, an endearing query on his face. Willow had no choice but to lead the way out into the hallway and into the room opposite.

It didn't take Peter long to assess what he found. He walked from one spot to the other, peering at the elderflowers, smelling the aromatic cordial and fingering the page in Willow's notebook where her grandma had carefully written the recipe in her best copperplate handwriting.

'So you need people to pick? And in huge quantities by the look of things. Maybe people to man the strawberry fields, and possibly people in here to keep the pans going?'

Willow smiled, watching Peter carefully.

'Leave it to me,' he beamed, with a glance out of the window. 'Right, time I was back out there I reckon.' He looked back at the room as he passed through the door. 'Would the day after tomorrow be okay?'

Willow was right, by the time two o'clock came, the strawberry field was scorching. In fact, everywhere was scorching, but that had its advantages too. The picked fruit had marched out of the door during the morning, but actual pickers were reluctant to venture out which gave Willow the perfect opportunity to shut up shop early and pop over to see Henry. She had pored over his designs the night before, and every time she picked up the folder, she found herself returning to one particular set of designs. The colours were striking, a vibrant lime green and a deep pinky-plum, and although the motifs and lettering were modern, there was something timeless about them too. She was sure that they would appeal to the market she was aiming at.

It was much cooler in the shaded lane and she walked slowly, taking the time to trail her fingers through the fronds of cow parsley along the verge, and inhale the gentle scent from the wild sweet peas which grew there.

Henry was in the garden when she arrived, standing among the tomatoes and sweet peppers which he'd planted to take full advantage of the warmth from the red brick wall that ran the length of one side. He waved a greeting.

'Warm enough for you?' he called, straightening up, one hand full of sweet cherry tomatoes.

'Only just,' she replied. 'But alas too hot for my pickers. Most of them have sloped off to a deckchair and a glass of Pimms, so I thought I'd come and harass you instead.'

'Lucky old me.' He grinned. 'Go on in, I won't be a minute. Dinner won't pick itself.'

Willow glanced at the array of vegetables and herbs in front of her. Whatever Henry was planning for his tea, she had no doubt it would be tasty. She followed the path to the wide French doors, both open, stepping over the two panting spaniels who were sprawled in the shade cast by the house.

Inside, the living room was cool and dark, and she took a seat, admiring Henry's artwork on the walls. All was quiet for a moment until the sound of a door opening caused her to look up.

A young woman stood in the entrance to the room, quite naked.

'Oh, hi,' she said, stepping into the room and looking around. 'Does Henry know you're here? I could fetch him if you like.' She made no move to cover herself.

Willow was never very good at judging people's age, but the lithe tanned body in front of her could be no more than early twenties.

Willow cleared her throat. 'Sorry. I met him in the garden. He said to come on in…'

'Okay,' she said with a smile, looking down at her feet as if seeing them for the first time. Funnily enough, her feet were not what was concerning Willow. 'I should probably go and get dressed. Aren't you hot?'

Willow managed a smile. 'A bit,' she said cautiously.

The young woman stared at her as if she was deranged, and with a nod and another smile disappeared back though the door.

'Right, so a cup of tea, is it?' asked Henry coming inside. 'Or something cold?' He was carrying a trug full of salad vegetables.

Willow was still staring at the door in the corner of the room, feeling hotter than ever.

Henry followed her line of sight.

'Ahhh,' he said slowly. 'I can see you've met Delilah.'

Willow gazed at him. 'Delilah?'

He nodded. 'As in *Why, Why, Why Delilah*… You know, the Tom Jones song?'

'I can see *why* Delilah, Henry, she's gorgeous… I just didn't expect—'

'She wasn't wearing any clothes, was she?' Henry grinned. 'She does that. She's a goat keeper,' he added, as if that explained it.

Willow remained seated, hoping for further explanation, but as Henry hopped from foot to foot, it became clear that it wasn't going to arrive any time soon.

'Henry Whittaker, you're a dark horse,' she said in her best school matron's voice. 'And don't tell me she's your sister; nobody has a sister like that.'

'No, she's not my sister.' He laughed. 'She's not my niece either.'

'So are you going to tell me what's going on, or not?' she retorted, getting up from the chair. 'This is the first time I've seen another female anywhere remotely near here, so don't go all shy on me now.'

Henry blushed a little. 'I'll go and put the kettle on.'

Ten minutes later, the three of them were sitting around the kitchen table, Delilah now ever so slightly dressed in a skimpy pair of shorts and vest top. She sat cross-legged in the chair, cradling her mug in her lap.

'So how did you two meet?' asked Willow. 'You're rather a long way from home if I'm right in thinking that's a Cornish accent.'

'You are,' smiled Delilah, 'but where I'm from, everywhere is a long way from home. I spend my life on the M5.'

'I can imagine. So…?'

Henry shared an amused glance across the table with Delilah. 'This might explain it,' he said, throwing his foot up onto the empty chair next to Willow. He rolled up the leg of his jeans to reveal bright green socks. 'Goat socks,' he said. 'At this precise moment I have about eighteen pairs, which is sixteen pairs more than I actually need.'

Delilah poked Henry's thigh. 'But you have to admit that the after sales service is spectacularly good…'

Henry sighed. 'It is… which is why I have eighteen pairs.'

'Oh, I see.' Willow giggled.

'We actually only met for the first time about three months ago,' adds Henry. 'Up until then, I'd ring Delilah to order another pair of socks and heave and sigh listening to her talk dirty to me in that fabulous accent—'

'While I would swoon listening to his cut glass vowels… in the end, I decided that although the poor man was pretty much keeping me in business, enough was enough, so I suggested we meet—'

'And the rest is history,' finished Henry.

Willow felt like a spectator at a tennis match, as she struggled to keep up with the conversation that batted back and forth, Henry and Delilah both finishing each other's sentences.

'Well, it's lovely to meet you, Delilah, although I shall thump Henry later for not telling me about you. How long are you staying for? Only if you're here for a few days, then you should come over to us for dinner one evening. I haven't cooked properly for anyone in ages.'

Henry exchanged another look with Delilah before replying. 'Willow runs a fruit farm,' he explained, 'but she also happens to be the finest cook for miles around, *and* she makes the most amazing ice cream.'

'To be honest, I'm not entirely sure how long I'll be here for,' replied Delilah with a rather coy look at Henry. 'We're sort of taking things as they come… dinner sounds a lovely idea, though, thank you.' She twiddled the ends of her jet black hair around her fingers. 'I don't suppose you make your ice cream with goat's milk, do you?'

'No, sorry,' replied Willow. 'It's rather a new venture. I think I need to stick with what I know for now, but who knows, maybe one day.' She suddenly felt very naïve in front of this confident young woman who obviously had a successful business herself. There was so much she needed to learn.

She sat up a little straighter in her chair. 'Actually, Henry, I'm sorry for hogging your afternoon, but the ice cream making is the reason I popped round. I've made a decision on the designs you produced for me, but I'm not sure where to go from here. I need packaging and marketing stuff, but I'm clueless about who to use, and what it's likely to cost. I was hoping you might be able to point me in the right direction.'

Henry's grey eyes sparkled at her. 'But that's brilliant news, Willow. Which designs did you go for in the end?' He got up from the table. 'Hang on and I'll get my laptop.'

It took a few moments for him to boot it up and navigate to the right folder, but almost immediately Delilah pulled her chair closer to his so that she could see the screen too. 'I've got Henry working on some new designs for me as well, but I'd love to see what else he's been doing. Frankly, I'm amazed he even found my company to begin with, my website is so out of date it's shocking, and while the stuff I produce is of the highest quality, the designs for the packaging and branding are total pants.' She looked at the screen for a moment as Henry scrolled through the images, her hand suddenly grabbing his to halt the movement. 'Oh, I like those ones,' she exclaimed. 'The colours are wonderful, and—'

She suddenly stopped, looking across at Willow, misreading her expression. 'Sorry,' she said. 'I get a bit excitable sometimes.'

Willow could feel a little tingle in her toes. 'Do you really like them?' she urged, 'only that set is the one I've picked. I could have one colour for each of the different flavours. So my elderflower ice cream and cordial could have this zingy green for example and—'

'Maybe this for strawberry?' finished Delilah.

The two women stared at one another for a moment, beaming smiles on both their faces. Willow's hand strayed to the tiger's eye pendant around her neck, where it remained, her fingers stroking the smooth polished surface of the stone.

'That's exactly what I was going to say,' said Willow. 'I don't suppose you know someone who makes brilliant, but not too expensive packaging, do you?'

Delilah gave Henry a gentle nudge to the ribs. 'Any chance of a biscuit my gorgeous lover,' she said in a thick Cornish drawl, 'an' we might be needing some more tea an all,' she added, blowing a kiss. 'Willow and I have a lot to talk about.'

Chapter Thirty-Seven

'I hope we're not too early,' said Peter, looking at Willow's astonished face. 'Only I wasn't sure how long this would take.'

She swallowed her mouthful of tea. 'No, not too early. I just… didn't expect quite so many of you,' replied Willow. 'But this is wonderful!' she finished, doing a swift tally in her head. Where on earth had Peter dredged all these people up from? And more importantly people who all looked pleased to be here.

'So who have we got?' she asked. 'Although I should apologise in advance because I'll probably forget half your names in the next five minutes.'

'Okay, so we have Callum, my brother,' Peter began, 'followed by Luke and Josh, twins obviously. Jennie, who's Josh's girlfriend, Lucy her friend, and Ollie. I can vouch for them all except Ollie, who's a drunken reprobate most of the time, but has promised to be on his best behaviour today.'

Willow had a feeling he was joking, but she wasn't entirely sure. She smiled, a little nervously. 'Right, well… have you all had breakfast?' A chorus of affirmation followed.

'And they've all got plenty to drink, snacks to eat and are smothered in factor 50.'

'Peter, what would I do without you?'

Willow downed the rest of her tea as fast as possible and snatched an apple from the bowl on the table. 'Right, do you want to follow me, and we'll get going? I'll explain what I need once we're outside, and then you can decide what you want to do.'

In the end, it was an easy decision. Peter declared that he was a strawberry man. It was what he knew, and he could help the others if they got stuck. He picked his 'team' of Callum, Ollie and Luke, leaving Josh, Jennie and Lucy to stay with Willow. After a few moments of discussion, Peter led his crew away, and Willow watched him stride out into the field with pride. She and her strawberries were in safe hands.

She led the others around to the side of the house and one of the long low barns that stood there. At the moment, it was mainly used for storage of outdoor equipment, but Willow had other plans for it long term. Inside it was dark and still, a warm musty smell rushing through the opened door, dust motes spilling out into the sunshine. Inside, she quickly found what she was looking for and brought the special hods over for everyone to see.

'I bought these a while ago from a market selling old farm equipment,' Willow explained. 'They're actually for picking apples, but perfect for all sorts of things.' She showed them the large bucket made from canvas and reinforced with metal strips. A wide canvas strap was attached at each side. 'You wear them across your body. They're surprisingly comfortable, and you get both hands free for picking, plus you don't have to keep bending down. I've only got two, though, so we'll have to share.'

'No problem,' said Josh. 'Jennie and I can share.'

'Great! I'll wear the other one, and let's get going, shall we? The elderflower's only in the next-door field, so it's not far.'

She stopped when they got to the hedgerow, and turned to face the group. 'I'm just going to point this out,' she started, 'because it's not as daft as it sounds, and definitely not 'cause I think you're all thick.' She held a frond of creamy white flowers in her hand. 'So this is cow parsley.' She then reached overhead to pluck another head of flowers from the bush above her. 'While this, on the other hand, is elderflower, and they are actually pretty similar.' She shook the head of elderflowers. 'And whereas this one makes a gorgeous fresh tasting drink, cow parsley tastes revolting. It also looks very similar to Hemlock which if you're unlucky enough to eat will kill you.'

She smiled reassuringly at Lucy who was beginning to look a little nervous. 'Fortunately, although the flowers look quite similar, the leaves on the elderflower are quite different… look.' She showed them the rounded leaves on the bush above her. 'So I know you'll all be fine, and since I like nothing more than to tease my husband who once picked a fine crop of both for me, I'm counting on you three not to let me down.' She grinned. 'We're also only going to pick half the flowers on each bush. That way we leave the other half to turn into beautiful elderberries come the autumn.'

'Are those the tiny purple berries that people make into wine?' asked Jennie. 'My grandad used to give it to us at Christmas. It was revolting.'

Willow laughed. 'I think they've had rather a bad press as far as homemade wine goes, but I make them into a cordial which is gorgeous, and a pretty fearsome liqueur too. Has you under the table in a matter of minutes if you're not used to it.'

By the time Willow even thought to check her watch again, nearly three hours had passed amid much happy chatter, laughter and the odd Taylor Swift song belted out from Jennie's iPod. Above her the sun continued to beam down on them as the skylark's distinctive call filled the air, and cabbage white butterflies danced to find their dinner. There was nowhere finer to be on a summer's day, and if this was work, Willow hoped she could do it forever. She'd lost count of the number of times the hods had been emptied into the plastic sacks she'd also brought along, and now half a dozen were full and ready to take back to the house.

She motioned for everyone to join her, taking off her hat, and shielding her eyes from the sun.

'Look at this lot, amazing!' she exclaimed. 'Thank you all so much. You've all worked so hard.'

She was met with three happy faces.

'Why don't we take these back to the house, and I can get you all some lunch? I made a special treat for pudding.'

The two girls exchanged grins. 'I've really enjoyed this morning, Willow,' said Lucy. 'I didn't think it would be half as much fun as it has been, and it's so beautiful here.'

Willow smiled to herself. Lucy who at first had been a little shy, and quieter than the other two, had soon relaxed in the fragrant air, with the sun warming her limbs and the light breeze ruffling her hair. Willow had seen it so many times before, but the magic of the countryside never lost its potency. She gave a slight shiver, acknowledging the dark clouds that hovered just out of sight, but she pushed them away. That was a battle for another day.

Having sent Josh out to fetch Peter and the other lads, she and Lucy poured out some drinks, while Jennie laid the table. It was simple food, but once it covered the table, the comments were full of appreciation. A fresh cob loaf stood in the centre, surrounded by a wedge of strong cheese, ripe tomatoes – the size of small apples – and a dish of plum chutney which glowed pinky-red in the sunlight. A huge strawberry Pavlova sat waiting to one side, a jug of fresh cream beside it. Mouths watered, plates were heaped, and bellies were filled. It was the perfect end to a perfect morning.

Willow looked up at the big clock that hung on the wall behind the table and then back down at the sea of contented faces. There were still a couple of hours to go before the children got home from school.

'Right then, who'd like to pick some gooseberries this afternoon?'

It wasn't unusual for Jude to get home from work late when he was away from the office. The clients who bought the huge estates his company sold were wealthy and liked to be wined and dined as part of the deal. Sometimes, they just liked to talk, about their holidays or their yachts, their art collection or the shares they'd just sold for a couple of million. Jude would do whatever it took to get the business, but he always let Willow know when he was going to be delayed. Always.

She hadn't even realised how late it was until her stomach gave a huge gurgle. Lovely though it had been, lunch was a distant memory, and now the girls were already in bed, and the quick half hour she had planned checking the elderflowers over before dinner had turned into nearly an hour.

With a sigh, she covered her precious crop and went back through to the kitchen. Her mobile phone still lay on the table, and she checked it again. The last message she had received from Jude was at six thirty, saying he would be home in about an hour. Whilst in reality this meant it would be nearer eight before he got in, it was now nearly nine. She opened the Aga's warming drawer and peered at the lasagne. It was now or never.

By the time she had finished her food, a curl of unease was working its way up her spine. This was not like Jude at all, and all her calls to his mobile had gone straight to his answerphone. She didn't know what to do. This had never happened before, and there was no one she could contact. He worked alone day to day, and although his father was a partner in the business, he would have no more idea about Jude's whereabouts than she did. Besides which, she would rather wait, alone and anxious, before she called that man. She drew up her legs on the kitchen chair, wrapping her arms around them. She would wait until ten o'clock, and then she was calling the police.

The room was fully dark when the sweep of headlights hit the wall opposite her. It was three minutes to ten. Willow let out a breath and rose stiffly from the chair, one leg refusing to work after being bent in the same position for so long. She resisted the urge to fly down the hallway. Whatever had detained Jude would not be helped by her ranting at him like a hysterical fishwife, but it would take all her acting powers to remain calm and reasoned.

Any anger she had, however, evaporated the minute she caught sight of him. At first, she thought he'd been in a fight; his clothes were dishevelled, his tie gone altogether. But then she saw the expression on his face and the breath caught in her throat. Like anybody, Jude had days when his mood was not as sunny as on others, but in all the years they'd been together she'd never seen him look so low, utterly defeated in fact. He looked as if he were barely hanging on by a thread, and then he turned away from her gaze, as if ashamed.

He carried no bag, no paperwork, no phone or iPad; all the things he had left the house with that morning and, as Willow followed him slowly up the stairs, he might as well have been a ghost for all the substance he had. She flicked on the bedroom light ahead of him, darting in front to try and engage with him in some way, but he turned a weary head towards her.

'Please Willow, don't. Just come to bed. Just be with me.'

By the time she had turned off the lights downstairs and locked up for the night, Jude was already in bed. His once immaculate suit lay discarded in a heap by the bed, only the watch she had given him the Christmas before was placed carefully on the table beside the bed.

She slipped on her pyjamas and crawled into bed beside him where he pulled her so that she lay almost on top of him, her blonde hair splayed out in a fan across his naked chest. He began to stroke it, and it was a long time before his hand finally stilled and he slept. Willow closed her eyes and waited.

Chapter Thirty-Eight

Jude had got up as usual at seven o'clock that morning, spent double the amount of time he normally did in the bathroom, and emerged as if nothing had happened the evening before. He ate wholemeal toast and honey like he always did, drank a cup of tea, followed by a cup of coffee as was his custom, and it wasn't until Willow sat pointedly in front of him that he looked up with a grimace.

'Oh God, that's better. I feel almost human again,' he said with a wry smile. 'Remind me never to entertain Mr Nakamura and his cronies again. They took me to some 'authentic' restaurant, and I've never felt so ill in all my life. I ate things that would probably make me feel sick just looking at them, never mind having them for dinner. Coupled with some heinous wine concoction. I'm a country boy at heart, I can't cope with too much exotica.'

Willow studied him for a moment, his face open and honest, just like it always was. He looked a little tired, but the desolation of the night before was nowhere to be seen.

'I'm really sorry I didn't let you know I'd be so late. Events overtook me rather, and the Japanese consider it extremely rude to use your phone in a restaurant. I was in a bit of a quandary really.'

'You could have called when you left the restaurant. I was really worried.'

'Willow, I was completely pickled. I was way over the legal limit and not thinking logically about anything. I can't believe I drove home.' He shuddered. 'It doesn't bear thinking about.'

He reached out his hand to her. 'Listen, I'm back in the office today, and there's every chance I could be finished by three. Why don't we take the girls and go out for a picnic tea?'

It was a lovely idea, and were it not for the fact that she was absolutely sure that not one drop of alcohol had passed her husband's lips last night, she would have accepted his peace offering without a second thought. His story was so convincing he even had himself believing it, but there was more to it than that; a lot more. Willow didn't need second sight to know that her husband needed her more than ever right now. Whatever was happening in his world, he was trying to shield her from it, just as he always did, only this time it was serious. This time he was scared.

*

Jude kissed his wife goodbye and left the house by the back door. He closed his eyes momentarily against the bright sunlight, and took a deep breath before continuing the short walk to his office. He wasn't sure that he had completely got away with it, but Willow was not the suspicious kind, and she was worried about him rather than looking to find some darker reason for his behaviour yesterday. With any luck by this evening, she would have forgotten about it entirely. Jude, however, was certain that the events of the previous evening would stay with him for a long time to come.

*

Willow hoped Peter wouldn't notice the bags under her eyes, although knowing him, he would and just wouldn't say anything. Now more than ever, it seemed important to get her new venture well and truly underway. She was beginning to feel panicked, which was not like her at all, but last night had spooked her. She had never seen Jude look so distraught, and the fact that he had lied so blatantly about what had happened was proof enough that something was very amiss.

She stood in the doorway to her new stillroom, hands on her hips surveying the stacked crates of elderflowers, and the bags full of flower heads that had yet to be checked over. There was so much to do and the only way through it was to start at the beginning and work methodically. She picked up three huge boiling pans in succession, filling each with water and setting them to heat.

'Peter, would you mind paring the zest from all these lemons, and then quarter the fruit when you've done that?'

He stared at the huge pile of waxy fruit on the table. 'Good job I've got no paper cuts,' he quipped.

Willow was weighing out quantities of sugar. 'Just don't pare your fingers at the same time as the zest,' she grimaced, 'then you'll know about it.'

'So, what exactly is it that we're doing here?' asked Peter. 'Talk me through it from beginning to end.'

Not only was Peter super-efficient, he was a fast learner, and as Willow explained how she made her cordial, she knew she would only have to tell him once.

He nodded in understanding. 'And how much are we making exactly?' he asked, eyeing up the syrup from a previous batch dripping through a muslin cloth into the bowl below.

'If I say until the elderflowers run out, promise me you won't run away.'

Peter stared at her impassively. 'Something tells me you don't just mean that pile of elderflowers there.'

Willow wrinkled her nose. 'Pretty much the whole field, and maybe the next one too...'

'I see. And how many lemons would we need for that?'

She crossed the room to the tall fridge standing in one corner and pulled open the door. A mass of bright yellow ovals covered every shelf. She closed the door quickly.

Peter sighed and picked up the zester, peering at the lemon in his hand.

'One...' he intoned, but when Willow risked a glance at him, he was smiling.

The morning passed in a blur of lemon-scented industry, until the last of the elderflowers had been checked over for bugs and stacked in the waiting crates, and every work surface held pan after pan of the summery concoction. They could do no more until tomorrow when the syrup was ready to be strained.

Willow, however, was not finished with the day yet.

'Do you want to make some ice cream?' She grinned.

Peter, who had a glass of water halfway to his lips, nearly choked before he had even begun to drink it.

'Now might not be the best time to mention that I don't actually like ice cream,' he said.

Willow grinned. 'In that case now might be the perfect time to mention that that doesn't matter in the slightest. Besides, I'll soon change your mind.'

She enjoyed the teasing banter she shared with Peter. He was easy to talk to, but he never let their chatter get in the way of hard work. The morning had taken her mind off the images of last night; not removed them but pushed them firmly enough to one side so that she was able to concentrate on the task at hand. She had to stay focused now. She had to be smart if this venture was ever going to succeed, and simply making gorgeous cordials or ice creams wouldn't be enough. She wasn't just trading in yet another food stuff; instead, she was selling the hum of summer hedgerows, busy with bees, the feeling of sun on bare toes whilst walking country lanes, the soft quiet dawn turning to the pale violet close of the day. It was everything she held dear, bottled, packaged and enticing. She was selling the dream. And not only was she selling it, but she also had to convince some pretty important people that they wanted to buy it.

She glanced back at Peter who had now finished his drink and was waiting for further instructions. He had asked nothing of her during the morning, beyond the odd check that he was doing things correctly, or what to do next, but she could sense his curiosity. It was pretty obvious, particularly to someone with Peter's intellect that her comment about branching out her business a little was not all there was to it, but she still wasn't sure how much she should confide in him. She trusted him, that wasn't the issue, but how did you explain to someone that everything you were doing, every decision you made was because of a feeling, a hunch, even a bad dream. It sounded kooky even to her.

She took some cream from the fridge. 'The ice cream isn't difficult to make,' she said. 'It's basically gooseberry puree mixed with elderflower cordial and added to whipped cream, but I find it has a happy spot when you're mixing. It's hard to explain, but under or over the happy spot and it doesn't seem quite the same somehow. I'll try and—'

Willow was interrupted by the sound of her mobile ringing. She glanced down at the table, her face crossed with anxiety when she noted who the caller was. She picked the phone up immediately.

'Maggie, is everything okay?'

She listened, nodding, for a few seconds, her expression growing more and more concerned. 'I'll come straight away. I can be with you in about ten minutes... Is Amy okay? She'll be so upset about her sister.'

Peter looked up sharply when he heard Amy's name mentioned and his eyes connected with Willow's as she lowered the phone.

'That was the school,' she murmured, her hand fluttering to her throat. 'Beth fell awkwardly in PE, they think she might have broken her arm.'

Peter took the phone from her hand with a glance at his watch. 'Go and get your bag and keys. I'll ring Jude, maybe he can pick Amy up later, otherwise I'll go.' He shooed her out of the room, already dialling the number. By the time she returned, it was all sorted, and he pushed the phone back into Willow's hands.

'Go on, go. We'll look after everything here until you get back. Just keep in touch, let us know how you get on, okay? And give my love to Beth.'

Willow gave him one final look before turning on her heel. Her mind was already elsewhere.

*

Peter watched her retreating back as she hurried down the hallway. It was every parent's worst nightmare, and he hoped that Beth was okay. He'd never really had any experience with children before coming to work for Willow, but Beth was bright as a button, and funny too. She'd had him in stitches one day trying to teach him tongue twisters. She was so much better at them than he was. Amy was quieter than her twin, a little more thoughtful perhaps, but just as adorable, and she would miss her sister dreadfully this afternoon. He didn't think he had ever seen them apart.

He turned back to the table and looked at the two large pots of cream that Willow had put there moments earlier. The navy-blue notebook lay a little distance away, and he picked it up thoughtfully. He'd never made ice cream before, but maybe this would help to keep him occupied while he waited for news about Beth. After all, how hard could it be?

The gooseberries were cooling by the time Peter heard the back door slam, and the sound of running feet. He knew that Amy would head for the kitchen first, and as he pulled open the door to the stillroom, he was met with her tear-stained face racing down the hallway to find him. She barrelled into his legs just as a tired-looking Jude came through the door. He looked a little fraught.

'I want to go to the hospital.' Amy wailed into his legs. He suspected Jude had heard nothing else since he picked her up from school, but he bent down as close as he could to her level, pulling her gently away so that he could at least see her face.

'I'm sure you do,' he said. 'I know if it were my sister that had hurt her arm, that's exactly what I'd like to do too.'

The tears halted for a moment. 'Then why can't I go? Daddy says I can't go.'

Peter took hold of her hand and started to lead her back down the hallway. He bent down to whisper in her ear.

'Shall I tell you what I think? I think daddy doesn't want you to go because then he'll have no one to look after him while Beth and mummy are at the hospital. Daddies get scared too, you know.'

Amy looked up at him, her blue eyes large and round. 'But you could look after him.'

Peter bit back a sigh, thinking quickly. 'But I'm looking after you,' he said.

There was silence for a moment while Peter was subjected to rigorous scrutiny by the six-year-old still holding his hand.

'Okay,' she replied. 'I'll look after daddy then… Do you think he'll want a biscuit?'

Peter grinned. 'I'm sure he will. I think he'll also like a very strong cup of coffee,' he added, with a quick look at Jude. 'But I can make that. You go and see if there're any jammy dodgers left.'

Amy skipped off happily to the kitchen while Peter smiled at Jude apologetically. 'Sorry about that,' he murmured. 'Best I could come up with at short notice.'

Jude looked exhausted, but he laid a hand on Peter's shoulder. 'No, thank you,' he smiled. 'Jammy dodgers… blimey, I haven't had one of those in years. Are they still as good as I remember?'

Peter nodded. 'Best get in there before they all go. I'll put the kettle on.' He followed Jude into the kitchen where Amy was already sitting at the table, biscuit tin in front of her.

'You know what, Ames,' said Jude, sitting down. 'I'm rubbish at drawing things. Would you help me make a get-well card for Beth? I think she'd like that.'

Amy shot Peter an exasperated look. 'Daddy, Beth won't want a rubbish card, will she? *I'll* make the card, and you can help.'

Peter turned away quickly so that she wouldn't see his smile.

Leaving the two of them at the table surrounded by card and felt tip pens, Peter went back to the stillroom wondering whether he had the nerve to finish making the ice cream. He'd read through the instructions in the notebook several times but was still baffled. *Mix together the whipped cream and gooseberry puree until it starts to sing* – what on earth did that mean?

He washed his hands and pushed a tentative finger into the gooseberries that he'd left to cool. Perfect. He checked the recipe again and then took up a bowl in a meaningful manner.

So far so good. He was now staring at a bowl full of whipped cream and one of gooseberry puree, mixed with the fragrant elderflower cordial. He picked up the second bowl, stared at the wooden spoon in his hand, and started to pour.

At first, the gooseberry puree cut swirls of green through the cream, but as his spoon moved back and forth, they began to turn a pale-yellow colour. He mixed some more, energetically this time and was rewarded with a higher pitched sound than before. It wasn't quite singing yet, but Peter could hear the difference and that was all the encouragement he needed. After a few more minutes, he stopped. The recipe was right. Some strange alchemy indeed, but if he had to choose a word to describe it, he would have said that the ice cream was happy, singing away in the bowl as he mixed. He'd already laid out a plastic container on the table, and now he moved it a bit closer, grinning with delight as he poured out his first batch of ice cream. He placed it reverently in the freezer, and sat back down at the table, a hum of excitement settling with him. He had done it.

Willow rang again just after seven. She sounded tired but relieved as she explained that they would soon be on their way home. The doctor had declared that no bones were broken, but Beth had sprained her arm, and it would still be sore for a few days. Now all she wanted to do was get home and snuggle up in bed with Matilda, her favourite bear.

Peter exchanged a look with Jude. He had stayed, not only to help look after Amy, but because he didn't want to leave without knowing what had happened to Beth. Now it was time for the family to be together again, and he didn't want to outstay his welcome. He dropped a kiss on Amy's head, telling her he would see her tomorrow and let Jude walk him to the door. He'd never really thought about his life in terms of being a father before, and yet the few hours he had spent with

Amy and Jude had convinced him that at some point in his life, there was nothing he would like better. He'd only ever seen Jude when he was coming or going, never for long enough to form an opinion beyond the fact that he was a bit of a flash merchant. He knew he worked hard for his family, but the clothes he wore were just that bit too nice for Peter's taste, the car he drove, just that bit too arrogant. But tonight, he'd seen a different person in Jude. He'd seen the person who wanted nothing more than to make his daughter happy.

*

Jude closed the door thoughtfully. He'd never really paid any of the students who came to help Willow much attention before. They went almost as soon as they arrived, and although he was on hand if there was ever a problem, Willow seemed to manage them perfectly well without his help. Peter was different though, and he let his thoughts meander through the various scenarios he now had in his head. He wouldn't discuss any of them with Willow however, not just yet.

With an ear cocked, listening out for Amy, he pushed open the door to the stillroom, a place about which Willow had said very little recently. He admitted that in the past he'd rarely ventured inside. It was more Willow's domain than his, and unless she wasn't around and he needed to find something, what reason did he ever have to go in there? Things had changed, though. There was a bustle about the place that he had only just allowed to register. Smells that, although he was used to them, seemed to be occurring more frequently. Willow didn't keep secrets but neither had she volunteered much about what she'd been up to lately.

He hadn't thought about what he would find as he entered the room, but he was transfixed by what he saw. A slow smile began to turn up the corners of his mouth as he stared around him. He had gone through hell last night. It had been far worse than he had ever imagined and afterwards he had sat for hours, practically motionless trying to remind himself that what he was doing was the right thing. He had crawled home to bed, and to Willow, who was all he had craved, but the cost of what he had done would be his to bear for a long time yet. This was good, though. This was a glimmer of hope for the road ahead, and Willow was in for such a surprise.

Chapter Thirty-Nine

'Peter, I could kiss you!' exclaimed Willow, grinning, as he backed away in embarrassment. 'Don't worry,' she added, 'I was only joking, you're quite safe! This is perfect, though. It tastes wonderful...' She winked at him. 'Almost as good as I could make myself.'

The tub of ice cream lay on the table in front of them, a spoon sticking out of its depths.

'I was a bit mystified by the thought of it singing to me, but bizarrely, once I'd got to that point, it did seem to make sense. I might have been dreaming, though.'

'That's grandma Gilly's notebook for you,' she replied. 'It's full of all things magical.'

Peter didn't doubt that it was. He eyed the silver moon on the corner of the cover. He'd had a little peek at the pages beyond the instructions for the ice cream, and some of the 'recipes' were certainly not for things you'd want to eat...

'So, what's next?' he asked. 'In the grand scheme of things, I mean.'

Willow made a face. 'It's not a very grand scheme at all. In fact, I'm making most of it up as I go along.'

She laid down the pencil she was doodling with. It was another hot day, and her long hair was loosely wound into two plaits. She blew a puff of air upwards, trying to ruffle the line of her fringe. 'I should have a plan, shouldn't I?' she asked. 'I should have all this laid out like a military campaign, so I know exactly what I'm doing.'

Peter pulled the spoon from the ice cream, a generous dollop still attached to it which he made no effort to remove. Instead, he stuck the whole thing in his mouth and closed his eyes, letting the ice cream melt and trickle around his mouth. A small dribble escaped.

He opened one eye. 'Am I now wearing this?' He sighed, knowing that his beard had mopped up any excess.

Willow giggled. 'We should really put this back into the freezer.' She held out her hand for the spoon, which Peter offered up reluctantly.

'Do I take it that you now like ice cream?' she asked.

Peter ignored her. 'So tell me what it is you want to accomplish. Really accomplish, that is. Rather than what you're pretending, which is that you're just fooling around making a few pots of ice cream here and there.'

Willow picked up the tub of ice cream and got up from the table without saying a word. Peter thought at first he'd upset her, but when she turned back from the freezer she had a gentle smile on her face.

'I am *so* not a businesswoman,' she said. 'I mean, look at me. Bare feet, plaits, and a smock. And yes, before you say it, I know I run a fruit farm, but that's different. I don't have to convince anyone to eat the strawberries, or gooseberries or whatever, people do it all by themselves. I don't change the product in any way, after all, why mess with perfection? I simply grow the fruit, and people come and buy it.'

'I'm sure it's not quite as cut and dried as that,' interrupted Peter. 'You need to know what you're doing for one thing,' he added.

'That's very kind of you, but really Mother Nature does most of it.' She paused, gathering her thoughts. 'What I want is a business that's sustainable all year round. I want to gather everything we have here, and take it out there...' she waved a vague hand at the window, '... to people who don't have these gorgeous things on their doorstep, who don't get up every morning and gaze out on fields sparkling with the morning dew. Who aren't as lucky as we are. I want to share it, but in the process I want to give our family a future, here on this land, so that it never has to become a field full of houses, or offices or a car park. That's actually the most important thing to me, but I'm not stupid enough to think that we don't need money to survive, or to grow, and I know people won't want to buy the things I make just because I say they're good. I'll need to convince them… I just don't know how.'

She sat down at the table with a thump. 'I have ideas for all the things I want to make, I know how to make them. I have someone who makes packaging to put them in, and I have designs for said packaging. I just don't have a bloody clue about what to do next. How to get it out there.'

Peter rubbed the end of his nose. 'And this business?' he began, 'how big is it going to be? Are we talking about shed loads of investment? New premises? Staff?'

Willow snorted. 'God no. Just enough for us, our family, no more. Small, selective, self-sufficient, an extension of our lives here. We have the space and if we need somewhere a little bigger to work from, there're always the barns outside. I grow a lot of what we eat… and we can live pretty cheaply really. We don't need masses of money… we never have.'

Now we're getting to the heart of the matter, thought Peter, watching her expression. 'So start-up costs are relatively small. You've sourced your equipment. You have a worthy range of products, now what you need is marketing and exposure, would that be right?'

Willow eyed him cautiously.

'Only it strikes me that you have what you need right under your nose, and I'm wondering why you haven't asked him.'

Peter might be mistaken, but he thought he detected a slight blush at his words.

'Ask who?' replied Willow. 'Oh, do you mean you? That would be perfect, Peter, I—'

He held up his hand. 'No, I don't mean me… although I do almost have a degree in Business and Management. I meant Jude actually. He's a salesman, isn't he?'

'Well, not really,' frowned Willow. 'That makes it sound like he sells double glazing… not that there's anything wrong with that of course,' she added quickly. 'But what Jude does is a bit different. He sells land, huge farms, estates, I mean he even sold an island once. He has a very specialist knowledge, and...' She caught sight of Peter's stony expression and ground to a halt. 'Yes, at the end of the day I guess he is a salesman,' she accepted.

'So what's the problem, Willow?' asked Peter softly. 'Why won't you talk to him about any of this? And don't say it's because it's a stupid idea and he wouldn't want to be bothered with it.'

'Okay then, I won't.'

'I'm trying to help here you know, and yes, I do have some ideas about how you could market and develop the business, but you and I both know I'm not the solution. I'm only here until October and then I go back to uni, so what use would I be then? What you need is a proper partner in the business who can help you longer term. Jude might be busy, but surely he'd see the value in what you're doing? He'd be proud, wouldn't he? He'd want to help?'

Willow bit her lip. 'I know you're right. But I also know that Jude is a stickler for detail and he never goes after anything if it doesn't feel right, if the numbers don't stack up. I have to present this whole thing as a viable business, up and running, with a business plan, forecasts, and projections if he's ever going to take any notice of it. Otherwise he'll discount it out of hand.'

'Okay, I get that, but what's the problem; you'll have all that soon.'

Peter stared at her, waiting for a reply, watching while she took a calming breath.

'I trust you and I need your help, Peter, but if I tell you why I can't say anything to Jude at the moment, you have to promise me you won't repeat it. I haven't told a soul about this, not properly anyway.'

His normally pale complexion coloured quickly. 'Willow, how can I possibly do that when I don't know what it is you're going to say? It could put me in an untenable position.'

'I know, and I shouldn't ask, but I need your help.' She raised her hands in a helpless gesture. 'There's nothing more I can say. Once you know and understand why I feel the way I do, you can't unknow it. It has to be your decision. I'm not going to try to convince you.'

Peter had never been in such a position before. Sure he'd had friends tell him secrets, who hadn't, but this was different. From what he could see, Willow and Jude had a happy marriage, but if there was something that Willow felt she needed to keep secret from her husband, then it must be important. The other night while he'd waited with Jude for news about Beth, he had heard Jude's soft words about his wife, affectionate words, caring words; a loving inflection in his voice that could never be faked. He wasn't sure he wanted to hear anything that might call that into question.

Willow had said she wouldn't try to persuade him and, as he looked at her downcast face, he realised that unwittingly perhaps he had led them to this point. He couldn't blame her now for trying to explain when that was what he had asked her to do. He liked Willow. He loved her business and the way she lived her life, and now she was asking for his help.

'Go on,' he said slowly. 'What is it you need to say?'

She gave a nervous smile. 'You're going to think I'm an absolute nutter, but to be fair you wouldn't be the first…' She took another deep breath. 'I see things sometimes… or feel things. Things which I know other people don't see or feel, but which give me a particular insight into a situation that's happening now… or in the future.' She glanced out of the window as if drawing strength from the view. 'Have you ever walked down our lane in the other direction, up towards Fallowfield?' she asked. 'The house just past the huge horse chestnut?'

'Only once or twice, although I'm not sure I really took much notice of it.'

'Middleton Estates own it. We have a tenant living there: Henry, and although you can't see it from the road, on the other side of the clearing is Jude's office. Just past that is a five-bar gate that leads onto a track through the trees, at the other end of which are fields as far as you can see.'

'Which the company also owns?'

Willow nodded. 'I had a dream the other week that it was all gone. All the fields, the grasses, the hedges, torn up and replaced with row upon row of houses. Huge jagged craters left in the mud like an open wound.' She gave an involuntary shudder. 'Peter, it terrified me to see all of that meadow-land gone, ripped aside through greed, houses crushed together...'

Peter reached out a tentative hand to touch her arm in comfort.

'I know that's what Jude is planning. He's going to sell the land to some developer and build houses on it. I can't begin to imagine how much money it will make him... but however much it is, it will never be enough for his father. Andrew only ever taught Jude fear. Fear of being poor, fear of being despised by others, richer and more powerful than him, and all Jude ever wanted from his father was to be loved. But there isn't enough money in the world to make him love Jude, not properly, not like a father should: unconditionally, wholeheartedly. But Jude hasn't figured this out yet,' she said bitterly. 'His father will be behind this somewhere, egging him on, justifying his actions. Telling him you're only as good as your next million.' A tear dripped down her cheek. 'I can't let Jude do this to himself. I have to make him see that he has a life here, a good life, with people who love him for who he is. I have to show him that enough really can be enough.'

This wasn't what Peter had expected to hear from Willow, but curiously, it made sense. Now that Willow had said it out loud he could see the desire in Jude, the mercenary streak that ran through his veins, the way he dressed, the way he spoke sometimes. Jude was a person who liked life with a gilt edge. Peter fished in his pocket for a hanky, passing it to Willow and feeling his own emotions welling up. Willow wasn't like that. Whatever she had would be enough, and she'd give you her last bean if you asked for it. She wanted a successful business, but it wasn't money that motivated her, it was love. Love for anything that lived, breathed, or grew, but especially, love for Jude.

'Will he take your strawberry fields as well?' he asked gently.

Willow looked up sharply, her nose still buried in Peter's hanky. '… I don't think so,' she replied, and then stronger, 'no, I'm sure he wouldn't do that… not to start with anyway, but it will come in time. What's to stop the developer wanting more and more?'

Peter thought quickly. 'So, assuming what you've said is true, your idea is to give Jude a viable alternative to his plan so that he doesn't sell the land. A business which ultimately you would run together, and one which he can see has a chance of being a success? He would stand to lose a huge amount of money, though, Willow. Do you really think it might work?'

She wiped her nose again. 'I don't know,' she whispered. 'But it's the only chance I've got.'

'You're going to have to speak to him about all this some time; you do know that, don't you? You might have got it all wrong, and—'

Willow shook her head urgently. 'I know, but not yet. I need to get things sorted out, Peter, I haven't got much time. I don't know how far advanced his plans are, or how much time I have on my side. It could only be a matter of weeks and, if I show my ideas to Jude now, without any of the assurances I know he'll look for, then I might as well not bother. I need something solid to divert his course of action, not a half-baked plan that would simply reinforce the notion that his own pursuits are the only realistic option for our future. I either need more time, or more results, and that's all there is to it.'

There was no knowing what amount of time they had, Peter could see that. All this still might be for nothing, but they had to try, surely?

'Have you got a pen and a notebook I can scribble in? I need to know exactly what you've done so far.'

Chapter Forty

Jude turned his car into the secluded parking area with a flourish, covering the small distance to the guest parking spaces far more quickly than was necessary. His powerful car swung around, coming to a halt immediately beneath a security camera, one of several that ringed the car park. It didn't matter whether you were inside the building or outside, appearances were what mattered.

He levered his long legs out of the car, and reached into the back for his jacket. His Ralph Lauren suit clung in all the right places, the jacket settling effortlessly along his shoulders, the crisp shirt he'd chosen, just a little tighter than he would normally wear. He'd debated buying a new suit for the occasion but decided that this would deliver the wrong message. He didn't want to look as though he was trying to impress; he simply wanted to be impressive, and far better to arrive wearing an old favourite that showed how accustomed he was to fine clothes than to look like some jumped-up barrow boy. He straightened his cufflinks and closed the car door with a clunk.

The cameras tracked him silently as he walked. He wouldn't need to announce his arrival. By the time he pushed open the door into the elegant glass atrium, Emily would have alerted her boss to his presence and would rise to greet him, enquiring politely about his journey and escorting him personally up to the third floor. The board room would already be set up, and her order for fresh coffee would take only a matter of seconds as he approached the building. Edward would be ready for him, as, no doubt, would Olivia. He only hoped he was ready for them.

His face had held a gracious smile for the whole distance across the car park to the reception area, and only now, as he reached out a hand for the door, did he allow himself to clench his jaws together momentarily. By the time he met Emily's outstretched hand, the smile was back. The next hour would possibly be the most important of his career, and he pushed the memory of the last conversation with his father away, thrusting it deep into a place where, today at least, it would not surface. He concentrated on Emily's face, not only on what she was saying, but what her eyes told him too. Secretaries always knew what was going down, and he'd never met one yet who'd been able to hide it.

Olivia met him as he stepped from the lift, her brown eyes twinkling mischievously. She was wearing a bright red dress, clingy and low cut, and Jude let his eyes wander its length for just a moment longer than casual interest might dictate. He met her gaze with a smile, leaning in for the customary kiss on both cheeks.

Her cheek was soft against his, as she pressed her body up against him, one hand lingering against his arm as she slowly stroked its length. When she finally pulled away, her eyes flashed like a cat in the night, and Jude let a soft sigh whisper into the space between them.

'Jude, you're looking even more ravishing than the last time we met. How will I ever keep my hands off you?'

He placed a hand in the small of her back as she turned around, applying just enough pressure to the base of her spine. His other hand was already extended towards her husband who he had spied walking soundlessly across the deep carpet to join them.

'Edward, a pleasure as always,' he smiled.

The hand that shook his was cool despite the warmth of the day.

'Jude,' he nodded in return, and then taking his wife's arm, 'Shall we?' He motioned towards the board room.

Inside, the table which would easily accommodate twelve was laid for just the three of them. A black jotter marked each place, a white coffee cup at its top right-hand corner. Apart from the carafe of fresh coffee, the table held a marble platter with milk, sugar, and a plate filled with a dozen or so small pastries. The only other thing on the table was a sheaf of thick white paper.

As Jude sat in the space indicated, Emily materialised back into the room, holding a trio of iPads, one of which she set up on the table in front of him. The others she passed to Edward and Olivia before soundlessly leaving the room. It was like a dance, a bizarre mating ritual, but Jude knew the moves, and he played them effortlessly.

The door closed behind them with a soft click as he waited for Edward to speak. His heart was pounding.

'Well then, Jude, how about it?' He grinned. 'Is today a good day to make an obscene amount of money?'

'It's always a good day for making money, Eddie, but obscenity can sometimes take a little longer.' He flashed a candid smile. 'And I never sign anything on an empty stomach. May I?' he asked, indicating the tray of pastries.

Olivia slipped out of her seat and began to pour the coffee. 'Help yourself,' she purred. The pastries were not the only thing being offered on a plate.

'I've taken the liberty of summarising the key points of our agreement,' said Edward, 'which you can find in front of you, although you and I both know we could recite them in our sleep. I want to be sure that you're happy with everything, Jude. It's important to me that there are no doubts from your perspective; Jennings Pemberton has built its reputation on integrity and, important though this deal is, for both of us, I've no wish to jeopardise what we've worked so hard for on a detail overlooked, or a technicality. Please take all the time you need before signing.'

Jude smiled. Edward was smooth, there was no denying it, but the fact of the matter was that Jude would not be sitting here today if he were in any way unsure about the deal on the table. Jude paid his lawyers a great deal of money to make sure that every detail was locked down, and indeed Jude himself had set the terms of this deal. There was never going to be any deviation from its specifications, he simply would not allow it. Today had been a very long time coming, and Jennings Pemberton were certainly not the first organisation with whom he had sought to broker a deal. It was gracious of Edward to make it appear that they were doing him a favour, but really it couldn't be farther from the truth. Even the parcel of land he'd thrown in as a sweetener had been chosen with the utmost care. Completely disingenuous on his part of course; he was well aware that there was every possibility that planning permission would be granted on it, but it didn't hurt to feign ignorance. Punters liked to think they were getting one over on the seller, and for all his integrity, Edward was no different.

He sipped his coffee, savouring the rich taste. 'I'm happy to sign, Eddie,' he said. 'I trust you received Andrew's instructions yesterday?'

'On the dotted line, Jude, all present and correct.'

Jude lifted the cup to his lips once more, letting it hide the outward breath he released. Andrew's co-operation had been by no means assured, and after their argument of the other evening there was a small, but none the less, significant risk that he would veto the agreement at the last minute. Jude was mightily relieved to see that Andrew's mercenary tendencies still held. Cold-hearted he might be, but he was no fool, and given the choice of either signing and accepting the new arrangements or losing a good deal of virtually free money, was there really any other choice open to him?

Edward reached inside his jacket pocket to retrieve a midnight blue fountain pen that exactly matched the colour of his tie, and slid it along the table towards Jude.

Jude looked down at the sheaf of paper on the blotter in front of him. He scanned the pages with a practised eye, and flipped to the last page with a casual flick of his wrist. He signed his name on the bottom without a second glance.

As if a spell had been broken, the calculated atmosphere in the room relaxed, and jackets were removed, ties were loosened and the conversation flowed amiably. Olivia rubbed her foot along Jude's calf a total of three times and Jude enquired politely how their eldest daughter's

GCSEs had gone. Forty-nine minutes after he first entered the building, Jude bid a cheerful goodbye to Emily in reception and walked back out to the car park. Moments later, he swung out past the security cameras with just the same panache as when he had entered.

He waited until he was several streets from the offices of Jennings Pemberton before pulling his car to the side of the road, opening his door and vomiting the two almond pastries and Olivia's unwelcome attention and cloying perfume into the cool grass of the verge.

Chapter Forty-One

It was difficult to see how Freya was managing to type anything on her laptop. It was precariously poised on a pile of papers, resting at such a slant that it bounced up and down each time she typed. Willow hovered in the doorway for a moment, unwilling to break Freya's concentration, but also fascinated to see her working in such a haphazard fashion. As she watched, Freya lifted up her laptop, peered at the piece of paper directly underneath it, and then carried on typing completely oblivious to how absurd she looked.

Sam leaned towards Willow. 'She's been like that for hours. Every time I come in, the paper level has risen another inch. God knows where it's all coming from. In fact, if you hadn't arrived, I'd be worried I might lose her altogether.'

'I can hear you, you know,' came the disembodied voice from behind the laptop. 'Sorry, Willow, I'll be with you in a minute... I just want to finish this sentence... while it's all in my head.'

'I'll put the kettle on.' Sam grinned, crossing the room.

Willow looked around her at the homely kitchen. When they were children, she used to come here at least once a week after netball practice. Freya's dad would make them hot chocolate and they would sit and giggle their way through copies of *Just Seventeen*. She'd never dreamed that years later they would still be here, hatching plans and schemes of a different kind. But it felt right; the happy energy in the room was still here after all this time, as if nothing had changed, and even Freya herself didn't look much different to how she had then, frantically trying to finish her homework before school the next day. When Freya's father had died last year, it had looked for a while as if she might lose both the farm and her childhood home, but today, with Sam at her side, their future was secure. She could only hope that her own plans would bring about a similar resolution for her and Jude.

Freya's dark head bobbed up from behind the screen, and she laid the laptop to one side.

'Sorry about that, but I've been trying to nail this particular paragraph all morning, and the perfect words suddenly came to me.' She got up from the table and gave Willow a hug. 'I'm like a thing possessed, but then I guess you feel that way too,' she added.

Willow smiled at Sam as he handed her a cup of tea. 'There never seem to be enough hours in the day. Everything I do spawns more and more jobs... I've never been so excited, though. I can't stop thinking about stuff, and even though things are getting done, I've a horrible feeling I'm getting carried away.'

Freya nodded repeatedly. 'Oh yeah,' she said. 'Been there, done that... still there in fact.' She laughed. 'Look, I'll show you.'

She took Willow's arm, just as Sam butted in. 'I'm going to leave you two for a bit and take my tea somewhere a little more peaceful, but I'll come back and check on you in about half an hour, Willow, just to make sure you're still with us. If you need me to come and rescue you before then, just shout, okay?' He winked at Freya. 'Go easy on her... and remember to breathe.'

Freya picked up her pencil preparing to throw it as Sam ducked out of the room. 'Cheeky sod, he's just as excited as I am.'

'So what are you up to now?' asked Willow, sitting down and peering at the assortment of leaflets and brochures on the table.

Freya turned the laptop screen around to face her friend.

'The Appleyard Community Juice Pressing Scheme,' she announced proudly. 'We're not short of a few fruit trees here in Herefordshire as you know, and it suddenly struck me what a wonderful resource we have. There are loads of people around here who'd like to make their own juice but haven't got the right equipment. Even a single tree in your garden is enough — one bucket load of apples could make about five bottles of juice, and we'll pasteurise it too, so it will last for about a year.'

Willow looked at the vibrant images on the screen. She scratched the side of her nose. 'But don't you want people to buy the juice *you* make?'

'Of course.' Freya grinned. 'But this way we get the best of both worlds. We'll make and sell our own juice products, with a little help from you of course, and by aiming these products at carefully selected retailers, we won't be saturating the market locally which will give the range more of a specialty feel to it. People will still have to pay for the pressing service, so that will generate additional income, keep our machines running and, with any luck, score us some brownie points with the local community, especially if we stress the fundraising possibilities for groups who want to press juice for a profit themselves.' She looked down fondly at the screen. 'It might also result in even more sales, perversely. Just suppose you press your own juice, proudly take home your bottles and then drink them over the course of the next few weeks. Where are you going to get more from, now that you've developed a taste for the fresh stuff?'

'Ah... clever,' said Willow. 'You know that actually makes sense. What a brilliant idea.'

'I know,' replied Freya, beaming. 'I'm a genius. Seriously though, it does make sound business sense, but I like the whole idea of the community thing too. I feel like I've been given a second chance with Appleyard, and I'd like to keep that luck running if I can.'

Willow looked down at the table again. 'And this is research, is it?'

'Mainly,' replied Freya. 'Information from other companies offering a similar service, but I've also got brochures here giving all the technical specifications for our equipment as well. We might be asked all sorts of questions by prospective users of the scheme, and I don't want to be caught napping. We could need to be pressing as early as August, and that doesn't give us much time to get all our marketing information out there and be ready for business.'

'So you need to know where I am with Willowberries?'

Freya nodded. 'I just love that name.' She sighed. 'We make such a perfect combination, don't we? Appleyard Juices and Willowberries nectar, it's almost as if it was meant to be – I mean who wouldn't want to buy us?'

Willow fished in the bag she had brought with her, carefully pulling out a cardboard box and laying it on the table in front of her. Wrapped around it was a vibrantly printed sleeve of cardboard the exact colour of a dusky Victoria plum. A froth of white elderflowers trailed across one corner, curling around the lettering that formed the company name. She looked at Freya's astonished face.

'Go on, open it,' she said.

Freya moved her laptop further to one side and slid the box towards her. 'I daren't, it's too beautiful,' she replied, running her fingers across the surface. 'Is this one of the sample boxes that you were talking about?'

Willow's smile was wide. 'They turned out better than I could ever have hoped. They were Peter's idea, but Henry did all the design work of course, and his girlfriend gave me the name of the people she uses for packaging.'

'And Merry has sent these out to the list of folk that she knows?'

'Some of them, yes, about twenty in all to start with. It was a pretty long list, but we picked some retailers, some hotels and a couple of restaurants too. All people she's dealt with before and recommends. Fingers crossed we get one or two bites.'

Freya looked down at the box in front of her. 'I'd eat *this*.' She grinned. 'It looks good enough.'

Carefully, she removed the sleeve from the outside, and levered open the lid of the box. A subtle waft of summery fragrance rose up. She inhaled happily. 'Mmm, what's this?' she queried.

'Elderflower oil, dabbed onto the bottom of the box. I thought it would help to appeal to all the senses,' said Willow.

'Oh God, I'm fairly drooling…'

She lifted out a small bottle from the box, a lime green label swinging from its neck. *Drink Me* it read.

I am elderflowers, gathered when the sun warms the blooms and
bees dance in the hedgerows.
I am steeped with sugar and juicy Sicilian lemons.
I am Willowberries Elderflower Nectar.

Next a tiny jar emerged with a label bearing the instruction *Eat Me.*

I am fat strawberries that dribble down your chin, gathered from a
field where skylarks sing.
I've begged a little lemon juice, sugar, and elderflower cordial to
keep me company.
I am Willowberries Strawberry and Elderflower Preserve.

Freya set this gently to one side, bringing out the last of the tiny
containers, this time a small pot with a vibrant plum label. *Imagine*
me, it read.

I am gooseberries, golden orbs bursting in the morning sun.
I am singing with sugar and elderflower cordial and whipped into
soft velvety peaks of double cream.
I am Willowberries Gooseberry and Elderflower Cream Ice.

She sat back in her chair, for a moment totally lost for words. Willow
was studying her, trying to read her expression.

'The labels are just a little bit of folly,' supplied Willow. 'I thought they
might add to the sense of magic; you know like Alice in Wonderland...'

'Willow, these are inspired! I've never seen anything like this, but
what a fantastic idea, it works beautifully.'

'There's some literature in there as well, giving details of the available flavours, ingredients, as well as how they're made. I've tasted so
many cordials and eaten so much ice cream this week I'll be the size
of a house soon, but fortunately for my waistline, this is the final list,
well for the time being anyway. We've settled on eight flavours of ice

cream to start with and six different cordials, together with nine types of preserves and curds.'

It had taken Willow quite some time to decide which of her favourite recipes to concentrate on, but she knew that if they were to have any chance of success she had to keep things simple. The number of flavours was sensible, and as they were seasonal, it would give them the opportunity to concentrate on each, one at a time, until they were really up and running. They were a mixture of the traditional and the more exotic, a little risky potentially, but Willow wanted to provide not just the familiar, but the enticing too. Her lemon and rose geranium cordial might sound unusual, but she'd buy a bottle just for the colour alone.

'These sound amazing.' Freya grinned, looking at the stylish literature. 'I can't wait to try them.'

'Well, some of the flavours I can get to you straight away, but the rosehips for example won't be available until the autumn. You'll just have to take my word for how gorgeous it is.'

'The main thing is that I get an idea of what you're going to produce. There will be plenty of time for us to experiment with our fruit juice blends later in the year. We won't be harvesting for months yet, but that's the beauty of it. It will give you time to start producing, and we'll be busy juicing other people's fruit until our own are ready to harvest.'

'I'm going to see Merry later to take her some more literature too, so she can help promote Willowberries through the shop. I'd like her opinion on a few other things as well; she knows so much about merchandising.'

Freya sucked in a quick breath. 'Did she tell you she's got someone coming to see her from *Country Living*? How amazing is that?'

Willow stared at her. 'What, *the* Country Living? As in the magazine? How on earth did she manage that?'

'Sheer fluke I think. A reporter did a piece on the shop for the local paper, talking about the artist who owned it before and how Merry has breathed new life into it by paying homage to him. Someone from the magazine spotted the article whilst they were staying with some relative or another for a wedding down here. I haven't got the whole story. They only called yesterday, and Merry was a tad excited when she told me.' She grinned at Willow. 'I could hardly understand a word she was saying…'

'I bet.' She laughed. 'What wonderful publicity for her, though, and such a stroke of luck.'

'Merry seemed to think that Christopher himself might have had something to do with it.' Freya winked. 'I did point out that he'd been dead for a couple of years, but that didn't seem to deter her.'

'Maybe she's found her guardian angel,' replied Willow. 'Stranger things have happened.' She thought back to the bleak time in Freya's life just after her father died and the transformation that had been brought about by her dark, curly-haired stranger.

Freya nodded, clearly understanding her meaning. 'Stranger things indeed,' she said. 'So who's your guardian angel then, Willow?'

A worried frown crossed Willow's face. 'I'd like to say maybe my grandma Gilly, but I'm not sure there's anyone watching over me right now,' she said seriously. 'I'm running out of time, so if they're out there, it would be nice if they could make their presence felt a bit sharpish.'

'Are you still having those dreams?' asked Freya, a concerned note to her voice.

Willow nodded. 'More and more. Always the same. And Jude is definitely up to something, he's like the proverbial cat on a hot tin roof, and he's working harder than ever. I've barely seen him.'

'Maybe you should talk to him, Willow. Then at least you'd know where you are, and what you're up against.'

Willow shook her head violently this time. 'No. Not until I'm certain. Not until I'm ready with all of this. I have to prove to him that this could work for us.'

Willow closed her eyes momentarily. She was getting scared now. The dreams were getting stronger and stronger, still most often at night, but now during the day as well, with an intensity that made her feel quite sick. She had been washing up a couple of nights ago when Jude had come into the kitchen and slid his arms around her waist. The sudden shock of the images which had forced their way into her mind had nearly taken her legs from under her, and had Jude not been there to catch her, she would have fallen. It had taken all her powers of persuasion to convince him not to call a doctor, so how could she confide in him now? He'd think her ill, or worse, mad, and she would never be able to convince him that her fledgling business was worth pursuing.

She gave Freya a bright smile, knowing that she disproved of her silence as far as Jude was concerned. 'I'll have a chat to him soon; I'd like to get a few more things underway first, that's all, and then I'll hit him with my amazing ideas and business prowess. He won't be able to believe it.'

The look on Freya's face was far from convinced, but she returned Willow's smile anyway.

'Give my love to Merry, won't you,' she said, changing the subject. 'I can't wait to hear all the gossip about the magazine.'

'Merry will be going nuts, making sure every little detail is perfect, but she's been such a star helping me out, she deserves to have a massive success on her hands.'

'So do we all,' remarked Freya. 'Don't you think? It's been quite a year one way or another, and it's not over yet, not by a long chalk.'

Chapter Forty-Two

'These are literally walking out of the door,' said Merry, standing back proudly to admire her display. 'I'd say a good part of the village is having strawberries with their tea tonight, and I can't say I blame them. Don't they look gorgeous… and the smell…' She breathed in deeply.

Willow fanned her face. It was warm in the shop now that the afternoon sun was streaming through the door, but Merry was right, it brought out the smell of the ripe fruit beautifully.

'I've been telling everybody who comes in that we're going to be selling more of your produce soon, and so far, the reaction has been very positive. I think it might be the weather, but people's eyes light up when I mention ice cream or your cordials. You're definitely onto a winner there.'

She motioned for Willow to follow her through into the back room.

'I thought I could put the freezer here, and by moving this stand around, I can fit in some shelving next to it where I can display your full range in time. What do you think?' she asked. 'Of course they'll marry beautifully with Freya and Sam's juices come the autumn.'

Willow stared at the room around her, feeling quite overcome with emotion. 'I'm absolutely gobsmacked, Merry. I can't believe that you've done all this for me. It's perfect.' Her eyes were shining, but she made no move to wipe the tears away.

Merry clasped her hands. 'It's perfect for us too, you know. The shop needed something to make it stand out—' She caught sight of Willow's face and laughed. 'Yes, apart from the décor! We needed to find a niche in the market that would set us above being simply the village shop. I wanted this place to be something special, and you and Freya have provided the perfect start for us. I've spent the last few days touring the villages and towns locally, and I've found the most amazing suppliers, from cheeses, to wines and everything else in between, and all from small businesses within a twenty mile radius. I want to turn us into a gourmet food centre. We can offer the products online and do food demonstrations and—' She stopped suddenly. 'What's the matter, Willow? Are you okay?'

Willow was aware that her mouth had dropped open. She closed it, a huge grin immediately swamping her face as a tide of excitement swept over her. 'I don't suppose you need any extra space for these demonstrations… or courses even…'

Merry narrowed her eyes. 'Why, what are you thinking?' she asked.

'Only that Peter and I were chatting the other day, like you, trying to come up with something that might make us a bit different from the competition. Purely by chance, one of his friends gave us the most brilliant idea.'

'Go on,' said Merry, intrigued.

'I had a few of Peter's friends over for a day recently to help us pick elderflowers and gooseberries. One of them, a young girl, seemed quite nervous to start with, but as the day went on, forgive the pun, she really blossomed. I've just had a message from her to say thanks for giving her the opportunity to help out, and how much she had enjoyed the experience. It struck me that we could offer residential cookery courses or retreats, perhaps in exchange for help to make our products. We could incorporate all kinds of things so that people learn new skills or have a chance to brush up on old ones, and while we're doing that, we get a ready workforce. We've got that huge barn we could transform as time goes on, and if any of your suppliers would be willing to come and teach their skills as well, then—'

It was Merry's turn to have her mouth drop open. 'Oh, my God,' she said slowly. 'We have to make this work, Willow. *Country Living* are going to love this! They want to talk to me about what we've already done here, but also what plans we have in the future to develop the shop. They're very keen on the flourishing rural business angle. If we can come up with ways like this of linking all our businesses, it would be perfect.'

'When are they coming?' Willow breathed.

'Next Friday, a little over a week away. We've probably just got time to pull something together for them. It doesn't have to be concrete, but we would need to show how it might work, how we would set it up in principle, what resources we have, that kind of thing. Would that be possible, do you think, or are we just plain mad?'

Willow gave an excited squeal. 'Mad!' She laughed. 'Mad as March bloody hares, but we have to do this, Merry, we have to!'

The journey back into town passed in a blur of wild ideas, and Willow had parked the car before she realised that she couldn't even remember turning into the High Street. She was desperate to get back home and speak to Peter, but she needed to stop and get some extra cash out for him. It was payday at the end of the week, but he had put in so many extra hours of late that a little bonus was the least she could do.

Willow snatched up her bag from the passenger side and was only about fifty metres or so from the bank when she realised that Jude was standing on the pavement outside, and he wasn't alone. He shook Henry's hand, his left arm reaching out to grip his shoulder in the classic configuration of a deal just sealed. She would have waved, had her ears not been filled with a sudden roaring, and for a moment she was completely disorientated.

Somehow, she made it back to the car, where she sat for a little while, shaking, before starting the engine and drawing away as slowly as she could. She needed time to think and had no desire to be seen by anyone she knew, least of all her husband. She drove at a snail's pace along the back road and eventually stopped the car just over the bridge into their village, throwing open the door and drawing in lungs full of fresh air.

She breathed deeply for a few minutes, trying to calm the voices in her head. Voices that mocked and derided her. How could she have been so stupid, so complacent? So very wrong.

After a few minutes, she drove off again, more purposeful this time, heat gathering at the back of her neck, and a burning anger swelling inside her. In the past, her dreams had been little more than pointers, a heightened sense of intuition perhaps, but always clear in their meaning. They had never sought to mislead her or caused her any real anxiety, but these past few weeks had been so different. The visions had been vivid, powerful even, consuming her senses for several minutes at a time, and in the last couple of days not confined to night-time either, when her perception was surely at its greatest. But still she had missed something, perhaps the most vital thing of all. She had seen a glimpse into a future, of that she was sure, but until today, she had mistakenly believed Andrew to be at the root of it all. It had never crossed her mind that it might be someone else… She needed to see more, had to know if what she'd seen today was the truth, and there was only one place she could do it: by the very fields that were the source of her vision.

The driveway was empty as she turned up to the house, and she abandoned the car at an angle, keys still in the ignition. In a matter of minutes, she had reached her destination and she stood in front of the five-bar gate that lead onto the track and the open land beyond.

It was here that she had first seen the horrific sight of their fields torn asunder to make way for row upon row of houses. The meadow-land with its wild flowers and grasses, home to so many, all gone; ripped away to make homes of a different kind. She put her hands on the gate, dropped her head and closed her eyes.

She had expected the vision to come to her straight away. Sometimes at night now it clamoured for her attention so much she had to fight to push it away, but now all she felt was a deep and languid peace, quite the opposite from what she had been expecting. It confused her even more. Here, in the very place she had seen in her dream, the images should be stronger than ever, but even as she sought to empty her mind of chatter all she could see were the tall heads of the grasses gently swaying in the breeze, livestock nibbling at the fresh green shoots of spring and the march hares leaping in their ritual dance. There was nothing of the carnage that had filled her head so recently. She felt her breathing begin to ease until all that filled her head was the rushing of the wind in the trees.

A light touch on her arm made her jump.

'Willow?'

She opened her eyes to find Delilah looking at her anxiously, her voice gentle. She had the feeling it wasn't the first time she had spoken to her. The two dogs milled around her as she stood, a nervous smile on her face.

'Are you okay?' Delilah asked. 'You look like you're away with the faeries.'

Willow swallowed hard, looking backwards and forwards between the gate and the face in front of her. Maybe Delilah was right. Maybe that's exactly where she was. In the land of the faeries, being deluded by visions and a certainty that what they showed her was the truth. Too busy chasing dreams instead of dealing with the reality that was under her nose. And now she was more confused than ever. She had believed that what she was trying to achieve was the right thing for her and her family, for the way in which they lived their lives. To help Jude turn away from a downward spiral into money-grabbing materialism, towards living a simpler, more nurturing and sustainable way of life. In doing so, she had reached out for help to someone she had thought to be a friend. She never imagined for one minute that Henry would be the one to betray her.

Warm fur brushed against Willow's legs and she became aware of Delilah's anxious face still studying her. She needed to be anywhere but here.

'Sorry,' she started. 'I came over a bit faint there for a minute. I'm okay now, though.'

Delilah regarded her suspiciously. 'Are you sure, 'cause you still look a bit peaky to me.'

Willow waved an airy hand. 'Honestly, I'll be fine. I didn't have much for lunch, and I think the heat got to me a bit.'

'You could come inside and have some water,' added Delilah. 'Sit down for a minute.'

The dogs were still milling aimlessly.

'No, don't worry. You go and enjoy your walk. I'll just wander home and have a glass of something cool.' She smiled as reassuringly as she could, beginning to back away down the lane. 'I'll catch you later,' she added. 'I haven't forgotten about my offer of dinner. We should fix something up.' She gave the dogs a final pat and turned away.

*

Delilah watched her walk a little way before turning in the other direction. She pulled her mobile from the pocket of her shorts and dialled Henry's number. He answered almost straight away.

'Are you still with Jude?' she asked urgently.

'No, I've just left, why?'

'It's almost as if Willow knows,' whispered Delilah, 'but I thought Jude wasn't going to say anything to her just yet. Has he changed his mind?'

'No,' replied Henry. 'The only people that know are us and Jude, I'm sure of it. Beside there's no way Jude would say anything until the deal goes through, he wants it to be a surprise.'

There was silence on the line for a moment.

'Is everything all right?' Henry prompted.

'I don't know… it's weird. I've just met Willow in the lane by the gate. She was staring right at the fields, and the look on her face was… I dunno, but she didn't look happy. She gave me some story about feeling faint, but she didn't want any help.'

'That does seem a bit odd,' agreed Henry. 'Jude is sure she'll be over the moon when she finds out… are you still okay, though?'

Delilah couldn't help herself and gave an excited skip. 'Lover, I'm blinkin' ecstatic!' she gushed.

She could hear Henry's smile as he replied. 'Well, then, we'll just have to wait and see. And that won't be long; Jude said he could get the call from his bank as early as tomorrow. I'm still sure Willow doesn't know anything about it, and when she does find out, I'm pretty certain she'll be as excited as we are. Perhaps it's like she said, and she just felt hot, that's all.'

'I'm sure you're right,' answered Delilah. 'After all, it can't really be anything else, can it?'

Chapter Forty-Three

It felt to Willow as if she had been sitting in the same spot since yesterday. There seemed little point in doing much else.

The door to her potions room as Peter had once called it, remained firmly closed. She had gone in there early this morning to retrieve grandma Gilly's notebook, but apart from that she had no intention of stepping inside. The last batch of elderflowers would wither and turn brown during the day if they were left unprocessed, but Willow didn't care if they were unusable. It seemed fitting somehow that the fragrant frothy white heads would lose their strength and wither and die. It was much how she felt herself.

Jude had been his usual loving and attentive self last night, playing with the girls after tea, a quiet game, mindful of Beth's arm which was still quite sore. He had them in fits of giggles as he read their bedtime story with his repertoire of silly voices which they loved. It had been easy to pretend that everything was fine during the early evening when there were things to be done and Willow could keep busy but, as soon as the girls were in bed, he had come straight to her side. She looked tired he had said, working too hard, and had offered to run her a soothing bath. Willow had never known Jude to behave in any other way, but now she caught herself watching him, questioning his motives. Was it attentiveness, or guilt at his betrayal? Keeping her sweet until the time when he would have to tell her what he had done.

Eventually, after she feigned a migraine and her replies became ever more monosyllabic with each question, Jude had left her to the quiet solitude she had wished for. He had slept curled around her back though, just as he always did, but instead of welcoming the warmth and comfort his arms provided like she would normally do, he had felt heavy, and confining, pinning her to the bed, and she longed for some space to think and to breathe. She hated the way it made her feel.

This morning her tiredness had been real, her face pale and drawn, and even though Jude needed to get to his office early, he promised to look in on her at lunchtime. It was now nearly eleven o'clock, and she had not moved for some time. Another message from Merry flashed up on the screen of her mobile, at least the fifth since yesterday. She picked up her phone to tap out a reply.

Hi, sorry not to reply earlier, but Amy is really poorly bless her, and I can't leave her today. I'll ring you later, so we can fix up when to meet, hope that's okay? Still madly excited! Xx

Pressing send, she tossed her phone back onto the table with a sigh. She had bought herself time with her lies, that was all, but some time fairly soon she would have to make a decision. In all the years she had been married to Jude, they had never even argued, and she certainly had never had cause to doubt their relationship, it was simply not on her radar. Now though, with one fell swoop, everything she believed about their life together had been called into question. It wasn't only Jude's duplicity that she was struggling to deal with, but her own, for wasn't she just as bad? She had kept secrets too, convincing herself that what she was doing was right without even discussing it with Jude, not once. In all honesty, Jude probably thought he was doing the right thing for his family, just as she did herself, so which of them was right? They were both as bad as one another, she thought bitterly.

She'd been such a fool to think that her stupid business venture would be the thing to make the difference to their lives. So blinded was she by her ego and fanciful dreams that she had forgotten how to share, to talk, and to love. She could never agree with what Jude had done, but how would he feel when he found out how she had been planning to ambush his plans too. To discount them out of hand by thrusting her own, better idea under his nose. She loved Jude so much, always had, and a life without him was unthinkable, but for the first time in her marriage she was worried for their future. A single tear, the first she had shed, made its way down her cheek, and as it dripped from the end of her chin, a bout of crying gripped her so fiercely she could scarcely breathe. She lowered her head to the table and howled like a wounded animal.

Some time later she awoke, much to her surprise, to find she was lying beneath the cool sheets of her bed. She vaguely remembered Jude talking to her, when she was still slumped at the table. The tears had dried up by then, but she was listless and unresponsive, and he had led her to bed without protest. He had brought cool flannels for her forehead and sweet drinks in the dimmed room, and then left her to the effortless escape of sleep.

She lifted her head weakly to look at the clock beside her bed, astonished to discover it was early evening. Panic lurched in her stomach at the thought of the girls worried and alone after school, but a burble of laughter reached her from along the hallway, and she realised that they were having their evening bath. It had always been the same, she remembered. Any time she had been unwell, or simply exhausted with the twins' demands when they were tiny, Jude had been there, without a second thought, caring for the girls, and for her. He worked so hard himself and yet any free time he had, he devoted to them, never to himself. He'd been the best father and the best husband she could wish for. A lump rose in her throat.

A cool breeze ruffled the curtains at the window, and she let the air play over her skin. She closed her eyes again, pressing her head deeper into the pillow. She would have to deal with all of this soon, she knew that, but not today. She was so tired and all she craved now was to be released from pain. She slept.

*

There was no lightning this time to illuminate the scene, no pouring rain, but instead a blazing sun shone down, bouncing off the stark pale streets intersected by rows and rows of houses. Tired gardens drooped in the heat and a haze shimmered from the cars as they passed. A young mother wheeled a pushchair, sweat collecting on her back as she bent to the child inside who was hot and fretful. There was no shade anywhere.

And then she saw it. The huge oak tree that had always guarded the entrance to the fields. A tree under which she had played with the girls, collecting wildflowers, having tea parties with their dolls, making daisy chains and lying on their backs staring up at the sky, making shapes from the clouds that floated past. The same tree was now fenced off, contained, unreachable, and undesirable. Willow woke, heart pounding, her own sweat gluing her nightdress to her body. The vision was just as clear as before and she tried to slow her breathing.

As her eyes adjusted to the darkness in the room, she became aware of movement beside her, and ragged breathing that was not her own. A sliver of moonlight lay across Jude's body and without thinking Willow slipped her hand into its light, feeling the comfort it brought. She crept soundlessly from the bed and pulled back the curtains, letting the silvery rays flood the room. It was a full moon; how could she have forgotten?

She climbed back into bed, moving closer to Jude, seeing the sheen of perspiration on his face as he dreamed. His eyelids fluttered, his mouth parted as he fought against the images in his mind. His fingers opened and closed on the sheet beside her, seeking solace, seeking comfort from her, and as she slid her fingers into his, she gasped as his terror filled her too.

Willow stared at her husband, a man she had loved for most of her life, and for the second time that day wondered how she had been so foolish, how she could have got it so completely wrong? Her dreams had plagued her for weeks, visions that were so real, they had haunted her, waking in her a terror of what they could mean; but as she looked at Jude's face, struggling and in pain, she realised that the fear had never been hers to begin with, and neither were the dreams. They were Jude's.

Chapter Forty-Four

A missing PE kit had cut a huge swathe through Willow's available time this morning, and she barely had time to talk to Jude beyond vehement assurances that she was now fine and that he was not to worry about her. He rushed out of the house as soon as he could, claiming he needed an early start.

They had slept entwined together, just like they had in the early days of their relationship when they could scarcely bear to be apart for more than a few minutes. Jude's breathing had eased in time during the night as his dream passed, and Willow held him close, stroking his cheek and gazing at the face of the man too scared to share his fears with her for dread of seeming weak, a failure in her eyes, just like he had been in his father's his whole life. All he had ever wanted was to be loved, and although hate was not an emotion that Willow agreed with, in that moment she had never loathed Andrew more.

She knew now that the business deal that Jude was on the verge of was not one to sell their land, but somehow to save it. She had no idea why or how this had come about, or indeed where Henry came into it, but, given the urgency she now sensed in Jude, she realised the axe was about to fall one way or another. Whatever happened, Willow would not let another day pass without speaking to Jude and discovering the truth. Yesterday, she had convinced herself that her fledgling business was sheer folly, an exercise in flattering her ego and nothing more, but now she wondered whether her original thoughts had been right; that Willowberries might possibly be a viable alternative for their future.

The room at the end of the hallway beckoned to her once more and, scooping up a pile of letters from the doormat, she slowly walked its length, savouring the moment before she pushed open the door and breathed in the sweet smell of summer. Once inside she tossed the letters onto the table and smiled broadly as if greeting an old friend. It was time to get down to business.

One of the first things she needed to do was find Peter. She had shamefully left him to his own devices over the last day or so, and she couldn't blame him for keeping out of her way. Yesterday, she had told him she had a migraine and, whether or not he believed her, she had probably been quite short with him. He hadn't appeared at all yet this morning. She had an apology to make, but she also needed to ask him something very important. She gathered up the crate of elderflowers that had indeed withered the day before and carried them out of the back door. Dead things had no place inside a house for the living. This afternoon she would replace them, and another batch of cordial would be underway.

She collected a stray mug from the table and picked up the letters again, scanning the envelopes for anything more exciting than the electricity bill. She was still staring open-mouthed in shock at the letter in her hand when Jude came flying through the back door, her shouted name on his lips.

There was a moment's hesitation as he grinned at her before scooping her up and whirling her around. A stray splash of coffee flew from the cup and splattered against the wall, but neither of them saw it.

'Oh God, Willow, I've done it!' shouted Jude. 'I'm finally free... we're free!' he bellowed, too excited to restrain himself. He set her down momentarily before grinning like a loon and picking her up once more. He buried his face in the side of her neck, kissing her over and over.

Willow giggled. 'Put me down,' she managed through her laughter, struggling to hold onto the things in her hands. 'What on earth has got into you? The last time I saw you this excited... well, I can't actually remember ever seeing you this excited before.'

He did as she asked, stepping away slightly to look at her better. His chest was heaving, his eyes shining, and yet bizarrely he looked calmer and more relaxed than she had seen him in weeks.

'Do you want to come and sit down and tell me what it is that's got you so worked up? I don't think I can stand the suspense.'

Jude raked a hand through his hair. 'Yes... no... I don't think I can. I don't think I can sit still for that long.'

Willow put her hands on her hips and gave him her best 'I'm standing no nonsense' stare. 'I'll superglue your trousers to the chair if I have to.'

Willow's heart was pounding too, she realised, but her own news would have to wait a while. Whatever Jude was trying to tell her must surely be connected with the source of their dreams. She had a feeling she might remember this moment for some time to come.

She sat at the table and waited for him to join her, watching his face expectantly, but his expression hardly changed. He looked overjoyed, and excited, but something else glittered in his eyes, and as his gaze met hers, she understood what it was. He looked jubilant.

'I don't really know where to start,' he began, 'and I know I probably should have discussed this with you before, but when I tell you I hope you'll understand why I didn't.' He paused for a moment to gather his thoughts. 'It's complicated, but maybe I should start at the end and work backwards.'

Willow nodded encouragement as Jude took a deep breath.

'I've sold the business,' he said, laying down the sentence in the room like an unexploded bomb. 'I no longer have any share in Middleton Estates,' he added as if his previous statement wasn't clear enough.

Whatever Willow had expected him to tell her, it wasn't that. Her mouth hung open slightly as she tried to take it in. That didn't altogether sound like their land was safe after all.

'But what about Andrew?'

A cloud crossed Jude's face for an instant. 'I'll tell you about that later.' Willow was about to ask a further question, when Jude jumped in again. 'And I know that probably sounds like the most horrendous news you've ever heard, but you're not to worry. Financially, the deal was a very good one, so we're not going to be penniless for a good while yet; besides it's more a matter of what I want to do with the rest of my life, or more importantly what *we* want to do with the rest of our lives.'

Willow's letter was growing hot in her hand. 'And what do you want to do with the rest of your life?' she asked cautiously.

Jude plucked the letter out of her grasp and took both her hands in his. He raised them to his mouth and gently kissed each one in turn.

'I want to spend some more time with my gorgeous wife, and find out just how incredible her talents are. I want to watch our girls growing up instead of blinking and waving them off to university as virtual strangers, and I want never to have to wear a tie again… well, not often anyway.' He grinned. 'But most importantly, I want to nurture our family and the land around us. Other people can buy and sell property and land for huge sums of money, but I'm not going to be one of them, not any more.'

Willow watched Jude as he spoke, a mixture of emotions playing across his face. Mostly excitement, but now also a little nervous, as if unsure how his momentous decision would be received.

'Well, I'm not sure that I want you around all day, under my feet, getting in the way, making a mess…'

She winked at his astonished face.

'… Actually, I can't think of anything nicer,' she admitted. 'To be honest, I wish you'd done it years ago – all this striving for an even bigger pot of money that we didn't need, when pretty much everything we could wish for is right here…' She gave a twinkly smile. 'And anything else is on next-day delivery from Amazon.'

Jude visibly relaxed. 'You really don't mind then? I know I should have talked things over with you before, but there was so much to go wrong, and even up until the last minute, I wasn't sure it would all go through. I didn't want us to start to believe in the kind of life we could make for ourselves and then have it all torn away from us if things didn't work out. I didn't think I could bear that for you.' He rubbed a thumb over the back of her hand. 'Although… by some weird stroke of fate, I think you might be one step ahead of me anyway… or have I got that wrong?'

Willow blushed, a sheepish smile on her face. 'I'm guilty of keeping things to myself too,' she said. 'I've been exploring some new ways of expanding the business here, things that complement the fruit farm. I kind of hoped that if I got it off the ground, I'd have a viable idea to put to you… and now might be the perfect time to tell you what I've been up to, especially as this arrived in the post this morning.'

She handed Jude the letter with a slightly shaking hand, not yet having had a chance to fully absorb its contents herself. She waited anxiously while he read it, wondering what he was thinking. It had been so wrong not to share any of what she had been up to the past few weeks, she knew that now, but at the time it had seemed right; a decision which now seemed silly and misguided.

Jude's raised voice broke into her thoughts.

'Bloody hell!' He grinned. 'I've been reading about these places in one of the business magazines I subscribe to. The bloke that owns them is an organic farmer and he started with just one small guesthouse at his own place, which his wife ran, but now they have eight, very select and very exclusive small hotels, which are currently on the lips of every famous blogger and YouTuber around.'

'I know!' Willow grinned back. 'I've been experimenting with a range of ice creams and cordials, and to cut a long story short, Merry has been sending out some sample packs to people she has contacts with.'

'And they want to talk to you about supplying all their hotels, not just the kitchen but the guest rooms too… Willow, this is amazing!' he burst out, excitement mounting once more. 'I said you were a woman of spectacular talents.' He paused for a moment. 'I don't suppose,' he started, more seriously, 'that you might need a little help from a chap who's pretty good at marketing, and making the tea and whatever else you need, and who has suddenly become comprehensively unemployed?'

Willow beamed the smile she had been waiting a long time to deliver. 'I don't think there's anything I'd like more,' she said, holding Jude's look. 'I've no idea how all this is going to pan out, or how busy we might get, but I'd much rather be doing it with you by my side.'

She took a breath, wondering how best to frame her next question. 'This might sound a bit weird, even for me,' she began. 'But I've had some… dreams lately, they only started a few weeks ago, but last night I woke from a particularly vivid one, only to realise that they might not have been my dreams after all… but someone else's.'

Jude shifted uncomfortably in his chair. 'Go on,' he said.

'And don't ask me how, but it's almost as if I was picking up on your thoughts… although I'm not sure thoughts is quite the right word. They were a bit stronger than that.'

'What kind of thoughts?'

Willow pulled at the end of her plait. 'Maybe I had better just come out with it. You'll either laugh, or…' She sat up a little straighter. 'I've seen images of the land up beyond Henry's house, at some point in the future I'm guessing. Only not as it is now, but torn up, built on, a mass of houses and roads and I—'

Jude visibly paled, swallowing hard. 'How could you possibly know that?' he whispered. 'How could you know what I've seen… what frightened me more than anything in this whole business?'

Willow clutched at his hand. 'It terrified me too, to see the meadows all gone, everything destroyed.'

'It'll never happen, Willow, you have my promise. I've seen to it that Andrew never—'

'Andrew?' echoed Willow, confused. With all that had happened over the past couple of days, she had forgotten her original belief that Andrew was behind the sale of their land, but now Jude had sold his share of the business, it didn't make any sense. Her thoughts were churning.

'But what about Andrew's share in the business? And you've done some sort of a deal with Henry, I know you have. I saw you both outside the bank yesterday, shaking hands. What was that all about?'

Jude gave a wry smile. 'Ah, Henry...' he said. 'Yes, that was... unexpected. But listen, let me tell you about Andrew first. As you can imagine, he wasn't over the moon when I told him I wanted out of the business, but in the end he really had no choice.' He cleared his throat before continuing. 'You'll remember the night a few weeks back when I came home really late, and in a bit of a state to put it mildly. I made out I'd been led astray by some Japanese businessman, when actually what happened was that I presented my father with the details of the sale I'd already negotiated. After a... heated discussion... we agreed that from here on in, I was no longer fit to call myself his son.'

Willow's hand flew to her throat as her eyes filled with tears. 'Oh Jude, why didn't you tell me?' she said, anger flaring. 'How could he do such a thing?'

'Because he's an unfeeling sanctimonious bastard I suspect. He's never loved me, Willow, I know that now. I've spent my life trying to please him, to make him take notice of what I achieved in the hope that he might deign to throw me a crumb of affection, but it's never going to happen. Now I've woken up to the fact, I'm rather surprised to find that I'm looking forward to taking my own decisions and living my own life without his influence.' He smiled at Willow again. 'Despite what he thinks, I happen to believe that I've made some very sound choices in my life so far.'

Willow searched Jude's face as he regarded her calmly and with more than a little affection. He was telling the truth, and it must have taken a lot of guts to face up to it, let alone come to terms with it. Willow couldn't pretend to be anything other than overjoyed to have Andrew out of their lives for good, even though its legacy must be hard for Jude.

'I know he's never liked me, but—' She stopped suddenly as she realised what Jude's words would actually mean for them. 'But what about the house, and the land? My strawberries! Oh, God, Jude, we'll have to leave and...' She couldn't bear the thought of it, not now, not when she had come so close to making things happen.

Jude took hold of her hands again and chuckled. 'No, we won't, and believe me that's absolutely the best bit. Wonderfully ironic too; it was your strawberries that were his downfall in the end.'

Willow gave him a quizzical look.

'There've been many occasions over the years when Andrew has suggested selling the meadows, but this time he'd even gone so far as to suss out the potential for getting planning permission, and snaring a buyer who was happy to do a deal on a speculative purchase. No doubt, had the sale gone ahead, Andrew would have done everything in his power to make sure planning was granted and the resultant kick back from any houses built would have netted a small fortune. There was only one problem with the proposed sale – well two actually.'

'And they were?'

'Well, first, that I was dead set against it, but second, and more importantly, that to build any houses on the land, you'd need to have an access route… and the only two possible routes would be through our strawberry fields or up the lane behind Henry's house. Of course the best one would be through our fields, or rather, as Andrew put it, "through that silly little business of your wife's". He even asked me to have a chat with you and talk you out of running it.' Jude held up his hand as he caught the expression on Willow's face.

'In the end, that was what made me stop and think. Apart from the brazen cheek of it, he made me realise how important our fields are and that in fact we have a proper future here together which is worth more to me than anything I could ever earn. It made me even more determined not to sell the land.'

Willow nodded. 'So you needed to find a way to get Andrew out of the business…'

'… No, the other way around. I needed to find a way to get *me* out of it, and everything we have here along with me.'

'But how did you do that?'

'It was quite simple in the end. I just played to his love of money. Andrew can't run the business, he doesn't have the skill, and he never has had. So despite what he thought of me, he needed me plain and simple... or someone else who could take my place, keep the company afloat, and keep Andrew's investment paying out at a nice steady rate. Without that someone else, the company would fold, and bang would go Andrew's income. Middleton Estates is currently holding two huge parcels of land that I acquired some years ago. Bought speculatively, but shrewdly, and which have now fallen into areas ripe for development. In fact, one has already had planning permission granted on it. If we simply sold the company outright, Andrew would get his payout, admittedly, but by staying in the game, he stands to net a huge fortune from the building of the houses too. So it wasn't much of a choice after all. I've sold my share in the company to a third party, and Andrew gets to keep his millions. He might be a materialistic bastard, but he's not stupid.'

Willow gazed at her husband, trying to take in everything he had told her.

'But you've given up all that money too...' she said.

'Yep,' grinned Jude. 'I decided it wasn't worth as much as I thought it was.' He kissed her nose. 'And besides, I'm not that magnanimous. I made sure I got exactly what I wanted.'

'Which was?'

'A certain sum of money—' he winked '—but more importantly, my price included this house, the strawberry fields, all the meadows, the office...'

'Henry's house?'

'Yes, that too. It all belongs to us now.'

'You really have worked all this out, haven't you?'

Jude picked her letter up from the table and waved it at her. 'As have you if I'm not very much mistaken.' He read the letter through again. 'I even love the name Willowberries – it's just perfect!'

'Do you really? It seemed right somehow, but I probably wasn't thinking properly at the time. I mean, we should have something that reflects both of us, shouldn't we?'

Jude leaned forward and kissed Willow squarely before she could say any more. 'No, I like it just the way it is,' he said, eyes shining. 'And our buyers are going to love it!'

Willow returned his kiss, her stomach fizzing with excitement at the prospect of what was to come. She was about to show him some of the things she had been up to when she remembered what she had to say to Jude. On the face of it everything seemed perfect, but there was still the possibility that things could come crashing down around her ears. She looked up into Jude's clear blue eyes.

'I have an apology to make,' she said. 'I've been going out of my mind these last few weeks, what with these dreams, and fears about what was going to happen. Everything has been so confusing, I almost didn't know what to believe... but I should have talked to you about it. I should have told you my ideas for this place, asked for your help and support instead of arrogantly going ahead with what I believed was right. I feel like I haven't trusted you, like I've let you down...' Her eyes filled with tears.

Jude touched her cheek, his eyes shining with emotion too. 'No, I should have told you... shared all of this with you before, but I was so scared I couldn't make it happen. I wouldn't have been able to bear it for you if we started to believe in what our lives could be like and then have it all taken away from us. It would have been the cruellest blow, and I thought it better if you didn't know.'

'Promise me that whatever happens in the future we will never keep secrets from each other again?'

Jude nodded gently. 'I promise... although there is just one other tiny thing I ought to tell you,' he added quietly, 'but it's a good thing, I swear!'

'Is this about Henry?' urged Willow. 'Please tell me it is. I still haven't figured out where he comes into this.'

'Well, no one was more surprised than me, but a couple of weeks ago, Henry came to see me offering to buy his house. Outright, in cash for a quick sale. I really had no idea, but he's completely minted... Anyway,

I had to tell him what I was planning, but I swore him to secrecy. I didn't even know myself at the time if it would be possible, but the more I thought about his offer, the more it made sound sense, for all of us. Yesterday, once I knew the deal was going through, I was able to firm things up with him. That's when you saw us in town I guess.'

Willow blushed slightly remembering her wild thoughts of the day before. 'Well, that does explain that,' she said. 'Although he's never mentioned anything about buying the house before...' Her eyes suddenly widened. 'Hey, I wonder if this has anything to do with Delilah?'

'Well, he's asked to rent the first meadow from us as well.'

'Really? Whatever does he want that for?'

Jude smiled slowly. 'To keep goats on of course. Or, more accurately, for Delilah to keep goats on. I rather think they've fallen in love.'

'Oh, of course!' exclaimed Willow, and suddenly everything in her world fell into the most magical and perfect place.

Chapter Forty-Five

It was the end of a very hot and very busy week, but sprawled in the meadow under the big oak tree, Willow had never been happier. Excited chatter and burbles of laughter reached her as she looked around at her group of friends enjoying a long cool drink in the evening sun. A slight breeze rustled the tall heads of the grasses that fringed the field and tickled their skin as they walked by, each of them revelling in the knowledge that, albeit for different reasons, life was about to get a lot more interesting.

As a result of the article in *Country Living*, Merry now had more customers than she knew what to do with, but she was taking it all in her stride and looking forward to being able to make all the dreams she had for their shop come true a little quicker. And of course more customers for Merry, meant more people to buy Willowberries' ice creams and cordials; not that it looked as though they were going to need many more customers just at the moment, because plans for their cookery courses and working holidays were coming along nicely too…

Henry and Delilah had to be peeled apart from one another at regular intervals as they forged ahead with plans for their new life together, and Freya and Sam had plans too, having finally decided to set a date for their wedding – after the harvest had been safely gathered in of course. The honeymoon would have to wait a while, but they would be pressing the first of their fruit together as man and wife and that was the most important thing. It all had the most wonderful symmetry about it, thought Willow.

Even Peter, who was lying flat on his back staring up at the evening sky would be a part of everything. Her idea to ask him to play a greater role in the development of Willowberries had not been hers alone. Jude had also spotted his potential, and, with a bit of frank discussion, Peter had been delighted with the offer Jude had made him. It had taken a while to organise, but by switching his course, he could finish his degree part-time, commuting the now much shorter distance to uni on the days he needed to attend and, on the others, honing his business skills. So far, he was shaping up to be a very fine apprentice indeed.

Willow waved a nonchalant hand as a bee passed a little too close to her drink for comfort.

Merry giggled. 'See, it's so good, even the bees want it back,' she said, raising her own glass as if in a toast. 'May the bees always pollinate your flowers, Willow,' she added.

'I might have to start giving them a bit as a thank-you present,' she replied. 'Especially if we do decide to start making honey and ginger ice cream. Got to keep 'em sweet,' she said, laughing at her own joke. She looked at Merry's happy face for a moment, knowing that she was just as contented.

Beside her, Jude cleared his throat, topping up her glass.

'I think it's time for a toast,' he said, raising his voice above the general hubbub. 'What do you all say?'

Sam pulled Freya from where she was lounging against him into a more upright position. 'I think that's a fine idea,' he agreed. 'Come on, Freya, what shall we drink to?'

'Only one thing we can drink to, I reckon.' She giggled. 'To all of us, to the future!' she cried.

'To the future!' they chorused.

Willow looked at her husband over the rim of her glass. His skin was golden from days spent outside, his lithe body relaxed, and his beautiful face so often turned towards her that she found herself blushing. Far from causing a rift between them the events of the last few months had brought them closer together than ever. To have him by her side day by day was more than she could ever have wished for.

*

Jude took a sip of his drink as he watched his two daughters playing a little distance away. He took Willow's hand as he looked out across the fields and watched the sun sink lower in the sky, feeling nothing but relief at the knowledge that he had been saved.

Jude Middleton was a very lucky man. He may have been afraid of being poor once upon a time, and he may have been afraid of not being loved, but for the first time in his life, Jude Middleton was no longer afraid, of anything.

AUTUMN

Chapter Forty-Six

From her vantage point just beyond the war memorial, Laura was able to watch Freya come and go with interest. Laura had seen her several times over the past few weeks and, at first, Freya had been completely oblivious of anyone's presence; but on a couple of occasions now, Laura had been caught unawares and Freya had seen her, giving her a beaming smile. She was only glad that today she had chosen to leave Boris behind. The dog had a habit of drawing attention, purely down to his enormous size, whereas Laura was tiny enough to lose herself behind a gravestone or in the shadow of a hedge. His absence gave Laura the opportunity to observe Freya unnoticed.

She'd only ever met Freya's father once or twice, but she knew the family – everyone did hereabouts – and a quick check of the headstone that Freya visited had confirmed what she already knew. She didn't exactly remember him dying, but she had seen the freshly dug grave well over a year ago and had felt for Freya. Death was never an easy thing, especially for one so young and alone, and although Laura didn't know Freya at all, she knew of her, and in Laura's world that was generally enough. The family were well liked locally; they had a history and a tradition in the town which Laura approved of.

In all the time since his death, the grave had been well tended and yet she hadn't seen Freya in the churchyard until these last few weeks. People were creatures of habit and, as with most regular occurrences in their lives, like shopping, or going for a walk, visiting the grave of a loved one was most often undertaken on the same day or days and at roughly the same time. It was one of the things that made Laura feel safe; that way she knew what to expect. Something must have changed for Freya to alter her pattern of visits, and it wasn't until a few days ago when Laura had both arms plunged deep into a hedgerow, rooting out the juiciest blackberries that she realised how busy Freya must be with the apple harvest. Since then she had kept a wary eye.

*

Freya smiled as she pushed open the gate to the churchyard. The slanting early-morning sun had risen just high enough to touch the cobweb that hung from the lichen-covered wood and light up its dew-drop-covered strands like a diamond choker.

She took a deep breath in the damp air. She loved mornings like this when the mist swirled about her feet as she walked, knowing that in an hour or so it would lift to reveal a beautiful day, full of the colours she liked best. For now, the churchyard held a muted beauty and, as she made her way between the graves, she let her thoughts wander towards the coming day.

October was when the hard work really began at Appleyard. The orchards had been quietly soaking up the sun and the rain all year, and now the apples were so ripe the trees were ready to offer them up like a gift; a reward for Freya's continued care and patience. Only this year had been different of course. This year her father no longer walked the rows of trees, but instead her beloved Sam. Her heart lifted at the thought that in a few short weeks she would be visiting this church again, but by the time she left, it would be as Sam's wife.

One short year ago, it had all been so different. She had come to the churchyard then, alone and frightened for her future, trying to cope with the all-consuming grief of losing her dad, and the threat of losing Appleyard, the house she had lived in all her life; her livelihood, and her stronghold. It had taken the wisdom of a curly-haired stranger to change all that, not only to bring Sam back to her, but life back to the orchards too. It was at about this time of year that Amos had arrived, walking up her drive to offer help with the harvest in return for food and a bed in her barn. He'd stayed until Christmas, until the wind had blown him on his way again, but there wasn't a day when Freya didn't long to see him one more time, to thank him for all that he had brought her.

She stopped in front of a small, neat headstone, tucked into the corner of the cemetery, and bent to her knees.

'Morning, Dad,' she said with a warm smile. 'And how are you this morning? It's going to be another beautiful day.'

She put down the bag she was carrying, her fingers automatically moving to collect the wilted blooms that filled the vases in front of the headstone. She lifted them to one side ready to dispose of. Then she rummaged in her bag for a pair of secateurs and began to gently clip away the faded heads of the bedding plants that she had planted in the late spring.

'I've brought you some Cyclamen today, Dad. I know you'll look after them much better than I can. I still can't manage to keep them alive, but I liked the colours.'

Freya's fingers were a little cold, but she worked quickly, keeping up a steady stream of chatter as she did so. Sometimes, she had the place to herself and sometimes not, but it never bothered her that others might be able to hear what she was saying. This was her time with her dad, and that was that.

'You should see the fields, Dad; they look amazing. I wouldn't be surprised if we don't start harvesting a couple of weeks early. The late burst of sunny weather we've been having is more than we could have wished for, and the juice presses are working overtime at the moment. That's why I've come so early today, so I hope you don't mind, but I've got to get back to give Sam a hand. Right, I'll be back in a minute.'

She gathered up the clippings and brown petals into a couple of sheets of newspaper and rose to take them to the small composting heap at the rear of the church. A trail of footprints through the dewy grass lay off to one side, and she followed their direction, trying to catch a glimpse of their owner.

Over the past few weeks as Freya's days had become busier, and her visits to her dad were earlier in the day, she had noticed another frequent visitor to the churchyard; a young woman, who looked much the same age as she, though tiny in stature. They had exchanged smiles on occasion, or at least Freya had, but they'd never spoken, and for some reason she intrigued Freya. It was her dog that Freya had noticed first: a huge Irish wolfhound that was almost as tall as the woman herself, and after that Freya found herself looking out for the slight figure with the beautiful heart-shaped face and huge almond eyes. She had an air of sadness about her, which was not all that unusual given the setting, but in all the times Freya had seen her, she had been in a different part of the churchyard, tending to a different grave, which was perhaps slightly odd. She lay flowers and wreaths, talking all the while just like Freya did, but whether this was to herself or the occupants of the ground beneath her, Freya didn't know.

Today, apart from the footprints in the grass, Freya could see no sign of her, and placing her wilted flowers and clippings on the compost heap, she returned to finish her own tidying.

Ten minutes or so later, she was done. She couldn't stay too long; the day was going to be lengthy as it was, and the sooner she got back to Appleyard, the sooner she could give Sam a hand with the myriad tasks that needed attention.

'I'll be back on Sunday, Dad, so you make sure you keep out of trouble until then, won't you?'

She touched her fingers to her lips and placed them on top of the white marble headstone for a moment before getting to her feet.

'Bye Dad,' she called.

The sun was fully around the side of the church by the time Freya made her way back down the main path to the lane outside. It lit up the wet grass, setting it sparkling and she stopped for a moment to watch a robin whose beady eye was also on the ground, although for an entirely different reason. As she watched, it flew to perch on a gravestone for a second before swooping to the freshly turned earth in front of it. The little bird darted off again, a prize worm in its mouth, but not before something else had caught Freya's eye. Aside from the late flowering geraniums planted there, a beautiful wreath had been laid upon the grave, and Freya's feet moved towards it before she could stop herself.

She had spent the last few weeks endlessly searching through images on the internet and in wedding magazines for something which resembled the idea she had in her head; an idea which was refusing to go away until satisfied. None of the pictures she had seen had quite captured the look she was trying to achieve and, with their wedding at the end of the month, she was getting short on time. All the wedding flowers she'd seen were too ordered, too uniform; she wanted hers to be exuberant, a little unruly even, but above everything else, a celebration of the season and their harvest. The wreath lying in front of her was all these things and more, and Freya's heart began to beat a little faster. This was exactly what she had been looking for.

With a quick glance around her, she dropped to her knees, reaching out with tentative fingers to trace the outline of the leaves and to touch the vibrant berries and fruits; bright orange hips, the rosy red of crab apples, the deep purple damsons. Freya had never seen anything quite like it. It looked home-made and, although some of the leaves seemed to have been preserved in glycerine, the rest of the wreath looked as if it had been plucked from the hedgerow that morning. Her head darted up again, scanning the churchyard for any sign of life, but whoever had laid this wreath was long gone; Freya was on her own.

She checked her watch, grimacing at the time, and reluctantly stood up. She must get on with her day, but one thing was suddenly very clear in her mind; even if she had to stake out the churchyard, somehow, she would get to know the maker of this beautiful wreath, and she had just over three weeks to do it.

*

Laura liked having the churchyard to herself. This early in the morning there were rarely any other visitors, and those that had come, so far, had obeyed the unwritten rules of the churchyard. Grief was such a personal thing. It was private, unobtrusive. It swathed those suffering from it in a cloak of invisibility, made them unapproachable, even among their own kind. People didn't talk about death. Eyes remained downcast, conversations were muted, and voices kept low; this had always been Laura's experience, until Freya started coming to visit.

She had never got close enough to Freya to make out what she was saying, but she could see her lips moving and her arms waving, and she knew that during the whole time she visited her dad, the words never stopped. Nothing unusual about that as such; lots of people talked to their loved ones during visits, but what was rare was that Freya didn't seem to obey the unwritten rules. She laughed, she seemed to speak in a normal voice, her mouth was open and expressive, not closed and tightened as most people's were when they whispered or spoke softly, embarrassed. She spoke to her father as if he was standing next to her, even cocking her head to one side and listening for his reply. Freya greeted other people in the churchyard too, and not the scurrying polite head nod that most people achieved, but a broad, smiling greeting, and it unnerved Laura a great deal.

Today though, as Laura watched the young woman leave the churchyard, she had seen something else. Something that she recognised in herself, and which intrigued her even more. Freya had stopped by one of the wreaths Laura had made, and in that singular moment it was as if for Freya everything around her, save for the wreath, had paled from view. It was a sensation Laura often felt herself, particularly on a day like today when the colour of the landscape, or of a particular leaf transfixed her with wonder. Freya had reached out, almost holding her breath and the reverent look on her face echoed something deep within Laura. In a matter of moments Freya had gone, but she had left behind something that Laura hadn't felt in a long time, and a tiny, but nonetheless vital spark began to glow.

Chapter Forty-Seven

Laura was just about to pop another chocolate into her mouth when two hairy feet landed on the work surface beside her as Boris made his presence known. Reluctantly, she returned the chocolate to the tray in front of her, moving it swiftly out of the dog's reach. Despite the fact that they would do him no good at all, he seemed particularly attracted to these and, whenever she made them, would try every trick in the book to try to pinch one. So far, she had managed to evade his wily ways.

'Is that my shopping?' she queried the dog, with a glance at her watch as she moved out into the hallway. Sure enough she could see the outline of someone through the frosted half glass in her door. The figure was too tall to be her usual delivery driver, but she pulled open the door anyway.

A rather nervous-looking young man stood there with a stack of plastic crates on a trolley.

Sometimes, Laura played a little game with them, when she was feeling in a particularly ruthless mood, but today had been a good one, so she smiled benevolently.

'Can you just pop them here?' she said, indicating a spot just beyond her door mat. 'That'll be fine.'

She gave Boris a stern command to sit while she ferried the bags back and forth to her kitchen, each time returning to give the delivery man a polite smile as he handed her more. When she had finished, she held out her hand to sign for the delivery and bade him a cheerful goodbye. He hadn't spoken once, but at least he hadn't shouted.

She realised her mistake as soon as she picked up the last bag. While it contained some breakfast cereal, a bottle of washing up liquid, a bag of rice and some lentils, it did not contain her two loaves of bread. Why on earth had she let the driver go without checking things first like she usually did? It didn't happen very often admittedly, but, on the few occasions that something had been missing from her order, it had always been discovered, still on the van, in a rogue bag that had somehow become separated from the rest. Now she would have to go and buy more. The making of a delicious leek and potato soup had also been on the day's agenda and she couldn't bear the thought of eating it without fresh bread.

Laura picked up a clean tea towel and draped it over the chocolates, snatching up one at the last minute and stuffing it into her mouth. She reached up to the hook on the back door and took down the dog lead that hung there.

'Come on, Boris,' she called. 'Walkies… again!'

It was just over a mile and a half into the village, so by the time she got back she would have lost most of the afternoon, but at least it meant she wouldn't have to go out again later in the day. A couple of new books had been delivered yesterday, and she was looking forward to an evening of reading. Taking this particular route into the village also meant that she could check to see how the sloes along the edge of the Williams' wood were coming along. By her reckoning, they should be pretty much perfect.

*

Stephen wasn't entirely sure he was enjoying exercise yet, but he had stuck at it, and it was getting easier. He was notching up several miles a day on his bike now, and even Long Lane hill didn't torture him quite as much any more. He was almost at the top now and looking forward to cresting the rise. On a day like today it was easy to see why people enjoyed cycling. The wind was almost non-existent; the air still warmed by the sun but with just enough bite to feel refreshing, and the view from the top of the hill would make everything worthwhile. The road sloped downwards, straight and true before disappearing around a sharp left-hand bend at the bottom. On one side, rich red earth stretched out in glistening furrows as far as he could see, and on the other, the deep blue of the sky was filled with majestic red, orange and yellow leaves from the trees that bordered the road.

He heard the car before he saw it, the engine roaring as it changed up into third and then fourth gear. He didn't think it was behind him, but as yet Stephen couldn't see where it was coming from. It was unusual enough to meet cars down this lane; it was narrow and there was a much quicker road away from the village that took most of the traffic, but the vehicles that did use it were never travelling this fast. His bike was building up speed as he travelled downhill, and he braked automatically, trying to retract his feet from the toe clips that held his feet fast on the pedals. One came loose almost immediately, but Stephen had always found the other much harder to disengage. He hadn't been riding for that long and didn't quite have the knack yet. Something told him that he would need to stop soon, though, and pretty quickly, judging by the speed the car must be going. With his feet stuck in clips, there was only one possible outcome and Stephen knew from bitter experience that it would be painful.

He was still wrestling with his pedal when the car shot around the bend at the bottom of the road. By now, Stephen was almost halfway down the lane himself and as the car tore into the thick hedge at the side of the road, he could see that the driver had lost control and out of instinct yanked the steering wheel away from hedge, propelling the car onto the other side of the road and straight into his path. As he frantically tried to free his left foot, he leaned on his own brakes, making for the other side of the road. A flash of colour caught his eye as he swerved, an automatic yell leaving his lips in warning as, too late, he registered the slight figure in front of him calmly picking something from the bushes.

*

Laura felt a sudden hard shove as something made contact with the middle of her arm and she was pushed roughly to one side, spinning around so that she crashed through the bush, landing sprawled on her back. She was vaguely aware of something hurtling past her and, as she flailed her arms around to try and slow her downward movement, an even bigger shape shot past, only metres from where she lay. She stared at the road in shock, her heart pounding, a sharp stinging in her arm from the thorns which had torn at her skin as she fell. Within moments, a gentle wet nose poked at her as Boris came to her side, licking her face. She struggled into an upright position, chest still heaving, to see what had cannoned into her.

The cyclist was lying on his back too, his bike to one side, the front wheel buckled, the rear still spinning wildly. He'd obviously gone straight over the handlebars, and Laura flinched at the memory of doing this as a child. She got cautiously to her feet, but apart from the pain in her arm and a slight soreness in her backside, she was unhurt, more shocked than anything. She crept to the side of the prostrate figure, fervently hoping for no blood or broken bones, stopping dead when she saw him. She recognised his face instantly. Of all the people who could have crashed into her this afternoon, it would have to be Stephen bloody Henderson; arrogant pig. And what on earth was he wearing? She could feel the heat of her anger beginning to rise as she stood looking down at him. He might have really hurt her, careering about the countryside on a bike he clearly couldn't control properly. If he wanted to look like an over-stuffed sausage in that ridiculous Lycra get-up that was up to him, but she certainly didn't want to be involved in his midlife crisis.

She was about to walk away when both his eyes suddenly shot open and he lurched upwards, looking about him wildly, his breath coming in short pants. He struggled to focus, eventually homing in on her face as his brain seemed to catch up with the rest of him.

'Jesus, are you all right!' he exclaimed, trying to get to his feet. 'I could have killed you!'

Laura studied his face, unsure of what to say. In fact, she didn't want to say anything at all. Stephen's face was all screwed up, his jaw clenched. He certainly didn't look like he was sorry.

'I'm fine,' she stated, beginning to look around for the bag she had dropped. There was no way she was hanging around for a minute longer than necessary. She spied it caught up in the branch of one of the bushes, and was about to retrieve it when she felt an arm tugging at hers. She wheeled around.

'I said… what on earth were you doing just standing in the bushes like that? You're lucky I saw you at all.'

He was shouting now, his face contorted.

'I was picking sloes, not that it's any of your business. What on earth were *you* doing riding that thing around when you clearly can't control it? And… if I'm not much mistaken, you were on the wrong side of the road.'

Stephen stared at her as if she had grown another head. 'Me? *I* was out of control? Didn't you see the bloody car going ninety miles an hour down the road? The one I swerved to avoid, the one that narrowly missed you? Are you blind or something?'

Laura bent down to retrieve her bag, picking up Boris' lead which was trailing on the ground. She turned back to Stephen and looked him squarely in the eye.

'No,' she said. 'I'm deaf.' And then she walked away.

Chapter Forty-Eight

Laura had only gone a matter of yards before she felt a sharp tug to her arm once more. Anger leaped into her throat. She turned swiftly.

'Will you stop grabbing my arm?' she snarled.

Stephen had the grace to step back slightly, looking momentarily abashed.

'And before you ask the bleeding obvious, I can lip-read, that's how. So, I can 'hear' what you said, but no I didn't hear the car tearing down the road, or you screeching across the road, or squealing your brakes or shouting, or any of those things that probably happened. Is that enough of an explanation for you, or do you need me to go on?'

Stephen stared at her. 'No, that's enough of an explanation,' he said, and she could see that he was no longer shouting. 'I had no idea, I'm sorry.'

'What? Sorry for hurling me into the middle of a prickly bush or sorry because I'm deaf?'

There really was no answer to that, and Laura didn't expect one. She glared at Stephen for one last moment and then turned her back on him once more, stomping off down the lane. There was no tug to her arm this time.

*

Behind her, Stephen gazed after the slender figure, still trying to catch his breath. God, if she was this beautiful when she was angry, imagine what she would look like when she smiled.

*

Laura made it home in near record time. Even Boris, sliding in through the door after her, flopped onto his bed in the corner of the kitchen with a reproachful eye.

'And you can stop looking at me like that as well,' she muttered, fetching the dog a bowl of water.

She managed to fill the kettle, set it to boil, and place the teabag into her cup before the tears came. She had done it again. What on earth was the matter with her? She had never been like this before David died.

She prodded the tea bag viciously. She didn't really know what it was that made her act the way she did. Her walk had been lovely, the loaves she carried in her bag were fresh and fragrant, and she had enjoyed the balmy autumn air. On the face of it then she had been in a good mood, so why on earth had she felt the need to take Stephen apart the way she had? After all, despite the fact that she hadn't wanted to listen to what he had to say, it sounded as if he had come to her rescue in a roundabout way; even if that had necessitated shoving her to the ground. Her memory of the events leading up to their encounter was patchy, but Stephen hadn't fared too well himself. She could have offered some gratitude, or even a solicitous enquiry after his own health, but instead she had berated him for something which was obviously not his fault at all.

Anger seemed to come at her from nowhere these days, boiling up when she least expected it, and when it did, the resulting embarrassment only served to make her worse. Instead of apologising for her behaviour like any normal person, she cranked her abuse up a gear and then walked away; running back to the safety of her little cottage, to her warm kitchen, where she was alone and could ruminate on her shortcomings at length. Her anger scared her. Everything scared her, and today was another stark reminder of how vulnerable she was.

She took her tea to the table, wrapping her arms around Boris who had magically appeared at her side. The sloes were still in a bag by the sink where she had left them, but her impulse of earlier in the day had waned, and she couldn't be bothered to deal with them now. The dog's fur was warm and comforting, and it seemed easier simply to sit where she was for the time being and let herself be soothed.

It was some time before she moved again, reluctantly getting up to prepare the fruit. She made it a rule never to pick more than she needed, or to waste what she carried home. If nature had seen fit to provide such bountiful produce, then she was only allowed to pick, never plunder. This batch of sloes was destined for the freezer first, where it would sit for a couple of hours until covered with a layer of ice. So far, the autumn had been warm, and the first frosts of the year had yet to appear, so the sloes would benefit from their assisted freezing, releasing their juices and flavour into the alcohol she would steep them in much more readily as a result. It wasn't until she was running water into the sink to give the fruit a good wash that she remembered the connection between Stephen and Freya.

*

Stephen's journey home took much longer than Laura's. Although he too had anger to fire his pace, he was considerably further from home than she was, and his bike might as well be left to rust in the hedgerow for all the use it was now. Walking was not the simple option it first appeared to be either, given that the only footwear he had with him were his cycling shoes complete with cleats.

When she had first stomped off, Stephen had watched Laura's retreating back with a mixture of desire, shock, amusement and burning anger. He was reeling himself with the force at which he had been thrown from his bike, but whichever way he looked at it, he didn't think his responses to her had warranted the bitter words she had flung at him. His shoulder was aching badly, but as he watched her stalk away, getting smaller and smaller, he felt an odd emotion he hadn't experienced for quite some time: compassion. He would have run after her were it not for his shoes, and even though he knew he would probably be attacked for his audacity; he had an overwhelming desire to explain, to soothe, to heal whatever had caused her to behave the way she had, and that wasn't like him at all.

He pulled his mobile from his pocket and peered at it closely; thankfully it seemed no worse for having had his bodily weight thrown upon it. He dialled his brother's number and waited for Sam to pick up. It rang for a while before it was answered.

'Hi Stephen.' Freya sounded breathless. 'Were you after Sam, only he's a bit busy right now?'

Freya sounded like she was standing in the middle of football stadium. 'What on earth is all that noise?' asked Stephen.

He could hear Freya smile. 'Thirty-two school children, all getting high on apple juice,' she replied.

'What?' Stephen shouted.

'Miss Kennedy's class from the primary school,' she explained. 'Year six have been tending the school garden this term, so they get to come and press the apples from their tree. You would never believe how exciting it is… I'd forgotten what it's like to be ten!'

Stephen groaned inwardly. He'd been banking on Sam effecting a swift rescue mission, but it sounded like they were up to their ears. He quickly explained his predicament.

'Stephen, that's awful! Did you see the car?'

'Not clearly. A dark blue four-by-four I think, which could fit the description of any number of cars around here. I was too busy trying not to get killed to take any more notice than that. And the driver was lucky he didn't end up wrapped around a tree, to be honest.'

'But it sounds as if you might have been. Are you sure you're okay?'

Stephen grimaced. 'I'll live,' he replied, circling his shoulder experimentally. 'Bit sore in places but nothing serious. Sadly, the same can't be said for my bike. I think the best course of action might be to put it out of its misery rather than let it suffer.'

Freya laughed. 'Well, at least you can still smile about it. Look if you can give me twenty minutes, I'll be there. Where exactly are you?'

*

Sitting on the verge to wait for Freya had been a serious mistake. Stephen was now so stiff he wasn't sure he could actually get up, and his shoulder throbbed painfully. He gave his bike a dirty look. This cycling lark was supposed to be a way of getting fit, not ending up feeling like he was a hundred and two. Perhaps some rigorous walking might suit him better, or even, if his knees could stand the strain, some gentle jogging. God forbid he should have to resort to sucking in his stomach in some fancy gym.

Stephen was still pondering the state of his girth, when Freya drew up. He levered himself off the ground through gritted teeth and hobbled over to join her.

'Do you want to chuck the bike in the back?' she called.

Stephen looked back. 'Not really,' he said. 'Can't we just leave it there?'

Freya stepped down from the pickup. 'No, we can't,' she said. 'Go on, jump in, I'll sort it out. You might feel differently in the morning.' She gave him a big smile, but not before Stephen had seen her trying to stifle a giggle at the sight of him in Lycra. She didn't know quite where to look.

'So what exactly happened?' she asked, once the bike was stowed and they were on their way.

Stephen recounted the afternoon's events. 'I couldn't help it, Freya. She was standing right at the edge of the road, but I didn't spot her until I nearly mowed her down, she was almost completely hidden by the canopy of trees. What's worse is that I dread to think what might have happened if I hadn't shoved her out of the way. The car was travelling so fast, and fishtailing around the road, he could easily have taken her out, no problem at all.'

'And she was deaf, you said?'

Stephen nodded. 'Hmm, and beautiful.' He sighed. 'Possibly the most beautiful girl I've ever seen, but as first meetings go, it wasn't what you'd call auspicious. She let me know in no uncertain terms what she thought of me.'

'I bet she did,' said Freya, prodding hard at Stephen's arm with her free hand.

'Ow!' he protested. 'What was that for?'

'Just checking,' she replied. 'It would appear that you do have a soft spot after all.'

Stephen glared at her. 'Very funny,' he huffed. 'She could have been seriously hurt.'

Freya was instantly contrite. 'I know. I'm sorry, Stephen. I shouldn't take the mickey. You should probably go to the police you know.'

'And say what? I didn't see the car well enough to make an identification. I'm fine, our mystery girl is fine, and that's pretty much all there is to it.'

Freya thought for a minute. 'Yes, I suppose. There ought to be something we can do, though. It doesn't seem right that something so potentially serious is just ignored.'

Stephen stared through the windscreen at the road ahead, lost in his own thoughts for a moment. When he eventually answered, his voice had a soft almost wistful tone to it. 'Well, there is one thing I'm going to do,' he said. 'And that's find her... whoever she is.'

Chapter Forty-Nine

Laura was up early the next morning. She had checked her diary before she went to bed the previous evening and would have to be out early if she was to get all her deliveries made before she visited the churchyard. In the dark days immediately after David's death, her neighbours, Stan, Millie and Blanche had been her lifeline. They were just as cantankerous as she was in many ways and her grief-stricken protestations that she didn't need to eat or drink had fallen on deaf ears. She had been practically force-fed chicken soup, beef stew and shepherd's pie, and although Laura had fought them almost every step of the way, in the end she had been grateful for their kindly ministrations and their present arrangements had grown from there.

All three of her neighbours were somewhere between the ages of sixty-five and eighty, with Blanche, Laura suspected, being the eldest. She had never liked to ask their ages, as all three were fiercely independent and as sprightly as someone half their age and, unlikely though the friendships were, they were firm.

Stan lived the closest to her, although still a good half mile away; a keen vegetable grower with a very sweet tooth and an intense fondness for her chocolate-coated boozy damsons. Three doors down from him was where Millie lived. She was the youngest of the trio and a stalwart member of the WI. Her cakes were to die for, although alas her jam was not, and so in return for her sweet treats, Laura left Millie with plain labelled jars of apple and ginger or raspberry jam. So what if on occasion she passed them off as her own; Millie's secrets were safe with her. Blanche lived in the next house, with her motley collection of chickens that had all been rescued from some place or another. With Blanche's tender care, they laid the biggest eggs Laura had ever seen, and as Blanche liked nothing more than a drop of sloe gin each evening, purely for medicinal purposes of course, the trade was a steady one.

Laura was well aware that these arrangements allowed her to stay outside the real world for much of the time, but she was also able to keep a watchful eye over her friends and, in an age that often felt unkind and uncaring to Laura, it helped to assuage her guilt over the darker aspects of her own character. Hiding from the world was not the answer of course, but life was certainly much easier this way.

It took Laura nearly an hour-and-a-half to make the round trip this morning despite the fact that Blanche wasn't in. Her friends were early risers like her, and it was nice to share a cup of tea with them, talking about their plans for the day and their love of the coming season. She returned home laden with runner beans, some courgettes, and a honey cake. With her bounty deposited safely in the kitchen, Laura was finally ready to set out for the churchyard. She slipped down the path to one of the sheds at the end of her garden to collect her tools and a garland she had made a couple of days earlier. The conkers in it were gleaming like newly polished mahogany, and she smiled to see them. Mr and Mrs Roberts were going to love them too.

*

'Morning, Dad,' called Freya. 'I hope you don't mind me visiting two days in a row, although actually…' she lowered her voice to a whisper, '… it isn't you I've come to see at all, sorry.'

She perched on the little stool she had brought with her for the days when the grave didn't need tending and she just wanted to sit and chat.

'Sam thinks I'm barmy of course, but then, no offense Dad, he's a bloke, so what does he know? To be fair, he's been pretty good with all the other wedding arrangements, but you know him as well as I do, and he hasn't got a creative bone in his body, has he? I know exactly how I want my bouquet and the other arrangements to look and, as I was leaving here yesterday, I saw the most beautiful wreath.' She sighed, looking around her once more. 'Even though it pains me to say it, it was much better than anything I could make, and I know that whoever did would be the perfect person to help with the wedding. Unfortunately, I don't know who that is.'

She cocked her head to one side as if listening. 'So you need to help me out here, Dad, because I'm pretty much lying in wait to see if I can spot whoever made the wreath, and if you don't talk to me, I'm going to look a complete loon.' She gave a wry smile. 'Yeah, I know. Thanks for the obvious witty response.' Her head whipped around as she heard the lychgate creak open, but it was only the wind; she probably hadn't fastened it properly.

A tiny robin swooped in front of her, a small worm in its mouth, and she followed the path of its flight, watching as it disappeared behind a rather ornate memorial at the far end of the churchyard. She smiled, turning back to speak to her father once more, before looking up again to where the robin had flown. *I wonder*, she thought.

'Excuse me for a minute, Dad.'

Freya had done a circuit of the graveyard as soon as she had entered it this morning, but there had been no one else there, and she had wandered among the graves looking for more evidence of the wreath-maker's work. It was a large cemetery, with a newer area off to the right of the church, where Freya's dad was buried, and with the original, older graves dotted around the rear of the church and along a low boundary wall to the left. At the far end of the wall however, an arch led through into a separate much older space where there were larger memorials and family plots; even a small crypt for one of the most notable village families. It was obvious that some of these plots were still being well cared for, and even though Freya had not seen any other wreaths, it set her thinking.

Since her arrival she had seen no one else enter the churchyard, even though her view of the gate from her father's grave was uninterrupted. Now she wondered whether anyone would come into the grounds from the footpath through the fields that ran alongside this older area. There was still an old stile at one end and, although it was now partially hidden in the yew hedge, it was possible that people still used it. After all, robins were known for being friendly little birds, especially if the person they were keeping company was digging...

She followed the tiny bird as it darted to and fro between two of the larger memorials, and immediately she could see the source of the robin's excitement. Between two of the graves a triangular flower bed had been freshly dug and planted with winter flowering pansies. A small fork and trowel lay close by, along with a green canvas bag. Of their owner she could see no trace, but as Freya grew closer, a gentle voice floated up from behind one of the headstones.

'Hello, little one,' it said.

Freya smiled, knowing instantly who the voice was talking to. It was exactly how she addressed robins herself whenever they perched close by. Judging by the tilt of their heads, they always seemed to know they were being spoken to, and she loved the gleam in their intelligent black eyes.

She moved forward a little hesitantly. Freya didn't hold with whispers and tiptoes in the graveyard; to her, the place was as much about the living as the dead, but she did respect other people's need for privacy. She didn't want to blunder into someone's precious time with a relative, but neither did she want to creep up on them without announcing her presence. Of course, the person behind the gravestone might well not be the one she was looking for, and then a rather awkward conversation would ensue.

Freya sauntered past the flower bed, stopping to look at it in admiration before moving beyond the grave and on towards the memorials as if she wanted to study their inscriptions. As she turned, she was now able to see the figure who had previously been hidden from view. Her back was towards her, but Freya instantly recognised the woman she had seen here before. She was tending the grave, arranging the stems of some bright orange and purple dahlias in a vase, and at her side lay the most beautiful foliage wreath.

Freya cleared her throat, but there was no response. Instead, the woman began to speak herself.

'There you are now, Mrs Roberts. Didn't I tell you he would bring you your favourite flowers next time? The most beautiful colours they are too. A deep burnt orange and purple the exact same colour as a red cabbage.' She paused for a moment to adjust a stem. 'He's definitely a keeper,' she said. 'Any man who goes to the trouble of finding you your favourite flowers is worth hanging on to I reckon. What do you say?'

The flowers were certainly beautiful, and Freya smiled at the words. They were just the sort of daft thing she would say to her dad. The voice continued.

'And you look absolutely beautiful, Ethel, doesn't she Ted? That must be the prettiest dress I've ever seen. Brings out the colour of your eyes too. Speaking of which...' She reached down to lift up the wreath from beside her. 'I made this for you. After all it's not every day you get to celebrate an anniversary, is it? I hope you like it.'

Freya couldn't help herself. 'I think it's perfect,' she said, realising too late that she had intruded into a private conversation. She expected to receive a withering glare, but the woman moved only to lay the wreath in front of the headstone.

'Now you two have the most magical day, won't you?' she said, as she began to rise. 'And remember... don't do anything I wouldn't do!'

The smile was still on her lips as she stood and turned, dying the instant she saw Freya. A hand rose to her chest.

'Oh my God, you made me jump!'

Her sudden surprise jolted Freya too, and she put out a hand towards the woman as if to steady them both. 'I'm sorry,' she said swiftly. 'Really. I didn't mean to.'

The young woman gave a wary smile. 'It's okay, no permanent harm done.' She regarded Freya curiously with narrowed eyes. 'Were you talking to me just now? I'm sorry, I didn't hear you.'

'Well, I was very rude, butting into your conversation like that, so it's as well you didn't.'

The woman looked confused. 'My conversation? Oh, with Mr & Mrs Roberts.' She swung around to face the grave once more. 'Bless them. It's their wedding anniversary today – eighty-six years, would you believe it?' She gave Freya a quick smile. 'Actually,' she said, 'I don't know them at all; theirs is just one of the graves I'm paid to look after, so for all I know, they hated one another's guts, but I like to dream, you know…'

There it was again, thought Freya, the wistful sadness that she had glimpsed on her face before, in those huge brown eyes.

'I think it's lovely, the way you talk to them. I do the same with my dad whenever I visit. One of these days I swear he'll tell me to shut up, but for now I just chatter away. That way I feel like he's still with me somehow, if that makes any sense.'

'It makes perfect sense,' said the woman. 'I've seen you I think, haven't I? On the other side of the church,' she said shyly.

Freya nodded. 'My dad died in April last year,' she replied, dropping her head. 'Although some days it feels like it was yesterday.'

Silence stretched out for a moment before Freya looked back up again to find the woman staring at her. She smiled. 'I'm Freya, by the way.'

There was a slightly puzzled frown. 'Freya?' she repeated, looking for an answering nod. 'Okay. Well, I'm Laura.'

The two women looked warily at one another, Freya feeling a little embarrassed until she remembered what she had wanted in the first place. She coughed a little self-consciously.

'I hope you don't mind me asking, but is it you who makes the beautiful wreaths I've seen? The one just there, and another over by the lychgate; I noticed it yesterday.'

'Oh, the garlands?' Laura blushed. 'The hedgerows are bursting with such lovely stuff at the moment, it seems a shame not to share it.' She looked around her. 'It's nice to use flowers and plants on the graves, but the garlands are a little bit different.'

'I think they're absolutely beautiful,' said Freya. 'In fact, they're the nicest I've ever seen.'

'Thank you.' Laura blushed again, tipping her head to acknowledge the compliment. 'I enjoy making them, that's all.'

Freya could feel her excitement of yesterday beginning to return. 'Do you make other things as well, arrangements I mean, or is it just the garlands?'

She was dismayed to see Laura's face close up a little.

'Not really,' she said. 'I just fiddle with things, when I see something that I like, but they're just for me... or for my friends here.' She indicated the grave behind her.

It was a funny choice of words, thought Freya, noting that Laura's hands were now clasped around her elbows as if she was cold. She decided to back off a little.

'I make wreaths too, at Christmas time,' Freya said. 'But they're far more traditional than yours. I can't always find the things I want, or enough of them at any rate. I sell them you see, at the Mistletoe Fair in Tenbury Wells, but they have to be pretty uniform, so I need plenty of raw materials. I've used fruits and berries in the past, crab apples too, but I don't really have the time to seek them all out any more.'

'You have the orchard, don't you?' cut in Laura. 'Out on the Witley road.'

Her question surprised Freya. 'Yes,' she began tentatively, 'Appleyard. Do you know it?' she asked.

Laura bit her lip. 'I know of it,' she said eventually. 'There's a place about three fields over where you can find crab apples, or huge orange haws. They're usually still about, even at Christmas.'

Freya smiled. 'Maybe you could tell me more one day.' She gave a quick glance at her watch. 'I have to get going in a minute, but I expect I'll see you here another time.'

'I'm here most days,' replied Laura quietly. 'Except at the weekend. I never come then, it's too... busy,' she said. She crossed to pick up her bag and tools. 'I should be off as well.'

Freya had to say something now or she had the feeling that the right time would never present itself. She gave a nervous smile.

'Laura, I hope you don't mind me saying… well, asking really, but I didn't come here by chance this morning; I came to see you.' She continued quickly at the sight of Laura's horrified face. 'Only because I meant what I said – I do absolutely love your garlands, but also because I've been looking for someone who could make things like this for a while now. I'm getting married soon, and these would be perfect for the wedding. They'd tell our story so beautifully…' She trailed off, unsure how to frame her question without it sounding too scary. In the end, she decided to simply spit it out. 'Would you consider helping me with our wedding flowers…? It's in three weeks.'

Laura's expression was unchanged.

'Look, you don't have to give me an answer now. It's a lot to ask, and I know I'm a bit of a bull in a china shop sometimes, but will you think about it at least? I'd pay you of course, and we could talk about it…'

Laura held her look for a moment, and Freya could see the turmoil reflected in her face. She was glancing about her as if checking she had everything she had brought with her, swapping the bag into her other hand.

'I'll think about it,' said Laura. 'But I'm not very good with people since…' She stopped abruptly. 'I'll think it about it,' she repeated, with the ghost of a smile. 'Thank you.' And she turned to go.

Freya watched her making her way to the stile and back to the fields. 'It was nice to meet you,' she called after Laura's retreating back; but there was no reply.

It wasn't until she had said goodbye to her dad and collected her stool that the penny dropped. It suddenly came to her why Laura hadn't appeared to hear her at times, why she wore a slightly intense expression whenever Freya was speaking, how she studied her face, and how her replies were not as quick as they might have been. She was lip-reading. Laura was deaf.

Freya thought of the last conversation she'd had with her future brother-in-law. Now what were the chances of that?

Chapter Fifty

Stephen had apples to harvest, he shouldn't still be sitting in his kitchen, but unaccountably he couldn't move from his laptop. He had never felt this way before, but now that he did, he was revelling in the experience. He was also beginning to realise that if this was how he felt, then this 'thing', which he had hitherto believed to be a made-up, or certainly overrated, emotion must be true. It suddenly made him understand people a whole lot better.

Take his brother for example. Sam had been head over heels in love with Freya since the minute they clapped eyes on one another at primary school. Of course, back then, Sam hadn't recognised what love was; he and Freya were simply good friends until his hormones kicked in, and Freya's too for that matter. Stephen had watched them over the years, from his vantage point of superior age, and thought them soppy and foolish with their plans and declarations. It hadn't stopped him feeling jealous, though, of the affection that Sam received, and of the easy relationship he shared with a woman instead of the furtive fumblings that Stephen managed. And because he couldn't understand it, because he could never have it, he set out to take what was not rightfully his.

He had wooed Freya and seduced her with make-believe affection and lies; promises he never intended to keep. Everything bigger and better than his brother could ever hope to give her. She had fallen for it too, right up to the point where they were about to walk down the aisle, Sam long since fallen by the wayside. But something had made Freya stop, and when she stopped, she started running.

It had taken a very long time, right up until a year ago in fact for Stephen to be forgiven, and for Freya and Sam to finally get back to where they were always meant to be: together. Stephen had begun to acknowledge a different way of living since then. He'd had a great many lessons to learn, but slowly he was beginning to understand that things happened to other people not because they were favoured, or lucky, but because they worked for them. He realised, in fact, just how much of a prat he'd been in his life, giving in to jealousy and sullen, petty anger when he should have been forging his own future. For much of it, his had been a wasted life, but Stephen was determined to do better from now on, and two days ago, he had come across the most perfect, and most beautiful incentive.

It wasn't a very promising start, Stephen would be the first to admit, but really, if you looked at it from a slightly different point of view, he had saved the woman's life. Perhaps, in time, she would see it that way too, and they would laugh about how they had both behaved badly, saying things they hadn't meant, jumping to the wrong conclusions. There was no possibility that Stephen could have known she was deaf, but now that he did, he was determined to make up for it. He just needed a way to impress her somehow. That and hope that fate would allow them to meet up again, and she would stay in the same room with him for long enough to make it count.

He opened a new internet tab on his laptop and typed 'British Sign Language courses' into the search engine. So far that morning he had watched about thirty YouTube clips, searching for some simple words or phrases that might be relatively easy to learn. Even just 'hello' or 'thank you' would be a start, anything that might let her know that he wasn't a hot-headed idiot all the time...

*

'I should never have gone,' said Freya, as she and Sam sipped a welcome cup of tea. They'd been hard at it since early morning, but several hours' work had resulted in an enormous pile of perfect apples, ready for pressing. The afternoon, if they were lucky, would see the bright crisp juice, bottled and ready to be collected.

'It was a rotten thing to come out with when I didn't even know the girl. She must have been petrified having me throw that at her.'

Sam looked at Freya over the rim of his mug. 'And did she seem petrified?'

'Not exactly, but she didn't seem that happy either. She was obviously really shy, and now I know why. I'd never have asked her if I'd known.'

'Why would her being deaf make any difference?'

'Well because... imagine how she must feel?'

'Chuffed to know how much you liked her work?'

Freya gave an exasperated tut. 'Honestly, Sam. I was obviously making her very uncomfortable. I mean, she spends her days talking to dead people for God's sake, probably so that she doesn't have to hold embarrassing conversations with complete strangers who don't know a thing about her, and yet make wild suggestions at the drop of a hat.'

Sam merely smiled. 'Or,' he said pointedly, 'she could be very lonely but unsure about how to make things any different. It must be quite isolating being deaf; think about that for a minute. And now here you are, the first person in ages who's taken any notice of her, and not only that but showered her with compliments, and made her what could be a very exciting offer. Have you thought of it that way?'

He took hold of her hand. 'I'm wondering who's the more embarrassed here, Freya; are you sure it's Laura? Don't treat her any differently just because she's deaf, that's possibly the real reason she shies away from people; because she's so fed up with people treating her that way.'

Freya sighed. 'How did you get to be so wise, Sam Henderson?'

'Probably because I'm getting married to you, Freya Sherbourne. Isn't that why we're having this conversation? To convince you of something you already know is true. Don't give up on her, Freya, maybe she needs you more than you know.'

'But she didn't come to the churchyard today.'

'Perhaps she was busy. You could always try again tomorrow.'

Freya flashed him a huge smile before leaning over and kissing him deeply. 'I love you,' she said.

*

Two miles away Laura was having the exact same argument with herself, and with Boris when he could be bothered to listen. The dog's head was resting on the table as he sat beside it, his eyes swivelling to the left and then the right as he watched Laura pacing back and forth across the kitchen.

'I should be thrilled that someone likes my garlands so much and, more than that, she's even offered me paid work – for a wedding of all things! Do you know what this could mean for me, Boris? Money. Money to help me get other things off the ground instead of sitting in my kitchen wasting my life away like the sad, lonely widow I am.'

She stopped pacing for a moment to look the dog squarely in the eye.

'I shouldn't even be having this conversation with you. I mean, it's obvious what the answer is. I should run after her as fast as I can and bite her arm off. But instead I'm having a deep and meaningful conversation with my dog because I'm scared, and pathetic and frightened that as soon as I'm among people again, they'll start saying all those horrible things about me that put me here in the first place.'

The memories of that time leaped out at her unbidden. It was a time and place that Laura never wanted to go back to, but even as her eyes began to smart with the pain of it all, a part of her knew that she had to go back to start going forward again.

'See, it's different with the others, my friends; they're outcasts like me, because their age makes them different, makes them less able. But they're patient, they speak slower, and it's not half so exhausting having a conversation with them. Besides, Blanche is pretty deaf too, Stan has a dodgy hip and Millie's memory isn't what it once was; but none of us needs to apologise. We all know what it's like to have bits of us that don't work properly, and that's okay. We're still us.'

She sat down heavily with a sigh.

'I might not get a chance like this again. There was something… something I can't explain about Freya, but it's like she understood me. She wouldn't think it weird that I tramp the fields all day and forage for stuff. *She'd* think it was magical; she'd want to do it too, I know she would. No one has made me feel like that about what I do in a long time, Boris, a very long time indeed.' She puffed out her cheeks. 'And yet I still bloody chickened out.'

She got up again and walked over to her larder returning with a large bowl of pale knobbly fruits.

'Right,' she said in a decisive fashion. 'Tomorrow I'll go. Did you hear that, Boris?' The dog watched her with his large brown eyes, licking his lips as he did so. 'Tomorrow I *will* go to the churchyard, and I *will* meet with Freya and find out what it is she'd like me to do. So, if I look like I'm chickening out, I give you full permission to push me out through the door with a very wet cold nose.'

She gave a satisfied nod.

'And now that's decided, I'm going to tackle these beautiful quinces. Stick your nose in there, Boris, aren't they some of the best things you've ever smelled?'

Chapter Fifty-One

Freya's heart leaped as she walked through the church gate the next morning. Laura was waiting for her on the other side, her huge dog beside her, and although she looked pretty terrified, Freya acknowledged that she'd found her own legs a little wobbly at times as she walked up the lane.

Two days ago, she had chatted away to Laura the same way she would to anyone else, but although she knew that today ought to be no different, she felt clumsy and tongue-tied. *Whatever you do, don't try and compensate for her deafness by shouting at her* was Sam's less than helpful advice. She had worked that out herself, but she still felt she ought to try to make things easier for Laura, she just didn't know how. The more she thought about their encounter, the more she could see her old friend serendipity at work. The fact that Stephen had quite literally bumped into Laura as well, only served to strengthen her feelings.

She gave Laura a tentative but she hoped friendly smile. The last thing she wanted to do was scare her off.

To her surprise, Laura responded with a massive grin of her own.

'Thank God, you're here,' she said. 'It took me all of yesterday to work up the courage to come. If you hadn't turned up, I would have felt the most enormous prat. I'd probably have gone home and had the most almighty blub as well.'

'Me too,' replied Freya. 'I'm so glad you came.'

The two women looked at one another for a moment, the early morning sun slanting a band of gold between them. It would be all right, thought Freya, and her nervousness faded.

'Well, this is Boris,' said Laura, patting the dog's head, which came easily to her waist. 'He's very big and very hairy, but other than that the least scary dog I know. In fact, he's a real pushover, but don't tell him I said that.'

Freya smiled at the hairy beast. 'It suits him,' she said. 'Very distinguished.'

When there was no reply, Freya lifted her head a fraction to find Laura squinting at her. She blushed.

'I said his name suits him.' She smiled. 'He looks very distinguished.'

There was a nod and then, 'I'm sorry, I…'

'Distinguished?' Freya repeated, trying not to shout.

'Ah, okay,' said Laura, 'I've always thought so. There's definitely something of the aristocrat about him.' She flashed Freya a grateful look before looking down and fiddling with the buttons on her coat.

'Perhaps I should just come out and say it…' began Laura. 'It might save us both a lot of embarrassment, and I can see you've worked out for yourself that I'm deaf. I probably should thank you first for not shouting. You won't believe how many people do, it's instinctive I know, but people's faces and mouths contort when they do that, and it makes lip-reading so much harder. Speaking normally is best.'

'I'll probably get it wrong a lot of the time, but I won't mind in the slightest if you tell me.'

'You might, when it's the nineteenth time I've done it,' said Laura with a wry smile.

Her words were light, but it struck Freya how utterly exhausting it must be for her to have a conversation this way, having to prompt people constantly to repeat things, having to study people's faces to such an extent that you see every flicker of irritation written there.

'How long have you been deaf?' she asked.

'Since I was about eighteen,' replied Laura. 'I had a brain tumour… everything's fine now,' she hastened to add. 'Luckily for me, it wasn't particularly nasty, it just decided to grow in a rather unfortunate place, that's all. Come to think of it when you have a brain tumour, pretty much everywhere is unfortunate, but when it grew large enough to operate on, it had to come out. There was a substantial risk to my hearing, but a risk I had to take if I was to keep my other faculties.'

'The lesser of many evils. Not a huge comfort I would imagine.'

'It could have been worse,' said Laura.

Freya nodded sadly. 'I suppose,' she agreed. 'And would you normally sign…? If you had the choice, I mean.'

Laura smiled. 'Yes,' she said, her hands flashing in front of her. 'It's a lot easier… for me anyway.'

'Maybe you could teach me,' said Freya, wincing as the words came out of her mouth. 'Or maybe I should just shut up and tell you about our wedding plans and what I had in mind for the flowers, and we can take it from there? I've brought one or two pictures I can show you too.' She shot Laura an apologetic look and was pleased to see she looked a little relieved. One thing at a time, Freya reminded herself, one thing at a time.

'We could go inside if you like,' said Laura. 'There's a small room at the side of the church with a table and chairs, and you could show me what you've brought.'

Freya followed Laura who led the way to a small anteroom just off the main entrance. Boris loped in by her side and immediately made for the only rug in the room beneath the small oak table. She gave a little shiver which had nothing to do with the coolness of the building, but instead to a flowering of nerves in the pit of her stomach. She would be here in three short weeks, walking through the huge oak door as a bride and leaving an hour later as Sam's wife. Between now and then there was an extraordinary number of things to attend to, and even though it wasn't a big wedding, Freya wasn't sure how on earth she would manage to pull it all off. If Laura would agree to help her, it would be a huge weight off her mind.

She sat down, waiting for Laura to follow suit before fishing in her bag for the photos she had brought.

'These aren't really right, but it's the colours I like and the general look I'm aiming for.' She straightened up, placing the pictures down on the table.

Laura sat looking at them, an expectant look on her face. It was only when a lengthening silence began to stretch out that Freya realised her mistake. She gently touched a hand to Laura's arm.

'I'm sorry,' she said, once Laura's eyes were on her face. 'I was talking at the same time as bending down. I forgot you wouldn't hear me.'

Laura looked back at the pictures. 'People have a tendency to talk to the thing they're discussing, rather than each other. Tap the table or my arm when you're going to speak, that way I know to look at you.' She smiled. 'I like these, though, except they're a bit too regimented for my taste. Too confined. I like my arrangements to be more unstructured, messy even sometimes...' She frowned. 'Sorry, what was it you said?'

'The same as you,' answered Freya, feeling excited at the connection between them. 'I like the colours of these, but they're way too formal.'

Laura nodded. 'And what are we talking about here, in terms of decoration I mean. What do you need help with? The church, your own flowers?'

Freya screwed up her face. 'Erm... everything. The church yes, and my bouquet, but we're having a marquee back at Appleyard for the reception as well, and I'd love to have flowers there too. In fact, not just flowers, but fruits, leaves, berries, that kind of thing.'

At the mention of the marquee, Laura's eyes widened. She looked shocked, and yet Freya didn't think it was extravagant, not by modern standards.

'It won't be huge, the marquee I mean. It's just that we've nowhere else to put people. The barn is full of equipment, and—'

'How many people will there be?' interrupted Laura. She blanched suddenly, shooting backwards in her chair. Her hand flew to her mouth. 'I'm sorry, Freya. I can't do this. I shouldn't have come.'

Laura was almost at the door by the time Freya had registered her sudden change of mood. She struggled to get up, hampered by the straps of her bag which had become tangled in the chair leg.

'Laura, wait!' she shouted, without thinking. She looked beseechingly at Boris who looked rather startled at the sudden movement. 'Can't you stop her?' she asked. There was nothing for it but to chase after her. God, Laura was fast.

She was halfway down the path before Freya caught up with her, catching at her arm as gently as she could. She turned Laura to face her and was horrified to see that tears had already stained her pale face.

'Whatever is the matter?' she asked. 'I'm sorry, I didn't mean to upset you.'

Laura stared at her as if unseeing.

'It's my fault. I should never have come,' she hiccupped. 'All the villagers, all those people…'

Freya was confused now. 'What people? Who are you talking about, Laura?'

Laura's eyes searched her face for answers. 'In the marquee, and at the church. Everywhere. I can't be with those people,' she said, shuddering.

It wasn't so much what she said but the way she said it which struck a chord with Freya. Being shy was one thing, but this was something entirely different. She recalled Laura's words of a couple of days ago. How she wouldn't visit the churchyard at the weekend because there were too many people, how she wasn't very good with folk since… a sentence that had never been finished. Freya could understand Laura feeling awkward in company. Deafness was not visible on the outside, and her life must be full of misunderstandings and apologies, judgements made, often incorrectly, as people mistook Laura's silence or lack of response for rudeness. But feeling awkward, although understandable, was not the issue here; it went much deeper than that. Laura was afraid.

Without thinking Freya reached out and pulled Laura in towards her, wrapping her arms around the tiny figure but saying nothing. It was an instinctive gesture, and Freya, not prone as yet to maternal feelings, was surprised by it; but there was something about Laura that was so gentle, so vulnerable, and although they were of a similar age, it touched something deep inside Freya. At first, she thought she had made a massive error as Laura's whole body went taut, but almost immediately she inhaled a huge shuddering breath and her arms clung to Freya's coat as she fell against her.

A cold wet nose pushed itself onto the back of Freya's hand several minutes later, as Boris reminded her gently of his presence. He seemed as confused about his mistress's behaviour as she was, but Laura's choice of a dog known for its loyalty and generosity was no coincidence. She wondered how long it had been since Laura had felt the reassurance of a human touch.

After a few moments more, Freya gently moved away, pulling Laura so that she could look at her. She had shed the tears she needed to, but her look when she met Freya's gaze was still fearful.

'Perhaps you should come and tell me all about it,' said Freya. 'If you're ready?'

There was a weak smile, but Laura was indeed ready. She had waited a very long time to talk to someone.

'We used to live next door to one another, had done ever since I was five and he was six, and I guess we grew up together. It wasn't until we started secondary school that I really took any notice of him; David was simply always there. It was never serious; we went out together a few times, but that all changed when I was fourteen and diagnosed with a brain tumour.'

Freya was beginning to feel cold, and the hard, wooden chair wasn't helping, but she sat as still as she could for fear of breaking the moment. Laura had begun to talk the moment they were back inside the church again, sitting in the same room they had left only minutes earlier. She nodded encouragingly.

'It's at those times that you find out who your friends really are,' she continued. 'I remember clearly the day when I told my best friend, Chloe, the diagnosis. I'd been in and out of hospital for weeks having various tests, and missed a fair bit of school one way or another. Chloe was brilliant. Every day I was absent, she came around to our house to fill me in with all the gossip, or help me to catch up with my homework; but the very day I was finally able to confide in her the diagnosis, she looked at me and said "So, you're going to die then?"'

The spot on the wall held Laura's attention for so long that Freya was tempted to look there herself, but eventually the words started again, a quiet monotone that belied Laura's true feelings.

'She apologised straight away of course, but I'd caught her off guard, and she'd said the first thing that had come into her head – the thing she really thought. It was what she believed, and at the time, so did I.' She took another breath. 'It certainly spelled the death sentence for our friendship. She didn't walk away immediately, just sort of drifted further off each day, like a piece of flotsam caught on the outgoing tide, until I hardly saw her. And I let her go. I was too preoccupied to care, and where she and others left little holes in my life, David came and filled them.'

For the first time since she started talking, Laura raised her eyes and looked at Freya. The loneliness in her eyes was stark, as was the longing for warmth and life.

'I'm so sorry,' whispered Freya. 'That must have been an awful time for you. I can't imagine how you must have felt. School and just being fourteen are hard enough to get through, but add something like that into the mix... How ever did you cope?'

There was a slight pause as Laura weighed up what Freya had just asked.

'Strangely enough, it got easier after that. It was just David and me against the world. We didn't need anyone else. That's where I went wrong of course, but at the time I didn't think beyond the next day and the day after that; everything else was too far in the distance, and so it went on. Even when I found out about the operation and the risk to my hearing, David simply said we would learn sign language together, and so we did. It never crossed my mind that this was wrong…'

'What do you mean wrong, Laura? I'm not sure I follow you.' Freya put out a hand in reassurance.

It took Laura some moments before she could speak again, a sudden welling up of tears tightening her throat, and quickening her breathing. 'Because now that he's gone, I have nothing in my life, and no one. I built my world around him, and when he died, my foundations went too, and everything crumbled around me.'

Freya took in a sharp breath at the shock of Laura's words. Here she was, on the threshold of sharing a life with the man she loved, and this young woman had already lived a lifetime of love and grief. She was flooded with remorse. She left her chair and knelt beside Laura, taking both of her hands and folding them in her own. They were like ice.

'I'm so, so, sorry,' she said, making sure that Laura could see every word. 'I've been gabbling on about my own wedding without a second thought, and I never even stopped to think. I feel awful asking for your help, it was probably the most insensitive thing I could have done.'

'And yet I want to help,' whispered Laura, 'I just don't know how.' Freya cocked her head to one side, confused.

'I want to live,' Laura continued, her tear-stained face pale, but more animated now. 'I want to feel alive, to be a part of things; have friends and do things normal people do, but I've shut myself away for so long it feels like an impossibility.' She clasped at Freya's hands. 'I'd love to help with your wedding. It's such a wonderful celebration of life, of everything that's important, but how do I face people again, when most of them are the reason I've shut myself away?'

There was something tickling at the back of Freya's mind. Something that she should know about, a memory that should never have been forgotten. And then, as she looked at Laura's beautiful face, it came to her. She squeezed her hand.

'Is your last name Ashcombe?' she asked.

There was a tiny nod as the two women leaned forward in a hug.

Five years ago, most of the farming community had turned out to attend the funeral of young David Ashcombe, a worker at the nearby Drummond Orchard, one of the largest cider producers in the area. There had been talk of dodgy working practices on the estate for years, but the general consensus was that Francis Drummond believed himself above the law and, in this case, he had seemed to get away with it. David had been killed while helping to clear damaged trees after a severe storm. The handbrake on the tractor trailer he was using had failed as he was stacking cut logs on the back. It rolled backwards crushing him to death. Laura had argued publicly that David talked frequently about badly maintained machinery, but the enquiry found it to be a simple case of operator error.

Freya's heart went out to Laura. There was nothing simple about a death, particularly of a young man with his whole life ahead of him. And the legacy that death had left behind was far from simple either, the proof was in her arms. She straightened up.

'Then we must do something to change your situation, Laura. I can't think of anything better than to have you help with our wedding, but it can't be allowed to cause you any more anguish. Let's focus on the thing you love doing most – making amazing floral arrangements and everything else we can take step-by-step and day by day. There's no need for you to have to meet anyone *en masse*. In fact, for now it'll just be me and Sam, and after that, well, whatever we do, you won't be doing it alone. How does that sound?'

Laura took a deep and calming breath. 'It sounds… a bit scary, but a lot less so than it did. I can't thank you enough, Freya. I'm really not quite sure what came over me.' She frowned. 'I don't normally make a habit of crying all over people and being quite so pathetic but—'

Freya put out her hand out to interrupt. 'You know, I'm a firm believer that things happen for a reason… often when we least expect them. A very wise man once taught me that, and when it's the right time, it really is the right time. Let's go with that, shall we, and see where it takes us. I have a feeling it might be to a very good place indeed.'

Chapter Fifty-Two

'And I know what you're thinking, Stephen, but back off, okay. The last thing she needs is someone beating a path to her door and declaring his undying lust for her.'

Stephen grinned. 'Are you ever going to change your opinion of me, even though you know I'm a changed man and you love me really?'

Sam looked up from yesterday's newspaper, and arched an eyebrow. 'Don't push your luck, Stephen, this is Freya you're dealing with, don't forget. She has a memory like an elephant and—'

'You say anything about the size of my backside and you're a dead man!' she exclaimed, marching between them. 'Either of you.'

Sam winked at his brother and returned his gaze to the paper. 'What did I tell you?' he muttered.

'I'm serious,' said Freya fiercely. 'Don't even think of making any sort of advance towards Laura. She's going to need a huge amount of courage to take these first few steps, and I promised her we'd take things slowly. She certainly won't be looking for any romantic entanglements right now, especially not with someone who has all the subtlety of a brick.'

Much to Freya's surprise, Stephen nodded. 'I can't imagine what she's been through. Having David die in a horrific accident was bad enough, but then to have his integrity questioned the way it was… it's shameful. It seems such a long time ago now, and I'm still surprised neither of us recognised her, but I do remember folks talking about it down the pub for weeks, and not in a good way either.'

Sam raised his head in astonishment, catching Freya's eye with a knowing look. 'I don't suppose they meant any harm, but folks don't always think before they open their mouths, especially if they've got a few on board at the time. I think we can all remember the time when the three of us were the subject of gossip and speculation, and it wasn't a pleasant experience. The difference was that we had other people around to protect us, to some extent. Laura's been alone with her thoughts day after day.'

'I wonder if she even knows that there were people who stood up for her at the time,' added Stephen. 'I didn't know her then of course… still don't,' he rubbed his chin ruefully, 'but Drummond deserves to be taken down a peg or two. He did back then, and I don't suppose anything has changed.'

'And you're going to be the man who does it, are you?' remarked Freya, knowing what Stephen was like.

Stephen shook his head. 'Uh uh. Not a chance. Think what that would do to Laura. The whole lot would be raked back up again, and she needs to move on, not be tethered to the past by that scumbag.'

Freya smiled to herself, careful not to let Stephen see. He wasn't a changed man, but he was definitely changing. Gone was the angry, arrogant bully who Freya had despised for so many years, and in his place, was a happier and more mature man. She looked at Sam affectionately, knowing that a few short months ago the brothers could hardly bear to be in the same room as one another, let alone trade jokes and mock insults. Things were undeniably shifting; she could feel it.

As if Sam could feel her eyes on him, he looked up, shaking out the paper.

'What day were you nearly run off the road, Stephen?' he asked. 'Was it Monday?'

'Yes, why?'

Sam laid the newspaper flat on the table. 'Because you might want to take a look at this,' he said in a low voice, anxiety creasing his brow.

Sam's finger tapped on the article which was a third of the way down the page. The headline screamed out at Stephen.

Hit and run driver leaves pensioner for dead.

'Bloody hell,' he said, scanning the page for details. 'It happened about the same time, and the driver was thought to have left the village via the Witley Road... that's where we were.'

Freya came round the side of the table. 'What does it say?' she asked, quickly reading the article. 'Oh, but that's awful. You should have gone to the police, Stephen.'

'To say what? I really didn't see much, I was too busy a) trying to stay on my bike, b) trying not to crash into Laura, and c)... shouting at her,' he finished lamely. 'And apart from anything else, I didn't realise anything was wrong at the time, other than some idiot driver losing it on the bend. It wouldn't be the first time that's happened.'

'No, but you can't ignore what's in the paper; it's too much of a coincidence.'

Stephen rolled his eyes. 'I wasn't going to ignore it. Jesus, will you ever stop labelling me as a thoughtless bastard?'

He snatched up the paper, re-reading the article, while Sam gave Freya a pointed look. She dropped her eyes to the floor.

'What I was going to say,' said Stephen, 'is that although I don't remember much in the way of detail, perhaps Laura does. She was facing the road, and it's possible she saw more of the car, and sideways on too, which makes a difference. I should go and see her. Between the two of us, we might be able to come up with something.'

Freya frowned. 'This couldn't come at a worse time for her,' she said, thinking ahead. 'Suppose you are able to give the police something which would help identify who did this, imagine what a furore there'd be; reporters, families... courts. Laura would find it very difficult.'

'So it's okay for her not to go to the police, but different rules apply to me, is that it?' Stephen glared at her.

'I didn't say that,' she retorted.

'Maybe not, but you might as well have done. The police are appealing for witnesses; we're witnesses. What else is there to say? I know Laura will find it hard, *if* she's seen anything, which of course I don't know yet. But if there's anything that needs to be said, at least I'd be there to hold her hand.'

'Yes, I bet you would,' she snapped, as all her old feelings about Stephen came rushing back.

Sam lurched up from the table. 'Will you two stop it! For God's sake, Freya, give Stephen a break.' He took the paper from Stephen's hand. 'Besides which, my brother was speaking metaphorically, weren't you?'

He nodded sullenly.

'So let's calm down and get back to what's important here; that a serious crime has been committed, an elderly lady is very poorly in hospital, and you and Laura are potential witnesses. There's nothing else to discuss, you both need to have a long hard think about what you may or may not have seen, and then take it to the police. Let them be the judge of what's useful information.'

Freya sat down. 'I'm sorry,' she said. 'I just don't want Laura to get hurt, that's all.'

There was a long sighing breath as Stephen joined her. 'Freya, neither do I.'

His words sat between them for a moment until Freya looked up at him. There was a softness to his eyes that she wasn't sure she had ever seen before. She nodded gently.

'I don't have a number for Laura, though, only an address. We agreed to meet tomorrow to go through the ideas she's had for the wedding, but you should probably try to see her before then.' She hesitated for a few seconds. 'I could tell you how to get there,' she added, 'or I could come with you...'

Sam cleared his throat. 'Actually, Freya, I could really use your help this morning. Joe Jones is bringing his crop round at nine. From what he said on the phone, there's a lot of it.'

Freya knew when she'd been outwitted. She gave a conciliatory smile. 'Okay, Stephen, you can go on your own. Laura's cottage is on the Marlowes road, just before you get to the village. There's a lane off to the right with a post box on the corner. Laura's is the last of four houses. Clarence Cottage it's called.'

'Okay, I'll find it.'

'Oh, and one more thing?'

Stephen looked up at the query in her voice.

'Before you go, change out of your running gear.'

He sucked in his stomach automatically. 'Aye aye, boss.' He grinned.

Sam waited until Stephen had closed the back door behind him before pulling Freya up from her chair.

'I'm very proud of you, you know.' He smiled, finding her lips with his.

Freya pulled away slightly. 'I don't know why,' she said. 'When I'm such a pig. I can see Stephen's trying really hard, but he still manages to rile me quicker than anyone I know,' she added.

'You'll get there,' he replied. 'It's taken Stephen a long time to square up to his shortcomings, but now that he has, we need to trust him, hard though that may be. He's learning to trust himself too, don't forget.'

'I know.' Freya sighed, looking at her watch. 'Right, come on then, we'd better make a start if Joe's coming at nine.'

Sam pulled her in closer. 'Actually,' he muttered, 'he said he might be nearer half past... we've got forty minutes or so to wait...' he said, kissing her again.

'Oh, I see.' Freya winked, kissing him back.

*

Laura was in the middle of making a very long list when she realised that someone was ringing her doorbell. She had a light in every room that alerted her to the fact, but engrossed as she was, they could have been standing there for quite some time before she noticed. She gave an audible tut. She was in full flow, ideas coming thick and fast and the last thing she needed was an interruption. She hastily scribbled another item on the bottom of her list in case she forgot it.

She had on her best *I can't stand here talking all day* face on as she opened the door, which deepened further when she found Stephen on her doorstep.

'What are you doing here?' she asked without thinking. It came out rather more bluntly than she had intended.

'Hello,' he signed slowly. 'How are you?'

Laura stepped back in surprise, suddenly understanding why Stephen looked so uncomfortable. He was nervous, and it was such a contrast to what she expected from him, that she didn't know how to respond.

'Fine, thanks,' she signed back.

There was immediate alarm in his eyes, and she smothered a smile. 'Is that all you know?' she asked, dropping her hands.

Stephen offered an apologetic grin. 'Pretty much,' he said. 'That and goodbye, please, thank you and sorry.'

'I can see we're going to have a scintillating conversation,' she said drily, rather enjoying watching him squirm a little. 'An interesting collection of words.'

'It was all I had time for,' he admitted. 'But I can learn more.'

A faint tingle of alarm began to sound in Laura's head. She was touched that he had even tried to learn her language, but she didn't want to encourage him. She could understand him perfectly well as it was.

'Stephen, why are you here?' she asked. 'It's very kind of you to learn a few words of sign language, but there's really no need, I can manage.'

Stephen seemed to examine her doormat for some considerable time before he spoke again.

'I wanted to see if you were okay, after what happened the other day. Apart from throwing you to the ground, I was very rude and obviously upset you. I didn't intend to.'

Laura had replayed their encounter over and over again in her head, and was rather ashamed of her own behaviour too, although she didn't want to admit it to him.

'It was the shock I expect,' she replied. 'I wasn't at my best either, so perhaps we should forget it ever happened. No harm done as it were.'

Stephen's face clouded immediately. 'Under normal circumstances, I would agree, but it might not be possible I'm afraid… Look, can I come in, there's something else I need to discuss with you.'

His manner had gone from relatively relaxed, albeit in a rather nervous kind of way, to pompously formal in a matter of moments, and although part of her felt intrigued, for the most part, Laura was wary. What on earth could Stephen want with her? Against her better judgement, she stepped to one side.

'We'll go in the kitchen,' she said.

Boris stood up the moment Stephen entered the room, crossing to Laura's side where he stood in front of her like a hairy protective shield. It had the desired effect; Stephen stopped dead, hovering in the doorway unwilling to go any further.

'What's that matter with you? Don't tell me you're afraid of a big dog?' she mocked, hands on her hips.

'Only ones that growl like that,' replied Stephen, trying to keep his face towards Laura, but with one eye on the dog. 'I'm just wondering if there's a bite on the end of it.'

Laura dropped to her knees in front of Boris so that she was on a level with his nose. 'Did you growl at the nasty man?' she cooed, putting her arms around the dog's neck. 'I know he pushed me over, but you can let him in okay, you don't have to eat him.'

She stood up again, waving an airy hand at Stephen. 'Go and make friends, Boris,' she said.

Stephen took several steps backwards as the dog covered the distance between them in an instant, thrusting its wet nose into the crotch of his jeans, before licking his hand.

'I suppose you enjoyed that?' Stephen remarked, trying to extricate himself.

'Of course… although in all seriousness, he was just trying to protect me,' she added, trying to soften the blow to Stephen's pride. 'He'll be fine now. Just come on in and have a seat. I'll make some coffee, shall I?'

Stephen nodded. 'No sugar, thanks.'

She turned her back, reaching for a couple of mugs, and adding coffee to both. She was trying to decide what to say next and by keeping her back to Stephen, she knew she was effectively forestalling any more conversation until she was ready to speak. He probably deserved an apology for her behaviour the other day; he also deserved her thanks. She was well aware that being thrown in the bushes was a small price to pay for not being run over, but she really didn't want to make a big deal of it. It was bad enough that he was here at all. She certainly didn't want him to visit again.

The coffee made, she had no further excuse to keep her back to Stephen, and she turned round, expecting to see him waiting patiently at the table. Instead, he was on the other side of the room, inspecting a garland she had made a couple of days earlier and hung in her favourite spot on the wall facing the doorway. The morning sun had picked out the stems of Honesty, like slivers of silver. He held out a hand to touch one of them while she watched.

He turned to look for her, wanting to speak, and dropped his gaze in embarrassment when he realised she was staring at him. She could see his lips start to move.

'I can't tell what you're saying if your head is down,' she said gently, blushing slightly as he also coloured.

His head jerked up again. 'I'm sorry... I didn't think, this is harder than... But this is beautiful,' he said. 'I wanted to tell you. Especially this,' he added, reaching out to touch the seeds once more. 'What's it called?'

'Honesty,' answered Laura.

Stephen swallowed. 'Oh,' was all he managed.

Laura carried the mugs back to the table and sat down, indicating for Stephen to do the same. She was about to speak when he leaned forward to touch her hand.

'You made that, didn't you,' he said. 'It's what you do.' He rubbed a hand across his mouth that was creasing into a smile. 'I should probably explain how I know that as well shouldn't I, before you think I'm some sort of psychic nutter. My future sister-in-law mentioned that she'd met you, and that you're going to help with her wedding flowers...' He looked at her apologetically. 'I have a bit of an unfair advantage, don't I, especially since we've never been properly introduced, but—'

'I know your name's Stephen,' interrupted Laura.

'Oh. Did Freya mention me?'

'No, I just know who you are.' She let that sit for a moment. 'And I expect that you know my name is Laura, because you've put two and two together, and after all how many deaf girls with big dogs can there be around here?'

As soon as the words had left her mouth, her eyes flickered closed in irritation. She had promised herself she wasn't going to do this. Stephen looked quite uncomfortable, and she almost missed what he said next.

'It wasn't quite like that,' he added. She could see the line of his jaw tightening.

She took in a deep breath and smiled. 'No, I know. Sorry, that came out wrong.' His teeth were still clenched.

'So, anyway, now that we don't need to introduce ourselves, I should at least say thank you for the other day,' she said as brightly as she could. 'I realised later of course that you were actually trying to do me a favour by pushing me in the bush. And if you hadn't, then either you would have hit me with your bike, or Giles would have run me over. On balance, the bush was the much better option.'

Stephen had just taken a mouthful of coffee and almost spat it across the table at Laura. He wiped his mouth as a trickle of it escaped. 'What did you say?' he gulped.

'Well, there's no need to sound quite so surprised,' Laura retorted. 'I'm trying to apologise but if you—'

There was another touch to her hand, and she snatched it away.

'No, you misunderstood me, don't be cross, Laura. You said a name just now, what was it?'

There was a very urgent expression on his face, and Laura wondered what on earth she'd done wrong.

'What, Giles, do you mean?' she asked tentatively.

Stephen muttered something she couldn't quite make out, which probably meant he was swearing. He lowered his head to his hands, and she tutted in exasperation, flapping her hands at him.

'What did you say?' she urged. 'Why do you want to know about Giles?'

A pair of hazel-coloured eyes met hers. 'I said bloody hell,' answered Stephen. 'Because I only know of one person around here called Giles, and that's Giles Drummond. I just hope to God I'm wrong.'

Stephen searched her expression, looking for her confirmation. He swallowed hard when he saw it.

'And you just said that Giles would have run you over… Are you absolutely sure the person driving the car that day was Giles? It couldn't have been anyone else?'

'Well, it's possible, but I wouldn't have thought so. What's the matter, Stephen? Why is it such a big deal, I mean everyone knows what Giles is like: too much like his father; too much money and too little sense. He has never been able to handle that car; it was ridiculous buying someone so young a machine that powerful. And half the time he's pissed out of his brain which doesn't help either…'

She sat back as the colour drained from Stephen's face.

'What is it, what's he done?' Her voice was like ice.

There was something like regret in Stephen's eyes. 'Do you get the evening paper?' he asked. 'Would you have yesterday's?'

Laura shook her head, unwilling to say any more.

'The reason I ask is because there was an article in it about a suspected hit and run. An elderly lady was knocked down and left for dead, and it happened about the time that I was forced off the road. No one saw the car properly, but it's thought it left the village on the Witley Road.'

Laura sat up in shock, trying to process what Stephen had just said, and then it came to her, just why Stephen was here, exactly why he had come to see her. Anger straightened her back like a ramrod.

'You must think I'm stupid as well as deaf,' she snarled. 'You didn't come here to see how I was at all, did you? With your pathetic attempt at signing and your *look at me I'm such a nice guy* act. You don't care about me one jot!' Her eyes flashed dangerously.

He baulked at this. 'That's not fair, I—'

'No,' she shouted.

'What do you mean, no?'

'No, as in, no, I won't help you. I'm not going to the police.'

'Laura, someone was seriously hurt. How can you not want to help?'

'Jesus, Stephen, are you completely thick? Who's going to listen to me? Giles Drummond is the son of the man who killed my husband. He ruined my life once, there's no way I'm going to let him do it again.'

She glared at Stephen across the table, bile rising in her throat as tortured memories of the past few years came flooding back.

'I think you'd better leave,' she said coldly.

Stephen blinked in surprise. 'What, that's it? You're not even going to consider it? How can you be so callous, Laura? She could die.'

'I might as well have, for what that man did to me.'

'But we're not talking about Francis now, we're talking about his son. Someone who has, in all probability, committed a horrific crime. You can't just sit here and do nothing.'

'Watch me,' Laura spat. 'And if you're so holier than thou, you go to the police. You can still tell them what you know.'

Stephen shook his head several times. 'I don't believe you,' he said, getting up from the table. 'We all wanted to help you, but I never thought for one minute you weren't worth helping.'

'Get out of my house!' she shouted, launching herself out of her chair and pushing at his arm.

Stephen strode from the room, his long legs taking him to the door in seconds. He yanked it open and was about to slam it shut behind him when he suddenly turned and grabbed both Laura's arms.

'And you got it wrong, for what it's worth. I did come to see how you were, but I won't bother you again.' And he signed the word goodbye.

Laura stared after him, tears pouring down her cheeks before she slowly closed the door and sank to the floor.

Chapter Fifty-Three

Not even the sight of squirrels playing on the lawn the next morning could lift Laura's spirits. She had moved through the rest of the day before like an automaton, making chocolates, steeping more blue-black damsons in brandy, and as the golden afternoon sun had dipped behind the hedgerows, she tore up the list she was making for Freya's wedding and cried some more.

She should have known it would come to nothing, but she'd so wanted to believe that things could change. She had seen something in Freya that spoke to her, awoke a spark in her that she hadn't felt for a long time; but now all the hopes she'd had were like scalded sugar in the bottom of a saucepan, turned bitter and fit only for the bin.

Her head was full of jagged images from the past: David's coffin, impossibly small to contain a whole life, and Francis Drummond standing over her, laughing, a gobbet of spit clinging to the end of his chin as he told her she would never win. She hadn't, and though time had done its best to ease her failure, with one fell swoop she was right back where she had started; except this time it was worse, because now she had nothing to fight for, not even David's name.

How could she possibly go to the police when all they would think – all anyone would ever think – was that she was trying to settle old scores? The thought of helping Freya with her flowers had been enough to completely unnerve her, it meant coming face to face with the people who had mocked her so cruelly; but she had allowed herself to dream, to think that things could be different and that with Freya's help, she might finally escape the past. How foolish she had been. Her bed last night had been cold and unforgiving, but she had lain in it anyway, wishing for sleep to steal her misery.

She poured a cold cup of tea down the sink, watching the brown liquid swirl across the white porcelain of the big butler's sink. As usual, it gathered in the corners, but this morning she didn't even have the energy to wash it away. She would just have to put one foot in front of the other today and count off the hours. The graves still needed tending, and there among the undemanding dead, she might at least find some peace. She lifted her eyes to the notebook which still lay on the table, a stark blank sheet waiting to be filled. She had no idea what she was going to say to Freya later.

Stan's chocolates were in the fridge, and after Laura had collected these, together with a pot of jam for Millie and Blanche's gin, there was no further reason to hide in the house, and pulling on her jacket, she crept from the house.

She half expected Stephen to be lying in wait for her, ready with a barrage of reasons why she should change her mind, but the lane was quiet as she reached her gate. It was a beautiful autumn morning; the sky tinged pale pink and purple as the sun crested the rise of the fields beside the house. The bright orange ball hung in the still air, its golden rays filtering through the swirls of mist which clung to the grass. Within an hour the sky would be the clearest blue.

It would be a perfect day for foraging, for seeking out scarlet haws in the hedgerows, or the dusky medlars which grew in the garden of a house behind the church. A day for hurrying home to make rowan jelly and damson ketchup, but Laura knew she would do none of those things, not today.

The smile was pasted on her face as she walked up the path to Stan's cottage, but his eyesight was not what it used to be, and she doubted he would notice. She could claim a busy day, and both deliver her chocolates and collect whatever he had to offer her in a matter of minutes. No one would be any the wiser.

Her knock at the door went unanswered, and Laura automatically made her way along the path to the side of the cottage and into the back garden. It was quite usual to find Stan there, even this early in the morning, crouched beside one of his precious vegetables, or sitting in his greenhouse, letting the sun warm his bones through the glass, but she was surprised to see Millie this morning too, and Laura felt her mood sink even further. Millie's presence could only mean one thing, and Laura was in no mood for a gossip this morning, but she gave her customary wave and went to join them.

'Beautiful morning,' she called, remembering to smile.

Millie's face fell immediately. 'Oh dear,' she said, twisting a hanky around her fingers. 'You haven't heard, have you? I didn't think you had. I did call around, but perhaps you were out...'

'What haven't I heard, Millie?' she asked, thinking back to yesterday evening when she had studiously ignored whoever had come to her door.

Millie looked hesitantly at Stan. 'Perhaps you should tell her,' she said.

Now that she was nearer, Laura could see that both of her neighbours were not their usual selves this morning. Millie looked quite upset, and Stan wore a distracted air; fidgety, not the calm, relaxed persona she was used to.

'It's Blanche,' Stan began, for some reason over emphasising the words. He had probably intended to make sure she understood them, but instead the reverse was true, and for Laura it was like listening to a transatlantic call with a lag on the line. Her brain took much longer than normal to relay the message so that she nearly missed what came next altogether. She held up a hand.

'Say again, Stan. I missed that.'

'She's in hospital,' he enunciated. 'With a broken hip and wrist.'

'She's lucky to be alive,' added Millie.

Laura stared at both of them, trying to wade through the fug in her brain. 'But I only saw her yesterday... No, not yesterday... what day is it today?'

'It's Saturday, Laura,' replied Stan, with a worried look. 'The accident happened on Monday, but none of us knew until Tuesday night when her daughter came round.'

Laura tried to piece her week back together. 'That's right, I came to see you all, on Tuesday... except Blanche wasn't in.' Her hand flew to her mouth. 'Oh my God.'

Stan patted her arm. 'Don't upset yourself dear, none of us knew. She'd been in hospital over a day before we found out.'

'But is she okay?'

Laura studied their faces, but neither of them said anything, just a glance flickered between the two of them.

'It's... difficult,' said Stan eventually, 'because of her age. The bones will heal, but the shock, well, you can imagine... and the doctors are worried about the risk of blood clots.'

The pit of Laura's stomach fell away. 'I've got to go and see her, where is she?'

Stan looked nervously at Millie. 'Up in Hereford, but, Laura... will you be all right? The police are still investigating what happened, and you know how nervous you still get around folk. There were reporters there too we heard, to start with, although maybe not now...'

'Police?' asked Laura, shocked. 'Why were the police involved? When you said she'd broken her hip, I assumed she'd fallen—' She stopped as she caught sight of Millie's face which was starting to crumple.

'What happened Stan? Tell me.'

'They're not sure, they think she was hit by a car.'

A slice of pain shot through Laura's head. She thrust the bag she was carrying at Stan. 'I'm sorry, I've got to go.'

Somehow, she stumbled back down the path to the front of the house, where she leaned heavily on the gate post, breathing hard. There was a wild rushing sound inside her ears, something which always happened when she was really stressed, but it was disorientating, it made her feel sick. She took several deep breaths waiting for the panic to subside. How could it be Blanche? Her lovely neighbour who had never harmed anybody. It was happening all over again – why was it always the good ones who got hurt?

If she thought she was angry yesterday, it was nothing compared with the boiling rage that hit her now, a wave of adrenaline-fuelled fury. And it was directed towards one person only: Giles Drummond. Her legs started to move of their own accord, flying first across the tarmac and then the open fields beside the church. She ran through the churchyard and out towards the Witley Road. By the time she got to Freya's house, her chest was burning, but she carried on. She hadn't reached her destination yet.

*

'All right, all right,' Stephen grumbled, fumbling with his trouser leg. 'Will you give me a minute, or I'll be bloody well naked.'

His wet feet refused to slide through his jeans, but eventually they made contact with the floor, and he stood up. He jogged down the stairs, doing up his fly as he went. The doorbell was still ringing.

'For pity's sake, what's so urgent,' he started, as he yanked open the door, the words dying on his lips when he caught sight of the figure standing there.

Laura was breathing heavily, eyes wild and darting, bleeding slightly from a cut on her cheek, the very last person he expected to see. A sheen of perspiration gleamed across her forehead as she stood there, her tiny figure diminished by the grand dimensions of the porch she stood under.

She held out a trembling arm. 'You've got to help me,' she said, the rest of her breath rushing from her in an anguished gasp. She looked like she was on the point of collapse.

Without thinking, Stephen pulled her through the door and into his arms. He realised too late that he would probably receive a swift and excruciating knee to the groin, but as Laura sagged against him, the seconds stretched out, and the threat of imminent pain receded. Instead, he gently rested his chin on the top of her head and wrapped his arms around her, fingers splayed but unmoving, as her tiny body shuddered against him.

He stared at the opposite wall in the hallway, focusing on the creamy expanse of paintwork and willed his body not to respond. But her fingers felt so good against his bare back, her hair against his chest… No! He sucked in a breath and thought about a song he had heard on the radio a few minutes ago, trying to repeat the words. Gradually, as Laura's breathing eased, and what Stephen realised were tears trailed off, he found himself relaxing. He had no idea what had brought her to his door, but whatever it was, she had asked for his help, and right now that's all he needed to give her. Whatever comfort she sought, Stephen would provide it.

It was an unusual feeling for Stephen, offering comfort to another, and not one he'd had much experience of before. Of course, he had held women in the past, snuggled up to them, but it had always been either a prelude to sex, or during its aftermath, and he could never understand the accusations levelled at him: *Why does it always have to lead to something else? Why can't we just have a cuddle?* As he felt a peaceful calm envelop him and his breathing match that of Laura's, he suddenly got it. He understood what he had been missing all these years, and despite the rather unpleasant memories of yesterday, he would stay like this forever if he could.

Whether he liked it or not, this little spitfire of a woman had stolen a march on his heart, and as this thought struck him squarely, he also realised that he would never be the kind of person who Laura deserved in her life. With all she had gone through, and the hurt that she was still suffering, his loud opinions and crass behaviour would overpower her. So, on the day that Stephen discovered a tiny glimmer of what it was like to fall in love, he also realised that Laura must never ever find out.

*

He'll think I'm an absolute nutter, thought Laura, and it was this which finally made her pull away from Stephen's warm embrace. When she had heard the news about Blanche, she had thought only of getting to Stephen, to tell him, to ask for his help. The anger that had engulfed her had long since gone, but in its place was a steely determination.

The Drummonds had ruined her life and stolen David's, but to leave an elderly lady for dead was more than Laura could bear. She had fought against Stephen yesterday, shock and fear replacing calm reasoning, but the last few days had taught her one thing. Just as the Drummond family had a hold on her past, the Henderson family seemed to have an equal hold on her future. She was waking up from the self-imposed sleep she'd been in for years, and although she didn't understand why things had changed, she certainly recognised that they had. There was only one person who could help her bring Blanche's assailant to justice, and that was the very man she had kicked out of her house...

She gave a low moan of embarrassment. What on earth was she going to say to him now?

'You're wet.' It was the first thing that came into her head. She cringed even more.

To her surprise, she felt Stephen's chest rippling. He was laughing. She looked up at his dripping wet hair.

'I've just got out of the shower.' He grinned. 'In fact...' He looked down at his bare torso. 'Maybe I should go and get dressed. I'm practically naked.'

Laura only caught the last of his sentence as he raised his head. 'Naked?' she asked.

'Yes, me,' said Stephen unnecessarily. 'Well not quite, but...'

Laura stared at the pale smooth skin that had felt so nice under her cheek. She blushed.

'I feel such a prat,' she groaned. 'You're going to think I'm completely loopy; what with my performance yesterday and then coming round here this morning, like... like I just did.'

'There is a somewhat marked difference in your behaviour,' replied Stephen. 'I'll give you that.' He cocked his head at her. 'So I'm guessing that something important has happened to bring about this change.' He watched her for a second or two. 'I tell you what, why don't I go and put some more clothes on, and if you like, you can make yourself a hot drink. I'll show you where the kitchen is.'

Laura nodded, glad of the opportunity for a little more time to compose herself. She followed Stephen through a door and then another, smiling politely as he showed her where the kettle and mugs were.

'And the tea and coffee are here,' he motioned, before leaving her to it.

She watched as he padded across the wooden floor, his feet bare, the bottom of his jeans slightly too long, frayed and trailing on the ground. The denim clung to his legs. Laura raised a hand to her brow. I must be in shock, she thought, that's the only explanation. But he had felt so good. She pressed the switch on the kettle. No, it wasn't Stephen that had felt so good, she corrected herself. It was simply the fact that he was a man. Tall and solid, safe even, and it been such a long time since she had been held like that. Despite the circumstances, her body had responded to a basic human need that she had been denied for so long; the simple comfort that touch can bring, that was all.

By the time Stephen returned, she was feeling more herself. Two cups of coffee stood on the work surface and she handed him one. 'No sugar, I think. Is that right?'

Stephen smiled. 'Thank you.' He'd combed his hair, and was now wearing a soft pale green shirt. 'Shall we sit down?'

He led her through to an enormous conservatory filled with plants: orchids, ferns, and a huge Stephanotis whose glorious heady scent filled the air. She looked around her in amazement.

'Are these yours?' she blurted out.

Stephen looked amused. 'Well, this is my house, so...'

'I know, sorry. I just didn't think you would have plants for some reason.'

'Well, I do grow plants for a living,' he replied. 'Sort of, well, trees obviously. Although granted I do take their produce, mash it mercilessly into a pulp and make wild booze from it which I sell for inflated prices.'

Laura turned to gaze out of the window at the rows and rows of apple trees which could be seen in the distance.

'You should adopt that for your marketing literature, you know. It's quite catchy.'

Stephen crossed the room to stand in front of her. 'And you should turn back around again so you can hear me laugh,' he said.

'Sorry,' she said automatically. 'It's not really fair, is it?' She went to sit down on one of the deep squishy sofas.

'I need to apologise… again,' she added the minute she sat down. 'I can't begin to imagine what you must think of me and worse, I can't really explain my behaviour. Talk about hypocritical. But I'm sorry for shouting at you yesterday, for being utterly unreasonable, for coming across as a callous uncaring bitch, and for throwing you out of my house.'

'You forgot the bit where you questioned my integrity.'

Laura sighed. 'Yes, that too,' she added sheepishly, but Stephen was smiling.

'I tell you what,' he said, joining her on the other end of the sofa. 'I'm going to let you into a secret, which might not actually be all that secret, but over the years I've gained a reputation for being an arrogant womanising bastard.' He took a sip of his coffee. 'Feel free to contradict me anytime,' he said. Laura said nothing. 'See, I knew I was right. But the thing is, people usually have a reason for behaving the way they do; I know I did. It's personal to them, but other folk can't always see it for what it is; they only see the behaviour on the outside, never looking at what might have caused it.'

He checked to see she was still following him. 'The worst thing is when you decide enough is enough and try to change; people are often unwilling to give you a second chance. I don't blame them for that, but it makes it bloody difficult when you're trying to convince them of your newly reformed character. I mean I might not live that long.' He stared into his mug before looking up again. 'Look, what I'm trying to say is that I think I understand a lot of what you must have been through in the past, and how that might make you behave at times. And if you can accept that I do understand, maybe you can also accept that I can draw a line under it and start again, without the need for apology or explanation.'

Laura's heart was beating ever so slightly fast again. It seemed impossible that what Stephen was saying was true, and yet the way his eyes gazed into hers at times, she really did believe he could see into the little boxes she had stashed away in her mind. The ones that no one was allowed to open. She looked at his face now, concerned, but sincere, nothing more, and she felt her shoulders drop a couple of inches more.

'Can I ask you a question?' said Stephen, the tips of his fingers lightly tapping the mug he cradled in his lap.

She nodded, swallowing.

'When I came to see you yesterday, I was in a bit of a panic myself. I'd only just realised that we were potential witnesses to a crime and, apart from checking that you were okay, I did want to see if you could remember anything from that day. You totally floored me by saying that you actually knew who was driving the car which nearly hit us. The reasons you gave for not wanting to go to the police were valid ones, and yet today things seem... very different. You were obviously upset when you arrived here this morning, and if you don't want to talk about it, that's fine, but you asked for my help. Am I right in thinking that something has happened since yesterday to cause your change of heart?'

Laura smiled. 'That's very tactfully put,' she said. 'I like that you referred to me as 'upset' when you could have described me as howling and weeping like a wild banshee.'

'I thought about it.' Stephen's gaze was level.

She took a deep breath. 'I know the lady who was knocked down. I only found out today when I went to visit her, but her name is Blanche; she's a neighbour of mine and rather partial to my sloe gin. The thing is she's the sweetest, kindest lady, who wouldn't hurt a fly, and the thought of her lying there because of that evil cowardly scumbag is more than I can bear. I let the Drummond family get away with a terrible wrong in the past because I didn't have the strength to fight any more. I'm not sure I have now, but if Blanche can fight for her life, then so can I... only I'm not sure I can do it on my own.'

'So I'll help you.'

Laura stared at him. 'Just like that?'

'Just like that,' he replied. 'Besides which, you're forgetting that I'm a potential witness too, so I'm obliged to help, plus, I'm looking for a lost cause to support so that folks can see I've redeemed my wicked ways. I think you might do nicely.'

Laura's cheeks grew hot again. 'You're teasing me now,' she huffed. 'Stop it.'

'Only a smidge.' Stephen grinned. 'After all I need to keep you sweet – my future sister-in-law will have my guts for garters if I do anything to jeopardise her wedding preparations.'

'Oh my God!' exclaimed Laura, putting her mug down with a thump. 'Freya. I'd completely forgotten about her. I'm supposed to be meeting her this afternoon with some ideas, and I've got nothing prepared. What am I going to do?'

'I don't know. What do you need?'

'Only half the hedgerows between here and Much Marlowes.'

Stephen wedged his mug between his knees and waggled both hands. 'I'm not fit for much fancy stuff, but I can pick, will that help?'

Chapter Fifty-Four

Laura held her breath. 'What do you think?' she asked.

The table was covered in flowers, fruit, berries, greenery and indeed a sample from every hedge and field for miles around it seemed. At the far end, Freya sat in absolute wonder, clearly trying to take in everything she had been shown..

'It looks incredible. The colours, the smells... Everything is so enticing, I want it all,' she said, laughing.

'We might have gone a bit overboard,' admitted Laura, smiling at the memory of Stephen's eagerness as he gathered and picked the best of what the countryside had to offer. 'But I wanted to show you what the decoration in the marquees could look like. I have some very strong ideas for your bouquet, and these will be echoed in the more formal church arrangements, but I thought the reception could take something a little less structured. The beauty of these extended garlands is that they just grow out of whatever comes to hand at the time. There's no uniformity to them, but instead each area is worked up with a variety of colours and textures, whatever fits, pretty much.'

'What do you think, Stephen?' asked Freya.

Laura smothered a smile at the memory of Freya's raised eyebrows as she caught sight of Stephen casually leaning up against her sink earlier. A long and rather ponderous explanation for his presence followed which, in Laura's opinion, made it seem far more suspicious than it really was. In truth, she wasn't sure why he had stayed either but, as the day had worn on, her determination of the morning had begun to fade and her doubts chipped away at her again. It was only Stephen's cheerful chatter that had kept her from succumbing to her fears, and she knew that without him, she would be feeling very different.

Now, Freya's reactions to her ideas were more than she could ever have wished for. By the time she and Stephen had returned from hunting out and collecting the various plants she wanted to use, it was the middle of the afternoon, which hadn't left her much time to think about her ideas and make up a few samples. To be honest, she had been winging it for much of their conversation, but she and Freya were so much on the same wavelength that Laura had needed only to start a sentence to have Freya finish it.

She suddenly became aware that Stephen was staring at her. He had come to join them at the table after a while, but so far had said very little.

'Sorry, did you say something?' she asked, pulling herself back to the conversation.

'Only that I've never seen anything quite like this before. And could I please have another chocolate?'

Laura pulled the tray out from beneath her notebook. She pushed it towards him.

'To be fair,' he added, 'I'm not one to frequent florist's shops on a regular basis, so I have no idea what wedding flowers are supposed to look like.'

Freya slapped his arm. 'Don't be so rude,' she said.

Stephen looked indignant. 'I'm not being rude. You asked for my opinion, and I gave it. I have no idea what brides like these days, but in my humble opinion what we've seen here is truly beautiful. Even I can see that. The sweets are lovely too.'

'Yes, well, I'm not supposed to be eating those,' said Freya, 'or I'll never fit into my dress. But they are gorgeous. What did you say they were?'

'Blackberry and coconut cream truffles,' replied Laura.

Freya closed her eyes briefly as she let the sweet melt in her mouth. 'Well, you'll have to let me know where you get them from. When the wedding is over, I'm going to pig out on these.'

'I make them most weeks, so just let me know when you want some. It's not a problem.'

A dribble of chocolate threatened to escape Freya's mouth as she swallowed hastily.

'You make these, did you say…? Oh my God, I have a friend who's going to love you.' She licked her lips. 'She runs a shop which sells gourmet handmade produce among other things. These would be perfect for her.'

Stephen leaned forward. 'Merry, of course! Why didn't I think of that? That's a seriously good idea, Freya. In fact, I'm sure Merry would be keen to stock all the other gorgeous things that Laura makes, I…' He sat back, catching the expression on Laura's face. 'Okay, one thing at a time… sorry, back to the wedding.'

Laura smiled. 'So, are you happy for me to go ahead, Freya?' she asked, steering the conversation back on track. 'If you can give me a couple of days, I can work up some proper designs for your bouquet as well, and then I'll need to get things finalised. With only two weeks to go, I'll need that time to plan how and when I'm going to get it all done.'

'I'm more than happy. You won't believe how lucky I feel to have found you,' gushed Freya. She looked as if she was about to say something more but then stopped herself. 'Are you sure you're okay with all of this? I know we're asking a lot of you.'

'I honestly don't know,' Laura admitted. 'But I do know that I couldn't have gone on like I was. You've given me an opportunity to change my life, and I've got to have faith that whatever will be, will be for a reason. And a good one, I'm sure.'

'Even so, you'll promise you'll ask for help if you need it,' said Freya. 'Or just to talk, you know, if things get tough.'

'I will, I promise.'

'And tomorrow I will metaphorically be holding your hand every step of the way,' said Stephen, with a glance at Freya. 'So try not to worry about that. The police will be sympathetic to your feelings I'm sure.'

Laura gave a weak smile. She was tired now, almost overwhelmingly so, and despite Stephen's assurances, the thought of the following day loomed large.

'Come on, Stephen, we must go,' announced Freya. 'Laura looks exhausted, and I've still got a million and one things to do today as well.' She looked at the table, still covered in piles of paper and foliage. 'We'll help you clear up first, though, if you like.'

Laura waved away their suggestion, suddenly longing for her own company. It had been quite a while since she had been with people for such a length of time, and it was exhausting just following the conversation. 'No, it's fine. I might have a bit more of a play in any case. I'll clear it away later.'

Freya came forward to give her a hug. 'Take care,' she said afterwards. 'And thank you.'

Stephen hovered awkwardly by the door. 'See you tomorrow,' he said. 'I'll pick you up at nine.' He was about to follow Freya back out into the hallway when he suddenly turned back to her. He made a sign with his hands.

Laura's eyes widened in surprise. 'What did you say?' she asked.

'Thank you,' said Stephen, repeating the sign.

She could still see the expression on his face several minutes after she closed the door behind them.

Chapter Fifty-Five

'That's a pretty serious accusation to make, Mrs Ashcombe.'

Laura could feel her pulse begin to quicken once more. 'I am aware of that,' she bit back. 'I might be deaf, but there's absolutely nothing wrong with my eyes.'

The two police officers exchanged a look as Laura felt a gentle touch on her arm. She glanced at Stephen, who smiled warmly.

'From the moment I mentioned our accident to Laura, it was clear that she recognised both the car and its driver,' he said. 'And that was before she even knew about the hit and run incident. It's hardly an accusation.' He looked between the two men sitting opposite them. 'You appealed for witnesses to come forward, and we have. Until the day we were run off the road, I didn't even know Mrs Ashcombe personally, although I am of course aware of the history between her and the Drummond family. The two things are entirely unconnected, however.'

The policeman directly opposite Laura sat back in his chair, looking at her with a frown. 'And yet the last time you entered this station, it was on a charge of assault.'

Laura hung her head. She could feel Stephen's eyes on her, but really, what was the point? What was she even doing here? She felt a wave of anger balling in her chest as though it would explode from her at any minute. She drew her legs underneath her, making ready to stand. She needed to get out of here.

The pressure on her arm increased. 'When was this?' asked Stephen, as she looked up. She shrugged away his touch.

'Does it matter?' she replied. 'I told you this whole thing was point-less.' She glared back at the policeman.

'It probably doesn't matter, no,' said Stephen, 'in that it clearly has nothing to do with the reason we're here today… But it might help me to understand why it looks as though you're not being taken seriously. And that actually matters a very great deal.'

Laura held his gaze. She could tell from the way his lips pursed that there was a real force behind his words, and although his face was turned towards her, she understood that he was not talking to her alone. She glanced across the table, where the policeman's previously relaxed pose had been replaced with a more businesslike stance. She licked her lips and swallowed.

'I was shopping,' she said calmly, 'just before Christmas. Something I try very hard not to do, but it was a bit of a special occasion. Usually, I go home to Mum and Dad's, but last year my neighbours all persuaded me to stay here and join them for Christmas dinner. I'd had to go to the big Tesco.' She bit her lip as her face was suddenly flooded with heat. 'That's when Francis started having a go.'

'What do you mean "having a go," Laura? What did he say?' encouraged Stephen.

Laura was quiet for a moment. It would sound stupid, she knew. Pathetic even. But to her, it had meant a very great deal. Staying in Much Marlowes for Christmas had been a big step for her at the time and had pretty much taken all her courage. Explaining it to complete strangers, however, would never do justice to how she had felt. She dropped her head, running a thumb over the smoothness of her fingernail. She was still staring at her hand when Stephen's fingers slipped over her own. She looked up in surprise.

'What did he say, Laura? Was he rude? Hurtful?'

She nodded gently. 'He made fun of me, it's what he always does. Goading me for being on my own; a sad and lonely creature he called me, saying it's no wonder no one wants me, looking up at people the way I do with my big doe eyes. Like I wouldn't say boo to a goose…

Then he made some stupid joke about geese and Christmas and that what I needed was a good stuffing...' The tears sprang to Laura's eyes. 'It was too much... especially coming from him, and it's not like it was the first time he'd done it either. I just couldn't bear it any more.'

Stephen's fingers tightened over her own. 'Bastard...'

The policeman nearest to her raised his hand. 'I understand that you were upset, Mrs Ashcombe. That was very clear to see when you came into the station, but it still didn't give you the right to assault the man.'

'I did not assault Francis Drummond. I threw a turkey at him, which is hardly the same thing. And you and I both know that the only reason I got dragged in here in the first place was so that you could keep your boss sweet; everyone knows he's been in Drummond's pocket for years. I bet you had a good laugh about it with him, didn't you? About how you ticked me off, and told me to behave myself. It's Drummond that needs keeping on a lead, not me.'

The two men exchanged looks. 'I rather think we're getting off the point here...'

'And yet it was you who brought up the subject of the assault, I believe?' interrupted Stephen. 'And as such, perhaps you could have the decency to listen to what Mrs Ashcombe has to say. At least, try looking at it from her point of view.' He turned to look Laura straight in the eye. 'I would imagine that for someone who's deaf, shopping in a supermarket just before Christmas must be hell – aside from the usual irritations, imagine what it must be like with people pushing past you, coming from nowhere because you can't hear them – glaring at you because they think you're ignoring them. Shop staff with even less time than usual tutting and sighing at their 'awkward' customer, never realising that you can't understand them. I bet their facial expressions hurt just as much as any words.' He paused for a minute to check that Laura was following him. She nodded slightly.

'Then, add to that the pain of having to spend another Christmas without the person you love, forcing yourself to be jolly and sociable which, by the way, only ever serves to reinforce the fact that you're by yourself, and you probably don't even come close to the way Laura was feeling that day. So, when a bully like Francis Drummond turns up, towering over her five-foot-three, shoving his face in hers and making rude and spiteful comments, it's no wonder she lost her temper.' He sat back in his chair, turning to look back at both policemen before returning his gaze to Laura. 'Now, given all that, she still finds the courage to come and report a crime, knowing that she probably won't be believed. And she does so not because she has a grudge against the Drummond family, but because an elderly lady has been knocked down and seriously hurt, and it's the right thing to do. I've validated everything she's described this morning about what happened on Monday, except the identity of the driver which I couldn't see. What more do you need to know?'

Laura leaned up against the wall outside the police station, gasping for breath. 'I'm sorry, I know I shouldn't be laughing, but you should have seen your face when I said I'd thrown a turkey at Drummond. It was priceless.'

Stephen caught both of her hands, pulling her upright. He faked hurt for a moment. 'I thought I'd hidden it pretty well,' he said, pretending to pout, although the corners of his mouth began to turn upwards despite his attempts at restraint. 'You have to admit, it sounded really funny the way you said it. Did you honestly throw it at him?'

'I did. It caught him square in the back of the neck,' said Laura, grinning again. 'It just came over me in a wave; I was so angry. I watched him walk away for a moment and then, boom! I picked up the nearest thing and hurled it at him – sent him sprawling. That's why he made such a fuss of course, because the place was heaving, and he went down like a sack of spuds. He did this *poor me, I'm just an innocent defenceless man struck down by a lunatic woman* routine. I couldn't tell half of what was being said of course, so I just kept shouting at him until the security guard came and hustled me away. I think they thought I was a spurned lover or something.'

Stephen was properly laughing now, his eyes shining in amusement. 'I wish I'd been there to see it—' he said, and then he stopped. 'Although if I had, things might have been a little different of course…' And there was that look again, the one that Laura couldn't define, but that was beginning to make her feel hot all over again.

'Anyway,' he continued, pulling away a little. 'I'm glad the bastard got what he deserved, even though it's meant you've had more of a tough time of things.'

Laura nodded back towards the police station. 'Will they do anything, do you think?'

'Oh yes, I think they got the message,' he replied, smiling. 'The local police probably don't see much more than a few kerfuffles outside the Red Lion on a Friday night. It's pretty quiet around here, and they're local lads after all, soaking up all the town gossip just like anyone else. Their attitude was somewhat different by the end of our conversation, don't you think?'

'Thanks to you,' Laura remarked. 'That was some speech.'

Stephen thrust his hands into his pockets and swallowed hard. 'I wanted them to treat you properly, that's all.' He dropped his head and mumbled something Laura couldn't catch.

'What was that?' she asked, deliberately forcing Stephen to look up again.

'I said, it's only what anyone would do,' he repeated.

Laura held his look for a second before replying. 'Really?' she queried. 'Only no one has done anything like that in the last five years.' She looked up and down the street again, conscious of Stephen's eyes on her face. 'I tell you what,' she said, breaking the awkward silence. 'Why don't I buy you a coffee as a thank you? And the biggest piece of cake we can find. It's the least I can do after you stuck up for me like that.' She was pleased to see Stephen looked relieved.

'Deal,' he said, with a quick glance to his watch, 'and then I've got to go and see a man about a disco of all things, I'm afraid. I'm Sam and Freya's official wedding entertainment co-ordinator, God help them.'

Laura smiled. 'Yes, I must get back too. Wedding bouquets to design and all that.' She cleared her throat. 'Is Mrs Muffin's Tearoom okay? It's the only place I've ever been in.'

Stephen offered her his arm. 'That will do fine,' he said. 'I'll avoid the rock cakes, though. That way if the conversation takes a turn for the worse, I won't end up with concussion.'

Chapter Fifty-Six

Stephen drummed his fingers against the steering wheel. He'd been stuck behind the tractor for what seemed like an age now, and whilst he hadn't made any firm arrangement over what time he'd call in to confirm the disco booking, he was later than he'd planned, and getting later by the minute.

It was partly his fault of course. His joke to Laura about the rock cakes had set her laughing again, and it had been so good to see her serious face lift and relax. If he was honest, he was also rather relieved at having managed to turn the conversation back to something more light-hearted, rather than focusing on his behaviour at the police station. That conversation had danger written all over it, and he had been anxious to move away from all that it might have implied. Laura didn't need those kind of complications in her life right now, and Stephen had been so surprised by how he had felt sitting next to her in the station that he had shoved these thoughts firmly to the back of his mind.

Of course, this lightening of the mood, welcome though it was, had also meant that a quick coffee had turned into the best part of an hour-and-a-half as the conversation flowed. Now, he couldn't remember half of what they had talked about, and that was something he didn't want to think about either. He wasn't used to feeling like this, hadn't in fact at any time in his life so far, and the thought was more than a little unnerving. He didn't know what to do with himself. He focused on his driving, and switched on the radio. He knew the road ahead like the back of his hand and there was no way he was going to get past this tractor. He was here for the duration, and he might as well try to find something to distract himself with.

He fiddled with the radio until he found a station playing eighties songs. As a small child, their kitchen had always been the place for music, his mother's tinny radio blaring it out from its permanent place on the windowsill. He'd never really bothered much with music over the years, and they were still the songs he knew best. As he'd grown older, he'd swapped the kitchen for the pub, or gone to clubs and parties. Records had been the background to much of life, and yet he was ashamed to think how little he'd appreciated what he heard. In a few minutes, he'd be finalising the music for his brother's wedding reception, and he had no idea what he wanted, what Sam and Freya would want. It was a stark reminder that so much in his life to date had been given so little thought. The only things he had cared about were his own selfish desires.

He caught sight of himself in the wing mirror as he peered around the tractor and looked away. He had taken so much for granted: wealth, his home, his family. Even women, attracted at first by what they saw on the outside. They never stayed long of course, once they got to know Stephen, but that had never mattered. Plenty of sex and no commitments had suited him just fine. But now he wondered what it must be like to have none of those things? To love someone so much that the pain of being without them was almost unbearable, to have to fight for every penny, to feel alone almost every day, because an invisible disability distanced you from the world. Even the joy of music or birdsong was denied you. He pulled up behind the tractor as it stopped at the end of the road and switched the radio off. He had time to make a difference, he thought, as he turned the opposite way to the tractor and accelerated out onto the clear road. Not much time admittedly, but it would have to be enough.

'It's a good job, I've known Sam since we were five,' joked Ash, 'you're bloody hopeless.'

Stephen pulled a face. 'Tell me something I don't know,' he said, frowning. 'Actually, tell me it's not a problem and that you know exactly what music to play despite my lack of input.'

Ash chewed the end of the pen he was holding. 'Maybe now might be the time to tell you that I bumped into Sam at the petrol station last week, and he gave me a bit of a heads-up. He mentioned you might be clueless.' He smiled. 'In the nicest possible way of course… so we'll be fine. I'll get them all up and dancing, don't worry, and I've come up with the perfect song for their first dance so even that's sorted.'

Stephen looked up sharply. 'Oh God, is that a thing?' he groaned. 'How was I supposed to know that?'

Ash grinned. 'I think you might need to brush up on your best man's duties… although I don't suppose you ever thought you'd be needing to, what with… well, everything that went on—' He stopped for a moment, his face falling. 'Sorry, mate, I didn't mean…'

Stephen shrugged. 'It's okay,' he said. 'It was a long time ago. A lot of water under the bridge, and me and Sam are good now. Freya too, actually.' He swallowed.

'Yeah, he mentioned that,' replied Ash, with an answering nod. 'I'm glad that things worked out…'

'Me too. Freya and I… well, it would never have worked. I know I've been a dick most of my life, but I'm genuinely glad she's with Sam; it's where she was always meant to be. It's just unfortunate that despite my best intentions now, Sam still has a shit best man.' He pulled his wallet from his jacket pocket. 'At least I can do one thing, though, and that is pay you. What did we say, two hundred and fifty quid, wasn't it?' He pulled out a roll of bank notes and placed them on the desk in front of him. 'And you know where you're going, don't you? The marquee will be up from the Thursday before, so you can set up whenever suits you.'

Ash pulled out a money tin from a drawer beside him. 'Yeah, I'll shout if I have any problems. Hang on a sec, and I'll print you out a receipt.' He turned his computer screen back towards him and clicked the mouse that lay on the desk beside it. A printer behind him whirred into life, and he passed the single sheet of paper it produced across to Stephen. 'Cheers, mate. Another one to add to your pile, no doubt.'

Stephen glanced at the paper before folding it in half. 'Thanks, Ash,' he said with a grimace. 'Now I'll just go and worry about all the other things I'm supposed to be doing.' He rose from his chair and crossed the tiny office from which Ash ran his business. The door was half-open before he noticed the poster that was stuck on the back. He stopped for a moment, before turning back towards the room. 'This is something new, is it?' he asked, tapping the poster.

'Oh, aye,' nodded Ash. 'Got to move with the times, my friend. Actually, they've been really popular. Good for a giggle and all that, especially when folks have got a few on board if you know what I mean.'

Stephen looked down at the receipt in his hand. 'Yeah, I bet,' he said, thinking out loud. 'I don't really know much about them,' he added. 'How do they work exactly?'

It was probably the worst idea he'd ever had. It was rash at the very least, but now that he'd done it, he couldn't get the idea out of his head. The thought of Laura's face when she realised what was happening, what it might lead to… Stephen groaned out loud and shifted uncomfortably in his seat. He rested his head on the steering wheel and took deep breaths. Dear God, what on earth was the matter with him? He couldn't sit in their driveway for long; any minute now Freya would look out of the kitchen window and spot him. But how on earth was he going to go inside and tell her, and Sam for that matter, that he'd just completely hijacked their plans for their wedding reception? And that wasn't all he'd done either.

He lifted his head and glanced down at his groin, checking that he had everything under control. Knowing how protective his future sister-in-law was of Laura, there was no way he could enter their kitchen in his current state. He was in for an earbashing as it was. He refocused his mind very firmly, and reluctantly climbed from the car.

As it turned out, the kitchen was empty when he pushed open the door, and a bout of loud yelling through the house brought no response either. Freya and Sam must both still be outside, which was a pity; he'd rather hoped that he'd be able to get either one of them on their own. He doubled back on himself, past the car and across the yard to the big barn that lay along one side of it. This too was empty, but as he neared the large open doors on the far side, voices floated through from outside. He groaned again. This was really not going well.

She had her back to him as he emerged outside, but he could hear her soft voice trail off as she caught sight of Freya's expression which changed to one of greeting as soon as she saw him. Laura turned around, and he saw her cheeks coloured pink by whatever excitement had lifted her voice too. She was holding a bouquet in her hands.

'I'd forgotten you were coming!' exclaimed Freya, giving him a beaming smile. 'Because look what Laura's brought over to show me. Now I'm that bloody excited I can't stand still.' And as if to illustrate her point, she gave a little hop. 'What do you think? Isn't it the most beautiful thing you've ever seen?'

Stephen, who was looking at Laura, could only nod. It wasn't until Freya took the bouquet from Laura's hands offering it to him that he realised he was supposed to say something. He took the bouquet, feeling the coolness of the blooms against his skin, the rosy apples mingled with creamy flowers, scarlet hips and dusky blackberries. There wasn't anything he *could* think of to say.

'It's just a rough one,' said Laura. 'You know, to give you the idea of how it might look, what we might use.'

Stephen nodded again. 'It doesn't look rough,' he managed. 'It looks perfect... I couldn't quite grasp what you meant when you described it to me this morning, but now...' He was aware of Freya staring at him from the corner of his eye, but he couldn't look at her.

'I'd forgotten that you two had already seen one another today,' said Freya, taking hold of Laura's arm. 'How did that go? Come on, we can go and put the kettle on, and you can tell me all about it.' She beamed at Stephen. 'And bring that, I don't think I can bear to let it out of my sight.'

Fortunately for Stephen, Laura and Freya were so excited that he hardly needed to say a word, which was just as well considering that his ability to speak had somehow deserted him. Unfortunately, however, Laura's excitement at Freya's reaction to her flowers spilled over into her recounting their time in the police station that morning, and so instead Stephen had to sit squirming at every mention of his name.

'Well, I hope they string the bastard up,' declared Freya. 'And well done you, Stephen, for sticking up for Laura. I had no idea that all this with Francis had gone on before, but then I don't suppose many people do. I hate the way he does business and most of the growers around here would probably say the same, but that's entirely different. I had no idea what a horrible man he was personally.' She took a sip of tea from the mug in front of her. 'As far as Giles is concerned, I've always thought there's truth in that old saying that *the apple doesn't fall very far from the tree.*' She took Laura's hand. 'Have you heard how your friend is doing?'

Laura shook her head. 'No, I was planning on going to see her tomorrow,' she replied, running a finger around the bottom of her mug. 'I've been putting it off, to be honest… I don't have very fond memories of that hospital.' She gave an apologetic smile. 'But I must go, Blanche was very good to me when David died.'

'Well, Stephen can go with you, can't you, Stephen? That would help, surely, having some company.'

Stephen couldn't believe it. He tried to glare at Freya without Laura noticing, but of course she had her eyes fixed on his face, so it was impossible. It wasn't that he didn't want to go, far from it in fact, but simply that the way he was feeling right now, being around Laura for too long probably wasn't a great idea. If only Freya hadn't blurted it out the way she had. Perhaps if she'd run it by him first, he could have tactfully made an excuse, or at least let her understand some of his… difficulties… but there was nothing for it now. He fixed a bright smile to his face.

'Well, that sounds sensible. I'm more than happy to go with you, Laura, if that's okay with you of course.'

And just as he knew she would, she smiled and accepted his offer.

'Would one o'clock be okay?' she asked. 'Only visiting starts at two.' She gulped down the last of her tea. 'Right, well, I must be off while there's still enough light to pick some more sloes. Thanks ever so much, Stephen. I'll see you tomorrow.' She leaned over to give Freya a hug. 'And we must meet up again soon too. I'll need some more apples for one thing.'

The door hadn't quite closed before Freya placed both elbows on the table and leaned forward, her hands making a cradle under her chin.

'You know it pains me to say it, Stephen, but I think Laura rather likes you. I've still got my eye on you, mind, but what you did today was really generous, and it's definitely earned you some brownie points. Now, what did you come over for again? With all the excitement of the wedding plans, I've completely forgotten.'

Stephen eyed her wearily from across the table. 'Nothing really,' he said. 'Just a bit of a catch-up, that's all.'

Chapter Fifty-Seven

Laura dragged a tissue across her lips, grimacing at herself in the mirror. Since when had she ever worn lipstick? Once upon a time, she told herself, a very long time ago, and she had no intention of starting again today. It wasn't as if Blanche would even notice, so she could stop fooling herself that her neighbour was the cause of her madness. The trouble was, she wasn't fooling herself; she knew exactly what the reason was, and his name was Stephen.

She stared at her reflection angrily. *Yes Stephen, no Stephen, three bags full Stephen*, she mimicked. For heaven's sake. Anyone would think she was a hormone-laden teenager the way she was carrying on, and most importantly what would Stephen think? He must be horrified by her behaviour. The first sign of a man who doesn't want to run a mile from her, and she throws herself at his feet. And what's worse is he's just being friendly, she reminded herself; no doubt because she was providing the flowers for his future sister-in-law's wedding, and wasn't that what the best man was supposed to do? Keep the *staff* sweet, chat up the single bridesmaids, and so on. It was a role that almost had its own job description, and she had fallen for his charming charade. Pathetic.

She tugged at her fringe and thrust her hairbrush back into its pot. She just had time for some toast before she'd need to leave for the hospital. And she'd make sure there was no necessity to stop for coffee and cake today either. Having Stephen accompany her to the hospital would certainly make things easier for her, there was no doubt about that, but that's where it ended. They were going to visit her dear friend, and that's what she should focus on. She peered at herself again, narrowing her eyes in appraisal. It's just that yesterday had been such a good day in many ways, and she really couldn't remember the last time anyone had made her laugh like that...

Boris alerted her to the ring of the doorbell, bang on the hour, and although she had been pacing the floor for a good ten minutes, she made sure that it took her at least another minute to answer the door. She was so determined to be welcoming but not gushing, friendly but not overly so, that the expression on Stephen's face when they finally came face to face threw her completely.

'Oh,' was all she could manage. 'Is everything all right?'

He gave her a searching look. 'Can I come in?' he asked unnecessarily, hovering slightly on the threshold.

Laura opened the door wider, allowing him to pass, and stared at his broad back as she followed him down the hallway. They came to rest in the kitchen, Stephen standing rather awkwardly with one hand on Boris's head, who despite the tension in the air was trying to surreptitiously chew his fingers. Stephen didn't seem to notice. He waited until Laura was standing facing him before he spoke. He must have cleared his throat because she saw his Adam's apple rise and fall a couple of times before his lips started to move.

'I wanted to apologise for yesterday,' he started, 'because I think it may have given you the wrong idea...'

Laura's heart sank. Even though she had been thinking much the same thing all morning, she would have preferred to be the one to say it. The thought distracted her for a moment.

'Sorry, say again, I missed the first bit.'

Stephen smiled softly. 'No, I'm sorry,' he said. 'I was talking about the police. I think I rather took it for granted that Giles was guilty, and perhaps you did too? Of course, all the police said they would do is look into the matter, and it never occurred to me to think anything else. I'm afraid it was my fault you ended up with the impression that it would all be okay – it was me, trying to be the big I am as usual.'

Laura stared at him. What on earth was he talking about? She frowned then as the meaning of his words sunk in. 'I'm not sure I'm following you,' she said. 'Isn't everything okay? And anyway, what do you mean *taking it for granted that Giles was guilty*? He is guilty; I saw him!'

'Laura... Giles has a watertight alibi for Monday, the police questioned him yesterday. They rang me this morning to tell me.'

She opened her mouth and then closed it again. 'But that's not right,' she blurted out. 'How can it be?'

Stephen's expression was full of contrition, and something else too. Something she really didn't like the look of.

'I don't know, Laura, I know how positive you are that Giles was driving the car that day, but... I'm not quite sure where that leaves us now.'

Her cheeks began to burn. 'Don't you dare!' she fired at him. 'Don't you dare say you believe me when you clearly don't. And if you ever look at me like that again, I swear I'll throw you out. I don't need your pity.'

'Laura, I—'

She turned her back on him. 'Leave me alone,' she said, trying to stop the rush of tears that were threatening to spill down her face. She stared at the wall, her fists clenched, fighting to stay in control.

She wasn't sure which emotion she felt the most. There was anger certainly, both at the police for giving her news she didn't want to hear, and at Stephen for swallowing what they'd said without challenge, and for pitying her because she'd got it wrong again. But there was also sorrow, because she'd let Blanche down, and because she *had* got it wrong again, clearly. Just when she felt things had begun to look a little brighter, she was right back where she'd been before; the pathetic deaf girl making a huge fuss over nothing again.

She shook her head, trying to clear her confusion. This wasn't right. None of this felt right; she'd been so sure. The minutes stretched out without interruption as she stared ahead, feeling her emotions swirling round her. She tried to pick one to focus on, but they were as elusive as butterflies.

A few more seconds ticked by, moments which became increasingly uncomfortable. She'd led them both into an impasse she realised.

Either she would have to turn around, or Stephen would have to do something to attract her attention. Both these options would feel stilted and unnatural and, worse, require some kind of capitulation, and she wasn't ready to give in, not yet. Any minute now there'd be a tug to her arm, just as there had been on the day of the accident. She waited but none came, and she could feel her anger beginning to rise again.

She whirled around, an accusation ready on her lips, and was astonished to find the kitchen empty; both Stephen and her dog had gone. Her anger subsided in seconds as a healthy dose of remorse replaced it. She hadn't meant for Stephen to leave, not really, and anxiety quickened her heartbeat as she realised that she couldn't bear for him to have left.

They must have gone out into the garden. From there, the side gate led out to the path beside the house and back down the driveway. Stephen could so easily be halfway down the lane by now. She flung open the back door and rushed outside. Seated on her small bench under the kitchen window was Stephen, his long legs stretched out in front of him, his eyes closed against the warm autumn sun which slanted across the lawn. One hand rested on Boris's head which lay gently in his lap. His eyes flew open as he heard her stumble out, his legs scrambling to tuck themselves beneath him so that he could sit up straighter.

'I thought you'd gone,' she said, her eyes wide with panic.

'No,' said Stephen with a soft smile. 'I'm still here. You said you wanted to be left alone, that was all.'

'Did I?' she replied, 'I don't remember.'

Another smile. 'You did. You were quite clear.'

Laura pressed her lips together. 'Oh... I was worried that you'd gone, as in completely gone.'

'Well, I thought about it... but I hazarded a guess you didn't mean for me to leave you alone forever and, as you didn't actually throw me out, I thought I'd stay. There is still time to throw me out of course.'

She nodded slightly, not knowing what to say. She should apologise she knew that, but she couldn't quite find the right words.

Stephen shuffled imperceptibly sideways on the bench. 'Perhaps you should come and sit down while you think about it,' he said. 'It's quite nice and warm here in the sun.'

Boris lifted his head as if to make room for her too. There really was nothing else she could do, so she edged onto the seat, keeping her knees pressed together.

'You should close your eyes for a bit; stretch out,' said Stephen, releasing his legs out from under the bench again. He laid his head back against the wall. 'It's such a beautiful day.'

Laura did as she was told. The gentle heat was soothing, and she could feel her tension begin to slide away. After a few minutes, she felt Stephen's fingers brush against her own. She opened her eyes to find him looking at her.

'Would you possibly do something for me?' he asked. 'In return for my being such an obedient soul.'

She nodded. 'I might.'

'Sit here quietly – quietly mind – without interrupting, while I try to explain what I attempted to a few minutes ago. Only this time I'm going to do it as I originally intended; without upsetting you, or giving you the impression that I don't believe you, or, God forbid, that I pity you.'

Laura's stomach gave a lurch, but she nodded again, her mouth firmly closed.

'I feel really awful about yesterday,' began Stephen. 'I was furious with the way you were treated by those two policemen, and I think I lost sight of the reason we were there, ironically the same thing I accused them of. I was so determined to prove a point to them... and if I'm honest... well, I wanted to score a few brownie points with you too. That's my innate macho arrogance getting the better of me I'm afraid.' He rubbed a finger along a furrow in his brow. 'When we came back outside, it felt like we'd scored a victory, and I never gave much thought to the consequences of our visit – because to me you were never anything other than one hundred per cent certain of Giles' guilt, and therefore so was I. It never even occurred to me that the police would find differently, and, if they did, how difficult this would be for you. And now I don't know what to say, because they *don't* believe Giles is guilty, and you *do* feel awful, and that's probably all my fault.'

Laura looked down at her hands in her lap, and those of Stephen lying inches away from her own. Slowly, she moved one hand to cover his.

'I'm sorry too,' she said. 'Just not half as eloquently as you. But, I am very grateful you're still here, and that I haven't managed to frighten you off completely, despite my best efforts. I'm just not sure how to say the rest of it.'

'Well, how about if I say that I think I already understand, and we'll work the rest out as we go along. How does that sound?'

Laura grinned. 'Much better than anything that will come out of my mouth...'

Stephen returned the smile. 'Right, well, are we going to sit here all day or are we going to see Blanche?'

Laura stared incredulously at Stephen for the second time that day. 'You're actually still going to come with me?' she asked, 'After the way I've behaved?'

'I know, sometimes I surprise myself. I thought I would have shouted a few profanities by now and gone down the pub. Instead, I find myself still here which is pretty impressive given my poor track record in being a kind and compassionate human being. Funny old world, isn't it?'

The heat was rising to her cheeks again, but this time not in anger. She looked at Stephen's easy smile. 'I'll get my coat, shall I?'

*

The journey to the hospital was silent for both of them, which was fine by Stephen. It gave him time to analyse the whole new barrage of thoughts that were swirling around his brain. Laura wasn't so much complicated as like a tangled ball of string. He wondered idly if he would ever be able to unpick all the knots, or indeed why he would want to, which was the strangest thing.

He had felt genuinely shocked at the news the police had given him. He honestly had not given a thought to Giles's supposed guilt or not. He had believed that it was simply a matter of letting time take its course before the inevitable arrest came; but now he felt more confused than ever. He didn't doubt Laura's certainty for a second, but he could see clearly how now, more than ever, that her previous dealings with the Drummond family stood every chance of being dragged up again, and that thought worried him a great deal. There was still the matter of a serious unsolved crime of course, and as furtive glances at Laura in the car had confirmed, she was still distraught at what had happened to her friend.

It wasn't only concern for Blanche of course. For Laura, the trip to the hospital was taking her right back to a time she had fought hard to forget. It was bound up in tortured memories of her husband teetering on the edge of life, unable to respond to her, leaving Laura unsure whether her final words to him had even been heard. He had learned the story from Freya; how David had clung to life for two long days, the medical staff doing everything they could to heal his broken body, even though his death had been all but guaranteed from the moment he had been brought into hospital. Without her hearing to help her, Laura had missed so much of what had been going on, and had had to fight for every scrap of information she could get. It must have been a hellish void. He risked another glance at her, determined that if she needed support, he would provide it. Just so long as she actually wanted it of course...

The walk up to the orthopaedic ward seemed to take forever, and Stephen willed every turn of the corridor to lead them to their destination. Laura was palpably tense, and more than anything he longed to take her hand, but her closed body language shouted *don't touch me* louder than words ever could. He too was beginning to get a little nervous about what they might find when they entered the ward.

In the end, he need not have worried. They eventually found Blanche at the end of a small bay, tucked into the corner under a huge window and beaming at a vivacious blonde who sat beside her bed. He hovered for a moment, unsure what to do for Laura's sake, until Blanche's visitor caught sight of them and got up immediately, a welcome smile on her face.

'Mum, you are popular today!' She laughed. 'Look, someone else has come to see you.' She held out her hand. 'I'm Elizabeth, Blanche's daughter,' she added by way of explanation.

Stephen stood back to let Laura shake the proffered hand. 'Hi,' she began shyly, 'I'm Laura, one of Blanche's neighbours…'

The smile widened in recognition. 'Yes, I think we've met once or twice, haven't we? And of course, I've heard all about you, or rather I've heard all about the magical properties of your sloe gin.'

Laura gave Stephen a hesitant look. 'I thought about bringing a bottle along with me today… but I didn't think it would be allowed…'

'You're probably right. Pity though, eh, Mum? You'd have liked a drop of that.'

Stephen glanced at Blanche who was lying flat on her back but, apart from a bright pink bandage circling her wrist, looked surprisingly none the worse for wear.

She waved at Laura with her good arm. 'Come and sit down, dear,' she said, patting the chair beside the bed where her daughter had been sitting. 'That's all right, Elizabeth, isn't it? That way I can talk to Laura properly.'

Elizabeth flashed Stephen a knowing smile. 'Perhaps you and I could go and find some other chairs?' she suggested smoothly. 'That way Laura can have Mum to herself for a few minutes without us all gabbling at once.'

Stephen felt his shoulders relax. 'If you're sure, you don't mind. We've rather barged in on your visiting time.'

'Oh, I've been here most of the day, don't worry. We're just waiting for the doctor's round so that mum can be discharged. She's coming home to me for a bit, until she's properly on her feet. Come on and I'll fill you in.'

She led the way back down the ward, her heels clicking on the floor. Despite the fact that Elizabeth wasn't too far off being old enough to be his own mother, she was a very attractive woman, and at any other time Stephen would have admired the sway of her hips in her tight jeans, or the cashmere jumper which clung to all the right places, but not today. He was only concerned with how Laura was feeling.

'That was very kind, thank you,' he said, as they reached the corridor outside.

Elizabeth turned. 'Not at all,' she replied. 'Mum told me that Laura's deaf, but aside from that I've got a bit of an ulterior motive I'm afraid. That's why I wanted to talk to you by yourself.'

Stephen looked back down the row of beds.

'Oh?' he said.

'Since her accident, I've been in to see Mum most days, and she's really quite worried about Laura. To be honest, I'm rather ashamed that I hadn't realised what good friends they are, or that Laura had been calling in on Mum nearly every day to check on her. Physically, mum's going to be fine. She's as tough as old boots actually, but the doctors are more concerned about her up here at the moment.' She tapped the side of her head. 'At her age the shock of the accident and a bad fall can be a real setback, and couple that with the fact that she's not going to be going at the same speed as she used to, the effect on her mental health could be disastrous. A young lad came to visit Mum earlier today and since then she's been quite distressed about Laura's well-being. That's why I'm so glad to see her; it might help to put Mum's mind at rest… particularly now that you've come with her. Mum mentioned that Laura was on her own, you see.' She gave Stephen an apologetic smile. 'Are you——?'

'No,' replied Stephen quickly. 'I'm Stephen – just a friend. I live in the same village and we… it's a long story.'

Elizabeth gave him rather too long a look for his comfort. 'Well, whatever, Mum will be glad to see you. Perhaps now she can see that Laura has someone to call on if she needs to, it will help assuage her worries. She seemed quite concerned about her living by herself, and being so vulnerable.'

They had come to rest by a stand of chairs, and Stephen automatically plucked two from the top of the pile. 'What do you mean?' he asked. 'Laura lives quite independently.'

'Yes, exactly,' Elizabeth replied. 'Mum wasn't worried that Laura couldn't cope or anything like that, more that it had something to do with this chap. I don't think she particularly liked him, although he seemed perfectly pleasant, but she mentioned something about an old family feud. Was he some dodgy boyfriend or something?'

Stephen looked at her concerned face. 'Laura doesn't have a boyfriend, she's a widow.'

Elizabeth touched her mouth automatically. 'Oh, I'm sorry,' she replied. 'I didn't know. Well, it can't have been that then.'

'No, I guess not,' replied Stephen. 'But, as you say, a good chinwag will do them both good.' He adjusted the grip on the chairs and motioned with his head. 'After you,' he said, his mouth set in a thin hard line as he followed Elizabeth back down the ward.

He did his best, but there was no way he could keep changing the subject; he was running out of things to say. So he sat, anxiously waiting for the moment when either Blanche brought up the subject of her earlier visitor, or Laura asked about the accident. Discussion of either one was guaranteed to reveal the identity of the 'mystery' young man who had come to see Blanche, at which point it would propel Laura through the ceiling. All Stephen could do was hang on until it did, and do his best to deal with the fallout. That, and pray for a miracle.

'He must think I'm soft in the head, or something,' Blanche deduced after a few minutes of animated discussion. 'As if that lad would even think about somebody else, let alone come and visit an old biddy in hospital, and one he hardly knows at that.' She looked across at Elizabeth. 'And I'm not surprised one little bit. His father's just as bad, as you very well know, Laura.'

Elizabeth looked confused. 'I'm sorry, Mum, I'm not following you. Are you saying that this lad who came in earlier is the one who knocked you down? Because that's a very serious accusation. I thought you didn't see the car?'

Blanche tutted. 'I didn't, but why else would he come to see me? He wanted to see if I remembered him of course; no doubt worried he's going to get into a whole heap of trouble. I think I did pretty well not letting on.' She smiled gleefully.

All of three of them exchanged looks; Laura now sitting up ramrod straight and Elizabeth opening and closing her mouth.

'But Mum, you have no proof. You can't make wild accusations like that, he could have come for any number of reasons…'

It was inevitable really, Stephen knew that. And the fact that he'd seen it coming a mile off didn't help. The conversation had been brewing like a volcano waiting to explode, and there was nothing Stephen could do to stop it. He looked at Laura, stricken, knowing exactly what was going to come out of her mouth any minute now.

'Did he actually say anything out of the ordinary to you, Blanche?'

The old lady shook her head. 'No… but then he wouldn't, would he, not with Elizabeth here. Of course, he didn't stay long, there was no point really. He couldn't get what he came for.'

To his astonishment, Laura chuckled. 'Would you listen to yourself, Blanche! I think you've been reading too many Agatha Christies.' She glanced at Elizabeth. 'I'm sure the police are doing everything they can to find out who did this, but for now the most important thing is for you to forget all about the accident and concentrate on getting better. Have some lovely time with your daughter and get fit and well again. After all, I shall still need a good home for my sloe gin, and who else is going to drink it?'

Elizabeth reached over and squeezed her mum's hand. 'She's right, Mum. I'm going to enjoy spoiling you rotten, so you're not to worry about a thing.'

'And I shall be making sure that Laura's well looked after whilst you're not around to keep an eye on her,' said Stephen. 'So, no fretting about that either.'

Laura checked her watch. 'We should get going really. You've had a busy day already, and we don't want you to be too tired to enjoy getting out of this place.' She got up and planted a kiss on Blanche's cheek. 'You behave yourself now and do what Elizabeth tells you. I'll see you very soon.'

A few moments later, after general goodbyes and promises to keep in touch, Stephen found himself hurtling down the corridor after Laura, trying to keep up with her. Much as he hated doing so, the only way he could get her to slow down was to catch her hand. She swung to face him.

For a moment, he thought she might be about to belt him one, such was the look of fury on her face, but then to his amazement her face broke into a wide smile.

'Sorry,' she said, almost breathless. 'You're right, I should stop, calm down… otherwise…'

'You'll nail the bastard to a tree?' suggested Stephen.

Her shoulders dropped. 'Something like that,' she said with a wry smile. 'You're also sure that it was Giles who came to visit today?'

'I'm afraid so, yes,' replied Stephen. 'I think it was pretty obvious.' He looked at her flushed face for a moment. 'You know that was a stellar piece of acting back there – letting Blanche think she was imagining things. It was a kind thing to do.'

'Well, I could hardly agree with her, could I? Imagine how she would feel.' She tilted her head to one side. 'You know something, Stephen Henderson…' She paused for a second as if thinking of what to say. 'Nah, don't worry, it doesn't matter.' And with that she took hold of his hand again, and started to walk. 'Come on. We've got things to do, and first on the list is to call the police. I think they might be very interested to learn of Giles' antics this afternoon.'

Chapter Fifty-Eight

Freya wiped a dribble of melted butter off the end of her chin. 'Just think…' She sighed happily. 'In four days' time I will be making your bacon sandwiches as Mrs Henderson. What do you think of that?'

Sam took another huge bite of his breakfast, chewing slowly and thoughtfully. 'Will you be changing the recipe at all?' he asked eventually. 'Only if you do, I fear it may be grounds for divorce.'

'And why would I mess with perfection?'

'Why indeed…'

They sat in silence save for the occasional slurp of tea, and the ticking of the huge grandfather clock which stood in one corner of the kitchen. Freya, who already had one eye on it, sighed again. How was it already seven o'clock in the morning? She'd been up since four and the To-Do List, which sat ominously in the middle of the table, still had just as many items to get through as it had when she first woke up. 'I could go back to bed; I don't know about you.'

Sam put the last of his sandwich down on his plate. 'Jeez Freya, again? I'm not sure I can keep up with your demands.' He winked cheekily, and Freya stuck out her tongue.

'Oh, ha, ha,' she replied, ignoring his expression. 'Not a chance, mate. We've still got far too much to do… In fact, I'm thinking of imposing a ban on sex until after the wedding – seeing as it was you who suggested it would be a good idea to get married in the middle of the harvest…'

'Freya Sherbourne, you bloody liar! It was all your doing, as well you know, romantic fool that you are.'

'Me?' she queried, with mock innocence. 'It can't have been me. I would never have suggested anything so daft.' She met his look with eyes that danced with good humour. 'Come on, eat up, we haven't got all day.'

'Mutter mutter, grumble grumble; bloody slave driver,' said Sam with a smile, getting up from the table. He offered a solicitous hand to his soon-to-be wife. 'Listen, about the whole sex thing, maybe we could renegotiate...'

Freya was pulling on her wellies when a thought occurred to her. 'Have you heard anything from Stephen yet?' she asked.

'Probably a bit early,' replied Sam, shrugging on his jacket. 'I'll give him a call in a while if we still haven't heard. He did say he might pop over with Laura today anyway, now that the marquee's here. She needs to measure up, apparently. Besides there are no guarantees that the police's stance will change, even with Laura's further statement. Granted they're viewing Giles's visit to the hospital as suspicious, but they still need something more concrete to go on before they can act. We just have to hope that they do decide to investigate further; taking a look at Giles's car will be the crucial thing.'

'Laura must feel happier about things though, surely? At the very least the police seem to be taking her more seriously, and rightly so, it's a big thing for her.'

Sam regarded her squarely as he zipped up his jacket. 'Hmm, although the potential repercussions worry me somewhat. She's still very vulnerable.'

Freya stopped in her tracks. 'What do you mean repercussions?' she asked, looking up.

'Well, think about it for a minute. Laura's husband died five years ago and yet, according to Laura, Francis Drummond still takes every opportunity he can to make fun of her or threaten her even. Doesn't that strike you as odd? I mean, why bother, after all this time?'

'Because he likes to throw his weight around. He's a bully, you know that.'

'He is,' continued Sam, 'but bullies usually have something to gain by their behaviour. Often they're cowards, or vulnerable themselves, using their actions to hide the truth from the world. It's almost as if he needs to keep Laura under control, subdued, if you like. But what do you suppose would make him want to do that? What possible threat could Laura pose to him?'

Freya's eyes widened. 'You're scaring me now, Sam. Are you saying you think Laura's in danger of some sort?'

'No, I think that's a tad melodramatic, but it does make me curious. And now that she's made an accusation against Francis's son, which looks as if it might stick, I don't suppose he'll be feeling particularly charitable towards her.'

'Then we should say something to Laura, warn her.'

Sam took her arm gently. 'I think Stephen has it pretty much covered,' he said with meaning, giving Freya a long look.

She stared back at him. 'You've discussed this with him, haven't you?' she accused. 'That's what you were talking about for ages on the phone yesterday; nothing to do with the wedding at all.'

'It was mentioned, yes, but don't go getting on your high horse about all this...' He gave her a small smile. 'Stephen really is the best person to deal with this as far as Laura's concerned. I'd say he's got to know her pretty well over the last few days...'

Freya opened her mouth to speak again, but Sam dropped her arm, and turned for the door.

'And not the way you're thinking either, so you can take that look off your face. I've honestly never seen Stephen behave this way before, about anybody. He obviously cares about Laura a great deal, and I think he deserves some respect, or at the very least, our trust.'

With that he walked out into the yard, leaving Freya staring after him in astonishment, a small smile gathering at the corners of her mouth. Well, well, well. Now that was something she'd never expected to hear. Stephen might be acting out of character, but he wasn't the only one. In all the years she'd known Sam, she'd never heard him stick up for his brother like that before. Times certainly were a changing. She hurried through the door, pulling it firmly shut behind her.

*

Laura could hardly contain her excitement. At least she thought it was excitement. The bubbling, fizzing feeling in her stomach might well be sheer terror, she acknowledged. She gazed around her at the huge open space, at the multitude of tables and chairs that filled the marquee, and took a very deep breath. Then she closed her eyes.

She stayed that way for several minutes, letting images fill her mind, mentally roaming the hedgerows, seeking out the colours and the textures that would bring the pictures in her head to life. The tables, the great arch of the marquee entrance, the tented ceiling, all of it was a blank canvas waiting to be filled. When she opened her eyes, she gave a nod of satisfaction. She had several days of hard graft ahead of her, but it was going to look beautiful, more beautiful than anything she had ever created in her life before. And the thought brought a sudden rush of tears to her eyes.

She glanced at her watch to confirm that she didn't have the luxury of any more time here and, whilst it would have been nice to make some sketches, or measure one or two things, Laura knew that it wasn't really necessary, not for her. Her designs weren't that structured; they were organic, they grew out of themselves, and however hard she tried to think things through in advance, she knew that in practice she rarely looked at any plans she had made. Instead, she sat down with her raw materials heaped around her and let the strange alchemy begin. It made her fingers twitch just thinking about it.

With one final glance about her, Laura strode from the marquee. Stephen had disappeared almost the minute they got here, saying that he would only be in the way and she should have some time on her own to think about things without his interference. More like gone in search of a bacon butty she reckoned, but she couldn't begrudge him that. He had offered to help her today, and having done a recce on the church first thing this morning, now she needed to plunder what the fields and hedgerows had to offer, and that was going to take some time, and manpower.

She finally rooted him out in the kitchen, having a bit of a heart to heart with Sam by the look of things, but he jumped up the minute he saw her.

He turned to her and smiled. 'Are we sorted?' he asked, stretching out his back and giving his neck a flex.

'We are, although are you sure you're up for this? We're going to walk miles this afternoon.'

Stephen merely shrugged. 'Don't be fooled by appearances. I'll have you know this body is a finely tuned machine.'

Laura caught Sam's eye and winked. 'We'll see,' she said. 'Come on then, no time for dallying. It's a mile-and-a-half to the first place we need to go.'

'Not that I'm wimping out or anything, but you do realise there's a perfectly good car outside?'

She grinned. 'Perhaps I should rephrase that last statement. It's a four-mile drive to the nearest place you can park, and then a mile-and-a-half walk across the fields.'

Stephen looked back at Sam, and she didn't catch what he said next, but judging by the expression on his face when he turned back to her, she could guess.

It had been a shrewd investment buying Clarence Cottage all those years ago. Back then, she'd been an accounts clerk, and neither she nor David could have foreseen the direction her 'career' would take. They had fallen in love with the cottage primarily because of its cosy charm but, whilst they appreciated that it also had a large garden and outbuildings, they hadn't thought much beyond them at the time. Now, these sheds were filled with tables and, looking around her in the dimming light, Laura was grateful indeed. Their afternoon's work was heaped before them.

Every surface groaned with an array of greenery, fruits, grasses and grains, with hues of every colour ranging from vibrant oranges and reds, to dusky pinks and purples, lime greens, soft greens, and warming ochres.

Her hair was tangled with straw and cobwebs, her skin flushed by the sun and wind, and her fingers stained with sap and juice, but Laura felt profoundly at peace. She was knackered, but filled with an immense satisfaction, something she had not felt in a long time. She sat on a wooden chair beside one of the tables and smiled to herself. Usually, the fields and hedgerows were hers alone; she might see the odd rider or dog walker, but invariably her day was spent in solitude. This afternoon she had shared her knowledge with someone else. Where she'd walked, Stephen walked, out of necessity saying little, but at times stopping to ask her questions, and listening to her enthusiastic responses with a keen ear and a ready smile. He had followed her instructions for what to pick and how to pick it to the letter, and had worked solidly without complaint. His company had been easy, familiar even, and reluctant though Laura had been to admit it, she had enjoyed the afternoon far more because of it. When he dropped her home, his kiss to her cheek had been soft, nothing more, but the memory of it now, still brought a renewed flush to her cheeks. She shook her head in wonder at the changes she could feel within herself. Who would have thought that Stephen Henderson of all people would be the person to bring that about?

She glanced outside at the rapidly falling night and began to scoop up sheaves of tawny foliage from one of the tables. They would need to be steeped in a glycerine solution to preserve their colour and pliability, and the sooner she did it, the better the result would be.

The back door to the cottage was still open, the light from the kitchen spilling a welcome square onto the path which led up the garden. She was only a few feet from the door when the first brilliant flash lit up the sky, followed quickly by another, then another. She flinched automatically, unable to see clearly for a few moments, but her feet carried her safely to the door. Once inside she threw the door closed, and hurriedly dumped her cargo on the table. Boris was right where she expected him to be, cowering up against the side of the Aga, his brown eyes ringed with white. She sank to the floor, wrapping her arms around his neck. Bonfire night was ages away yet, but every year the fireworks seemed to get earlier and earlier and, big dog he might be, but he was still terrified of the noise and bursts of light.

She remembered firework displays from her childhood, how her stomach had contracted with the thud of the rockets, noise that seemed to come from nowhere even though it was expected, the sharp staccato crackles leaving her ears ringing. Of course, now, for her, the fireworks had fallen silent, but she could recall the noisy confusion as if it was yesterday.

Another burst lit up the darkened room, the intensity of it making even Laura jump. She could feel the fur in Boris' throat quivering and knew that he was growling. Her murmured words of comfort were having little effect, and he broke free from her hold, running at the window, jumping. She would like to give whoever was being so irresponsible a piece of her mind, but there was little point; she would never be heard. The flashes were coming almost continually now, until, blinded, Laura could scarcely make out the room in front of her. Boris was frantic, running up and down the room, and out into the hallway. She realised belatedly that the light which alerted her to a caller at the front door was flashing too, and it was then that the first slivers of fear began to replace her anger.

She got to her feet, trying to catch hold of Boris, but he was lunging at the window and she was almost knocked over by his huge size. He was trying to protect her, she knew that, but the dog was clearly terrified too. Her own heart was hammering in her chest, and it gave a wild leap as a masked face appeared at the window, illuminated for a second by the flare outside. Whoever was outside was in her garden! And then, as an icy trail snaked down her back, everything began to make sense. This was not kids having irresponsible fun, nor was it an early bonfire party. This was a deliberate attack on her.

Laura grabbed hold of Boris' collar and dragged him across the floor and out into the hallway. She kicked the kitchen door closed, whimpering, and came to rest in the corner of the hallway, her back against the wall, her arms trying to contain the terrified dog. It was at least darker in the hallway, with the doors closed and no windows to broadcast the light from the fireworks. The doorbell alarm was still flashing, but the light from it was nothing compared with the onslaught in the kitchen. She could only imagine the noise level, and knew this was what was making Boris so scared, and her so panicked. She also realised that it was preventing her from thinking straight.

She closed her eyes and tried to concentrate for a moment, weighing up what she could do. There was no way she could go outside. Apart from being terrified, without fully functioning senses she would be defenceless; and Boris, despite his size, was a gentle dog and not given to aggressive behaviour. And then it hit her; the cold truth was that whoever was behind this definitely knew her, and knew the best way to scare her too. She clung to Boris even tighter, knowing that she was trapped in her own home until whoever was outside had finished intimidating her. Only then might she be able to venture back into the kitchen and root out her mobile. She was beginning to feel slightly more in control when she suddenly realised that she had no memory of locking her back door. Granted, she normally did it automatically when she had finished outside for the day, but in her earlier haste she couldn't remember whether she had or not. The thought made her stomach leap in shock; they could be in her kitchen right now…

To her surprise, this new fear brought anger rushing to the surface. How dare they corner her in her own home? Cowardly bullies, she thought, that's all they were, and it was about time she stood up for herself. She flung open the door to the kitchen, realising a split second too late that the room was now pitch black. She cannoned straight into a hard body on the other side of the door, the shock causing her legs to buckle alarmingly. She felt a cry loose itself from her lips, and a pair of arms caught hold of her as she dropped; strong arms which held her up and then held her close. She breathed in a scent that had become so familiar over the last few days, and this time instead of evading Stephen's touch, she returned it, letting his solid warmth seep into her.

The tears came as she felt his hand move to cradle her head. She could feel his lips moving against her hair, saying words she could neither hear nor see, yet words her heart imagined. They clung together silently in the dark for several moments until Laura felt a sudden need to see his face, to talk, and to understand. Slowly, she disentangled herself and doubled back to flick on the light switch, flinching once more as the kitchen sprang into relief.

Stephen's face was dark with anger, but his eyes were soft on hers.

'They've gone,' he said. 'It's okay.'

He bent down, stretching out one hand in front of him, and as Laura watched, Boris slunk across the floor, half his usual height, his tail tucked between his legs, but with just the faintest twitch of a wag. He pushed his nose into Stephen's palm, his body quivering gently, from fear still, or a sense of delight, Laura couldn't tell. He sat on the floor pulling Laura down too and held the dog in a jumble of limbs between them. 'Who were they?' she whispered.

'I've no idea,' Stephen replied. 'Three of them, all wearing masks. It's a wonder they didn't kill themselves, letting off fireworks at such close range, but I imagine that when the police catch up with them, they'll be easy to spot; their clothes must be covered in burns, and stink too I shouldn't wonder.'

Laura nodded. 'And will the police catch up with them?' she asked.

'If they've anything about them, they will. Particularly as I told them a good place to start looking.'

She swallowed. 'You reckon it was Giles then?'

'Not personally. He's far too cowardly for that,' sneered Stephen, 'but he'll have found some thugs for hire. His sort generally do.'

'I can't believe he'd be so stupid. I mean he's now being investigated for a hit and run, right? How does this possibly make things any better for him?'

Stephen sighed. 'Well, he might be loaded, and he might think the world is his to command, but that doesn't mean he isn't thick as shit. Whereas you and I might approach a difficulty with rational thought and integrity, I suspect that when the Drummond family are faced with a problem, they simply require it to be got rid of; I don't suppose they're especially bothered about how.' Stephen sank his hands into the dog's fur. 'And of course there is another way to look at it...'

'Which is?'

'That by scaring you senseless, you might change your mind about what you saw on the day of the accident... that you might even retract your statement, telling the police that you simply got it wrong...'

'But that's ridiculous!'

'It's not actually... Because today they only scared you. They lit fireworks, knowing that the noise would terrify Boris and that the flashes and flares would disorientate you. By taking out Boris, it effectively made you very vulnerable, which is just what they wanted of course—'

'Yes, but...'

Stephen held up his hand. 'And if they could do that today... what might they get up to the next day, or the next...'

Laura stared at the gentle expression on Stephen's face. He couldn't possibly mean that, he was just being melodramatic; but the more she looked at him, the more she could see the truth in what he had said. A shiver ran through her. Despite all that had happened to her in the past, Laura still believed in a world that was kind and good. Things like this only happened in soap operas, not real life. And yet, it had happened. Giles Drummond had knocked down a defenceless old lady and driven away; left her for dead at the side of the road, and even now, when faced with the possibility of having to accept responsibility for his actions, he was trying to wheedle his way out of it. People did do bad things, she had seen the proof of it, and Stephen was right. She felt his hand cover hers.

'I'm not trying to scare you, Laura, but we need to think carefully about what we do next. I'm worried about you being on your own, and I know you're very capable, and independent...' he gave a wry smile, 'and you'll probably punch me for coming over all macho on you, but even though I know all this, I'm still not happy about you being by yourself. I don't want to point out the obvious for risk of permanent injury to my nether regions, but where Giles is concerned your deafness puts you at a real disadvantage, and he knows it.'

A few months ago, she would have been angry at Stephen's words, and his nether regions would most definitely have been under threat, but today, she simply smiled. She *had* changed over the last few weeks, and however much she wanted to dispute that fact, her current feelings were proof, and they would have to be faced up to very soon. She wasn't at all sure what she wanted to do about them, but for now at least the thought of Stephen not leaving her alone was stomach churningly lovely. A warm glow began to rise up from her toes.

'So what do we do now?' she asked, blushing.

'Well, our most pressing business is still Freya and Sam's wedding, and nothing must prevent that from being the glorious day it deserves to be, which also includes giving your decorations the chance to shine, by the way. As all your materials are here, and you're going to need help gathering more of them and transporting them too, I suggest that I bagsy your spare room… just for a few days until we see how things lie. That way I can help make sure that the wedding arrangements go according to plan, and I can be on hand in case there's any repeat of this evening. I dread to think what might have happened if I hadn't been around.'

Laura hardly dared to think what colour her face might be, but apart from that she suddenly realised what had been flitting about in her brain over the last few minutes.

'I was wondering about that,' she said. 'Don't think that I'm not stupidly grateful of course, but why are you here? I thought we'd said goodbye for the evening.'

'Ah…' Stephen smiled, patting his stomach. 'I'd like to say something worthy and heroic, but sadly it was a case of having got home, realising that I was knackered, starving, and couldn't face cooking, and wondering if maybe you felt the same? I was going to suggest a takeaway. The Indian place at the far end of the High Street is very good, it does home delivery too.'

The look on Stephen's face was priceless. 'Well, it's honest at least.' She grinned. 'And... actually not a bad idea. Now that I've thought about it, I'm starving as well. I could murder a good curry.'

She ruffled Boris's fur one more time and, laughing, struggled to get to her feet. Stephen followed suit until they stood rather shyly in the middle of the room.

'What about my other suggestion?' began Stephen, scuffing at the floor with his foot. 'Do you think perhaps I should stay for a bit?'

'Let's get some food sorted first,' she replied, 'then we can talk about it. I'll see if I can find a menu.'

She turned away so that Stephen wouldn't see her smile. She didn't want him to think she was a complete pushover.

Chapter Fifty-Nine

Stephen was not normally given to strong emotions, nor had he found it easy in the past to show them, but as Freya moved slowly down the aisle towards him, his throat constricted almost painfully. Beside him, Sam stood waiting patiently for his bride, and as she neared, Stephen's heart swelled with delight and pride.

Freya looked radiant, and more than that, thought Stephen, she was totally and utterly, blissfully in love. It shone out of her, in the way she walked, the way her eyes sparkled as she met those of the people sitting in the pews she passed, and the way she clasped her bouquet excitedly in front of her, a beautiful tribute to the life she had made with Sam, and one which they would now share forever.

Rosy apples jostled for space with huge deep pink peonies; eucalyptus leaves and sage sat between glowing hips and golden pears; pale roses met with dark dusky blackberries and huge speckled poppy heads. If Stephen hadn't helped collect all these beautiful things he would never have believed it for himself, and two rows behind him, Laura sat in the church, where he hoped she was also bursting with pride at her achievement. He had heard the gasps of astonishment from the congregation as they filed into the church, and it hurt him more than anything to know that she could not hear them herself. But she must surely see the delight on the faces, the fingers that pointed out her stunning decorations where the unusual and the traditional sat side by side in such perfect harmony.

A golden beam of afternoon sun filtered through the huge windows in front of him and warmed the stone flags onto which Freya now stepped. The light settled upon her and Sam and, as the vicar came forward to join them both in marriage, a wide smile settled over Stephen's face. He had come a long way since the days when he had fought Sam every step of the way; fought even to take Freya from him, and had she not come to her senses when she did, they would both have been condemned to an unhappy future. It had taken a long time for things to come right again, for Stephen even longer than Freya and Sam, but as he watched the couple in front of him now, he realised that things were just as they should be.

It was only a matter of hours since he and Laura had last left the marquee. They had worked into the wee small hours, dressing and pinning, arranging and perfecting, but now, as the wedding guests filed in to take their places, he increased his pressure on Laura's hand. The space looked amazing, and the expression on her face was mirrored by his own; a mixture of excitement, of childlike wonder, and an overwhelming relief that it did indeed look as good as they had imagined it would. Appleyard Farm was shining like a jewel today, and the woman by his side had been responsible for most of it.

The conversation was increasing to a steady hum, and Stephen knew that this was when Laura would feel most ill at ease. It was hard enough for her to follow what people were saying in a crowd, but when they were eating and drinking as well, it unwittingly made their speech almost impossible for her to decipher. For the most part, he could do nothing but stay by her side and make sure that she could at least understand his words. Beyond that he had one or two little surprises up his sleeve, which he hoped would be received in the spirit in which they were offered.

He almost hadn't told Sam and Freya what he had done, fearing they would laugh at him, or even be angry with him for making arrangements for their wedding day without their knowledge. But the fact that Freya had turned away when he told them, on the pretext of putting the kettle on, had meant more to him than her words ever could. He had seen the tears welling in her eyes, and although he knew he still had much to prove to her about his behaviour, her reaction was more than he could have wished for. He also had her and Sam's blessing which made everything all the easier of course. His speech nestled in his jacket pocket and he patted it for the umpteenth time that day. He almost knew it off by heart but automatically felt for it just the same.

He had arranged for Laura to sit at the top table, alongside him, and with Freya's best friend, Merry, who had acted as maid of honour, on her other side. He knew that Merry had owned a florist shop once upon a time and hoped that the two of them would have plenty to talk about. As they took their seats, he caught the eye of one of the guests sitting directly on the table opposite and gave a nervous smile. His stomach was in knots.

*

Laura concentrated on her food for a moment. The room was a confused jumble of words, gathered here and there as she looked out onto the sea of faces in front of her, but to her surprise she was still enjoying herself. It didn't much matter that she couldn't follow what people were saying all the time, because everywhere she looked, she saw smiling faces and the mood was infectious. Most eyes were quite rightly on Freya, but she saw many looking at her huge urns filled with the countryside, and bounty from the farm, and the smiles remained in place. She even caught the eye of a few people, folk she had known for years, only this time instead of looking away, or worse, pretending they hadn't seen her, they held her look, nodded and smiled. Something subtle had changed in their reactions, and with a jolt she realised that she was the reason.

Previously, her gaze had been a challenge, a dare to prove her suspicions right, and an opportunity to justify her own poor behaviour. She realised now that she had made people uncomfortable, embarrassed even, and had deserved the responses she got, simply because she had given people no other choice. A scowl was met with a scowl, just as now, a smile was met with a smile. It was a simple equation, but one which had taken her far too long to work out.

She realised that Stephen was talking to her again, and leaned in towards him. He had, as he suggested, moved into her spare bedroom and, whether it was the sight of his car, a constant companion to hers on the driveway, or the fact that he insisted they sit with the curtains open every evening in case anyone happened to glance in and see that she was not alone, she wasn't sure, but nothing untoward had happened since the incident with the fireworks. In fact, nothing untoward had happened at all, and Laura wasn't entirely sure if she was disappointed or not. They had got on well after the initial embarrassment of finding themselves sleeping under the same roof; beyond that their relationship had been friendly and companionable, but nothing more.

Now he seemed a little jittery, and she hoped it was simply nerves at the thought of his looming speech. Throughout the day he had been attentiveness personified, making sure that she was okay, that she wasn't too nervous herself, or feeling uncomfortable. At times, he had seemed to want to say something more than the words that had actually come out of his mouth, but the feeling passed again, and Laura was left wondering. As she looked at him now, she realised that she was not concentrating at all on what he was saying, but instead focusing on the full curve of his mouth, the slight dimple that appeared in his right cheek when he spoke, and the warmth in his eyes. She frowned and asked him to repeat what he had said.

'I'm sorry, I was miles away,' she added. And she was. She was thinking very much about kissing him.

She almost missed the start of Stephen's speech. She was deep in conversation with Merry, who was fascinated to know more about her business, and it was only when she stopped talking and touched Laura's arm, that she realised Stephen was tapping the side of his glass with a knife. She straightened up, and arranged her face into a polite smile. She would have to take her cue from the other wedding guests about when to laugh as she doubted very much that she would be able to follow what he was saying from this angle.

To her surprise, a tall, very elegant lady directly opposite her got to her feet and fixed Laura with a beaming smile. She was even more surprised when she signed *Hello, I'm Natalie.*

Tentatively, she signed back. Natalie smiled again, and then looked to Stephen, giving him a nod. There was a momentary pause and then her hands began to fly as Stephen started to speak.

'Well, this is a first for me,' she began to sign, 'and so before I launch into what might yet turn out to be the worst best man's speech you've ever heard, I'm going to ask you all to be patient with me. I know that most of you here are well aware of the gory details of my past as far as Sam and Freya are concerned, and could be forgiven for wondering how on earth I've ended up giving a speech at their wedding… So, I'm also going to ask you to be lenient with me too as I try to explain how I think that's happened. Firstly, though, I'd like to welcome you all here today, and of course thank you for coming. I genuinely don't think there's a soul left in the village, but Appleyard Orchard has been at the centre of our community for a very long time, and I know it means the world to Freya and Sam to see you all here. Without further ado then, I'd like you to raise a glass in toast to the deliriously happy couple… Freya and Sam.'

Laura raised her glass with a grin, watching the stream of bubbles in her champagne rising to the surface and popping. It was much how her stomach felt. She waited for everyone's attention to switch back to Stephen, all the while never taking her eyes off Natalie, whose hands moved back into position.

'I'd also like to make an introduction before I go any further… Some of you may have noticed that my speech today is being signed, so I'd very much like you all to welcome Natalie. She is a British Sign Language tutor from Hereford, and has very kindly offered to give me a hand here today, quite literally… and at very short notice too. Thank you, Natalie.'

Natalie broke off to give a little wave, before continuing with her interpreting. 'Some of you might already have worked out that the reason why Natalie is here today is sitting on my left. For those of you who don't know, her name is Laura and she's profoundly deaf. More importantly, she's responsible for today's stunning floral decorations, and as I'm just about to say some incredibly nice things about her, I thought she should be able to 'hear' them.'

Laura risked a tiny peep to her right, knowing that Stephen would be looking at her. She didn't want to blush bright red in front of all these people, but then would that really be such a big price to pay considering what Stephen had done for her? Her eyes met his, surprised to see that he was blushing too.

'When Sam first asked me to be his best man, I'll admit I was a little surprised; but I realised very quickly how humbled I was at being asked, and how generous Sam was being in asking me. That's just like Sam. He's always seen the good in me, even when we were young, and I spent most of my time being jealous of him and consequently trying to make his life as miserable as possible. For a long time, I pretty much succeeded, but a year or so ago, all that began to change when a very special person came back into Sam's life. That person was, of course, Freya. I think they first got engaged in primary school, and even then, it was clear that the universe had decreed they should be together. Despite my best efforts to keep them apart, fate intervened and brought them back together again, fortunately for me.

'I say fortunately because from the moment they did, it gave Freya the perfect opportunity to let me know in no uncertain terms what she thought of me, urging me to grow up and to start taking responsibility for myself. Much to my surprise, I listened. It hasn't always been easy, and I dare say I still get things wrong, but Sam and Freya are the kind of people who go the extra mile for anyone, even me, and that's really why I'm standing here today.

'I'll also admit that I didn't really get it, this whole love thing. I could see how much Sam and Freya were in love, but I never understood what that meant, what that felt like, or, perhaps more importantly, why I didn't or couldn't feel the same. It wasn't until recently when I quite literally got knocked for six that I began to feel these alien emotions. It's possible that the blow to the head I sustained might be the cause, but I'd be willing to bet it had a lot more to do with a beautiful young lady who came into my life very suddenly one afternoon, and since then, in my head at least, has refused to leave.'

Natalie broke off her signing, looking rather puzzled. She exchanged a look with Laura and gave a slight shrug as if in apology. Clearly, Stephen had stopped speaking for some reason and, as Laura leaned forward to see what the problem was, Stephen turned to look squarely at her.

'You're going to kill me,' he said with a grin.

Laura, whose heart was suddenly beating very fast, was still trying to process the rush of emotions that Stephen's words had already created when he continued to speak.

'Because I'm about to tell everyone here that I love you…'

Laura looked up in astonishment to see Natalie signing *Oh My God…*

Stephen began again. 'Laura has a huge soul, is kind and incredibly brave, but sadly, and for reasons best known to themselves, certain people have tried to break her spirit over the years, and she has been on her own for far too long. She has taught me a great deal, about myself, however, about what makes me happy, and what it is to share the life of another. I find myself being nice, and considerate, compassionate even, and believe me these are things that never came easily before. I think of her before myself, in fact I think of her all the time, and it's only now that I realise what it means to love someone else… So, as I say my closing words, in celebration of the love that Freya and Sam share, and with hope that it continues undiminished, you can be sure that I mean what I say, because, to both my surprise and yours, I finally get what this thing called love is all about. To Freya and Sam.'

Laura imagined that the noise in the room at this point must be deafening. She could see glasses being raised, mouths open in surprise, repeating Stephen's toast, whooping and calling, and hands crashing together, clapping feverishly. What would it be like if she could hear it all? It was hard enough trying to think inside a ball of silence, her brain frantically attempting to recall Stephen's words in case she'd got them wrong, but the look on his face seemed to suggest she had not. She looked over at Natalie, who was nodding and smiling from ear to ear, then back again to Stephen who wore a curious expression, almost as if he was waiting for a punch to land, but then as her mouth began to curve upwards, following the trajectory her heart was also taking, she saw his expression begin to mirror her own. The last thing she saw as he bent to kiss her was Freya, grinning like a loon over his shoulder.

Chapter Sixty

Stephen looked down at the piece of paper he was still clutching and dropped it on the table. It was the speech he had so carefully written and rehearsed and then completely ignored. He still wasn't sure what had made him do it, except that as he began to speak about Freya and Sam, he had suddenly realised how very simple things were when you loved someone, how very 'right' things could feel, and for a split second, had been utterly terrified that this might change. Without really thinking about where they were, telling Laura that he loved her had suddenly been the most important thing in the world.

Freya and Merry had immediately whisked Laura away, and they were now standing in a huddle, broad grins on their faces, hands flapping in their excitement. The memory of his first kiss with Laura still tingled on his lips, and if the shy but meaningful glances she kept giving him were anything to go by, he wouldn't have to wait too long for another.

Beside him, Sam refilled his glass.

'Get that down you,' he said, giving Stephen's arm a nudge. He took a swallow from his own glass. 'What an absolutely bloody amazingly stupendous day,' he added.

Stephen who, bizarrely, was now finding words difficult could only grin in reply, but he took a large glug of champagne anyway.

'Who would have thought it?' mused Sam. 'My brother finally becoming an adult, after all these years.'

'Don't be so cruel,' he said in reply. 'I'm still in a state of shock myself.' But he smiled at his brother, recognising the truth in his words.

'Actually, mate,' said Sam. 'I'm proud of you. Proud of what you've done too. I see now that you had an ulterior motive, but all this business with Drummond can't have been easy. Laura would never have had the courage to come forward as a witness to the hit and run if it wasn't for you, and now it actually looks as if that scumbag low-life is going to get his comeuppance. Have you heard any more?'

Stephen shook his head. 'Only what the police told me this morning; that they've impounded Giles' car pending an examination. They were very interested to hear of the incident with the fireworks the other night, and I have to say it's not looking good for Drummond.' He took another sip of his champagne, his eyes now firmly on Laura. 'I know none of this is over yet. It could rumble on for months; we might both have to give evidence, but all Laura ever wanted was for people to take her seriously, because of what's right, not because of some stupid grudge against the Drummond family... although God knows she'd have cause enough for that after the way they've treated her.'

'They're a powerful family; it's not easy standing up to bullies like that.'

'No... and I hope in time the villagers come to see the truth of it too. Francis has employed a good many of them over the years, but I think now, more and more folk might start asking questions, and come forward in support of Laura and her allegations over David's death.'

Sam nodded grimly. 'I'm sure they will,' he replied. 'Which is of course the very thing Francis was seeking to avoid. Anyway, let's not think about that now. The DJ is giving me the eye, I think it might be time for me and my wife to have our first dance.'

'Sounds good that, me and my wife,' replied Stephen, grinning at his brother.

'It sure does!' Sam winked.

*

'But I can't dance!' protested Laura, laughing. 'Trust me, it's not a pretty sight.'

'Well, I don't believe that for one minute. Anyway, this is different.'

Laura studied Stephen's face. 'It's a disco, people will be dancing. How can it possibly be different?'

He took hold of her hand. 'Come on, I'll show you.'

Before she had a chance to protest any further, Laura found herself propelled through an archway into a smaller marquee which was sitting just behind the first. The space was dim apart from shimmering rays of silver light which flitted around the room courtesy of a series of disco balls which hung from the tented ceiling. Inside, just as she suspected, people were dancing. She slowed her movement, feeling the tug against Stephen's hand as she ground to a halt. He turned to look at her, his face lit by an excited grin.

'It'll be fine. Come on, I promise you.'

'I can't, Stephen, I'll make a complete prat of myself.'

He angled his head at her. 'Or no one will notice what you're doing at all…' He moved a little closer. 'Watch for a second, and tell me what you see.'

She looked at him quizzically.

'I know, it sounds stupid. But honestly, just stand and watch…' He moved to stand a little behind her, pulling her into him, enfolding her in his arms. She leaned back into his warmth.

Her first, cursory glance, showed her nothing new; it was simply a room full of people who were dancing and laughing, moving their bodies in time with the music, just like she had done once upon a time. But then, as she watched, she began to pick out the details of what was happening. Two young girls were giggling madly, almost jumping with energy, their arms flailing above their heads. Next to them a middle-aged couple swayed together, her head on his shoulder, shuffling in the manner of every slow dance she had ever seen. She stared around the room, not understanding what she was looking at. How could some people be dancing to a slow record and yet others be leaping around?

A group of people moved past her, crossing slightly to the right where a chap standing behind a table smiled a greeting at them. He handed them what looked like a pair of headphones from a pile in front of him; bright purple and blue in colour, and when Laura looked back to the dance floor, she realised that everyone was wearing a pair.

She wriggled round in Stephen's arms until she was facing him again. 'What's going on? Why does everyone need headphones?'

'Because it's a silent disco. The headphones play the music, but without them on, no one can hear it in the room.'

Laura thought for a moment. 'But what's the point in that?'

Stephen brushed a curl of hair from out of her eye. 'Well, the headphones don't play the same music to everyone. They work by picking up wireless signals from the DJ's box of tricks, and he's broadcasting four different signals, which is why, if you look around the room, it looks a bit odd... People are dancing to different things.'

Laura turned to face the room for a moment and then back again. 'I still don't get it,' she said, frowning.

Stephen dropped a kiss on the end of her nose. 'Well, if no one else can hear what you're listening to, does it matter how you dance...?'

It took a moment for the meaning of his words to penetrate her brain, but when they did, a slow smile began to spread across Laura's face.

'Oh my God, that's bloody brilliant, come on!'

By the time they reached the centre of the floor, Laura was grinning from ear to ear.

'What shall we dance to?' she urged.

'I don't mind,' replied Stephen, 'I'll follow your lead.'

'Well, there is one song I remember dancing to when I was young – 'Wake Me Up Before You Go Go', by Wham. What do you think?'

'How about we go on three?' grinned Stephen, holding up three fingers. 'Three... two... one... Go!'

Laura felt the song flow through her mind, trying to move how she used to, letting the feel of it surge through her body, it had been such a long time... She closed her eyes and let herself go. A wild excitement began to fill her as her body became alive again, and after a few minutes, she opened her eyes risking a peep at Stephen. He looked a little self-conscious but nonetheless was moving in time to the music playing in his own head.

'Oh God, this is so silly!' Laura laughed. 'But it's the most fun I've had in... well, I can't remember when.'

Stephen started to answer, but clearly found that the combination of moving his arms and legs, trying to listen to imaginary music playing in his head, and speaking all at the same time was simply too much. He gave a series of odd movements as he tried to pick up the beat again, and then ground to a halt, laughing at himself.

The sight of him was too much for Laura. She collapsed in a fit of giggles that only got worse, the more she tried to stop them. She leaned against him, holding on for support, shaking with laughter and clutching onto her stomach which was beginning to hurt from the effort. It was some moments before she could speak again.

'I'm so sorry,' she spluttered helplessly. 'I shouldn't be laughing, but that was the funniest thing I've ever seen!'

'Perhaps I should wear the headphones after all; coordination has never been my strong point.' He looked at her then, a more serious expression on his face. 'Only trouble is, if I do that, I won't be able to dance with you or hear what you say.' He caught both her hands in his. 'Would you teach me how to sign, Laura? I mean it. And not just hello and goodbye, all of it. I want to be able to talk to you anywhere, and anytime, all the time.'

She leaned forward and kissed him gently, her body now up against his. 'I will,' she whispered, 'I promise.' She lay her head against his chest for a moment, before suddenly pulling away.

'You did this for me,' she said, her eyes wide, 'didn't you? I've only just realised.'

Stephen looked into her eyes, a soft expression on his face. 'Guilty as charged,' he said. 'I wanted you to have something today that was on your terms, something that wouldn't make you feel out of place, or different to everyone else. To be honest, when I booked the disco I wasn't planning on hijacking my best man's speech and declaring my feelings for you… but I had sort of hoped this might do it…' he trailed off.

'No one's ever done anything like this for me before,' whispered Laura, reaching up to touch the side of his face.

'Yeah, they have,' countered Stephen. 'A while ago maybe, but I'm sure they have.'

Laura studied his face. 'Perhaps,' she said. 'A long time ago.' She looked around, at a room full of people, all of whom smiled at her when she caught their eye. A few months ago, simply being here would have filled her with dread, but now it filled her with hope. Freya and Sam were off to one side, as were Merry and her husband. She could feel her past receding into the distance as if she no longer had need of it. Her future was beckoning instead.

She turned back to Stephen. 'I think I can hear a slow dance starting,' she said. 'So maybe now would be the right time to start your first lesson in sign language.' She pulled away slightly to make a sign with her hands, speaking the words at the same time. She touched a finger to his lips. 'No talking now,' she said.

'That was one of the very first signs I learned,' laughed Stephen. 'Call me forward, but that's one you won't need to teach me.' And he held her gaze with eyes that sparkled with emotion as he signed back the words *I love you*.

A Letter from Emma

Hello, and thank you so much for choosing to read *A Year at Appleyard Farm*. I hope you enjoyed reading these stories as much as I enjoyed writing them. So if you'd like to stay updated on what's coming next, please do sign up to my newsletter here and you'll be the first to know!

www.bookouture.com/emma-davies

A Year at Appleyard Farm was originally published as four separate seasonal novellas – *Merry Mistletoe*, *Spring Fever*, *Gooseberry Fool* and *Blackberry Way* – and they're particularly special to me, not least of all because it's in the first of these books, *Merry Mistletoe*, that we first meet my favourite character of all time, Amos Fry. In fact, I fell in love with him so much that I always knew that one day I would have to write his story and share it with the world. I never really knew what it was, but last year, when I had my idea for my summer book, *The Beekeeper's Cottage*, I finally got my chance and Amos's story was told. And I think I did him proud.

But these books are also special because they were written when my writing career was in its infancy. I had just got my first publishing deal with Letting In Light when I suddenly had an idea for a seasonal novella which became *Merry Mistletoe*. It was, however, never intended to become part of a series, but it was so popular that I was soon thinking about what could come next. I have a real passion for rural crafts and settings which evoke our glorious countryside, and so when I began to think about the next book, it made sense to set it in the spring time to take advantage of this. Summer and autumn soon followed.

It was always my intention once all four novellas were released to create an omnibus edition, but somehow I never seemed to find the time. And then I got really busy... But, I'm happy to say that, this year, my fabulous publishers offered to produce it for me, and it's been wonderful to read these stories again and bring them to so many new readers.

Having folks take the time to get in touch really does make my day, and if you'd like to contact me, then I'd love to hear from you. The easiest way to do this is by finding me on Twitter and Facebook, or you could also pop by my website where you can read about my love of Pringles among other things...

I hope to see you again very soon, and in the meantime, if you've enjoyed your visit to *A Year at Appleyard Farm*, I would really appreciate a few minutes of your time to leave a review or post on social media. Every single review makes a massive difference and is very much appreciated!

Until next time,
Love, Emma xx

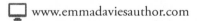

www.emmadaviesauthor.com

emmadaviesauthor

@EmDaviesAuthor